DESTINY OF TWILIGHT AND STARS

DESTINY OF TWILIGHT AND STARS

TWILIGHT AND STARS SERIES
BOOK ONE

BRIEGHANNA MAYE

INGRAMSPARK

Printed by IngramSpark

Title Font: Edgewood

Body Font: Crimson Pro

First Edition: February 2024

AISN: B0CQ659JHQ, EPUB

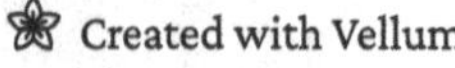 Created with Vellum

TRIGGER WARNINGS:

This book is a Dark Fantasy Romance and includes the following which may not be suitable if you find yourself sensitive to:

Implied child sexual assault, sexual assault, rape, narcissistic personality tendencies, body shaming, body dysmorphia, depression, PTSD, suicidal ideation, blood play, incest, descriptive torture, murder, flogging, death, explicit sexual scenarios, strong language.

PLAYLIST

Listen along and experience the ebb and flow of emotions along with the characters.

Leethe
Solana
Pyrus
Harmonia
Dalia
Nyxtas
Asphodel
Ancient Woods
Stefans camp
Dead Mountains

*Mom, you were taken away too soon and unexpectedly.
You were my heart, my soul, my inspiration, and my best friend.
When I started this book, you were the first one I sent my writing
to, and you told me of all my talents, my writing had been the
most impressive, that you had no idea that I had it inside of me
to create stories like this. Now you're gone, and you aren't
around to see the finished product, but I know that you're still
my biggest supporter, even though you're not here.
The world lost a star but the sky gained one.
I hope that this story makes you proud.
I will love you until the stars burn out and the universe
collapses, and even then I will keep on loving you.
I miss you so much.*

CHAPTER 1
ASTERIA

Tradition. It was the foundation of our Kingdom, our royal family. Ever since we rose to power, these practices were written, and after centuries of ruling we have not deviated from them.

"The strength of the Kingdoms comes from our reliance on the traditions laid down by our forefathers," my father droned on. I had been summoned by him early this morning for an important meeting—I should have known it would start with one of his speeches on the traditions of the Kingdoms marital traditions. "It is because of these traditions that we have been able to keep our families in power, our lineage pure," he stated. "That is why, after much discussion with your mother, we have decided it is time to find a suitor for your hand in marriage."

It was way too early in the morning for a conversation this serious. I hadn't even had breakfast yet, but maybe that was a good thing; this conversation had my stomach in knots. I knew this had to be coming soon. Being twenty-eight, there wasn't much time left to marry and become the subservient and silent wife, mother, and queen expected of me.

Some Kingdoms of Leethe practiced more modern forms of ruling, where a King and Queen served as equals, but not here. No, never here in the Kingdom of Pyrus. Here, we kept power within the family through an alliance with the Kingdom of Solaria, where my uncle, King Dameaon, rules. Our family had reigned over the two Kingdoms for ages, and keeping the crown within the bloodline was of the utmost importance.

"Father," I began, "I am more than aware that I must seriously consider marriage, but it has been months since we last hosted or attended an event with the rest of the Kingdoms. It makes it difficult to seek a suitor when there are no suitors around to be sought."

Father nodded. "That is why your mother, and I have arranged for a suitor. We have been in contact with King Dameaon, and his son, Prince Stefan, has also yet to wed. It has been decided that the two of you will wed in two months' time," he declared.

The weight of the news made me sick, and I was suddenly very thankful that I had not yet eaten. The finality in my father's voice offered no room for compromise, no chance of refusal. My world shifted and spun as I tried to process the news.

"Father," I pleaded. "Please, there must be some other arrangement. Please, don't make me do this. He... He is family. Are there no suitors among the heirs of the other heirs four Kingdoms?" My breathing became shallow and rapid as my veins filled with ice. This could not be happening.

"Asteria, do not argue with me!" He boomed. "You know your place and your duties, and I expect you to perform them flawlessly. You know the importance of ensuring the bloodline is not sullied. It is tradition, and it will not change for you."

"Please, Father, anyone else. Promise me to anyone else, just not him," I begged.

"*Enough*! I will not tolerate insolence. You will do as commanded, or you will face the consequences. The wedding is in two months. *You will* spend that time in the Kingdom of Solaria with your intended. *You will* learn what is expected of you as their future Queen. *You will not* disappoint me, Asteria, do you understand?" He had never used this harsh of a tone with me before. "Your things are being packed as we speak. You will leave this evening, so I suggest you take the morning to reacquaint yourself with your duties."

I didn't know how to react, so I bowed my head and excused myself. "Yes, Your Majesty."

Thoughts reeling, I walked back to my room with head down, lost in my dread. I didn't understand why there seemed to be such a rush—why two months from now? Why hadn't I been told about this? It was *my* future, after all. I had so many questions, but answers were something I knew I would never receive.

I couldn't stop rehashing my father's harsh words in my head. *It is tradition, and it will not change for you. You will not disappoint me, Asteria, do you understand?*

What happened this morning? I had been on the receiving end of my father's verbal lashings in the past, but even then, he had never been so harsh. This morning bordered on hatred; it felt more like a threat than a demand, and the echo of it sent chills down my spine.

When I arrived back at my chambers, I found my mother, Queen Elenora, sitting on the edge of my bed, two large trunks full of my belongings behind her. She stood and walked to me, her blue eyes full of what looked like guilt and regret.

"Darling," my mother said as she cupped my cheek, her voice full of sorrow. "Please understand that we love you. This was not a decision we made lightly. We have to consider the entire Kingdom's well-being when making decisions. There are things you do not yet understand, and I hope that someday, we are able to speak about them, but for now..." She squared her shoulders and adopted a stern voice. "This is what is best for both Kingdoms. We need this alliance to strengthen our ties and provide for our people. *Your* people."

I turned my head, moving away from her touch. How could she say that? There was no consideration for me, for my feelings, for my well-being. "What are you not telling me?" Something in her tone and her choice of words had a sinking feeling churning in my gut—there was more to this marriage than just a political alliance.

"I'm not sure what you mean." She lowered her gaze.

"Mother, there has to be something you're not telling me. Why is everyone acting so strange today? What is going on?" I pleaded with her, gripping her hands to try and meet her gaze.

Her face hardened as she looked back up at me. "It is time for you to step up and serve your Kingdom, Asteria. You have not held the interest of any suitor, so it was time for us to intervene."

I stepped back, dropping her hand, searching for a hint of the truth she was avoiding. My stomach sank, and without another word, I stomped into my bathing chamber and slammed the door behind me.

A weight lifted from my shoulders when I realized the servants had already prepared a hot bath for me. Thank Goddess because I needed it. I removed the silk dressing gown and cotton chemise I typically wore to bed and placed them on the stool next to the door. I pulled up my long onyx hair to keep it from getting wet, and tied it into a messy bun atop my head.

Sometimes, when the light hit my hair just right, you could almost see hints of blue in it, like a raven's feathers. It hung down my back, stopping just below my breasts. I had never thought much of my appearance, but I loved my hair, and it had become something of a security blanket.

Securing the bun, I stalked over to the tub and, without checking the temperature, stepped in. I exhaled through clenched teeth as I lowered myself into the scalding water. The servants must have known what today held, because the water smelled of lavender and chamomile oils. They had added bubbles and dried flowers to the steaming water, creating a calming atmosphere. As I sat, ruminating over the events of the morning, the tension in my body began to fade as if being drained by some invisible force. It's not that I didn't understand the need to marry. I even understood arranging a marriage for political reasons—a love match was something rare between royals—but Stefan? Not only was Stefan my cousin, but he was ten years my elder. Growing up, we spent summers in each other's Kingdoms, attending the same royal events and keeping each other company as we were the sole heirs to our kingdoms. I had never been particularly close to him. How could I be when there was such a large gap between us? Then, that day happened, and I haven't spent much time with him since. The memory sent chills across my skin, and despite the warmth of the water, I felt cold. There was a reason he had yet to wed; aside from his poor reputation amongst the heirs, he had never shown interest in courting women.

As he grew older, Stefan became known for his lack of empathy and his cruelty towards those he deemed lesser. For some reason, neither his parents nor my own seemed to notice how cruel he could truly be—most of the royal families were charmed by him. I couldn't deny that, when it suited him, he put on a good show. He was charismatic, and his appearance was flawless, not a single hair out of place. He had become a master at manipulating and steering conversations to get what he wanted, and the rulers were completely oblivious to it.

No, the heirs were the ones who knew his true colors, the ones who had seen the changes as we grew older. I'm sure if the topic of engagement to Stefan came up among the other families, the heirs would have intervened and refused the proposition.

I should have known this was my fate. Solaria and Pyrus had always been joined, marrying the sons of one to the daughters of the other. A part of me had hoped my stars would be different, that

I would break the cycle and find a love match. Alas, try as one might, there was no changing one's destiny. I let out a long sigh and decided it was time to get out of the bath; the bubbles were mostly gone, the flower petals had sunk, and the water was tepid at best.

At the sound of the water splashing, the maids came in and retrieved a warm towel from next to the fireplace to help me to dry off. I donned my clean dressing gown hanging next to the fire, let my hair down, and went to face my mother, who I could sense was still in my bedchamber.

"What is it you have left to say, Mother?" I huffed out, turning my back while I attempted to lace up my stay and slip into a grey, long-sleeved day dress.

"I just want to make sure that you are well. I'm sure today's news was a shock, and you don't have much time before you leave. So, are you? Well?"

It was so hard to stay angry at my mother. Despite her tendency to shield her emotions, she had always taken such great care of me. She taught me what was expected of me as a princess and as a lady, and despite my fathers' objections, she had allowed me to explore hobbies not typical of a princess. Most days, after my formal lessons, I would retreat to the castle garden, tending to the herbs and flowers before studying and training with the Kingdom's healers. I discovered my love for medicine and healing at a young age, and with that came a love of herbology and gardening. For many years, I dreamed of becoming a healer, traveling to all the Kingdoms and beyond to learn alternative methods. Most of my time was spent helping the healers make salves, elixirs, and tinctures for my people. As I got older, I dreamed of going with them to tend to the people in the villages, but as a princess it was not allowed.

"Astra?" Her touch startled me as she took over lacing the stay, tightening it in an attempt to conceal my full chest. I knew that she was trying to comfort me by using the pet name my family had given me as a child: Astra, the name of my favorite, star-shaped flower. I had gotten so lost in my thoughts, I hadn't answered her question.

"I am well, Mother. At least, I will be." I hesitated for a moment. "It's just...of all the heirs, Stefan?"

"What about Stefan?" she retorted, securing the laces. "He is a fine young man, and his father has raised him to be a strong ruler. You should feel honored he was willing to accept the arrangement."

"A fine young man?" I scoffed. "You don't know the first thing about this 'fine young man'," I snapped at her before I could stop myself. Instantly, pangs of regret hit me.

"What are you implying?" Her tone was offended. "We have known Stefan his entire life. He has been nothing but respectful and kind to us...to you."

"You don't understand," I muttered, mostly to myself, as I walked over to the trunks to observe what had been packed for me.

My mother placed her hand on my shoulder. "Did something happen? You've never shown such disdain for him before. I don't understand where this is coming from."

Shrugged off her hand, I plastered a soft smile on my face, and turned to her. "It is nothing, Mother. I think I'm just famished from missing breakfast and shocked from the news. I am well. You don't need to worry."

She reciprocated my smile, cupping my face as she ran her thumb along my jaw with a sigh. "I am so proud of you and the woman you have become. You are going to make an exceptional queen."

I finally let out the breath I had been holding as the door clicked shut behind her.

CHAPTER 2
ASTERIA

The journey would take three days and I would be escorted by a party of royal guards. My parents would be making the journey just before the wedding, meaning that for the next month, it was to be King Dameaon, Queen Phenelophe, and my betrothed, Prince Stefan. I shuddered at the thought of being alone with him.

The carriages left in the evening, like always, traveling through the night and the following day before stopping when the sun set. I always hated this journey; it was long, and the thought of being stuck alone in a small, dark carriage felt like a prison sentence. I requested I be allowed to ride my own horse instead of being sequestered in the carriage, but my request was immediately denied by my father.

"You are a royal, a princess, and soon to be, a queen. You will travel in the carriage. It is the safest place for you to be while journeying through the Ancient Woods. You know the journey is not safe, and making yourself an easy target is not the way a future queen should be thinking. Your safety is a priority. You should know this. It's..."

"Tradition," I interjected. "Yes, I know. I just thought some fresh air would be nice."

His jaw tensed, and I knew I had struck a nerve. Something had been off about him since that morning. I didn't know what was causing him to act this way, but his reaction and lack of fatherly compassion had me itching to push him further.

"What is going on with everyone today? Everyone seems like they are hiding something. Is there more to this arrangement? What are you hiding from me?"

He bowed his head momentarily before he met my gaze. "It is not a women's place to be concerned with the goings-on of a king's duties. You know this. Why must you always push for exceptions? Accept your role and serve your Kingdom, both this one and your future home." His tone hardened with each sentence.

I thought about pushing more, but I backed down with a sigh. "Yes, Father. Sorry to disappoint you."

I turned to look at the approaching caravan readying for our departure before moving my gaze back to my father, now accompanied by my mother. "I will miss you both. I will do my duty, and I will not fail you."

I bowed at the waist, a much more formal interaction than we usually shared as family. I looked up at my parents, expecting them to pull me in for a hug or return the gesture, but they remained standing. They could have been made of stone, their eyes the only things giving them away. Their dark blue eyes, were normally like the deepest parts of the ocean, that shined full of light and expression. Now, though, my father looked straight ahead, giving no insight to his feelings, my mother's full of enough emotion for the both of them. But her eyes did not hold the emotions I had expected; there wasn't sadness or love there. No, her eyes were full of fear, regret, and anger.

The carriage rolled to a stop behind me, and the sound of the door opening was my cue to leave. I climbed into the dark cabin, feeling like the closing of the door signified the end of my dreams, the end of my choices —the end of me. I looked back to see my parents one last time before the door closed, but the spot they had occupied was now empty, and the darkness of my temporary prison swallowed me.

Once we had been on the road for a bit, I laid down and tried to force myself to fall sleep; surprisingly, despite the rough ride and noise, I was able to drift off into a fitful rest.

"Astra, this way! Look at this willow tree; isn't it amazing?" Stefan's voice rang out all around me. *"Come here, look at this!" He grabbed my arm and pulled me towards the large willow tree sitting along the edge of the river that cut through both our Kingdoms. We were in the fields near the Solarian castle. Nearby farmers would stack hay bales along the edge of the field, and we would build forts, claiming they were our own castles. We would swim in the river, using a rope tied to a nearby tree to swing out into the water. Sometimes, we would just lay in the field and pick out shapes in the clouds, seeing who could come up with the most ridiculous ones. The willow tree was large—it had to be a hundred years old. At the start of every summer, it would be green and lush, its leaves creating a curtain so thick, it would block the sunlight – a sanctuary away from the world. At least, until he ruined it.*

"I'll race you to the willow. The last one there has to move to the Asphodel Kingdom!" Stefan took off running.

"Wait, Stefan, that's not fair. You cheated!" My voice was so much higher then, the innocent timbre of a child.

"Haha, beat you! Should I pack your trunk for you, or do you want to, Astra? I can arrange for a carriage to take you tonight!" he huffed out, smirking like it was some great achievement, beating a ten-year-old in a foot race.

"Stefan, please don't make me go! Don't send me away!" I pleaded with him as my eyes began to well with tears. Asphodel was the Kingdom of nightmares, and I was terrified at the thought of being sent there.

"Hey, hey, hey, I would never truly send you away. You know that,

don't you?" He pulled me in for an embrace and cupped my cheek, lifting my gaze to meet his. "I will always keep you by my side. You are my favorite girl." He sat down, pulled me into his lap, and embraced me. Something about this felt different than hugs from him in the past—I suddenly felt scared.

"Stefan, I want to go back to the castle now." My voice was so soft, it barely came out as more than a whisper.

"Don't you trust me, Astra? I've always taken care of you, haven't I? I will always take care of you."

I stood up, not wanting to be in the shade of the willow tree any longer. Something about his eyes had changed. He followed suit, standing as well.

"How about we play another game? Would that make you feel better?" I nodded. "Okay, this is a special game, only for us, okay?" Confused and not understanding what he meant, I agreed, starting to feel better that we were going to play again.

"Come here," he said. "We're going to play Royals. Except this time, we are going to rule together as king and queen, doesn't that sound fun?" I nodded. "But before we can be the King and Queen, we have to get married, so are you ready?" I agreed. I never got to play queen—I was so excited.

"Okay, stand here so we can get married." He moved me so my back was against the tree and stood in front of me, towering over me with a huge smile on his face.

My heart began to race; this didn't feel right. I didn't want to play this game anymore. Stefan put his finger to his lips, indicating that I needed to be quiet, before he leaned down and whispered into my ear.

"If you tell anyone about our game, we will both be in trouble. It's better to just keep quiet about this, okay? I don't want you to be punished for it."

The memories began to pull me down as I tried desperately to escape them. I didn't want to remember this.

Waking full of disgust, I lurched forward, banging on the roof of the carriage. I needed them to stop. I needed air. I needed to get out. I was going to be sick. The carriage halted, and before one of the guards could make it to the door, I threw it open and jumped out, running to the side of the road and vomiting.

"Are you well, Your Highness?" the guard who had been reaching to open the door asked.

"I'm fine," I huffed. "Just motion sickness. I forgot how rough parts of this journey are." I looked at my surroundings then; it was dark—extremely dark. The canopies of the tightly knit trees blocked out any moonlight that might have illuminated the path, and when I looked around at the royal guard, they all seemed on edge and worried.

"Where are we?" I asked.

The guard hesitated before answering, "We just entered the Ancient Wood, Your Highness. Are you feeling better? We need to move. We shouldn't linger in these woods too long."

I stood there another moment, listening, only there was nothing to listen to. Aside from the sounds of our breathing, the woods were completely silent. The hair on my body stood on end, and I turned to hurry back into the safety of my carriage. Perhaps the woods were safer than the thoughts and memories that prowled in the depths of my mind—even the royal guards could not protect me from the darkness of my past. The carriage lurched forward as we started moving again, throwing me back into my seat. I groaned; this was going to be a very, very long journey.

The caravan continued until mid-morning before stopping to allow the horses to rest and graze while the cook prepared food for the rest of us. The meal was simple and bland: bread, dried fruits and meats. My stomach protested at the thought of food, despite aching with hunger. I had not been able to quell the knot of dread sitting within it since I awoke from my nightmare. I could still feel the cold trails his hands left when he raked them up my body, the fear that overwhelmed my every sense as he pressed his lips to mine. Every time I closed my eyes and began to drift off to sleep, I would hear Stefan's voice.

If you tell anyone about our game, we will both be in trouble. It's better to just keep quiet about this, okay? I don't want you to be punished for it.

Me. I was the one threatened with punishment. I should have questioned why I would be the one deserving of punishment. It hadn't been my idea to play this game. I wasn't the one who had made the rules. He had been the one to steal something from me. Though he may have left my virtue intact, he took something from me that was not his to take.

As I grew older and began to understand the complexities of being a royal and the importance of maintaining alliances, I decided it was best to keep this information buried for the good of my people. My suffering did not outweigh the suffering of a Kingdom or the destruction of a family. It was just a touch; it was just a kiss. It wasn't as if he stole my virginity. So, I stuffed it down, put it in a box, and tossed the memories into a dark chasm in the back of my mind. I hadn't dreamt or even thought about that day in years, but I guess it wasn't surprising that the demons are trying to climb back out of the darkness following the news of my future.

"Your Highness?" A voice brought me out of my thoughts. "Here," a guard said as he placed a small plate of dried fruit and meat into my hands. I just shook my head, not feeling as though I could eat anything.

"You should try to eat. It's a long journey, and you need to keep up your strength," he persisted, working the plate into my hands.

I gave a curt nod and accepted the food. I inhaled deeply, enjoying the feel of the cool breeze on my alabaster skin. It was the end of summer and the autumn breeze was refreshing, the air cooler due to the dark oaks of the Ancient Wood swallowing the sunlight. Despite it being mid-morning, it looked close to dusk while under the thick canopy.

There were many rumors surrounding the things that lived in the Ancient Wood: stories of monsters, both human and animal, that roam the forest in search of their next meal. Yet, in all my years, I had never encountered anything while traveling these woods. However, the ominous tension one feels creeping in from the darkness beneath the trees made it easy to understand where such stories came from.

A crack from somewhere off the path startled me, and from the state of the horses, I would say it startled them as well. The hair on my arm rose as fear crept into my throat.

"Your Highness, I think it is best we carry on. We have much ground to cover before nightfall if we don't want to spend a night camping in this forest," said the guard who insisted on me eating. I stood and offered him my plate; I had hardly touched the food.

"Keep it with you. I am not sure when our next stop will be. I do not wish for you to become famished," he insisted. I did not have the energy to argue with him, so instead, I asked for him to retrieve my trunk of herbs and elixirs I had packed before we left. He reluctantly agreed, obviously not wanting to spend any more time here than necessary. I could sense his nervousness, draining and heavy, like a thick blanket stifling you in the summer heat.

I fetched a water bladder and returned to my carriage, igniting the lantern that hung above the window before leaning over and opening my trunk. I'd packed a variety of herbs, elixirs, and salves to bring along with me. I hadn't visited Solaria in months and did not know what state the castle gardens would be in. Some herbs were regional, so I made sure to pack extra of those. Most could be purchased through trade, but others were particularly difficult to obtain. Those are the ones I kept on my person in a small brown satchel tied around my waist. I was exhausted, and the constant knot in my stomach was beginning to take its toll. I felt weak and drained from fasting since the previous morning.

I rummaged through my jars until I found what I was looking

for: chamomile, lavender, ginger, blue lotus flower, hibiscus, and valerian root. The combination of herbs would hopefully settle my stomach and lull me into a peaceful sleep. The fear of experiencing another nightmare had me reaching into my satchel for one of my most precious and rare ingredients: the purple Astra flower. It used to grow wild across the Kingdoms, but it had all but been wiped out. No one seemed to know why the Astra plant became so rare, just that one day, it seemed to stop growing anywhere other than Pyrus, and even that was still a scarce occurrence.

I managed to stumble across a small handful one evening in late summer while out for a ride. The small flower buds would swell, looking bloated before they bloomed into gorgeous five-point flowers resembling stars. The flowers themselves carried almost no odor, but each part of the plant had a use. When added to a sleeping draught, the petals greatly increased its potency and, since the petals are essentially odorless and tasteless, most people wouldn't know if it was in their tea. The stems and roots, on the other hand, had a very bitter, acrid taste, and most people didn't have the knowledge to make them palatable. When properly prepared and added to elixirs, though, they had a strong healing effect.

Tonight, I needed sleep, so I began preparing an herbal mixture to drink as a tea after we made camp. I added the ingredients to my mortar and ground them into a fine powder before taking an empty jar to store the concoction for later.

Now, it was time to address the knot in my stomach. Taking more of the chamomile, I lightly crushed it in my hand and added it to the water I had before using the small knife from my satchel to cut off and dice a thumb-sized piece of ginger root to add. After gently shaking the water bladder, I opened it to add a small amount of honey for sweetness and to help tame the spice of the ginger root. I sipped on the mixture, careful not to drink it too fast at the risk of it having the opposite effect.

Before too long, I found myself reaching for the dried meats and bread that sat untouched from before. It was flavorless and cold, but that was probably for the best on my weak stomach. I hadn't realized how hungry I had become, and soon, the plate was cleared, but I found myself even hungrier than before. Defeated, I rested my head on the back of the carriage seat. *This journey is never going to end.*

The day wore on, each hour passing slower than the last. It was difficult to tell what time it was while in the forest, but I assumed evening was nearing after noticing more lanterns being lit by the guards. The monotony of horse hoofs and the sounds of the carriage wheels across the dirt path were broken up by a thunderous crack as the carriage pitched to the side. I was thrown to the floor, my head smacking against the seat across from me. Commotion sounded from outside, and the door of my carriage was flung open by one of the Solarian guards sent to accompany us.

"My Lady! Are you alright?" he hollered, panic in his voice. He was probably imagining the punishment that would await him should I arrive to Prince Stefan injured.

"I am well," I assured him. "What in Goddess' name happened?" I looked up to see him reaching his hand forward to help me up and out of the carriage.

"We hit a rut in the path. The carriage wheel broke."

Well, that would explain the commotion. I stepped out and onto the path, turning behind me to look at the damage when suddenly, the guard grabbed my face with one hand, jerking it toward the light of his lantern.

"You're bleeding." I reached up, touching the right side of my face that had been too graciously introduced to the carriage seat, wincing as I felt the small cut. I rolled my eyes at the thought of what my cousin might say or do when he saw the injury.

"I'm fine," I tried to reassure the guard, pulling my face from his grip. "Retrieve my trunk, and I'll make sure it is properly tended to." I paused, looking around at the scene. The carriage wheel was useless, and I didn't foresee anyone being able to repair it. The carriage itself sat on an awkward angle, tilting to the right side where it was no longer supported. It was quickly growing dark, and we were still surrounded by trees—we were obviously still deep into the Ancient Wood. "What will we do now?" I asked, turning back to the guard.

"It is too risky to travel with you exposed at night in these woods. We will set up camp here for the evening. One of the other guards has already ridden ahead to the next town to fetch a new wheel. We will repair the carriage tomorrow and continue our journey."

I nodded my head, already feeling a searing headache setting in from the impact. "Is there anything I can do to help?" I asked.

He shook his head. "No, Your Highness. We will have your tent set up shortly and I will fetch your things so you may tend to that wound. Your only priority tonight is to ensure that this," he lightly grazed the cut with his hand, causing me to flinch, "is cared for and does not become infected. The prince, would not appreciate his goods being damaged."

Once the camp was set up, a basin of hot water was brought to me, accompanied by a servant who set up a small circle of hot rocks near the center of the tent to heat the small space. On a small stump near the rocks, he placed extra clothing and towels for me to bathe. "Is there anything else I can fetch for you this evening, my Lady?" he asked.

"No, thank you. This is more than enough." I smiled at him and nodded, dismissing him. After he left, I removed a few herbs and salves from my trunk to clean up and tend to my wound. Looking in the small mirror in the lid of the trunk, I examined the cut. The bleeding had stopped, but the skin around it was already turning shades of purple and green.

Well, this is just beautiful, I thought. *Sure, let's tarnish Astra's best feature. Wouldn't want her to enjoy at least one aspect of her appearance.*

I took a cloth from the stump, dipping it into the basin of warm water to clean the cut. It wasn't too deep, thankfully, only about two inches in length along the right side of my temple, angling toward my eyebrow. The chances of it scarring weren't too bad, so that was a relief. Once the dried blood was washed away, I dabbed the cut with a bayberry and witch hazel tonic; it stung slightly, but it would help prevent infection. I carefully spread a salve made of arnica, camphor, and clove, hoping it would heal the bruising, stave off infection, and my favorite part, numb it.

As I undressed and bathed, I found myself thankful for the lack of mirrors I was usually surrounded by back home. I felt as though I had a pretty face with pale skin, a delicate nose, and soft lips, but my eyes were one of the few features I truly loved about myself. They were light grey with hints of light blue near the center. I always thought they looked like two full moons sharing a dark sky, especially against the black curtain of my hair, surrounded by my dark lashes and eyebrows.

At home the mirrors had a habit of reflecting and magnifying the things I hated most about myself. I was never secure in my body. I couldn't remember where the shame came from, but it clung to me like a shadow. I was always larger than what was deemed beautiful, and my curves weren't considered ladylike.

"A proper lady's body does not resemble a lady of the evening," my mother would tell me as she laced me into my stays in an attempt to flatten my chest. "We must disguise your shape if we are to ever find you a proper suitor."

Most of my dresses were made of layers of loose, flowing fabrics fitting only across the shoulder and part of my suffocated chest. The body of the dresses did well to hide the extra weight I carried in my stomach, as well as the fullness of my ass and thighs.

During a visit from another Kingdom, I returned to the castle from a group ride and walked through the tea garden in my riding pants and a flowing tunic. Whispers flowed through the castle about how appalling it was that the King and Queen would allow me to walk about in clothing that so blatantly accentuated my shapely, hourglass figure. I was made to wear a day gown when out riding or gardening after that. I hated seeing myself naked in the mirrors of my bathing chamber—the soft rolls of my stomach, my thighs that hugged each other as I walked, and my full breasts, all on display. The lighting always seemed to highlight the lines that stretched over the fullest parts of my body, another flaw in my appearance, according to my mother.

"Ahem." The sound startled me, and I quickly grabbed the nearest fur to cover myself. I turned to see who had made the noise, only to find a guard standing in the entry to my tent. My skin flushed, my face burning as a wave of embarrassment crashed into me. His eyes were pointed down, but the tension in his stance told me he had seen all of me.

Frustrated by the intrusion, I barked at him, "Don't you know better than to barge into a lady's quarters? Were you not taught an ounce of respect? What is it that you found so important as to inappropriately obtrude on me in this state?"

"I apologize, my Lady. I thought you may be hungry, so I brought you some food." It wasn't until now that I noticed the steaming bowl of broth with chunks of bread and a water pitcher in his hands. He sat the food and water down on the stump near the warm coals before he backed out of the tent.

"Again," his sarcastic tone obvious, "my deepest apologies for the intrusion." He paused, raking his eyes down my figure as if he could see through the furs I covered myself with. "Princess." He smirked as he left.

As his footsteps retreated, I heard a roar of laughter mixed with whoops and hollers.

"Oh shit! I didn't think you would do it."

"Fuck, what did she look like?"

"What's hidden under those dresses?"

"Did you actually see anything?"

I fell back onto the pile of furs that made up my bed. I was...I was...I didn't know what I was. I was embarrassed, angry, ashamed, scared, but mostly, I think I was disgusted at the objectification of my body. Seeing it bare had become a task, a challenge, a thing to conquer. As the laughter continued outside my tent, my emotions only spiked. Before I knew it, I was standing in the entrance of my tent, wearing nothing but the furs I clutched over my body, the bowl of steaming soup launching out of my hands and hurtling towards the back of the guard's head. The sound of the impact snapped me back to reality: it had missed its mark, finding a new target in the head of the Solarian guard who had helped me earlier.

Holy shit—what had I just done?

Before I could process my actions, the impact of his hand across my face sent me to the ground. "You stupid bitch," the guard hissed. "What the fuck is wrong with you?" The top of his shoulders and side of his face were scalded by the soup. "If you were any other woman," he inhaled deeply, gathering his composure, "a much worse fate would be awaiting you." His body was still tense, fists clenched—he was furious. "Just because you are royal, *Princess,*" he said, emphasizing my title, "does not mean you should forget your place. If you ever pull such antics again, I won't care about your title."

He reached down to examine my face, gripping it much more aggressively than he had earlier. I ripped myself from his hand as warm liquid trickled down the side of my face—he had opened the wound from earlier. After instructing one of the servants to fetch another towel, he leered down at me.

"Fix your face. Wouldn't want to ruin your prettiest feature."

The words were like a blow to the chest, seizing my lungs. My prettiest feature. How had he known exactly where to throw his venomous words to cause the most damage?

I didn't know how to respond. I had never been struck by a man other than my father, and it had been years since I'd received a lashing from him. The camp was silent as the rest of the guards watched, waiting to see my response. Unfortunately for them, they would be sorely disappointed, because I had none, no clever words or witty remarks. Just silence.

I got to my feet, careful to keep myself covered before walking back into my tent. *What just happened?* I changed into a pair of trousers and a tunic to sleep, feeling as though a gown wouldn't be enough to protect me from the eyes of the guards outside my tent.

I spent a few minutes cleaning the reopened wound, now worse than before. The bruise would be easy to heal quickly, but the cut would be a different story. This would leave a scar; it would be small, but it would scar, nonetheless. I took what little hot water was left from dinner and added a heavy amount of the sleeping draught. I drank it down as quickly as I could, before placing the cup back on the stump and crawling beneath the furs on my makeshift bed.

Tears rolled down my face, soaking my pillow, while I ran through everything that had happened up to this point. I didn't ask for or want any of this. I simply woke up yesterday morning and had my life stripped away from me without any warning or consideration of my desires. My mind was spinning—was it from the sleeping draught? I wasn't sure, but what I *was* sure of was that I had never felt more powerless, more alone, and something in my gut told me it wasn't going to get better anytime soon. My entire body felt heavy, weighed down by the thoughts and fears of what was to come.

CHAPTER 3
ASTERIA

The next day came too quickly, my eyelids heavy and swollen from crying myself to sleep. I dragged myself out of bed to see if the rest of the camp had risen, but to my surprise, the sun had not yet broken the horizon. I stepped out of my tent into the chilled air, inhaling deeply, trying to clear the ghosts haunting my mind.

Coffee, I thought, *I need coffee. Desperately.*

I navigated my way through the camp until I found the kitchen tent; the fire had been stoked recently, indicating that someone was around.

"My Lady, you're about early. Can I help you with anything?" the cook asked, walking out of his tent, clearly surprised to meet another person at this hour.

"Just some hot water, please," I replied. Coffee was a luxury and not easy to come by, but, fortunately for me, I had a stash of ground beans hidden in my herb trunk.

"Of course my Lady, right away." He disappeared momentarily to return with a pot of water which he placed over the fire. "Are you sure I can't get you anything else? We have breads and cheese.

I could heat up some broth, or maybe you would like some porridge?" He continued to list options while he tended to the fire, the water beginning to boil.

"No, thank you. I don't have much of an appetite this morning." He didn't seem sure of my answer, but he obliged me by handing me a cup of steaming water. The flames flickered, illuminating my face, and I knew by his mortified expression my wound had not healed as well as I'd hoped. I turned my face from the light.

"Thank you again, sir. You've been very kind and helpful." I nodded my head and departed for my tent. The camp began to stir as the sun slowly rose, and the haze of grey fog coating the forest floor started to roll.

When I entered my tent, I came face to face with the head guard, who stood in the center of my tent, obviously waiting for my return. I walked past without acknowledging him.

"You shouldn't wander around these woods alone in the dark, even within the confines of camp." His eyes tracked me as he spoke, and when I did not respond, the act visibly angered him. "Are you hearing me, Princess, or did the impact of my hand render you deaf? Maybe a second blow would fix it."

"What is your name, soldier?" I finally looked up at him.

"Valdin," he said on a rough exhale.

"Well, *Valdin*," I accentuated his name, "I'm just trying to remember my place."

"Excuse me?" Shock and anger caused his voice to tremble, only increasing when my response was a short and curt *okay*.

He had reached the end of his apparently short fuse, moving to tower over me. "We do not give short, shitty answers when asked a question, Princess." My title was like poison on his tongue. "Get your things together—we leave within the hour."

He turned and stormed out of my tent, finally allowing me to breathe. Not even the coffee was going to cure this headache.

Sitting in front of my trunk, I looked at my face. I understood the reaction from the cook now—I looked like I had been in a tavern brawl. My eyes were puffy, red and blood-shot from crying, my face paler than usual, probably from exhaustion. Still, the hardest part to take in was the right side of my face; the skin was a deep purple, fading into red along the edges of my hairline and the corner of my eye. The arnica salve hadn't worked as well as I'd hoped, no doubt thanks to the guard's strike. The cut bled slightly during the night, coating it in dried blood, while the cut itself seemed to rise from inflammation. It was grotesque and I averted my gaze, not able to stand the sight of my own ruined face a moment longer. I sipped on my fresh coffee, tuning out my thoughts as I dressed and prepared for another day of travel.

By the time the camp was broken down, the carriage had been repaired. Silently, I trudged through the straggling guards and servants. I had an overwhelming desire to be invisible—I couldn't handle the leering eyes of the soldiers on my injury. I kept my head down, my face hooded by the cloak that it was too warm for. All of the gawking made me uncomfortable; I never had enjoyed being the center of attention—it made me feel like an object on display.

Reaching the carriage, I climbed in, and what had felt like a prison the day before felt like a safe haven now. The walls protecting me from the judging gaze of the men who escorted me the rest of the way to Solaria.

CHAPTER 4
ASTRAEUS

"You're sure of this?" I asked the man sitting across from me, cloaked in darkness. It was hard to make out his features and, in turn, hard for him to make out mine. Most, if not all, of my meetings with commoners throughout the five working Kingdoms of Leethe were done with anonymity. It was easier to trade in secrets when my identity was kept concealed.

"I am sure. Invitations have been sent to the four other Kingdoms. The heirs of Pyrus and Solaria are to be wed in less than two months." The stranger spoke in a hushed tone. "It's disturbing if you ask me, marrying off your daughter to her cousin. That's bad enough, but the reputation of Prince Stefan..." The man blew out an exasperated sigh.

He wasn't wrong. It *was* disturbing, but I had an idea of why the arrangement was made. Prince Stefan had a violent streak for sure; he was also power hungry, as the rulers of Solaria and Pyrus always had been. They were the ones who led the human resistance against the magic wielders so many centuries ago. If I had to bet on it, I'd assume this marriage was a power play – a way to inherit both his Kingdom and the Kingdom of Pyrus. It was clever, I'll give him that.

"Have the three of the other Kingdoms all agreed to attend?" I questioned, wondering if this would be the opportunity I had been searching for.

"All have replied saying they will attend," he confirmed. This was perfect, but I didn't have long to arrange my plans and make the journey. I would have to move quickly if I wanted to return to Asphodel before the following evening. I thanked the informant before returning to my room, leaving a small pile of gold as payment.

This was it. I paced my room, unable to quell my thoughts. *The perfect opportunity to try and save Asphodel.* For years, the Forgotten Kingdom of Asphodel had been struggling to survive. The Great War had cut off all trade with the rest of the Kingdoms of Leethe, but we had persevered. We had found ways to work the land, but over the last few years, the crops had begun to fail, and what was left of our Kingdom was beginning to dwindle. Asphodel used to be a thriving civilization. Our people were the magic wielders; able to shadows to defend our people and the Kingdoms of Leethe.

Shadow wielders most often served as soldiers, capable of cloaking themselves in darkness, wielding shadows into creatures and weapons, giving them life and bending them to their will. But that was long ago, our magic had left us after the Great War. The true powers of our people were lost when the rulers of Solaria and Pyrus decreed magic wielders a threat that needed to be eliminated. We fought as hard as we could, but eventually, we had no choice but to flee, crossing the mountains that divided us from the rest of the realm. The other Kingdoms destroyed our trade routes and banned all interaction with our Kingdom, essentially sentencing us to death. As far as the other Kingdoms believed, we were gone. For years, they had been boasting about eradicating

Asphodel and its people, leaving the land across the Dead Mountains home to ghosts.

For years, I had been looking for a way to infiltrate Solaria and Pyrus, to find a weakness and exploit it. This wedding was the perfect opportunity. The only thing that could possibly get in my way would be my father, King Thetis of Asphodel. I would need his blessing before I could leave my Kingdom.

He has to let me go. I have to do this. Our people need me to do this, I told myself as I prepared for the journey home.

Crossing the mountain path into Asphodel from the Kingdom of Nyxtas was always my favorite part of the journey. The forests were peaceful, and the trail forgotten, much like the Kingdom itself, leaving it nearly untouched. The trees were full, and the canopy cast a gorgeous green hue over the forest floor. Covered in a myriad of flowers of different colors, it was a uniquely beautiful mosaic. The trail ran along the river that flowed from the glaciers atop the mountain; it was frigid, but the water was unlike any other.

I stopped along the bank, kneeling to fill the water bladder I'd slung over my shoulder and splash some across my face, shocking my system and waking me up. It was early and the trail was long, but the path I took was shorter than most, cutting through a cave system beneath the mountains. Few knew of its existence, and those who did could not navigate their way through the maze. My father showed me the way as a young child, teaching me how to notice the change in temperature, the feel of the air, and even the smells to help find my way.

I used the path regularly to meet with informants from the other Kingdoms. Keeping tabs on the other Kingdoms had been tasked to me—listening and looking for any opportunity to help restore life to Asphodel. For years, I had heard of feasible chances, but none that my father would approve of—until now.

I stopped as I neared the entrance to the cave, sensing that something was different, off. I crouched down, keeping to the high grass for cover, and placed my hand on the hilt of the blade strapped across my back. My senses were on fire as I tried to identify the threat I knew was near. The hair on the back of my neck rose as I heard it – rustling of grass behind me. I shifted, pulling my blade free and turning to face my attacker when my legs were swept out from under me. I fell to the ground, landing hard on my back, the breath knocked from my chest. Before I could process what had happened, the cold sting of a dagger grazed my neck.

"Tsk, tsk, tsk. A well-trained soldier such as yourself shouldn't be caught off guard, and he definitely shouldn't be taken down by his little sister so easily." Ardisia's sarcasm, along with her swift and easy takedown, grated against my nerves. I shifted my weight to throw her off then rolled away from her and stood.

"And a princess such as yourself shouldn't be outside the borders without a guard," I shot back at her. She knew better than to venture this far from the castle without protection. Seeing her out here alone infuriated me. "What the fuck do you think you're doing, Ardisia? You should be at home, helping Mother and Father tend to our people."

"I am helping tend to our people," she snapped back. "They are running out of meat. I can hunt, so I'm hunting."

I knew she was right; hunting within the borders was becoming difficult. The game was sparse and small: rabbits, quail, turkey. But we had hunters, men who had been trained specifically for this task. She knew better than to wander outside of the Kingdom alone. She knew how dangerous it was for her, and I thought she had learned her lesson.

"We have hunters. I understand you want to help, but you

must think about your safety. We can't risk you being hurt again." My voice softened as I spoke. I had struck a nerve—her face dropped momentarily, reliving her nightmare before she fixed her face.

"I can take care of myself. There is no need to worry." We stood there for a few moments just staring at each other, neither one of us willing to relent. Finally, I stepped forward, pulling her in and hugging her tight.

"I know you can, but I'm still your brother, and I will always worry about your safety." I looked down at her, a crooked smirk crossing my lips. "You will always be the little girl who ran through the castle singing about her imaginary friend. What was his name again?"

Her face flushed with embarrassment. "Don't you dare!"

She screeched as I ran towards the caves, singing, "Mr. Sunshine, oh my best friend, yes you are mine!" She chased behind me, laughing as we forgot about the seriousness of why she had been out there in the first place. Just for a few minutes, we forgot.

We wound our way through the cave system, teasing each other, trying to see who could embarrass the other most with ridiculous childhood stories. As we came to the end of the tunnel, we both fell quiet; this was my favorite part of the cave path. Exiting the cave, the sun shone brightly in my eyes, momentarily blinding me as they tried to adjust. When they finally did, I came to a stop, inhaling deeply.

In front of me, stretching for acres, was a sea of purple, shifting in the wind and filling the air with a sweet scent. Astra flowers. Though our magic had died out long before I was born, the flowers still grew abundantly here. I stood there for a few moments more, basking in the warm sun and floral breeze, enjoying the view of the Astra fields before venturing around them to the castle.

"So, did your meeting yield any good information?" Ardisia

asked, keeping pace with me and surely wondering if the rumors that had spurred the meeting were true.

"It did," I said, not wanting to disclose anything more until I had met with our father.

"So...are you going to tell me what you found?"

I looked at her seriously. "Isa, you know I can't, not until I've spoken to Father."

She rolled her eyes flippantly and sighed. "I know, but I thought I would try anyway." I shoved her lightly, causing her to stumble to the side. She looked at me, her mouth open, feigning offense.

"What?" I said, my voice serious but the playful smirk on my face saying otherwise. "My hand slipped!"

Within seconds, we were racing back towards the castle as if we were kids again. My sister and I had always been close, born only a few years apart. We spent a lot of time playing when we were kids, but as I got older, my responsibilities increased. Beyond my defense training, I had to learn about battle and war tactics and all the other intricacies of running a Kingdom, meaning we spent less and less time together. As I became more entwined in my duties, we grew apart. Some days, we felt more like acquaintances than siblings—but then that night happened, changing everything.

I regretted allowing myself to become distant from her, not being more involved with her life or giving her the chance to be more involved in mine. Perhaps things would have been different had I been more attentive. That night almost broke her, and I refused to see her break. I brought her with me to training, teaching her hand-to-hand combat, how to wield a sword and a dagger, how to hunt with a bow and arrow, anything I could manage to teach her. Our friendship as brother and sister was rekindled through the time we spent practicing. She picked it up quickly, training hard and daily until her skill almost matched mine. *Almost.*

We reached the castle, out of breath, clutching our sides from laughing, and I gave her one more hug. "I want a rematch. I don't want your head getting too big over one successful takedown."

She laughed. "You just need to make yourself feel better about being beaten by a girl."

WALKING into my father's study, I inhaled the scent of pipe tobacco, oak, and books. The scent always put me on edge; as pleasant as it was, it always meant a serious conversation was on the horizon.

I walked up to his massive wooden desk lined with maps and letters from other informants. It was through one of those letters that we learned about this engagement and why I had gone to meet with a citizen of Harmonia in Nyxtas.

As I took a seat, my father turned around to face me. Despite his declining health, he still managed to exude pure power–the perfect picture of a king. Naturally, we shared many features: we were both tall and broad shouldered, with the same square jaw and sharp cheekbones. Most distinctly, we shared the same emerald eyes, a dead giveaway to our lineage as descendants of royal magic wielders. On the other hand, my jet-black hair, full lips, and delicately straight nose were from my mother—a stark contrast that gave my face a softer appearance.

My father's voice rumbled through his chest; though soft, it demanded attention. "Well, son, what did you find out?"

"It's true," I started. "Princess Asteria has been promised to Prince Stefan. The other royals will be attending the wedding in just under two months."

He pondered my words for a few moments. "Knowing you, I

assume you have already formed a plan to capitalize on this rare opportunity?"

Settling back into my chair, I looked up at him, a coy smile on my lips. "Yes, Father, of course I have." I began to explain the details of my plan. "The royals from the other Kingdoms plan to arrive five days before the ceremony. Predictably, the prince has planned a variety of extravagant events leading up to the wedding. I would like to spend the time from now until those events in the Kingdoms surrounding Solaria, gathering information from the townspeople. My face is not known there, and I can easily live as a commoner. Before the wedding, I will sneak into the castle as a, where I can overhear royal gossip, bonding over drinks with the people who know their secrets best—their servants. After the wedding, I will return home, and if the information I've obtained is sufficient, we can plan our next move from there."

"And if you get caught?" he retorted.

"I won't. They believe our people died out years ago, the commoners believe us to be ghost stories. They would have no reason to believe I am anything other than a humble servant," I said confidently. He sat down, placing his elbows on his desk and lacing his fingers together before bowing his head and inhaling deeply.

"I will allow you to do all of this," he started, the corners of my mouth lifting as he spoke, "under one condition." He paused, lifting his gaze to meet mine, his eyes darkening as he finished. "I want you to kill the prince."

CHAPTER 5
ASTERIA

The wedding was fast approaching, and I was in hell. My days were filled with questions about what color this, and what color that, which flower here, what music there. I was drowning in taffeta and silks as the seamstress pinned my dress, trying to find the best way to hide my curves.

"If the skirt is big, then your waist will look small, and your hips will be hidden," she mumbled, with pins sandwiched between her lips. I just rolled my eyes; I was about to take one of those pins out of her mouth and shove it where the sun couldn't reach it.

"Maybe if we did a high neckline?" my mother suggested from the chaise lounge she occupied in the corner. "We could incorporate some extra boning around her chest as well. That would keep her breasts covered. Far more appropriate for a woman."

I needed two of those pins to shove someplace special. Still, I plastered on a fake smile, doing my best to play the part. My mother and father had arrived about a week ago—my mother jumped right into assisting with the wedding planning, while my father was hardly around, secluding himself to the study with Stefan and my uncle.

The torture of wedding planning was bad enough, but it was significantly worse now that my mother was here. She had an opinion on everything, whereas I had an opinion on nothing. The bigger the better seemed to be her theme: a bigger dress, a bigger cake, more flowers, more extravagance. More, more, more. I just nodded my head, agreeing to whatever she wanted; it was easier than arguing with her. I spent the daylight hours suffocated by white fabrics and an endless barrage of questions, and the nights...the nights were spent trying to avoid Stefan, who always seemed to be lurking around, knowing exactly where I was.

When I had arrived in Solaria, Stefan had spared no expense. The caravan had pulled to a stop in front of the castle, and I was greeted with something just short of a festival. More people than I had ever seen were gathered for the occasion. Predictably, standing front and center was *him*, clad in golds and burnt orange, his golden-brown hair reflecting the afternoon sun. His complexion was a rich, warm, deep amber, a stark contrast to my pale, rosy complexion.

As he opened the door to my carriage, a band struck up a lively tune, and the sky filled with flower petals as people began tossing them above us. Had you been a visiting bystander, you would have thought we had just been wed, not preparing to be. He reached out his hand, a gentlemanly gesture, and I graciously accepted, not wanting to give any cause for disappointment.

When I stepped out of the carriage and into the light, the smile faded from his lips as he noticed the wound along my temple. Reaching up, he ran his thumb across the scabbed mark, his face contorted in rage as he seethed through clenched teeth, "What happened to you?"

I opened my mouth to answer when Valdin interjected. "There

was a small accident, Your Highness. The carriage wheel broke, and she injured herself during the incident."

Something about Valdin's tone and the way Stefan looked at him made me feel as though there was some unspoken conversation between them. He wasn't completely lying, but the injury had been made significantly worse at his hand. Fixing his expression, Stefan pulled me close and wrapped me in his arms, kissing the injury.

"All that matters is that you're safe. I will take you to the healers to be examined." He made sure to speak loudly enough that any bystanders would hear his concern. His tone was sincere, but his honey eyes swirled with a darkness that caused my hair to stand on end.

He turned to the crowd, keeping me close to his side. "My beloved betrothed, your future queen, was injured during her journey and needs the attention of our most skilled healers. I am afraid the celebration of her arrival will regretfully have to be cut short. I do thank you all for being here to welcome Princess Asteria to her new home, but the well-being of my love comes first. Good evening and excuse us."

He ushered me forward through the castle doors, offering one last wave to the people gathered outside. However, as soon as the doors shut, hiding us from the world outside, he revealed his true nature. He whipped me around roughly, gripping my shoulders tightly he narrowed his eyes.

"Tell me, was Valdin's punishment enough, or do I need to reinforce your lesson?" I was shocked, my mouth falling open as I tried to find the words to speak. "I don't know what you did, but I will find out. You will not make the same mistake again. I suggest you learn your place in this Kingdom and as my wife very quickly if you wish to avoid future repercussions for your actions."

I struggled to reconcile the performance he had just put on in front of other people with the true monster in front of me. From that moment on, I did my best to keep my head down and play my part, looking for any opportunity to occupy my time and avoid interacting with him. It didn't work, though—he found great joy in cornering me whenever I was alone.

This night was no exception. After dinner, I slipped out of the castle and made my way to the courtyards. I was pleased to find that the castle had a beautiful flower garden, full of towering fountains and a large hedge maze. Occasionally, I would find myself wandering about and getting lost in the maze. Tonight, the weather was cool, the sky was clear, and the stars so bright that I found myself distracted by them. Without even realizing it, I had entered the maze, though my attention quickly returned to the present when I heard the trickling of the water fountain in the center. As I rounded the corner to the clearing, I saw him there, sitting on the edge of the fountain.

He had been waiting for me.

I turned to leave, but I didn't make it two steps before I felt his grip around my waist, pulling me back to face him. He held me tightly, his fingers digging deep enough to leave marks.

"Don't you look ravishing this evening, *wife*," he said into my hair.

"I am not your wife yet," I spat back at him, "and if I had any say, I never would be." I fought back, trying to force him to loosen his hold. He walked me backwards, forcing me back against the stone wall of the building that sat in the corner of the clearing.

"You might want to watch your tone with me," he said, boxing me in. "You *will* be my wife, and you *will* learn to respect me as a wife should." He inhaled, smelling my hair, making my skin crawl as a chill ran up my spine. "Lest you forget who you belong to."

He slid his hands down past my waist, tracing his fingers along the inside of my thighs. His full weight slumped against me, stopping me from moving as tears began to sting my eyes. "This," he said, groping me between my thighs, causing me to flinch, "belongs to me; you have always belonged to me, Asteria. You will be mine, whether you want to be or not."

A malicious grin crossed his face as his eyes darkened. He moved quickly, his hand around my neck as he pulled me in, forcing my mouth open with his tongue. I couldn't breathe, my skin ice as he moaned into my mouth. He was enjoying this, this display of power, claiming me as his. My stomach rolled as I tried to push him off me, which only seemed to excite him more.

After a moment, he relented, pulling back, only to drag his tongue up the side of my neck and whisper into my ear, "You better learn to fucking enjoy me." He pressed his arousal into me. "Because no other man will ever fucking touch you. No man will ever fucking want you." He ran his hand over my breast as he whispered his venomous threats. He stepped away, smiling as he raked his eyes up and down my body, huffing a quiet laugh before walking out of the maze, leaving me alone.

I fell to my knees, catching myself with my hands out in front of me. I heaved a sob. Unable to catch my breath I sat back on my heels, and shook from the fear and cold that had settled into my bones from his touch. I sat there for a moment longer under the star-speckled sky, head tilted up, crying silently into the night. *How am I going to do this?*

Because you have to. It's what's expected of you. Besides, what choice do you have? Where else would you go? The monster living in the back of my head had reared its ugly head again. *You'll never be good enough. No one will ever want you, want to be with you, want to love you. You get what you are given. This is the hand you have been dealt, so stop crying. You're pathetic.*

"Shut up!" I yelled into the dark, but I knew the voice was right —what other choice do I have? Picking myself up, I wiped my tears and walked straight to the bath waiting for me.

Things between Stefan only escalated after that night. I did everything in my power to avoid being alone with him, but it was an impossible task. He cornered me in the hall outside of our rooms, in the dark alcoves and crevices along the staircases. Any chance he got, he took the opportunity to pleasure himself by torturing me. His words became more poisonous, and with each encounter, he took more liberties with my body.

You are mine to do with as I please. You are going to be my wife. You need to learn what I like, what I want. This is what is expected after we marry. Admit you like it. Stop playing so hard to get.

His words haunted my dreams; they echoed in the darkest parts of my mind, feeding the monster that already lived there. The ghost of his touch lingering in places it was not welcome.

The wedding was in less than a week, and I couldn't sleep without nightmares of Stefan's advances. Even worse, days were filled with wedding planning, which he had now decided to attend. He was always standing close to me, touching me; placing a hand upon my shoulder, or around my waist, brushing a strand of hair off of my neck, or placing a kiss upon my cheek so that he could speak to me without anyone else hearing. To the eyes of others, we looked like the perfect pair, bonding over plans to wed, but in reality, each moment spent together was another opportunity for him to break me. Stefan knew that, and he took every chance to capitalize on it.

I couldn't take it anymore; I'd had enough of this charade. I ran to my father's makeshift study, throwing open the doors and not stopping until my hands were planted on his desk. He turned and looked at me, shocked at my intrusion he dismissed the others from the room...

"Daughter," he said, not even bothering to use my name. "What seems to be troubling you so intensely that you would barge in here unannounced?"

Breathing heavily, I pleaded with him. "Please, Father..." I began to cry. "Please, do not make me marry him. Please, do not force me to go through with this arrangement." All of the emotions

I had been hiding burst forth, demolishing the carefully structured wall I'd built.

"What?" he asked, confused. "You have been promised to the prince. The wedding is two days away, and you want me to call it off?" He got louder as his anger rose. "You are a princess, Asteria, not a commoner. You have a duty—to your Kingdom, to your people, and to me!" he yelled, slamming his fist on his desk, before dropping his head. "You have no idea how much depends on this marriage. You have no idea the consequences that will befall not only our Kingdom, but the entire realm should I allow you out of this arrangement." He was shaking now. "You will not question me again, Asteria, do you understand?"

I shrunk back, shocked at what he was saying. "Please, Father, tell me what is happening," I pleaded quietly, scared to speak.

Slamming his hands onto the desk once again, he looked at me, flushed with rage.

"No!" he bellowed. "I will not hear another word from you! Now stop this childish behavior and leave!" He turned his gaze away from me. "I do not want to hear from you again until after the wedding." For a moment, I thought I saw tears in his eyes, but I was too afraid to linger.

As I made my escape, I found the hallway full of servants who had undoubtedly heard the entire argument. As if that wasn't bad enough, I looked up to find Stefan leaning against the wall, one leg kicked up and his head shaking with laughter. Goddess dammit, he had been listening to the entire thing. I fixed my face and held my head high, straightening my spine as I walked past the row of onlookers. The moment I was out of eyesight, I ran to my room.

Once inside, I slammed my door shut, throwing myself onto my bed as I buried my head into my pillows and cried. I cried until I could cry no more, only to begin screaming into my pillows until my throat was raw. It was only after I had completely exhausted myself that I fell asleep.

When I finally awoke, the sun was streaming in brightly through the windows. My gaze stopped on a gorgeous yellow and white gown, the colors of Solaria—my gown for tonight's event, the final dinner and celebration before my wedding. My heart raced, and my head started spinning, but before I could spiral into a panic, my door opened to reveal my mother, along with a team of handmaids. They cleared the table near the fireplace and filled it with coffee, tea, fruits, and pastries.

"Good afternoon, sweetheart," my mother chirped. She walked over to me and lifted my chin to examine my face. "Goodness, we have a lot of work to do. Still, we will have you looking like the queen you were meant to be by the time the celebration begins."

I threw back my sheets, climbing out of bed and reaching for my dressing robe before heading for my chest of herbs. Opening the chest, I picked out some aloe vera leaves and chamomile flowers before going to the table and grabbing a few orange slices.

"Whatever are you doing?" my mother asked.

"Making myself the perfect queen everyone is expecting me to be," I said to her as I sat down and got to work. Grinding the chamomile flowers into a powder, I added them to the juice from the orange slices, mixing it all up to create a paste. I took the aloe leaves and sliced them longways, revealing the sticky, gel-like meat of the plant. Scraping out some of the substance, I added it to my paste to create a mask. After splashing my face with cold water, I slathered the mixture all over my skin, praying to the Goddess it would do the trick.

I let the mask marinate on my face while I sipped on a cup of hot coffee and picked at the fruits and breads. Seated opposite me, my mother sat silently, sipping on her tea for what felt like an eternity. I was too drained to fake being the happy bride anymore, and I was sure she was too uncomfortable to bring up why I needed to cake this concoction on my face in the first place.

I knew by now that she would have heard about the argument

between my father and me. I also knew that with the wedding tomorrow, she wouldn't risk bringing up the issue or dare to start an argument that could lead to my refusal to walk down that Goddess-forsaken aisle. So we sat there in silence, each waiting for the other to start a conversation—a stalemate if I had ever seen one. Finally, unable to take the awkward silence any longer, I moved to the bathing chamber. My mother followed me in, her supportive and eager mother façade back in full swing.

"So, what oils do you think we should use for your bath today? I do love your lavender and pomegranate combination. How about that?" she asked, reaching for the oils.

"No!" I stopped her. "No," I repeated calmly after clearing my throat. "I think something different for today." I loathed the thought of associating anything about this wedding with my favorite oils and scents. "How about we try mint and geranium?"

I handed her the oils so she could place them in the bath before I went to the small basin on the counter and rinsed my face. The mixture had worked well, the puffiness around my eyes had become nearly non-existent. The irritation seemed to have calmed thanks to the chamomile, and the orange did exactly as I had hoped, smoothing and brightening my skin.

"You are very talented with your herbs, aren't you?" she asked with a smile. I smiled a genuine smile, grateful for the compliment.

I climbed into the hot bath, feeling like I could die right there from the pure pleasure it brought. The combination of the cooling mint oil and the heat from the water was a somewhat euphoric sensation. I leaned back and inhaled deeply, allowing the oils to fill my senses and lift my spirits.

"Rest your head," my mother said, sitting on a stool behind me. I did as she requested, and she began to wash my hair using the same combination of soaps and oils she had used to prepare the bath.

As she massaged my scalp, the mint spurred on a strong tingle, but oh, it felt so good. I used to love when my mother would wash my hair as a child, when she would tell me stories and we would laugh and joke endlessly with one another. It had been years since I heard a genuine laugh from my mother; the thought made my heart heavy.

"I'm proud of you, Astra," she spoke smoothly. "I know this situation hasn't been ideal." *You have no idea*, I thought. "I understand how hard this must be for you. We have asked so much of you and not given much consideration for your feelings." Her voice began to shake. "You have no idea how hard this has been on your father and me, but I want you to know...if we thought we could offer you any other choice, we would. I know it doesn't make sense to you right now, and I wish I could explain it all, but it's so much more complicated and bigger than you will ever know." She was silent for a moment, the only sound was the water splashing as she continued to massage my scalp. "Despite your father's actions and words, he does love you. He is doing what he feels is best for everyone."

I sat up, pulling my head out of her hands and turning my body towards her. "What is happening?"

She stared at me for a moment before she shook her head and motioned for me to turn back around so she could finish my hair. She didn't utter another word until I was done getting ready.

I stood in front of the mirror, unable to fully recognize myself. I'd been prepared and dressed for formal events before, but nothing like this. This was over the top. Tonight, my appearance would demand attention, and I dreaded it.

My raven hair was done half-up, intricate braids woven around the golden crown that sat atop my head. The crown was made of two separate parts: the first being a simple gold tiara with canary diamonds accenting basic curves that met in the middle, creating a delicate point, and the second, a halo piece that sat further back on my head and seemed to erupt from beneath my braided hair–

golden spikes that varied in length rising from my head and creating the illusion that I had harnessed sun-rays as a personal accessory. The rest of my hair was curled and pulled over my shoulder, with golden tinsel was woven throughout the curls. My eyes were rimmed with black charcoal and painted with bronze and gold powders that matched the dusting of gold on my cheeks. I was disappointed to see that the unique silver-grey of my eyes were dulled by the choice of colors. Likewise, my lips were painted with a bland, pale color only a few shades darker than my natural skin tone.

Around my neck sat a gaudy gold choker inlaid with the same canary yellow diamonds as the crown. It was thick, heavy, and suffocating. The dress was a full-length gown of layer upon layer of flowing white fabrics, specially dyed so the white faded into a deep yellow at the base of the skirt. The dress was fitted around the bust, and the sleeves fell off my shoulders. The fabric gathered vertically along the top before flowing freely to the floor, ornate gold trimming along the sleeves and hem.

It was very pretty; it just wasn't... me. It was a dress designed to hide my curves and portray me as the perfect princess and future Queen of Solaria. From the golden sun crown to the fabrics boasting the colors of the Kingdom, I transformed into exactly what I was expected to become—a trinket for display.

I stood there trying to recognize myself, when my mother appeared behind me, a smile lighting up her face.

"You look absolutely perfect," she breathed. "I think Stefan will be very pleased."

Every part of me shuddered at that thought as I resisted the urge to roll my eyes—as if that were my only purpose, to please the prince. I plastered on a smile that did not reach my eyes and tipped my chin, acknowledging her statement. She turned me around, embracing me for a moment before holding me at arm's length.

"You, Asteria, are going to make a wonderful queen. Your father and I are so proud of you."

Her words of praise did not sit right with me. I knew they were hollow praises—honeyed words to sweeten the knowingly difficult and dark life I'd face after walking down that aisle tomorrow. The path that lead to my future husband, the orchestrator of my eternal dread.

CHAPTER 6
ASTERIA

The lively sounds of music flowed through the halls of the castle, stemming from the party celebrating the union of Pyrus and Solaria. According to my parents and, by all appearances, this was the political arrangement of the century: Solaria inherits rule over the Kingdom of Pyrus.

Dread pooled in my stomach as I rounded the corner and saw the him waiting there. I could feel his eyes boring into me, as if he were able to see beneath the layers of fabric straight to my skin. The air was thick with his desire, it poured off of him in waves that crashed into me, causing my steps to falter—a mistake that didn't go unnoticed. He sauntered over to me, his appearance pristine, the perfect facade to hide all the malice and deviance that lived within him. I was glad they had painted my face with so much color, because I could feel myself paling as he approached.

"After you, my queen." His voice was laced with the manifestation of all my nightmares. The music stopped as we walked through the door at the top of the stairs. The bustling crowd of royals in the ballroom halted their libations, turning their eyes on me.

I felt Stefan's arm loop through mine, pulling me tight to his side as the herald announced our entrance. My heart began to race as we descended the stairs into the crowd below; I could feel every pair of eyes on me, stalking my every move, picking me apart, judging me. The dance floor cleared as we neared the center, the silence deafening as Stefan threaded one arm around my waist and turned me to face him, lacing his fingers through mine.

Looking down at me, his golden eyes shifted to the deepest shade of amber—void of any compassion but full of malice, lust, and dominance. A sly smirk graced his thin lips, his face giving life to the words he need not say: "*You are mine.*"

The band started with a slow waltz, and we moved across the dance floor gracefully, never missing a beat, just as we had been taught. I felt his stare burning into my skin as I kept my face at an angle to avoid his gaze. As the tempo increased, so did the beating of my heart. The room suddenly seemed smaller than it had before. *Were the guests moving closer to us?* I felt flushed everywhere except where Stefan's hands gripped me. The chill from his touch and the heat from my nerves, combined with the drumming of my pulse, created a disorienting and grating sensation throughout my body. I felt the urge to bolt from the floor, every cell within me vibrating in warning. I eyed the exits, trying to determine the fastest escape from his claws when the music ended on a quick flourish of notes. Before I even had a chance to catch my breath, Stefan's hand was under my chin, lifting my gaze to his as he placed a strong, possessive kiss on my lips. I went to pull away but halted when his grip around my waist tightened and his teeth caught my bottom lip.

"Do not embarrass me, Asteria, or I will make sure you sincerely regret that decision."

I softened my gaze, looking up at him. "Whatever do you mean, my prince? I am here simply to serve."

I shifted my weight so that the heel of my shoe was planted on top of his foot. The low, guttural noise that echoed in his throat told me I'd hit my mark, but his face revealed nothing.

We made our way, arm in arm, to the dais where our thrones awaited us. We reached the platform and turned to face the crowd of guests here in our honor, and Stefan began to speak.

"Kingdoms of Leethe, I cannot begin to tell you how grateful we are to have you here in the Kingdom of Solaria, celebrating this momentous union. For years, I have searched for ways to fortify my Kingdom and, as many of you know, our strength has been dwindling."

Lies, I thought.

"As I looked to the other Kingdoms for solutions, I was encouraged by my father to look for this strength through a marital union. It was then that I realized the solution to not only the problems my Kingdom faced, but also the problems faced by Pyrus: a marriage, a political union that would allow us to rebuild, to solve our problems together. And, in return, allow us to be able to offer greater aid to you, the allied Kingdoms of Leethe. This union, this blessed marriage to Princess Asteria, will mark the beginning of a new era, of a more giving Kingdom, and of a stronger and more resilient realm!"

The crowd erupted in applause, cheering and congratulating Stefan for such a formidable alliance, for such a genius plan. He smiled and thanked those who approached the dais, and as I sat there, watching him woo the people in front of him, I understood what they saw in him.

Stefan wasn't unattractive. His honey brown hair was cropped short at the sides, the top long enough to brush back out of his face. He had a sun-kissed complexion, and his bone structure was sharp in all the right places. He stood a little over six feet tall, and it was evident he spent many hours training. I could easily understand why many women swooned in his presence. Even beyond his appearance, his easy, natural charm could work a crowd and command attention.

What these infatuated onlookers didn't realize, though, was that it was all an act, a carefully manicured mask to expertly control both people and situations. The true face behind that mask was one of vengeance, malice, hate, and evil—someone who was going to get what they wanted, no matter the cost. It was that face, the one without the mask, that I saw, that haunted me. *He* haunted me. While I was awake, while I slept, and as of tomorrow morning, he of my husband. A shudder rolled through me at the thought.

I excused myself to fetch a drink; it was going to be a long night, and if I planned to get through it, I was going to need more than a few of them. Turns out, it was surprisingly hard to avoid your fiancé at your engagement ball. Everyone expected you to be hanging on to each other at every moment, so every time I thought I had found reprieve, I was pulled back to his side. He ensured that every person knew I belonged to him. I was kept firmly at his side, his hand either snaked around my waist or anchored on my shoulder, and at times, he would even go so far as to pull me back against his chest. No matter how I tried to get free, I was caught in his grasp.

As the night wore on, it became obvious that Stefan had indulged in more than the appropriate amount of wine and whiskey. He was soon stumbling out of the ballroom, and I finally felt as if I could breathe. I spent another hour or so mingling around the ballroom, visiting with the other heirs. As the crowd thinned, I realized how tired I was. Turning in I started up the stairs to my room when I was startled by one of my maids.

"So sorry to alarm you my Lady, but are you retiring for the evening? Shall I ready a hot bath? Let me fetch the others, and we will help you prepare for bed," she continued. I was drained and quickly decided I couldn't handle any more people for the night.

"No, thank you. I will prepare a bath and get ready for bed

myself. It's been a long day, and I would like to be left alone for tonight, though I appreciate your attentiveness." She nodded her head and headed off in the opposite direction. I let out a long sigh of relief as I continued up the stairs to my room.

The hallway was quiet, and I basked in the much-needed silence. I entered my room, finding it empty, the only sound coming from the crackling of the fire, and the only light from its dancing flames. I stood there for a moment, being one with the darkness and silence; I breathed in the cool air, exhaling the stress of the evening. I began to prepare a hot bath, taking down my hair and slipping into a simple silk nightdress.

I was adding oils to my bath when a loud bang startled me. Jumping back, I dropped my jars of oil, shattering them on the floor. *What the fuck*, I thought to myself, stepping around the broken glass and into my bed chamber. Standing in the dim fire-light, I looked for the source of the noise when three more thunderous knocks on my door reverberated through the room.

I slowly stepped towards the door when three increasingly aggressive knocks came from the other side. I began to worry something had happened; why else would someone be so insistent at this hour? I reached for the lock, slid it over, and slowly turned the handle, fearing what waited on the other side.

Before I had the chance to open the door, it was flung open from the other side. Stumbling back, trying to regain my footing, I looked up to find Stefan standing in the doorway.

"What are you doing here?" I spat, furious at the intrusion.

His eyes were glazed over, evidence of all the alcohol he had consumed during the evening. He stumbled forward, pointing a finger at me. "I told you not to embarrass me tonight, Asteria," he scolded. "I told you not to embarrass me, and yet you did just that." His words were slurred as he began stalking toward me, eyes lit with rage.

I shrunk back. "I don't know what you're talking about. I did nothing to embarrass you. I did exactly what was expected of me." My voice wobbled as I tried to argue back, weary of where this was headed.

He scoffed, eyes growing dark, switching from blind rage into something between lust and possessiveness. "I saw how you looked at every other man tonight—like you were ready to get on your fucking knees for them. You stupid little bitch; did you think I wouldn't notice? Did you think there wouldn't be consequences?"

His voice rose as his tone shifted from menacing to sadistic. "You are *mine*. You belong to *me*. Do you understand that? No other man will look at you. No other man will think of you. No man will ever dare touch you, unless it's me."

He reached out, grabbing my hair at the base of my neck and pulling me to him. He forced my head back causing me to yelp in pain. He took that as an invitation and swallowed my scream with a brutal kiss, forcing my mouth open with his tongue as he backed me into the wall, pinning me like he had so many years ago, his full weight against me. This time, though, I would fight back. I pushed at him, beating my fists against his chest, screaming at him to let me go, but he just laughed at my efforts, grabbing my hands and pinning them above my head.

"Go ahead, keep fighting," he snarled into my mouth before bruising my lips with his. I wanted to scream again, but I couldn't; I wanted to breathe, but the weight of him against my chest and his unrelenting kiss were suffocating me.

I tried to knee him, but he spit out another callous laugh and just pressed into me harder, putting his thigh between my legs to block me from another attempt. He pulled away from my mouth, catching my bottom lip between his teeth and applying enough pressure to draw blood.

"I've dreamed of the ways I would ruin you," he said, inhaling as he moved his mouth along my neck and shoulders. I struggled against his hold, my heart pounding, my breath shallow and strangled. He switched his hold on my hands, trapping them within the grip of one so he could free the other. He ran his hand down the front of my silk gown, stopping to cup my breast and gasping deeply with pleasure as he did. I screamed, but it was cut off quickly when he clamped his free hand over my mouth and nose, hindering my ability to breathe.

"Scream again, and I will break your fingers, and I will savor every moment of it." His words were more a promise than a threat. "Do you understand?"

I nodded my head, and he smiled. It was a nightmarish smile, one conveying his victory. He knew he had won—he had his prey in his trap and could do whatever he wanted. He removed his hand from my mouth, resuming his exploration of my body until it found the hem of my gown. He slid it up my legs, over my thighs, and hitched it around my hips so my bare sex was exposed. He traced a finger through my folds, circling my entrance before he plunged it inside me, and I let out a cry of pain when he trapped my mouth with his.

He moaned with pleasure as he looked at me, watching the tears fill my eyes as he asked, "Who does this belong to?" I just stared at him, scared to make a sound. His hand that held my own found one of my fingers and slowly began to apply pressure. "Who. Does. It. Belong. To?" he snarled between clenched teeth.

I closed my eyes as I let out a small cry and whispered, "You."

He took that as his cue. Yanking me from the wall, he threw me down onto the bed and ripped my gown over my head before throwing it to the side.

"Not a fucking sound," he growled as he unsheathed himself, fueled by his dark desires as he lined himself up with my entrance. "You have no idea how long I've waited for this," he said as he brutally thrust into me. Feeling him tear my sensitive flesh, I desperately gripped the sheets in an effort to prevent myself from screaming. "I've been planning this since our first kiss. You remember it, don't you?" He leaned down, kissing me painfully before thrusting a second time. It was excruciating.

"You're fucking mine." He thrust again as pain shot through me.

"I own this." He moved harder as I stifled a sob.

"No one will ever fuck you but me." He shoved inside me again, even harder than the last. With each assault, I felt another piece of my soul, my self-worth, my humanity shatter.

I laid there, tears silently streaming down my face, until he finished, my mind trying to put me anywhere but here. He collapsed on top of me, breathing heavily and covered in sweat. Where he had found euphoria, I had found desolation. He rolled off me, sitting up and turning to me while I laid there, unable to move. I flinched when I felt his thumb sweep across my cheek and wipe away the tears there.

"Remember, Princess, you are mine." His tone was soft, but with a darkness behind it, and I swallowed another sob as he laughed under his breath.

"Before you go and try to accuse me of anything, remember that this is an expectation. You are my betrothed—my queen. You will come to our bed and please me whenever I desire. And if you refuse to come willingly, I will simply take it for myself. You will take my cock and you will like it, or you will be punished." He laughed again, louder this time. "You have no idea how long I've wanted this, how many people I've had to extort, how many arrangements I had to make, and now, you're mine. I own you, Asteria, and now that I've fucked you, no one else will want you. You are tainted goods." He leaned over and brushed a gentle kiss across my lips. "Goodnight, Princess. Until tomorrow."

With that, he stood, gathered his clothes, and walked out the door.

After he left, everything froze. Time stopped, and my heart stood still in my chest. I couldn't seem to take in any air, as if my lungs were refusing to work. Chills erupted all over my body as I relived the feeling of him touching me, the feeling of him inside me, the feeling of his breath upon my ear...claiming me, destroying me, breaking me. That's what he was doing—destroying me for anyone else, destroying me so I could never look at myself, trust myself, or love myself, again. Destroying me so that the only person who held power in my life was him.

Tomorrow, I would have to commit to a life with him in front of the entire realm. I couldn't be here. I couldn't do this. A lifetime of this? Reliving this night over and over until death claimed me? No, I couldn't. I wouldn't. I would rather die than suffer through his touch again.

Carefully, I gathered my composure and rushed to the bathing chamber. The fire from my earlier attempt at bathing was still flickering, and I filled the pails up with water, stoking the flames until the water was nearly boiling. I filled the tub before gathering new oils and soaps, pouring as much as I could into the tub. Hissing through my teeth as I stepped into the water, I submerged myself completely and held my breath until my lungs burned, yearning for air. When I finally broke the surface of the water, I inhaled deeply before grabbing the rough loofah and starting to scrub. I scrubbed and scrubbed until my skin was raw and red, I tried to cleanse every last remnant of him from my body, even still, I swore I could feel his touch etching itself into my skin, making my stomach churn.

Once my I had worn down the top layers of my skin, removing any part of me harboring him, I stepped out of the bath, wrapped myself in a bathing robe, and walked to a chest with extra linens. I ripped the sheets out, splaying them across my bed. In the center, I placed a change of clothes and a book of herbal recipes I'd been curating for years before tying it all up in a small, makeshift knapsack. I dressed myself in a pair of brown leather pants and a loose brown tunic, an outfit I would have once worn when working with the healers, tending the garden, or going out riding. I quickly laced up my riding boots and grabbed the small bag I often wore around my waist. Looking inside, I breathed a sigh of relief upon seeing the small jars of different healing salves and tonics. I grabbed the few pieces of bread leftover on a tray by the fire and a satchel of gold, stuffing them inside.

Throwing on my cloak, I tethered my knapsack to my back and reached for the door handle. As the cool metal touched my skin, I froze. What was I doing? Was I really going to run? Where would I even go? I had no map, no connections, no form of defense. Growing up, I had spent very little time away from the castle grounds. I wasn't allowed to train in combat or weaponry, and I had no survival skills. What was my plan? I didn't have one—there was no plan. I stepped back, doubting myself.

There's no way I can do this on my own. If I get caught, Stefan will make sure I pay for the indiscretion for the rest of my life. If I imagined a marriage to him was bad now, if he caught me abandoning my commitment, something worse than hell would become my reality. Tears stung my eyes as my hands trembled, my breathing strangled. I was trapped, an animal caught and caged, waiting for my next performance in this traveling show that had become my life.

I looked around the room, avoiding my reflection in the large mirror beside the bed. I couldn't stand to look at myself. Honestly, I'd never really been able to, but after tonight, I couldn't stomach the sight of myself more than ever before. Inhaling deeply and trying to shut out the events of the evening, I reached forward, flung open the door, and ran.

ALL I COULD HEAR WAS the thrum of my pulse in my ears as I crept down the hall, inching closer to the door to Stefan's room. I held my breath, fearful that if I made even the slightest noise, his door would open and I would be caught—my chance at escaping lost, a mere dream. I couldn't imagine the wrath I would face if he caught me trying to leave.

I snuck past his door, pausing to listen for any sign of life moving behind it. Hearing nothing but silence, I picked up my pace, still not daring to breathe until I reached the end of the corridor and turned the corner. A sigh of relief passed my lips as I leaned against the cold stone of the castle walls. I hadn't heard or seen another person yet, and all I could do was hope that at this late hour, the castle and all its occupants were deep in slumber.

As I approached the last set of stairs to the ground floor, I heard voices. They were hushed, as if to keep what they were speaking about from reaching unwanted ears. I pressed myself into the wall, hiding in the shadows as I listened, trying to place the familiar voices.

"Are you sure this is right, Ronan?" the higher of the two voices said. *Ronan? My father?* Confused, I dared to peer around the corner.

"Elenora, you know the story. You know what it means if what was predicted comes to pass. We cannot risk it." The voice rumbled through the silent hall, growing louder as the couple appeared from the shadows to cross the foyer toward the staircase I currently occupied. As they passed beneath a lit torch, my skin chilled; I was correct. The voices *did* belong to my parents, and they were headed directly towards me.

Panicked, I turned around, looking for an alternate escape route, but there was nothing, no other halls, and I couldn't risk bursting through one of the doors, not knowing who or what might be on the other side. Their footsteps grew louder, and I knew

I was running out of time to make a decision. I felt a breeze along the back of my neck; turning, I spied a cracked window.

Goddess help me, I thought as I pushed the window wider and looked down. The fall might not kill me, but it would definitely break something. I inhaled a shaky breath and stepped up onto the windowsill, willing myself to move. The ledge was small, just wide enough for my feet. There was a metal sconce off to the side, just within reach. The voices were louder now, the footsteps growing closer; it was now or never. I stepped out onto the ledge, reaching for the metal piece, but the stone was slick, and my feet slid from under me. Swinging out my arms, I latched onto the sconce, falling forward and slamming my face into the hard stone. I wanted to scream, but I swallowed the sound along with my fear as I pulled myself up, planting my feet firmly on the ledge.

The voices paused in front of the window—I had been caught, my efforts a failure. I expected to feel my father's hands grasping at my cloak, yanking me back inside, but they never came. I strained to listen over the sounds of the wind as the conversation turned to arguing.

"This can't be the only solution," my mother pleaded. "Surely there is something you can do to help her."

My father's retort was harsh. "There is no other option. He knows. He's known for years. If any other Kingdom knew the truth, do you think a marriage would be their solution?"

Me. They were talking about me and my marriage to Stefan. I didn't understand what they meant, though—what did he know? What information could my cousin have that would be so crucial and dangerous that it could force my father's hand? What did he mean, if the other Kingdoms knew, their solution wouldn't be marriage? What would it be?

"I know, but..." My mother was cut off by my father's sharp tone.

"Dead, Elenora, she would be dead. This is our *only* option.

This is *her* only option." A moment of silence followed before the sounds of receding footsteps echoed through the hall.

Dead. My father's voice replayed in my head. *She would be dead.* I stood there, clinging to the metal while the wind threatened to knock me down. Little did it know, I had nowhere left to fall—I had hit rock bottom. I shook my head, clearing my thoughts as I climbed my way back through the window into the now-empty corridor. More worried and fearful than before, I rushed through the hall and down the stairs, aiming for the servants' entrance to the kitchen.

Much of the castle's layout was still unknown to me; my two months here had been filled with wedding planning, which happened in only specific, dedicated parts of the castle. But I knew where the kitchen was, and once I was out the kitchen door, it was a straight shot to the stables. I was close enough now I could smell the herbs and seasonings. As I turned the last corner, my body slammed into something hard.

I was caught off guard by the impact, not expecting to run into anyone near the kitchens at this hour. I looked up at a man I had never seen before.

"Oh." My voice was startled, high-pitched. "I'm so sorry, I didn't see you there. Well... honestly, I didn't expect to see anyone down here this late at night. I'm sorry. Are you okay? I wasn't paying attention. I was in a hurry, and I just... I couldn't sleep, so I thought a nice cup of tea might help." I rambled on senselessly, fearing that I had just been caught.

He eyed me suspiciously, taking in my clothes and the knapsack tied to my back. His face was hooded in darkness, and I couldn't make out any features except his mouth—the mouth that was now tipped up into a smirk.

"Obviously," he purred, his tone telling me he knew exactly what I was doing. He just stood there, making no move to go around me or to allow me to go around him.

"Obviously," I uttered frustrated and on edge, "so do you think you could let me pass?"

He chuckled, the sound almost...sensuous. He stepped to the side, bowing dramatically and ushering me forward with a wave of his hand.

"Of course, My Lady." I stood there another moment longer, unsure what game this stranger was trying to play. Did he know who I was? I certainly don't remember ever seeing him around the castle before; he was tall, built, and from this momentary interaction, a serious pain in my ass. I had a feeling I would have remembered him if we had met before. He kept his head bowed, shadowing his features. I moved around him leaving him in the hallway as I stalked through the kitchen and out the door towards the stables.

I didn't care who he was or why he was there. I only cared that he didn't stop me.

CHAPTER 7
ASTRAEUS

I didn't expect to encounter anyone at this hour. It was late, the kitchen staff had stopped working hours ago, and the torches in the castle were mostly extinguished, signaling my time to move. I figured sneaking in through the kitchen and then finding my way to the servants' quarters, where I could find some appropriate attire for tomorrow, would be the smoothest plan of action. What I did *not* expect was to nearly be taken out by a maiden who, by all appearances, was on her way out indefinitely.

The woman was astonishing at first glance. Her damp onyx hair was pulled into a braid, as if she had just bathed. Her figure curved in all the right places; most women in this realm did not appreciate a full figure, striving to stay *very* thin. Seeing a woman who did not hide her curves behind stays and binders was rare and something I deeply appreciated.

The light from a nearby torch illuminated her face. Her skin was pale, her eyes the most captivating shade of grey. They were stunning to gaze into but also rimmed with tears. The skin around them was red, raw, swollen. Her lips seemed swollen too, bruised like they had been brutally kissed, and I noticed some discoloration on the side of her face. I had heard rumors of the men in these Kingdoms using brutality and physically harming their women, to take what they wanted–it was a disgusting culture. I wanted to ask her what was wrong, but it was clear she was in no mood to converse. Watching her become flustered as she tried to explain herself, I couldn't resist lifting the corner of my mouth in amusement, which only seemed to irritate her further. *Noted.*

Whatever was driving her to leave at this hour concerned me, but as her irritation and frustration seemed to fade into something deeper, something like fear and urgency, I stepped aside. Dropping my head low in an exaggerated bow, I motioned towards her exit with a flourish of my hand. She stomped away, clearly irritated by my presence. I looked up, sneaking a final glance at her before she crossed the threshold of the door. She did have an *exquisite* form.

Lurking through the halls of the servants' quarters, I found an empty room to occupy for the rest of the evening. After digging through the room, I eventually found a tattered blanket. It wasn't much, but it would make do for the next few hours. I laid down on the worn mattress and tried to find sleep until morning, but I found my thoughts drifting back to the woman with the grey eyes and all the pain and fear behind them.

I wanted to know who had caused those tears, the bruising on her face, who had been kissing those lips before hurting her. Even in her distressed state, she was beautiful. I closed my eyes and could see her clearly, her black hair falling over her shoulders. Her top had been loose, but the front was cut low, allowing my eyes to trail down the swells of her breasts. I imagined the feel of them beneath my hands, how her nipples would harden as I brushed over them with my thumb. I trailed down her body in my mind to the curve of her hips, yearning to grip them tight, controlling her as she moved on top of me; my cock twitched at the thought.

Fuck, I groaned to myself, palming my erection. *This is not the time.* I rolled out of the bed and adjusted myself in my pants as I walked to the small bathing chamber attached to the room to splash cold water on my face. The castle had plumbing, which meant running water, but they hadn't developed the means to heat the pipes like we had back in Asphodel.

I clutched the edge of the counter, my knuckles turning white. I could not clear my head; she kept clouding my thoughts. It was strange—never had I felt like this about any woman: the lust, the passion, the desire to touch her, please her, fill her. It felt like every other woman I had seen before was a farce, and now that I had seen *her*, I had seen true beauty. I had my history of flings. Nothing was ever serious, my responsibilities were far too important to be distracted with significant relationships. Even still, I'd never been so overwhelmed with desire before, and it was really fucking with my head. I drenched my face and hair in the cold water, trying to shock my system out of the heat consuming me. It helped, but the embers still burned. I forced myself to ignore the thoughts; I refused to give into the desire, refused to pleasure myself, no matter how desperately I wanted to. Eventually, I drifted off into a restless sleep, my dreams consumed by thoughts of her.

I woke early in the morning, drenched in sweat, my cock painfully erect, aching to fill the grey-eyed woman who was haunting me. I sat on the edge of the bed, pulse pounding as I clenched and unclenched my fists, my erection straining against my pants. I had to do something about this. I couldn't focus.

I stood, rabidly unfastening the laces of my pants. Freeing myself, I inhaled deeply as I gripped the base of my cock. I closed my eyes as I stroked myself, erection in hand, imagining those striking grey eyes peering up at me from beneath a curtain of black hair. My breath quickened, matching the pace of my strokes. Images of her body beneath mine flashed through my mind, of me filling her, thrusting fast and deep. I moaned my pleasure between my ragged breaths. Bracing myself against the cool stone, I felt my pleasure cresting. My head fell back, vision tunneling as I tipped over the edge.

"Fuck," I growled out as I found my release, my head dropping forward as my strokes slowed, my hips hitching forward with the lingering sensations of pleasure. I shook my head, reeling from the intense orgasm, when I heard a flurry of excitement outside in the hall. I had been so consumed in my own activities, I had momentarily forgotten the task at hand.

I straightened, grabbing the servant uniform I had found in the room, and headed to the bathing chamber. I splashed some cold water on my face, and cleaned myself up quickly before getting dressed. The fabric hung off me; the clothes having obviously belonged to a man much larger than myself, but they would have to make do. I stashed my dagger in the waist of my trousers and began lacing my boots.

The commotion gave me the perfect opportunity to slip into the thrall of people unnoticed and blend in seamlessly. I opened the door and snuck into the hallway, sliding into the flow of workers heading towards the kitchen. There was a tension in the air that did not align with the occasion–a combination of worry and panic, not the joy and celebration I had expected. Leaving the kitchen, I crept towards the dining hall, where I expected to find the majority of the royals at this time of day. I tuned my ears to the whispers that filled the halls.

"Do you think it was a kidnapping?"

"I can't blame her. I would have run too."

"The wedding has been postponed until she's found."

"Who would have taken her?"

Someone was missing and the wedding was postponed. *This might throw a wrench in my plan.* I opened the door to the dining hall, finding it empty. *Well, this is strange.* I began wandering the castle, trying to find out what had everyone so on edge. As I came to the top of the stairs, I heard yelling from behind a closed door at the end of the hall. I crept down the corridor, making sure to keep to the shadows and stay unseen while doing my best to decipher what was being discussed behind the door by three distinct voices, all men.

"Do you understand what is at risk if she is not found and promptly returned to me?" the first voice seethed.

"I understand, son." *Most likely Prince Stefan and his father, King Dameaon.* "We know what hangs on this union, and she will be found."

The third voice sounded hesitant to speak. "Stefan, can you think of any reason she would have fled? She seemed like she had accepted her duty and was more than ready to step up for the Kingdoms. Her mother and I made sure to stress the importance."

So her father, King Ronan of Pyrus, was the third voice.

A heavy object slammed into something. "Dammit, Uncle, do you think I could begin to understand the feeble mind of my cousin?" Stefan's tone was full of rage. "I don't care why she fled. All I care is that she is returned to me. She will follow through on the arrangement. She will marry me, and she *will* be my queen. She is mine"

"Of course she will," Ronan replied. "We will send the best of our soldiers to search for her. She couldn't have gotten far. She's not equipped to survive on her own. I vow to you, she will be found, and she will be your queen. We will do whatever it takes."

"Once she encounters the harshness and filth of the common-ers, she will come running back. One night among the men and women of these towns will be more than she can handle," Stefan's father added.

Stefan hushed his father and uncle. "She *will* return to me, and when she does, she will beg for forgiveness." His voice was strained, like he was forcing himself to contain his rage. "And she had better return untouched."

As the conversation continued, my mind went to my

encounter with the woman last night. Could it be possible that she was the princess? Running into Princess Asteria herself as she escaped–what were the chances? I needed to rethink my plans; killing the prince after their union was no longer an option.

Heading back to the room I had commandeered, I began to work out a new plan when the frantic loading of carriages caught my eye. The other royals were leaving, which meant using the wedding and its events to gather intel was no longer feasible either. Frustrated, I slammed the door behind me. What the fuck was I going to do now? All my plans had been ruined. I punched the door in frustration.

"Fuck!" I yelled, shaking out my hand, now throbbing from the impact. I needed some fresh air and a drink. Changing back into my own clothes, I found my way out of the castle and headed for the nearest tavern.

Hooded in darkness, I drank my ale, ruminating over my options. Returning home with no information and leaving the prince alive would surely disappoint my father. As the evening wore on, the tavern began to quiet, allowing me to tune in more intently to the conversations happening around me.

"I heard that the prince and both kings were having a heated discussion outside the King's study this morning after the princess was discovered missing," one of the patrons started. "They were arguing about some sort of arrangement that hinged on the wedding." I already knew that.

"You know the king is struggling to provide for Pyrus; his Kingdom is losing strength. They have been trying to keep up appearances, but their people have been struggling to produce enough goods for trade." Now *that* I didn't know; they had done a good job fooling the other Kingdoms, because what intel I'd managed to gather over the years had never mentioned this.

"I think this is just a power move for Solaria. They have the largest Kingdom now—or will, as soon as the princess is found and the wedding happens," a third voice chimed in.

"You don't think Prince Stefan plans to move into other territories once he takes the throne, do you?" the second voice asked.

"With the rumors of his hubris, it would not surprise me," the first voice replied.

"If he does, would that mean he's the one from the prophecy?" the third asked, a hint of fear in his tone.

Now there's a theory I hadn't heard of. I knew the prophecy of which they spoke; it had been passed down for generations by the Kings of Asphodel, and apparently the kings here as well. It was a prophecy of a change–a vision from a magic-wielding oracle who had been captured by Solaria after the war that stripped us of our power. It came after the magic disappeared, a prediction of the downfall of the Kingdoms and the reawakening of magic, something I did not foresee coming to pass in my lifetime.

"Change comes on two moons bearing the belt of Orion.
When the falling star is enraptured by twilight,
Darkness will fall upon the Kingdom.
Out of the dark, a star will rise to remake the realm.
Beneath shadow and light, a new era will emerge, and power once lost
will be returned.
For theirs is a destiny written in twilight and stars."

The thought of Stefan being the prophesied one to change the realms and return our magic had me stifling a laugh. While I may not be able to rid the realm of the prince as I had initially planned, at least I could get information on the Kingdoms. The commoners seemed to enjoy spilling their thoughts and opinions, so maybe I didn't need to pose as a servant after all. The commoners were more than willing to divulge their information over drinks.

I would bide my time, traveling through the Kingdoms as a

mere peasant, learning what I needed about the royals from the loose lips of their people. When the princess was inevitably returned to her prince, I would return to Solaria to complete my original mission. I would send a message back home regarding my change of course, and then prepare to head to the Kingdom of Harmonia. It was there I would start to gather intel.

I tipped my head at the barkeep as I threw a handful of coins his way before returning to the room I had rented for the night. I was going to need a good night of rest before my journey.

CHAPTER 8
ASTERIA

I rode throughout the night, not knowing my destination, and, quite honestly, not caring. I just knew I had to put as much distance between me and Solaria—between me and Stefan—as I could manage. I was vaguely aware of the location of the other Kingdoms, but with no map and no guide, I couldn't be sure which Kingdom I may land in.

Images of his attack—his *invasion*, flooded my mind, and I pushed my mare to go faster, ride harder, as if I could outrun my nightmare. After the unexpected run in with the mysterious man outside of the kitchens, I had made my way to the stables, where I found a strong mare who appeared to be well-trained. I found the saddle and reins that had been designated mine and I approached the horse carefully. I gently reached out my hand, allowing the horse to come to me and coaxing her with soft praises. She returned the gesture, bowing her head and nuzzling my hand before snorting in approval.

"What is your name?" I had whispered to her. She whinnied back at me, as if in response. "Freya?" I inquired, waiting for her reaction. She gave a nod of her head and a quick stomp of her hoof, which I took to mean yes. "Good. Freya. A strong goddess name for a strong, beautiful mare."

I leaned forward, putting my forehead to hers for a moment before opening the gate to her stall and leading her out. We had stopped in the shadows of the hay that lined the side of the building as I saddled her. Then, I gazed up at the castle, taking a deep breath before mounting the saddle and racing out into the night.

It was mid-morning before we paused to rest along a river-bank. *Surely, I am out of Solaria territory,* I thought to myself, looking at the landscape. We were bordering the Ancient Forest–unmistakable with its towering, dark oak trees, the river cut through the forest before winding through green meadows into what I was sure was the Kingdom of Harmonia. Hopeful that I'd crossed the border into Harmonia, I dismounted and headed for the river, Freya trailing behind me.

I was exhausted. So much had happened since I woke yesterday that it seemed like a lifetime ago. The Earth's pull seemed to increase with each step that I took, dragging my heels as I approached the crystal waters of Leethe River.

Named after the realm since it cut through most of the King-doms, Leethe had a much older meaning to it. The Leethe is said to be a river within the Underworld, and that drinking from it would erase the memories of your life. The lore came from reli-gious beliefs that were no longer followed. But many of the stories that had been passed down through the generations became tales still shared around fires and at bedtime. If only the lore were true of the river in front of me; I could drink from it, forgetting all the pain this night has caused me. Kneeling along the bank, I splashed my face with the brisk water a few times, trying to waken my senses, but it was a failed effort. I retrieved the water bladder I'd grabbed from the stables and filled it from the river before downing it just as fast. I was parched and hungry. There was no village that I could see—just an ocean of green in one direction, a wall of trees in the other, and behind me, a path I dare not retrace.

Looking at Freya, it was obvious she was just as drained as I was, quenching her thirst from the river before resting beneath the shade of an old oak. This seemed as good of a place as any to rest for a while, my body begging me for sleep, for food. I trudged over to Freya and leaned back against the trunk of the tree. The bark was rough, but the bed of grass beneath me and the cool breeze were blissful enough that I didn't care. I reached into my pack, pulling free a few pieces of stale bread; it wasn't much, but it would have to do. I choked down the dry bread, it didn't rid me of my hunger, but it quelled it enough that I leaned my head back, and drifted to sleep.

I was drowning. The roaring of the waves filled my ears, as the cold water slammed into me like rocks. My skin stung from the impact as thunder boomed above, rattling my bones. This is my end. I struggled for air, and just when I thought all was lost, I was enveloped in warmth. I reached out my arms, searching for the source of the heat when my hands met something solid and velvety. I was confused—why was there warm velvet in the ocean?

A nudge sent me tumbling, and I awoke laying on my side. *It was a dream.* I panted, trying to catch my breath. I felt another nudge and turned my head, finding Freya; she had laid down next to me to keep me warm. I wiped my face as the rain spattered all around us, my body drenched and cold. I sat up, exhaling as I leaned against the tree, taking a moment to remember where I was. *Right,* I reminded myself. *I left.* Teeth chattering, I hugged my cloak tighter to my body. I knew I couldn't stay here much longer, I had no supplies and no shelter. I stood, grabbing Freya's reins.

"Come on girl," I urged her. "We need to find a village."

I climbed up into the saddle, adjusting my hood to protect my face from the rain. *It's just rain. You can handle a little water.* I tried to convince myself, though it was hard to do when I was shivering so violently, I could barely stay atop my horse.

We kicked off at a brisk pace, hoping to find reprieve from the rain. We continued alongside the river for over an hour until we came to a bridge, then a fork in the path. *Which path to take?* I closed my eyes, inhaling deeply. *Which path to take?* I asked myself repeatedly.

Something stirred within me, a pulling sensation, as though an unexplainable force was telling me which way to go. *Right,* I heard a voice inside say. *Go right.* I couldn't explain what I was feeling; a sort of tingling sensation starting at the top of my head and diffusing down through my limbs. *Right. Right. Right.* Every shivering cell in my body began chanting.

"Ok," I said aloud, "to the right it is." Shifting my weight and leading the reins, I urged Freya to the path on our right.

The rain continued for hours, occasionally lifting, but as night fell, it became relentless. Between the darkness and the torrential downpour, I knew we couldn't continue much further, but as we crested a hill, lights flickered in the distance. My heart began to race at the thought of warmth, of food, of an escape from this storm. We carried forward—careful of her footing, Freya galloped along the path as quickly as she could. In a little less than an hour, we arrived at a small town. Riding through the streets looking for food and lodging, I eventually stumbled upon a tavern with a vacancy for travelers.

"Thank Goddess," I mumbled. Dismounting, I handed the reins and a few gold coins to a stable hand to care for Freya. "See that she's well cared for, and there will be more gold for you tomorrow." He eagerly thanked me before leading Freya back towards the stables.

I stepped into the tavern, loud and full of music with patrons drinking and dancing. The space was warm and smelled of braised meat and soup. My shivering began to calm, as my stomach began aching with hunger, my mouth salivating at the thought of a warm meal. I approached the barkeep, soaking wet, and held out a hand of gold coins.

"One room for the night please? With food and drink." His eyes slowly slid up and down my dripping clothes, which I now realized were also covered in mud, before returning to my face, where they quickly found the bruising on my cheek. *Dammit*, I thought. I hadn't considered how my face might look after it was slammed into the castle wall. I couldn't even imagine how I looked at this moment, but my appearance might be to my benefit—surely no one would recognize me.

"It's ten gold pieces for the room and food; you want a drink, it's an extra five," the barkeep gruffed.

Of course it is. I reached into my pack, rolling my eyes, and pulled out thirty gold pieces. "How about a hot bath and dry clothes?" I asked before sliding the gold across the bar. His eyes widened in surprise, snatching up the gold as he gestured to the end of the bar.

"Follow me, My Lady."

We weaved through the crowd of patrons, and I wrinkled my nose at the reek of stale sweat and ale. I trudged behind him, up to the second floor and down a long corridor, until we reached the last door on the right. He turned around, handing me a key.

"Here's your room. Food and drink will be brought up soon, as well as dry clothing and hot water for a bath. Enjoy, princess."

I paled, worried that he had recognized me.

"Excuse me?" I said sharply. "What did you just call me?"

"Princess," he said again. "Most women seem to take to being called princess, but my apologies. It won't happen again." With a quick nod, he stalked back down the hall.

Well, now I felt guilty for my tone, but "princess" wasn't a pet name—it was a royal title. I'd never heard of a woman of common status being referred to by such a title. Then again, I hadn't spent much time among commoners; my parents wouldn't allow it.

Chills erupted over my body once again as a draft from an open window passed over me. I quickly unlocked the door to my room and went inside, closing the door behind me. It was warmer here —the space contained a small fireplace that had been lit earlier. Now it was down to mere smoldering embers, but it was still emitting plenty of heat.

The room was small. It housed a small bed on one wall, while the bath was on the opposite, with nothing but a curtain to shield it from the rest of the room. I removed my cloak and my boots, placing them next to the small fireplace before stoking the embers and adding a few pieces of wood from the pile stacked against the wall. I hoped they would dry during the night with the aid of the fire's heat. The flames began to dance along the logs, and I held out my hands, trying to warm them and regain some feeling when I was startled by a knock on the door. Jumping to my feet and running over to open it, I found a woman on the other side, holding a tray of hot soup, bread, and cheeses, a pitcher of ale in her other hand.

"Your clothes and hot bath water will be up soon. Here," she said monotonously as she placed the food and ale on the small table next to the bed. She turned and faced me, looking me over before she gave a little huff and exited the room. Usually, I would have been offended, but the food calling for me tore my mind from her rude behavior.

I grabbed the tray and set it on the floor in front of the fire, sitting down alongside it. I picked up the bread and tore off a large piece before dunking it into the soup. I was far too hungry to care about manners right now. Shoving the dipped bread into my mouth, I moaned in pleasure; it was heavenly. I ditched the bread and brought the bowl to my lips, inhaling the scents of tomato and sweet basil. Tipping it back, I drank it directly from the bowl, the heat trickling down my throat, thawing me from the inside out.

Finishing the bread and the soup, I grabbed the pitcher, hesitant to drink it. Ale had never been a favorite of mine. I much preferred sweet wines, ripe with fruity and floral notes that warmed my belly as I drank them. I swirled the ale in the pitcher, wondering if it would cause the same warming effect. Without another thought, I tipped the pitcher back and gulped down the ale when another knock sounded at my door.

Abandoning my drink by the fire, I answered the door, finding two people this time—the grumpy lady from before and the barkeep from downstairs. They were carrying pails of steaming water, and the woman had a bundle of what appeared to be clothes under her arm.

I stepped aside, allowing them to enter. The barkeep filled the bath with hot water, and Grumpy asked if I was finished with my food. I told her she could take the plates, but to leave the ale. I think I was beginning to like ale. I didn't get the fiery sensation in my stomach that wine gave me, but my head was light, and I was feeling great. The barkeep asked if there was anything else he could do for me. I stood there thinking about it for a moment, but it was hard to focus on my thoughts when it felt like the floor was moving beneath me. *Oh, I am drunk*, I thought to myself. The barkeep huffed a laugh, "Well, that's not surprising," he said, holding the pitcher in his hand and turning it upside down. "Would you like me to send up another round?"

Wait, had I said that out loud? And when did I finish off the ale? I needed to slow down. Bracing myself on the mantle above the fire, I tried to focus on the couple standing in front of me. "No, thank you," I slurred. "I'm all set." I smiled at them, face feeling flushed, and it was like the world was just slightly tilted. They closed the door as they left, snickering as they made their way back down the hall. I hadn't expected the ale to affect me so drastically, but I hadn't factored in my exhaustion and how little I had eaten since fleeing the castle.

I stood there propped against the wall, trying to convince the room to stop spinning around me. Out of the corner of my eye, I saw the steam rising from the tub that had just been filled, and I willed myself to stand upright, fighting against the spell the ale had placed on my body, forcing it to comply. I stumbled to the tub and sat beside it—I was still in my wet shirt and pants, which clung to my skin like they belonged there, refusing to leave. Struggling with the laces of my pants, I laid back to try and force them down over my hips. It was tough, but eventually, they relented, and I kicked them over my ankles.

My skin was like ice. Despite the time I had spent in front of the fire, the heat hadn't been able to penetrate through the cold wetness of my clothes. I sat up, peeling my shirt off over my head and throwing it to the side before fumbling with the ties of my stay. Out of breath and shivering, I sat there on the floor, bare and exposed, before I gripped the side of the tub, hauling myself up and climbing in. The heat from the water stung as it worked to warm my skin. Leaning back and allowing the water to cover my breasts, I sighed, enjoying the sensation of my muscles releasing after the long and difficult ride.

I soaked in the tub until the water was no longer warm and the room had stopped spinning. Sitting up, I looked around and found some soaps the barkeep had brought. I poured the soap into my hands—it didn't carry any scent to it, just smelling of castile. I lathered the soap, making sure I reached every part of my body, cleaning the day off my skin before moving to lather my hair. I rinsed the suds off before pulling the stopper and allowing the water to drain from the tub. Reaching for the towel, I began drying off, the texture rough and scratchy against my skin, and the sensation caused me to squirm unpleasantly.

I searched the room for the clothes that had been brought to me before finding them on the bed. It was a simple cotton chemise, cream in color, with a deep brown overskirt and matching bodice. I set aside the garments, slipping into the just chemise for the night. I walked over to the fire, adding a few more logs before crawling into the bed and pulling the covers over my head.

I laid there, slipping into a constant thread of thoughts, each pulling in different directions. *Where was I going? How was I going to get there? What was happening back in Solaria? Were they coming for me? Was he coming for me?* Despite the spiral of dread, the physical and mental exhaustion combined with the comforting warmth of the blankets enveloped me, lulling me into a much-needed deep sleep.

CHAPTER 9
ASTERIA

The sun broke through the window the next morning, illuminating the room with its golden rays and shining light on my impulsive choices. I sat up, my muscles stiff and my head pounding thanks to the ale from the night before. I looked around the room before hanging my head in my hands, trying to think of a plan as the side of my face began to throb underneath my palm, *what the....*

I walked to the sink to investigate, looking in the mirror that hung above the basin, I gasped slightly. I looked...rough, to say the least. My hair was an unruly mess after sleeping with it wet, and my face was bruised from when I had slipped and slammed into the castle wall. *How had I forgotten about that?*

Sighing, I found my satchel of herbs and salves, looking for one with arnica to help heal the bruising. Finding the small copper tin, I inhaled the scent of eucalyptus and rosemary as I opened it. There wasn't much left, but it should be enough to help with healing my battered face.

I tenderly applied the salve to my face before dressing. The clothing fit; after lacing up the bodice over the chemise, I caught a glimpse of myself in the mirror. The fitted top showed my shapely figure more than any clothes I had owned before. The boning pushed my breasts up so that they were very much visible above the neckline of the chemise. The lacing tapered tightly around my waist, flattening out my stomach and accentuating my hourglass figure. My mother would die if she saw me wandering around in something so common, so figure-enhancing.

I had mixed feelings about what I was seeing in the mirror: part of me admired my curves, the way my hips sloped out from beneath the cinched top, the way my waist was displayed, shrinking in so that my full breasts and my round hips were the center of attention. I liked that I wasn't wearing something to hide what I looked like, but another part of me was embarrassed. I had never worn clothing like this; I feared the judgment of people outside of this room. Would they share the same opinions of my mother and other royals? That I was too large, my figure too un-ladylike, my curves too inappropriate? I rolled my eyes at myself; it wasn't like I had much of a choice—the clothing I had brought with me was still wet, and the ones I had worn were in desperate need of a wash.

I huffed as I gathered my soiled clothes, shoving them into the pillowcase from the bed. I gathered my waist pack and headed out in search of the barkeep. I found him behind the counter of the tavern. Towering over the bar top, his burly face was stern, as though something bothered him, but as he looked up at me, it seemed to soften slightly.

"Good morning. I hope your accommodations were to your liking," he said in a chipper tone.

"Yes, thank you," I replied, looking down at the pillowcase of clothing in my hand. "I am sorry to bother, but is there any chance you offer services to launder clothing?" I asked sheepishly. He looked down at the case and let out a breathy laugh, turning his head towards a door to a back room.

"Sofia!" he called out, and through the door walked the woman from last night. "Could you please take these clothes and get them laundered?" he asked, though it was more of a command than a request. She walked towards me, holding out her hand as a signal for me to hand her the bag. She took it without uttering a word to me, but before she could make it back through the door, I called out to her.

"Thank you for the clothing!" She paused, looking back at me, her eyes dropping to my feet before slowly climbing back up my body.

She only grunted as she turned and walked through the door, out of my sight. I must have made a face, because the barkeep chimed in. "Don't mind Sofia; she's harmless. Can I help you with anything else?" He began going about his business, cleaning the glassware that lined the wall behind him.

"Would you happen to have a vacancy for tonight as well? I'm in need of lodging for another night."

He paused, looking at me curiously, his tone incredulous. "Another night? Just yourself?"

"Yes, just myself. Is it going to be a problem, or are you able to accommodate me?" I snapped back, not appreciating his questions or his tone.

His eyes remained on his task as he shook his head. "Just unusual to see a lady traveling alone. You can keep your room another night—the rate will be the same."

I nodded at him, reaching into my pack and pulling out the coins. "The Apothecary—where is it located?"

I reached the market where the apothecary was located and looked around at the stalls. Finally, I spotted the shop I was searching for among the chaos; it was on the other side of the square. I weaved in and out of the crowd, smelling spices from the baker and herbs from the man selling roasted meats on one corner of the square. The music played by a madrigal in the center stirred something in me—it was soft yet powerful, the strings playing a slow but uplifting melody, the high notes strung out by a bow picking up in tempo, matching the beating in my chest. A discordant melody fighting for attention during the final crescendo caused a fracture in my feelings, pulling my emotions in different directions before the harmony resolved into a slow and quiet finish.

I found the apothecary where I was greeted by the shopkeeper. She was a middle-aged woman, the slight wrinkles around her eyes hinted at her age, but despite her years, she was breathtaking. Her copper hair spilled over her shoulder in a thick braid that reached her waist. Her eyes were a beautiful shade of green, and her light skin was dusted in freckles. Her skirts and matching bodice were a stunning shade of deep purple, layered upon a faded black chemise.

The colors only made her hair and eyes seem to stand out even more. "Good morning, Miss," she sang. "What brings you in today?" Her voice was soft and sweet, almost musical, and her movements were fluid as she danced towards me.

"Good day," I replied. "I'm running low on some of my herbs."

"Ah, well you're going to have to be more specific," she smiled back at me.

"Right." I flushed, not wanting to tell her the herb names, concerned that she may know what I needed them for. I breathed in deeply and listed off the ingredients I needed.

"Hmmm," she hummed as she danced about, gathering the things I had mentioned. "You know, if you add a little Queen Anne's Lace, it will increase the efficiency and potency of the contraceptive effects."

My heart dropped into my stomach. I had just recently started to take a contraceptive tea—when my marriage to Stefan was arranged, I went straight to the healers and collected what I would need. I was not going to be carrying his child anytime soon, so I began taking it in secret, knowing that if I were caught, the conse-quence would have been severe. I would have been denying my husband of an heir, refusing to do my as his wife and queen. I don't know why I was so embarrassed now; I wasn't in Solaria or Pyrus, and, as far as I could tell, none of these people knew who I was.

"No need to blush. Your secret is safe with me." She winked at me from over her shoulder as she reached for a jar. "I'm going to throw some in, free of charge, from one woman to another." She walked to the front of the store, where she packed my things up for me. "Here you go. It's going to be 5 gold pieces," she said with a smile.

I reached into my bag to pull out the coins for her when the door opened, and a member of the Solaria Royal Guard walked in. I could feel the blood drain from my face as the contents of my stomach tried to force themselves back up. I turned so my back faced the door, shielding my face from the guard. I heard his foot-steps falling closer, each thud of his boots against the wood flooring made my heart skip a beat.

I looked up at the shopkeeper, who glanced from me to guard. "Good day sir. How may I help you?" she asked in that musical lilt of hers.

"I'm looking for a sleeping draught," his voice seemed to echo through the shop, "And something to help soothe the aching muscles of my men."

Her lips parted in the friendliest of smiles before stepping around the counter. "Of course. It's not every day we get to assist the royal guard of Solaria. Isn't that right?" She placed her hand on my shoulder, and her gaze met mine. "My apprentice and I will make you the most efficient sleeping draught you've ever come across, and we'll get you a balm for your men."

She put her arm around me, guiding me to the back of the shop. "Stay here, and I'll come get you when he has left."

I stood there in silence as she went back out to assist the guard;

I didn't understand why she had helped me or if she'd known who I was. My knees began to feel weak, and I found myself backing up into a wall before sliding down and sitting with my head in my palms. I lost track of how long I had been sitting there when I felt a presence kneeling in front of me, and I lifted my eyes to find the shopkeeper just inches from my face.

"Why did you do that?" I questioned her.

"The way you paled when you saw him. I don't know how you know him, but any person who causes a woman's face to pale like that can't be good news. Plus," she continued, standing up and extending her hand, "I don't know why, but I feel drawn to you, like I've met you before, or I'm supposed to know you. Something put us in each other's path, and who am I to ignore the fates?" She shrugged, pulling me up.

"I don't know how I can thank you," I said, "but I am indebted to you."

"Indebted? Oh no, just a thank you is all I need. So, let's get you those herbs and you can be on your way, yes?" she said, walking back to the front of the shop. I followed behind her, utterly confused. I was not raised to believe in things like the fates, destiny, prophecies—the whole concept seemed unbelievable to me.

"Thank you again," I said as I retrieved the five gold coins I owed her.

She pushed them back towards me. "It's on the house today," she smiled.

"I don't understand." I looked at her confused. "Why are you doing all this for me?"

She leaned in, nearing my face as she held my gaze. "You have very unique eyes. Has anyone ever told you that? I don't think I've ever seen eyes like yours before." She smirked knowingly. "Like I said, I have a feeling we were supposed to cross paths, and I want to help you in whatever way I can. So please, allow me to give you this small act of kindness." The last statement sounded like a plea.

I didn't know how to respond. I'd never had someone do so much for me with such little acquaintance. "Will you tell me your name?"

Her eyes lit up, shifting to a captivating bright green. "Coralena," she said. "Lena to those I call friends. And yours?"

I paused, biting my tongue. I couldn't introduce myself as 'Princess Asteria of Pyrus' like I had been taught; it would be a reckless move. I didn't care how drawn to me she felt—I couldn't risk someone selling me out to the guards. I didn't know what to tell her, so I stood there another moment before settling on my nickname.

"Astra" I offered, and she seemed to be satisfied by that.

"Astra." She paused, seeming to ruminate on my name. "Such a beautiful and unique name. Well, *Astra*, I wish you well. Thank you for stopping by, and may the fates be with you." She gave me a clever smile as I walked towards the exit.

"Thank you for your kindness and all of your help, Coralena," I said as I pushed the door open.

"It's Lena to you. Until our next meeting, Astra." She winked at me before she disappeared into the back.

I walked out, not knowing what to think. I was thankful for her help, but all her talk of fates and feeling drawn to me made me uncomfortable. She had a gleam in her eyes as if she knew something about me, like she was keeping a secret.

I shivered the interaction away and disappeared into the crowded marketplace. I wandered in and out of the shops and through the stalls, gathering supplies I knew I would need: clothing, pelts, a satchel to carry things, as well as a bundle of oats for Freya. I was on my way out, hungry and desperate for a drink, when my attention was grabbed by a weapons stall.

I stopped, approaching to get a closer look at the item that caught my eye: a dagger, the most beautiful dagger I had ever seen. The blade was the deepest obsidian color, with tiny veins of purple flowing throughout it. The handle was crafted from the same unique metal, beautifully and ornately sculpted. It was covered in delicate scrollwork resembling vines, and the cross handles twisted from the body of the hilt, forming two leaves, one on either side. The pommel was a flower with five petals that resembled a star, and in its center sat a glittering amethyst gemstone.

"A special piece for sure," the merchant said, jolting me out of my reverie.

"I've never seen a metal like this before. What is it?" I asked, my eyes still exploring the weapon.

"It's a rare metal, mined from the Dead Mountains that border Nyxtas and Asphodel," he explained. "It's hard to find, and even harder to mine. Many people are too fearful to venture into the Dead Mountains to even try."

"Fearful?" I asked, looking up to meet his stare.

"Don't you know about the Dead Mountains?" He looked at me with something resembling shock painted across his face. "After The Great War the remaining magic wielders retreated back to Asphodel, and strange things began to happen in the Dead Mountains. People say they've been cursed, and others say they're haunted by the spirits of the Forgotten Kingdom."

I stared at him in confusion. I had learned of The Great War in my studies, but I had never heard of cursed or haunted mountains. I shook my head as I reached down towards the dagger, but he grabbed my wrist at the last moment.

"This is a special dagger, crafted for a special owner. I won't let it go to just anyone."

Yanking my wrist from his hand, I glared up at him. "What are you asking for it?"

"I won't accept less than a hundred gold pieces," he said, his eyes shining with greed.

"A hundred gold pieces?" I barked back at him. "What do you take me for? I am not an ignorant girl you can try and swindle or take advantage of. This is a marketplace in a small village, and by the state of your stall and clothing, you don't get much for your goods. If this really is as rare of a piece as you claim, it would have been crafted by someone special. I would assume it was forged by a master, which I have no evidence to believe you could have afforded yourself. Which means this weapon is likely stolen, probably from someone of status. So, unless you would like for me to call one of these guards over to report a thief, you will offer me a respectable price, and I will allow you to continue to run your third-rate stall."

The man stood stock-still, his spine stiff, his features morphing from greed and superiority to shock and fear. His jaw tightened as his eyes looked me over before shifting back and forth, noting the guards in the square. His fists unclenched, the color returning to his knuckles; I had hit my mark.

"Sixty gold pieces," he muttered through his teeth. I stood there for a moment, appearing to ponder his offer, stretching the moments as I watched the vein in his temple pulse and beads of sweat form across his head.

"Forty gold pieces, and you'll include that thigh sheath there." I pointed to a black leather sheath made to strap a weapon to your thigh. He exhaled, placing the dagger in it before reaching his hand out, leaving his palm open so I could hand over the gold. He snapped his hand closed and shoved the sheathed dagger into my hand.

"Leave," he grumbled at me.

"Pleasure doing business with you." I quipped, smiling at him while walking away and heading back towards the tavern for the rest of the evening.

My arrival was greeted by the smell of fresh baked bread and beef stew, my stomach growled, demanding to be fed. Sofia stood behind the bar cleaning, but when she saw me, she halted her greeting and rolled her eyes dramatically before turning back to her task.

"Good afternoon, Sofia," I chipperly greeted her. "Could I please have some food brought up to my room?"

She turned abruptly, facing me with a scowl. "Room service was a one-time thing. If you want food, you can eat it down here like everyone else."

Taken aback by the force in her response, I just nodded my head and turned towards the stairs. When I got to my room, I found the laundered clothes hanging over the fireplace to dry. I placed my goods from the market on the bed, pulling out the blade and admiring it again.

I didn't know why I was so drawn to it, but it was like it called to me, resonating with something deep in my soul. I ran my finger down the blade and across the tip, marveling at its sharpness. A bead of blood welled up on my fingertip—I hadn't even realized it had punctured the skin. The pain was delayed, manifesting after the blood had begun to trail its way down my finger. I sat there for a few moments, watching the blood cut its path across my skin, breathing in, allowing myself to feel the pain.

When I could no longer feel the sting, I went to the sink basin and washed my hands, watching the clear water cloud with swirls of crimson. I sheathed the dagger before leaning down and gathering the hem of my skirts, pulling them up and strapping the sheath to my thigh. I admired the way the onyx blade looked against my pale skin. I didn't have any training with a dagger, or any weapon really, but I felt safer having it on my person. The feel of the cool black metal against my bare skin was a little secret hidden beneath my skirts, beautiful and dangerous, just like I would become.

I RETURNED DOWNSTAIRS in search of food and drink, settling into a dimly lit corner table. The barkeep brought over a plate of braised meat and vegetable stew, the flavorful aroma making my mouth salivate.

"What will you have to drink?" he asked. I debated for a moment, unsure if I should imbibe this evening, but the ale had made me feel so good the previous night.

"I'll take a pitcher of ale, thank you." His lips curled up into a knowing smile as he nodded his head and left to retrieve the drink.

I needed to figure out where I was going to go from here. I couldn't stay in Harmonia with the presence of the Solarian Royal Guard. I thought back to what the weapons dealer had said earlier about the Dead Mountains, that most people feared venturing near or into them. That was the place; nobody would be able to predict I would dare travel past the Kingdom of Nyxtas. I hung my head, the weight of it and everything else resting in the palms of my hands.

"Looks like you've got a lot on your mind," the barkeep said as he set the pitcher and a pint glass down on the table with a thud before filling the glass and sliding it towards me.

"You have absolutely no idea," I replied, reaching for the glass. He just gave me a half smile and returned to his work.

The first pint of the ale was rough as it went down; I was still not used to the bitter taste. I much preferred the taste of wine, but if I planned to keep my identity and status concealed, I needed to get used to mimicking the behaviors and habits of the villagers.

By the time I emptied my third pint, the tavern had filled with people. The music from a small band in the center set a swift tempo to which the bodies surrounding them moved. The chorus of voices swelled from polite conversation to something disorganized and deafening. I didn't know if it was because of the weight-less, tingling feeling from the ale that had me enthralled with the idea of joining the dancers, but I found myself drifting towards the throng of bodies. The way they danced was so free, moving to the music without any care or choreographed steps. I had only ever experienced dancing at formal events, which consisted of waltzes and structured promenades. Not here—men and women held one another close, swaying and spinning, laughing and smiling, enjoying themselves.

As I reached the edge of the dancers, I felt a strong hand grip my shoulder, pulling me back. I slammed into something hard: a large body, a *man's* body. I stood in shock for a moment as a large arm slipped around my shoulder, pulling me closer, causing my neck to rest in the crook of his elbow. I felt the man shift behind me, his hot, ale-laden breath against the side of my face.

"Well, if it isn't the little barterer. You owe me, you little thief." I recognized the voice, and my stomach dropped.

I swallowed the lump now sitting in my throat. "I thought we clarified earlier that *you* are the thief, sir." I struggled to keep my voice firm; his hold around my neck tightened as he slid another arm around my waist, pulling me flush against his front.

"You think you're a clever girl?" His voice was tense and force-ful. "There are no guards here to save you and your smart mouth now. I want the money you owe me."

My pulse seemed to be keeping time with the music now. "I don't have the money," I managed to whisper.

He let out a low laugh that chilled my blood as he flexed, constricting my airway slightly. "You want to try that again?" His voice was low and menacing. I struggled to get air into my lungs, my hands reaching to grasp at his arm in an attempt to loosen his hold on my neck.

"I...I..." My voice was strained. "I don't have it." His grip shifted, his hand now forcefully turning my head so I could see him; his face was red and his jaw tense—he was pissed. His hold was painful, and his fingers dug into my jaw as he glowered at me. I tried to pull my face from him, but he held me firm.

"Then we'll have to work out some other method of payment, won't we?" His gaze dropped to my lips, then my breasts, and I suddenly regretted wearing this stupid bodice and skirt Sofia had given me. I knew that look in his eyes; I had seen it in Stefan's too many times in the past. My arms were pinned to my sides, and I could feel the dagger under my skirts; a lot of good it was doing me in this moment.

If only I could hike up my skirts and retrieve it, I thought, *then I could... I could...* My frustration rose, because I knew, even if I were to wield it, I didn't know what to do with it.

"Is there a problem here?" a stranger's voice piped in from in front of us, deep, smooth, and enchanting. Something about it seemed familiar, but I couldn't place it.

"No problem here. Mind your own," the merchant said to him, not breaking eye contact with me. A cough from the stranger drew the man's attention from me, and he looked up. His hand released my face, sliding down my neck, and squeezing just enough to threaten cutting off my oxygen again. The shift allowed me to turn to see the man who had intervened.

The stranger was tall, at least half a foot taller than me, and he was handsome. Goddess was he handsome. He had raven black hair that I swore almost looked blue when the light hit it, a mess of short, tousled curls, stopping just below his eyes. *His eyes.* A poet could write sonnets about those eyes, and they would not even begin to describe the depth and beauty of them. They were green, with contrasting hues of emerald and jade. It was hard to tell in this light, but they seemed to shift in color, like a spring meadow shifting in the wind. There was something else there, though: a depth and a darkness, unique to him. What had this stranger seen to give his eyes such depth?

His face was sculpted, a chiseled jaw and a strong chin, lightly shaded with a dusting of dark black hair. His cheeks balanced everything out, giving him a bit of softness and innocence that hinted at his age, which couldn't have been much more than mine. His lips were full, beautiful, and I couldn't understand why he was over here. Why was stepping into this? Why was he helping me? His face was set into a scowl as he eyed the placement of the man's hands, his possessive hold. I didn't know what drew this stranger in, but Goddess, was I thankful.

"Are you sure there's no problem? Because this maiden looks like she would rather be shoveling shit than be in your arms," the stranger said, his voice laced with malice.

"I think there's been some sort of mistake." The man's grip tightened. "This one's here with me tonight, isn't that right?" His grip on me constricted even further, hindering my breathing. I stood there in silence, not able to speak.

"The only mistake that has been made tonight, sir," the raven-haired stranger said through gritted teeth, "is that you seem to have placed your hands where they are not welcomed and do not belong. I urge you to remove them from this woman promptly, before I am forced to remove them from your body."

I stood there in silent shock. I could have sworn there was an undercurrent of excitement when he spoke the last part. Was he enticed at the prospect of removing another man's hands from his body? The thought sent a shudder through me, but the grip on my neck and waist seemed to solidify. I made a move to step forward and release myself from his grasp, but his arm clamped down further, halting my breath.

"I thought we had an agreement? We were going to have fun tonight, sweetheart," the man mumbled along my neck as I struggled for air. My lungs began to burn, and I reached up, trying to claw my way out of his grip, but before my hands could find their mark, his grip loosened. Suddenly, my back was drenched in warm liquid, I angled my head to see what had been spilled on me when I saw the dagger protruding from his neck.

I opened my mouth to scream, but nothing happened. I stepped forward, turning in time to see the man's body drop to the floor with a thud. I stumbled back, running into a wall or beam—I wasn't sure, just that it was solid. Something warm trickled down my face; I wiped at it, assuming it was a tear, but when I looked down at my hand, it was smeared in blood.

The world seemed to slow, my vision blurring as I stared down at the man who had threatened me, now dead. I felt arms embracing me, turning me to face the dark-haired stranger. He pulled me in, burying my face into his chest, keeping me from looking at the body now lying in a pool of his own blood—the same blood that now coated my own face.

The tavern erupted in activity, people screaming and running out the door. I felt the man's arms gripping my shoulders and moving me away from his chest. He lightly grasped my face, forcing my gaze upwards. As my head tilted back, I met the gaze of the beautiful green eyes steeped in concern. His lips were moving, and I realized he was talking to me. I hadn't even noticed that the sounds of screaming and crying had faded, leaving just the static noise of my panic ringing in my ears.

"Are you alright? Did he hurt you?"

I just stared at him, and he repeated the questions twice more, each time his voice filled with more urgency. When I didn't respond, he threw a satchel onto the bar top with a thud. The man behind the bar peered up at the stranger with eyes full of fear as he opened the bag, pouring out a handful of gold.

"Clean this up for me. Does she have a room here?" the stranger asked. The tavern owner nodded his head and pointed up the stairwell. His brow furrowed as he looked down at me.

"Can you walk?" he asked. I nodded my head, and without even thinking, I started across the tavern to the stairs.

When I reached the top, I realized that the man was following behind me, and I turned to him, full of concern and fear. *Why are you following me?* The man seemed to understand my unspoken words, because he stepped back and raised his arms.

"I just wanted to make sure you were able to get to your room safely," he swore.

"Why?" I asked, hesitant to believe him. "Why are you helping me?" It made no sense; this man was a stranger. Why was he so concerned with my well-being? He didn't seem to care for the well-being of the man whose neck now held his dagger.

"Aside from your obvious state of shock? I have a problem with men who can't keep their hands to themselves. He deserved what he got. I've been in this village for a while. You're not the first maiden to suffer at his hands, but you were the last."

"I...well... I... Thank you," I eventually ground out. I turned to my door when I stopped and turned back around. "May I ask your name? I would like to know who helped me."

"Rae," was all he said before he turned on his heels and started down the stairs. Just before he disappeared from view, he called back over his shoulder. "Goodnight, Little Star."

Closing the door to my room, I leaned against it before slumping to the floor. I looked down at my hands and my clothes; all soaked with blood. My face began to heat, and my eyes welled with tears. How do these things keep happening to me?

I forced my breaths to slow and my heart to stop pounding. As a calm began to settle over me, I mustered the will and strength to change out of my blood-laden clothes. There were already pitchers of water near the dying fire; the tavern keeper must have brought them before the incident. I needed to remind myself to thank him for his kindness and hospitality before I left.

I filled the bath with the warmed water and climbed in, the water streaked red as I began to scrub the grime from my skin and rinse it from my hair. Once I felt that I removed the evidence of the murder from my body, I dried off and quickly climbed into bed.

I found my thoughts drifting to the man who had come to my rescue: *Rae*. I couldn't make sense of it, but there was something familiar about him, something that made me feel safe in his presence. I would have remembered if we had met before; a face like his wasn't one to be forgotten, and yet, that sense of familiarity lingered. Though, as I combed through my memories, there was no trace of him to be found. Closing my eyes and drifting off into sleep, I exhaled, muttering a single word.

"Rae..."

CHAPTER 10
ASTRAEUS

"What the fuck were you thinking?" I muttered to myself as I paced back and forth across my rented room. My mind was racing, trying to sort out the events of the night.

"You killed him," I continued mumbling. "You killed him in front of half the damned village. That's definitely a great way to stay invisible." I slammed my fist against the door, the pain dragging me out of my spiral, allowing me to breathe and think straight. I sighed in frustration as I fell back onto my bed, dragging my hands over my face.

I didn't know what had come over me, but when I saw that man grab another innocent woman to harass, I couldn't sit back and let it happen. I went over to exchange a few words with the man, to tell him to leave the poor maiden alone, maybe break a finger or two, but that was all. Then, I saw those eyes, the ones that had been haunting my thoughts since the night I saw her running from Solaria. They were full of fear, pleading to be let go, but she didn't look like she was going to fight back—she was frozen. I

93

couldn't allow her to give up. The need to protect her was over-whelming.

The instant he tightened his hold around her neck and the fear in her eyes evolved to pure panic was the moment my last thread of composure snapped. My dagger was in his neck before I could even think. It was a fucking stupid move. I needed to get out of this village before I did anything else to attract unwanted attention. But how would I move forward from here? I knew I couldn't remain in this village, fishing for information, but hopefully I could move through the Kingdoms without any ransom posters of my face showing up in the villages. I began to pack my things so that I could slip out before first light, using the morning twilight to leave the village unnoticed. Goddess willing, I would make it to the next one in four days.

With my things collected and ready for travel, I stood at the small window, staring at the night sky. The stars seemed brighter tonight, the full moon illuminating the streets and buildings of the sleeping village.

What are the chances she'd be here and that I would run into her? Why can't I stop thinking about her? I shuddered a sigh of frustration and moved to the bed. I unlaced my boots, setting them aside before removing my shirt and loosening the ties on my trousers. I threw myself onto my back and folded my arms behind my head, breathing deeply. I swore I could smell hints of lavender and some-thing sweeter, like pomegranate, something like *her*, and it didn't take long before her face occupied my thoughts once again.

In my tranced state a plan suddenly emerged. A plan that seemed so obvious that I could punch myself for not thinking of it earlier.

She was the answer to my problems, the key piece to bargaining with Stefan using his influence on other Kingdoms. She would be how I restored trade and replenish my people. I heard the tantrum he threw after her escape, and I imagined he would give anything to have her returned to him. And she was within my reach. I just had to figure out how to get her back to my kingdom without giving away my ruse.

I laid there, running through different ideas and tactics, trying to decide on the one most likely to succeed. I mulled over what little I knew about her—I knew she wanted to escape, which meant she would have to navigate the realm without being recognized, which would be difficult with Stefan setting all of Solaria and Pyrus on a manhunt to find her. If tonight was any indication of her naiveté, she would need protection and training, or else she wouldn't last a week on her own.

It seemed easy enough, offering her protection and training while helping her flee her beloved prince. As a bonus, I could use the time as an opportunity to question her about the royal families, gathering the information from a direct source rather than eavesdropping on common folk. The longer I went over my plan, the more it seemed like a gift from the fates. I closed my eyes, smiling to myself, and on my last breath before falling into dreams, I whispered her name.

"Asteria."

I woke the next morning as the sun crested over the horizon, stretching my limbs so that I touched both the top and the bottom of the mattress. I began to prepare myself for my encounter with the princess, knowing I only had one chance to set my plan into motion. I sat up and placed my feet on the cool stone floor, sending shivers throughout my body. The weather was definitely changing; autumn was soon to be in full swing, and the long journey home was going to be difficult before much longer.

I found my way to the bathing chamber. It was cold—at some

point in the night, the fire had died out. *Great, no warm water.* I rolled my eyes as I braced myself for the brisk wash I was about to give myself. I opted for pouring my soap and oils directly into the basin and wetting a towel to scrub myself down as opposed to submerging myself into a frigid bath.

Afterwards, I stood in front of the small mirror, inspecting my appearance. My hair had grown longer than I normally wore it, the onyx curls falling in front of my eyes. I grabbed a bottle of scented oils and put a few drops into my hands, rubbing them together before pushing them through the mess of tangled curls. I did my best to tame them, raking them back out of my face, but it was a wasted effort as loose ringlets fell back across my forehead.

This will have to do, I thought to myself as I traced my hand across my stubbled jaw. I hadn't shaved since I arrived in Solaria; it was still short and close to my face, but it wouldn't be long before it became full and in need of a trim.

Warm beams of light broke through the window of the bathroom, telling me it was time to get moving. Gathering the rest of my things, I shoved them into my pack; knowing my time was limited. I quickly laced up my trousers and threw on my boots, looking around the room, I made sure nothing of mine was left. Grabbing my cloak, and securing the toggles at the shoulder, I quickly pulled the hood up so that it shaded my face. I quickly went over my plan one last time before I grabbed my pack and headed to the stables where my horse was being kept.

The stables were quiet, most of the horses sleeping, their piles of hay still wet with morning dew. As I wandered down the stalls looking for my steed, I heard a soft voice whispering praises to someone—no, not some*one*. Some *horse*.

"That's a good girl, Freya," the voice cooed. "I hope they've been taking good care of you in here. Look, I brought you some oats from the market."

I followed the voice, searching curiously for its owner. Coming to the end of a row of stalls, I turned the corner, careful not to make any noise, and there she was.

She stood in front of a beautiful white mare, stroking her mane and feeding her praises. I stopped, leaning against one of the empty stall doors as I watched her. She was breathtaking— hair cascaded down her back like threads of silk, cheeks rosy from the chill morning air, and her *smile*. She could light the darkest of nights with that smile.

She continued conversing with her horse as though it understood everything she said. I stood there watching her for a few more minutes as she fed her horse, Freya, more oats, talking about nothing and everything.

I couldn't stay silent any longer. "How often does she talk back?" I asked, a playful smile dancing across my lips. She jumped, clutching at her chest and whipping around to face me. It took her a moment to calm herself, her face relaxing when she recognized who had startled her.

"Well, she hasn't yet, but I figure it's because we don't know each other all that well, and I have a feeling her human speak is mediocre. She doesn't want to embarrass herself." She smiled, leaning towards me and dropping her voice to a whisper. "Between you and me, my horse speak isn't that great either, but she doesn't know that yet."

I laughed, and she laughed with me before she turned her attention back to Freya, who, to my surprise, was staring straight at me. Astra leaned forward, reaching her face to the horse's ear and whispering something I couldn't make out before giving me a mischievous smile.

I slowly stalked towards her, dipping my head and sliding my hands into my pockets. "Care to share with the class, Princess?" I asked her playfully. The use of her title seemed to throw her off her game momentarily, a flash of surprise crossing her face before she fixed it, masking her worry with a smile.

"Hmmmm," she hummed mirthfully. "I don't think so, it wasn't meant for your ears; it may injure your ego."

I raised my hands to my chest, clutching them over my heart and stumbling back as though I had been injured. "You wound me, Princess."

Her smile dropped, and this time, she didn't try to mask the worry. "Why do you keep calling me that?" she asked.

I closed the space between us, dropping my head and whispered against her ear. "Because that's what you are. A little far from Pyrus and Solaria, aren't we?"

Silence.

The air stilled as her breath quickened and the color drained from her face. She looked up, her eyes wide with fear as I held her gaze. She stepped backwards, but I reached out and grabbed her hand, holding her in place as she turned to run.

"I'm not here to turn you in, Princess," I said in a hushed voice. "I'm here to do quite the opposite."

She fought against my hold, trying to pull herself from my grip, "Let me go!" she demanded.

She reared back, preparing to rip herself from my hold, and being a gentleman, I did as commanded: I let her go. Not expecting her sudden freedom, the momentum she built as she threw herself back caused her stumble and trip over herself, and she landed so very clumsily in a pile of hay.

She glared up at me, ready for vengeance, and all I could do was laugh—which, of course, only further infuriated her.

"Woah there, Princess. We just met, and already you're trying to pull me down to roll in the hay with you? How very un-princess-like."

She flushed, her eyes going wide with embarrassment. "I.., You... Just.,." she grunted angrily as she fumbled over her words. "What do you want from me?" she finally hissed, the frustration in her voice clear.

I dropped down into the hay beside her. "I want to make you an offer." She gave me a skeptical glare; she didn't trust me, and I didn't blame her.

"Look," I said, leaning back onto my elbows. "I know who you are, and I know you ran from that ill-bread beast, Prince Stefan that you were supposed to be marrying. Am I right so far?" She shifted so that she was sitting with her knees pulled to her chest as she cocked her head, examining me as if she were looking for a sign that she should trust me. "I have seen the prince and how he treats the people. I don't blame you for running, but what's your plan? Tavern hop in the Kingdoms bordering his? It won't take long for the royal guard to find you if that's the case."

She turned her head, avoiding my eyes. "No," she said plainly.

"Then what?"

"Why would I tell you what my plan is? Why would I risk you running out of here to find the first royal guardsman you can and tell him where I'm going, just so you can collect a few coins?"

Well, she made a good point. "Now why would I do that?" I replied. "What good are a few coins when I could instead have the satisfaction of going to bed every night knowing I saved a damsel from a horrendous fate?" I let out a dramatic sigh as I fell back, a hand to my forehead as if I were a damsel in distress. I opened one eye, looking for her reaction. *Tough crowd,* I thought to myself as she sat there, stoic and emotionless.

"Fine." I sat up, meeting her gaze. "I want to help you out. I can offer you protection and freedom from your beloved prince. I know my way around the Kingdoms, and I'm very good at avoiding unwanted attention, with the exception of last night anyways. I can get you wherever it is you want to go, I'll keep you safe, and I'll train you."

"Train me?" she questioned.

"Yes, train you. You need to be able to defend yourself if you plan on abandoning your royal life. There are no guards to step in when you're being harassed, but there are thieves, bandits, and all sorts of dangerous and evil people out there. If you want to last any amount of time on your own, you need to learn to fight, to wield a weapon, to hunt, to provide for yourself. I can teach you all of that."

At least if she can learn some form of self-defense, she'll be able to try and hold her own against her cousin when I return her. What a way to sooth a guilty conscience, asshole. I kicked myself internally for allowing myself to even care.

She stood, dusting the hay from her trousers and tunic. *Now that is a view I would enjoy seeing every day,* I thought to myself as I admired her curves.

"What do you want in return?" she demanded.

"What makes you think I have any desire for a returned favor?"

"No one offers anything without wanting something in return, so what is it that you want?" her tone was stern.

"Princess, there's not much you could offer me that I don't already have or am incapable of getting on my own."

She loomed over me, searching my face for a hint at my motives. "I will not sleep with you," she finally said. "If that is what you are looking for in exchange for your assistance, then you need to look elsewhere. I will not trade my body for your help."

I was shocked—that thought hadn't even crossed my mind. Alright, thoughts of her body had most definitely crossed my mind, more than once, but never as a form of payment.

"What about my dagger plunging into that scum's neck last night hinted towards me wanting to trade for sexual favors?" There are many things I had done in my life that would make her despise me, but advancing on a woman who did not consent was not one of them. "Let's get one thing very clear here, Princess: I would never ask you to fuck me in exchange for a favor. I would never force myself upon you or take advantage of you in that way. And if, by some turn of events, I do fuck you, it will be because you begged for it." I stood as well, picking the hay from my clothing. "So, have you come to a decision? Do you accept my help?"

Her brows were furrowed as she looked at me with distrustful eyes. I waited for a response, and when she didn't give one, I turned, heading down the stable to find my horse.

"Wait!" she yelled behind me, and I halted, turning to meet her gaze. "You will promise to keep me safe and to take me where I wish?"

"Anything for you, Little Star." I smirked at her.

"Will you take me to the foot hills of the Dead Mountains?".

"The Dead Mountains?" I repeated. "What would draw you there?"

She paused, as if she hadn't thought her decision all the way through, "Solitude,'' she replied.

"To the Dead Mountains it is." I shrugged. "The journey is long, and it will be difficult. With autumn approaching, the nights will be long and cold. The trails can be treacherous, and accommodations will not be fit for royalty. Are you sure this is what you want?"

"Yes," was the only answer she gave.

"Ready your horse—we leave in thirty minutes. It's a four-day ride to the next village."

With that, I left to ready my own steed. Fate must be on my side, because like a moth to a flame, she fell right into my trap.

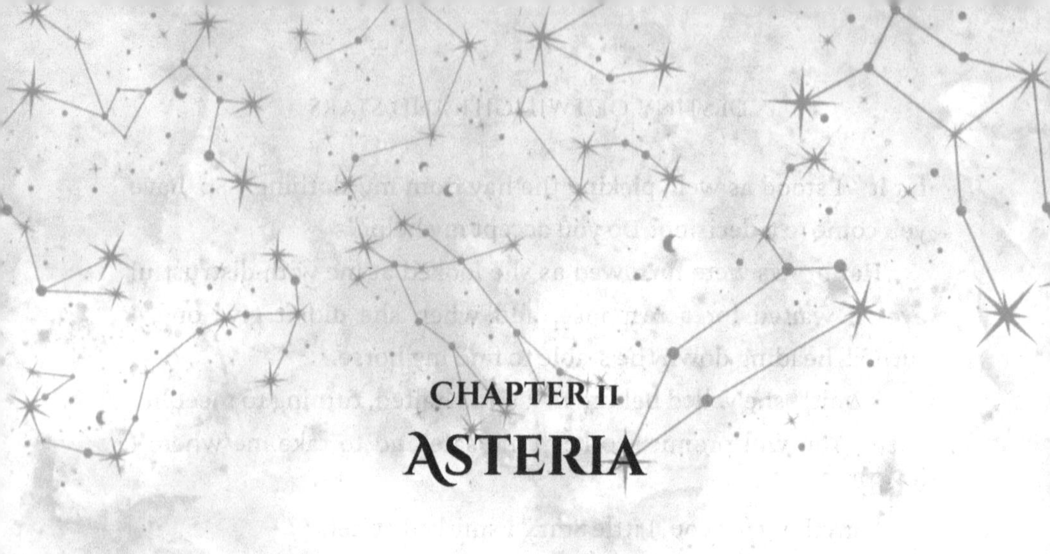

CHAPTER 11
ASTERIA

"I want to believe I can trust him," I whispered to Freya as I bridled her. "Something in me feels like I can, but his motivations concern me." I stood in front of her, my hands on either side of her face. I let out a long sigh and I pressed my forehead to hers. "What do you think? Can we?"

She lowered her head, pressing deeper into mine as she let out a soft sound, as if to say, *trust him.*

I fastened the saddle and was finishing tying down my pack when I heard a commotion coming from the stable entrance. I crept down the row of stalls until I got to the end. Peering around the corner, I saw a group of royal guards speaking to the stable hands.

Shit, shit, shit. I slowly stepped back, concealing myself from their view. I knew I should have left before first light, but I hadn't, and now, I may have lost my chance to get out of this village.

I had no idea how I would manage to slip past the guards unnoticed. I silently crept backwards when someone grabbed me from behind, placing their hand over my mouth to prevent me from screaming. Panic raced through my veins—I had been caught, and now I would be returned to Stefan. I would be forced down the aisle and imprisoned at his side for the rest of my life. My eyes watered as I struggled to breathe through my nose as I threw my head back, aiming to injure the assailant who held me captive. *Crack.* The back of my head collided with something solid, and the person released me.

"Fuck," the person said in a hushed tone. "Was that really necessary?"

I turned to see Rae rubbing his chin from the impact, blood trickling from his now split lower lip. I reached back, rubbing the crown of my head, which throbbed from the impact. Why didn't anyone ever talk about how much it hurt to hit another person?

"I'm so sorry," I pleaded, my voice soft and rushed. "I thought you were one of the guards."

"Nope, not a guard," he moaned, wiping the blood from his lip. "But next time, it might be if we don't get moving. Stay low, follow me, and keep as quiet as you can."

He crouched down so that he couldn't be seen moving through the stalls and began moving towards Freya. His horse stood next to her stall—he was huge, a war horse exuding power. His black coat reflected the early morning light as he shifted his weight impatiently from one leg to the other.

"How well can you ride?" he asked.

"Better than the average person," I replied. Growing up an only child I spent the majority of the time alone, and I often found myself in the castle stables. I would spend time talking with the horses, feeding them treats and tending to their coats. As I got older, I would take the horses out for long rides across the rolling hills and forests surrounding Pyrus.

Those rides were some of the few times I was free from the constraints of being who I was, free from what was expected of me. I had missed being able to go for daily rides these last two months. While I was trapped in Solaria I was not allowed to go riding without escorts, to *'ensure my safety'.* Looking back, I suspected it was to keep me from running.

"Grab her reins," Rae ordered, handing me the leather straps and motioning for me to follow him. I could hear the guards opening and slamming the door to each stall as they worked their way down the aisles of the stable. They were getting close.

Rae led us through the aisles, avoiding the guards with precision, heading towards the far back corner. I began to worry as I looked towards where we were heading I could see no way out. *What was he playing at? Leading the guards in a sick game of cat and mouse?*

"Where are we going?" I hissed, but he waved me off as he continued forward.

Slam! The sound of the stall door crashing reverberated through my skull; they were almost on top of us now. There was no way we were getting out of here without being caught.

Slam! Another stall door, this time causing me to jump and lose my balance. I fell forward, throwing my hands out to catch myself and letting out a startled yelp. *Fuck.* I knew what I had done before my hands touched the ground.

"There!" I heard one of the guards yell, and Rae moved instantly. With his dark hair and black clothing, he could have been a shadow. He was at my side almost immediately, hauling me up and yelling at me to get onto Freya.

I stepped into the stirrup and threw my leg over Freya's back, seating myself in the saddle. Rae was saddled and moving not even a second later. He took off, yelling for me to follow suit, and I did, kicking off as Freya jumped straight into a gallop.

We swerved in and out of the aisles of stalls, avoiding the majority of guards, and the ones we did encounter were struck down by Rae's sword before they could blink. The way he moved was mesmerizing—fluid and quick, like he anticipated every move before it was made. I was fixated on him as we continued, studying his every movement. We rounded the last corner, aiming straight for the back wall, and Rae urged his horse to pick up speed.

What is he doing? He is going to get himself killed. Even with the speed at which he rode, he wouldn't be able to break through that wall. I started to scream out his name, but my efforts were drowned out by the hollers of the guards tailing close behind us.

At the last second, Rae yelled out, and just before he collided with the wall, it moved. I was in shock as I rode through the opening where a solid wall used to be. I turned my head back, fearing that the guards had mounted horses and were following right behind us, but when I looked, there was nothing but the back wall of the stable. The opening was gone, not a single soul was tailing us. I couldn't believe it—how had he known there was a hidden exit? Who had he yelled to, signaling to open the wall, and why would they help us escape? My head was spinning with questions as we kept the strong pace, putting the village behind us.

Once the village was out of sight, and Rae was sure we were in the clear for the time being, we slowed our horses.

"Well, that's one way to get up and go in the morning, wouldn't you agree, Little Star?" he laughed, and I stared back, unable to joke at that moment. "I honestly prefer a strong mug of coffee to a life-or-death escape, but you take what you can get, I suppose." He smiled again, as if we hadn't just nearly been captured, as if our plans hadn't just nearly failed, as if I hadn't just lost my almost freedom.

"How did you know about the hidden exit?" I asked, unable to join in his light spirits.

"I told you—I've been in that town a while, and I'm very good at getting people to share things they're not supposed to." He winked. "Plus, I always make sure to have more than one escape plan, no matter where I am." He flashed me an arrogant smile, and I was equally both charmed and annoyed by it. Actually, I was more annoyed than charmed. Who was this man, and why was it necessary to have multiple escape plans wherever he went?

"Who are you?" My voice was laced with concern.

"Isn't that a question you should ask before running off into the wilderness with a strange man?" he chided. I wasn't amused, and he could tell.

He sighed deeply. "I am a man people hire to get information; information that people don't want to give." He paused, as if trying to decide if he should continue or not. "I get paid to keep other people's hands clean."

I just stared at him, unsure of how to process this information. "You're an assassin for hire?" My voice trembled slightly as I asked the question.

"Yes and no," he said with ease. "I get hired to extract information, not to kill people, but sometimes, one thing leads to another, and people wind up dead." He shrugged, his eyes forward on the path ahead.

I turned away, plastering my eyes on the path as well. I had just agreed to travel across the realm with an assassin. *That was some great investigative work you did there, Asteria. He saves you from one creep and you think you can trust him? Get it together, or you're going to get yourself killed.*

"What information were you trying to get in Harmonia?"

He laughed haughtily. "Information about you."

My stomach dropped. *Me? Who would want information about me?* Before I could ask more, he continued.

"Not so much about you specifically, but about your blessed union with your betrothed. Most people don't understand the arrangement. It's not a secret amongst the people that your cousin is a wicked human, and by giving you away to him, your father gives Stefan the right to rule over not only Solaria, but Pyrus as well. It creates a power imbalance between the Kingdoms. Many are worried about it."

My stomach dropped even further. "So, what did you find out?" *Did I truly want the answer?*

"Not much. No one seems to know why Stefan wanted this marriage so badly. The only reason anyone could think of would be to gain control of your Kingdom. That would make him the most powerful and richest king in the realm."

"Great information extractor, aren't you?" I rolled my eyes. He laughed at my comment, and the sound of it made me smile. The smile was superficial, though—his answers didn't settle the fear gnawing within me.

I knew there was more to the marriage arrangement than what he had told me; there had to be. The way my parents had acted so strangely when I questioned them about it, my father telling me that there was more resting on this marriage than I could understand, and the conversion I had heard between my parents the night I ran—there was something they were hiding. Something big. But I didn't have the slightest clue what it was. I opened my mouth to tell Rae what I was thinking but decided against it. The reasoning didn't matter. I wouldn't be married to Stefan, and he wouldn't rule Pyrus. There was nothing for the Kingdoms to worry about anymore.

"How did you move like that earlier?" I was curious. I needed to know.

"Move like what?" He looked at me quizzically, not sure of what I meant.

"Back at the stables. I've never seen a person move like that before, so silent and fluid, so fast. It was like you knew what was going to happen before it happened. At times, it didn't even seem human. You moved like a shadow. I couldn't stop watching; it was enthralling." Realizing what I had just admitted, I tucked my chin, hiding my face from his gaze.

His lips parted into the biggest smile, and he waggled his eyebrows at me. "Liked what you saw, huh?" If I had a rock, I would have used it to give him a bruise on the other side of his face to match the one blossoming from the impact earlier.

"No," I quickly and sharply replied. "I just meant... Can you teach me?" His eyes shifted, deepening in color as his face tensed, becoming stoic and serious.

"I already agreed to training you," he said. "It will delay our travels, though. We would have to train daily, if not twice a day, to get you where you're able to defend yourself." I nodded my head, signaling that I understood. "It's not going to be easy, and it's going to be painful."

Painful? Why would it be painful?

As if reading my thoughts, he said, "When I train, I train for real life situations. There will be no taking it easy. I expect you to train like your life depends on it, and I expect you to try and hurt me, because I promise that I will be trying to hurt you."

Suddenly, I wasn't so sure that I wanted to learn. "Can't you go easy on me until I learn what I'm doing? Give me some time."

He shook his head. "You'll be training to fight for your life. In a real situation, they're not going to wait for you to be ready. They're not going to go easy on you because you're not as skilled or prepared. They're going to hurt you, or worse. Do you understand, Princess? They won't care that you're a woman. They won't care that you're royalty."

I exhaled. "I understand." He was right—people didn't care. People would take what they wanted. People would do what they wanted. I knew that firsthand, and I had already promised myself that I wouldn't be weak again.

"I think you're going to do better than you realize," he said, thumbing his split lip and bruised jaw.

"Again, sorry about that." I gave him a sheepish smile.

"It's alright," he said, looking at me, his eyes darkening slightly as he noted my curves. "I liked it."

I felt the heat rise in my cheeks as I blushed from his intense gaze, having no doubt about what he was insinuating. The thought had a strange warmth swirling in my stomach that grew stronger as it traveled to more sensitive areas. I wasn't sure exactly what this was, but I knew I didn't want to explore this sensation in front of Rae. I cleared my throat and straightened in my saddle, facing down the path, trying to hide the way that had made me feel. I heard him snicker under his breath; somehow, he knew exactly what I was trying to hide.

We rode on, mostly in silence out of my embarrassment. We exchanged a few words here and there, but mostly, we just traveled down the path, our horses side by side.

It was early afternoon before we stopped to rest. Rae led our horses off the path, into a small clearing that had a small spring running through it. We dismounted and led them to the stream so they could drink and rest.

I found a place under a tall oak tree and sat down, leaning back against the trunk and breathing in the fresh air. The spot was peaceful, the breeze shifting the tall grass, carrying the scent of flowers and the promise of fall. The sky was clear and bright, and the flowers that grew in the meadow seemed to be reaching towards the sun. The sounds of the grass and trees rustling in the wind and the babbling of the spring nearly lulled me to sleep, but the thud of Rae's body planting itself to my right startled me awake.

"Tired?" he asked, passing me a bundle containing a piece of bread and a handful of fruit.

"Couldn't sleep much last night," I admitted, picking up the bread and tearing a small piece off.

"Couldn't stop thinking about me, huh?" he prodded my side with his elbow. "Yeah, I know. Most maidens I meet have that problem."

Goddess, did he really think that highly of himself? I closed my eyes, remembering the nightmares that had ripped me from my sleep many times throughout the previous night. It was always the same—it was always him, his hands, his lips, his face as he forced himself upon me. I would awake drenched in sweat, swearing I could feel his hands on my skin, leaving me cold and clammy. He had become a monster I couldn't escape, no matter how far away I ran.

"Yeah, something like that" I answered half-heartedly before I took a bite of a strawberry.

I leaned my head back, resting it on the tree and inhaling deeply. I released the breath slowly, trying to erase the memories from my mind and return to the present. I knew better than to dwell on that night; no good could come from it. Instead, I sat there, eyes closed, focused on my breathing, when I felt Rae staring at me. I opened my eyes, turning my face towards him and I was met by those striking green eyes. They were a softer shade of green now as they scanned my face, trying to read me and figure out what had forced me to retreat into my own head. I felt heated under his gaze, so I shifted myself, sitting up and moving out of his eye-line.

"What happened?" he asked softly, like he knew it was a fragile topic to approach.

"I don't know what you mean." I cleared my throat, shifting uncomfortably. This was not a conversation I was going to be having with him. I would not be bearing my darkest parts, and I would not have him look at me as broken and something to be pitied.

"Where did you go just now?" He sat up so that his body was even with mine and he was able to look at my face again.

"Nowhere." I stood, dusting myself off. "I told you, I didn't sleep much, that's all. I'm tired."

I looked down at him, his brow furrowed in concern. He opened his mouth as if he was going to say something, but he closed it and went back to his lunch instead. I looked at his face, the bruise on his jaw darker than it was earlier, and the split in his lip had reopened while he had been eating. A slight pang of guilt hit me for being short with him. It wasn't his fault; he hadn't been the one to ruin me, to break me, but it also wasn't his business to know my history, my troubles, my flaws. I wasn't some chipped porcelain doll in need of someone to fix me.

Exasperated, I left him there and went to fetch some things out of my bags. He didn't say anything as I walked off, which nestled the guilt a little deeper. When I got to the horses, I removed my smaller satchel before reaching into another one and removing a scrap of cloth. I kneeled onto the cool damp bank, opening the satchel and removing a few vials and tins before I returned to the shade of the tree.

Rae was watching me—I had felt his eyes tracking my movements from the moment I stalked off. As I turned to walk back to him, he bowed his head, as if to hide that he had been watching me. I watched him flinch slightly as he tried to eat the bread and fruit he had brought us for lunch.

I kneeled before him, sitting back on my heels, our knees brushed against each other, causing my skin to ignite from the contact. I selected one of the vials containing witch hazel and dampened the cloth before I reached out, cupping his chin and lifting his eyes to mine. Our gazes met, and for a moment, I could have sworn the breeze stopped and the Earth stilled. I cleared my throat, dropping my eyes to examine the split in his lip.

"I'm sorry," I offered again as I reached out, preparing to clean his wound. I almost gasped at the feeling of sparks between our skin; he seemed startled by it as well, but neither of us were willing to acknowledge it. He stared up at me, concern and confusion creasing his forehead.

"Witch hazel. It will help clean the wound and prevent infection. It should also help speed the healing." His confusion eased at my explanation, and I dabbed the moistened cloth to the oozing split in his lip. He jerked his face out of my hold, reacting to the pain.

"Don't be a baby about it." I rolled my eyes at him while I turned his face back to me. "It's witch hazel, not alcohol."

He huffed as he glowered at me, frustration tensing his lip and brow. "At least the alcohol could get me drunk."

I couldn't help but laugh at him, shaking my head while I continued to clean the wound, watching him flinch at the contact. Once the split was properly cleaned, I grabbed a tin of ointment, applying it to his lip. "This should help with the pain as well as healing. It contains camphor, arnica, chamomile, and beeswax."

I placed the ointment on his cut and lightly massaged it into the injury before swiping my thumb across his lower lip. I looked up, our eyes meeting, and the heat swirling in his eyes had me quickly dropping my hand, the act suddenly seeming intimate. He rubbed his lips together, spreading the ointment over them, and I couldn't help but watch. I found myself staring at his lips, wondering how it would feel to be kissed by them, how they would taste on my own. His were full and blushed ever so slightly, thanks to herbs in the ointment, and my full attention was on them. I pulled my lower lip in, biting it as the warm, swirling sensation in the base of my stomach returned, causing me to clench my thighs together.

Oh my Goddess. I shook myself out of this strange trance. Embarrassed, I dropped my gaze and handed him the tin of ointment. "Keep applying this throughout the day. You can put it on the bruises along your jaw as well to help them heal."

He took the tin from me. "Where did you get this stuff?" he asked incredulously.

"I made it," I stated simply as I returned to my original spot next to him, picking my lunch back up from where I had left it.

"Huh," he said, obviously surprised by my statement. "Where did you learn to do that?"

I sighed and popped a piece of fruit into my mouth, taking my time to chew it, allowing him to stew in quiet anticipation before answering. "I wasn't given many opportunities to socialize and make friends growing up. I was kept to the castle grounds, and there weren't exactly many kids wandering around them. When I wasn't in tutoring or etiquette classes, I found solace in riding and working in the gardens. As I got older, I became interested in the healing properties the plants and herbs provided. So, I began working with the Kingdom's healers, helping them to harvest and prepare the plants, and then learning how to use them to make different salves, ointments, tinctures, and so forth."

I paused, enjoying the cool breeze on my skin as I bit off another piece of bread. "I wanted to be a healer myself," my tone saddened thinking of the opportunities that I was barred from as a princess.

I stared down at my food, reminiscing on the time I spent working with the healers and in the gardens with my mother, showing her what they had taught me. Those were some of my best memories from home, the only thing I really had been able to choose for myself. Everything else had been laid out and planned from the time that I was born—everything leading up to that Goddess-forsaken engagement with Stefan. Still, regardless of my lack of choices, I had more or less been happy. I loved my parents, I loved the people of my court, and I loved the people of my King-dom. I had felt honored to be able to help preside over them, to provide security for them. It was really the only other thing I had pictured myself doing, aside from my dreams of being a healer.

I found my thoughts drifting back to the betrayal I felt for the marriage arrangement my parents had made, and the fact that if they had just talked to me about their reasoning, maybe things would be different right now. Wouldn't they? Maybe they wouldn't. Maybe all roads would have led to that night with Stefan, to me running away, to me sitting here under this tree with the most handsome man I had ever seen. I felt my cheeks begin to flush again, and I suddenly felt very exposed, like he could read my every thought. I could feel him looking at me, trying to follow where my mind had wandered, which made me feel even more self-conscious. I shook myself out of my thoughts and fixed my face, removing any hints of the despair and darkness that filled the voids in my heart and soul.

"So, that's where I learned how to make that healing salve. Anyway, we should probably be going. I don't want to risk The Guard catching up to us. I've had enough excitement for today."

With that, I stood, letting him sit in the silence of my absence as I moved forward, trying to quell in the ache in my heart and soul.

CHAPTER 12

ASTRAEUS

I reached up and dragged my hand down my face, sighing deeply as I watched her walk back towards the horses. This was going to be a long journey.

This is going to be so much fun, I sarcastically thought to myself as I stood and followed her to the riverbank. She stood in front of her horse, stroking her mane and whispering low enough that I couldn't make out what she was saying.

I walked up to Odin, roughly messing his mane before giving his shoulder a pat. "Ready to move on, pal?" He nodded his head with a snort and pawed his hoof at the ground.

Asteria rounded Freya, now standing side to side with me between our two horses. I turned towards her, grabbing the reins from her grasp and extending my hand out as an invitation to aid her into the saddle. She looked down at my hand as if the gesture were offensive before rolling her eyes and snatching the reins back. Placing one hand on the saddle horn and the other on the back of the seat, she hoisted herself up with grace. I watched her, every bit entranced by her movements. My eyes drifted up from her legs and vivacious hips to her waist and full breasts before catching her icy stare. I raised my hands up in surrender.

"My bad," I exclaimed as I stepped back, turning to my own horse and mounting the saddle. "Onwards and upwards, my fair maiden." I cast a devilish smile in her direction that was met with a look of indignation.

"All right then," I said as I kicked off, setting my horse in motion. I didn't know what it was about me that seemed to dig so far under her skin, but even more so, I didn't understand why I enjoyed it so much.

"So," I slowed my pace to match hers, our horses trotting alongside, "are you always this chatty?"

"I don't know, Rae. Are you always this annoying?" she shot back quickly.

"Only for as long as I've been alive," I said with a confidence only I could use when responding to an insult like that.

"Must you insist on conversing for the entirety of our journey?" she asked, not turning her head from the road.

"Well, no. I don't have to," I paused momentarily, "but I can, so I think I will."

"Just because you can do something doesn't always mean that you should, and in this instance, I think you should reconsider. We will journey together and train, but getting to know each other's deepest, darkest secrets and becoming anything more than acquainted travel companions isn't on my list of things to achieve. So, if you insist on trying to talk my ear off every waking minute, this is going to be a very long and miserable journey for us both."

Her attitude was something I shouldn't find so attractive, but the more she argued with me, the more I wanted her to. She was splendidly enticing when she was irritated. I sensed that she was avoiding confronting something, and I had a fairly good idea what it was. She still hadn't seemed to realize that I had been the person she encountered during her escape from the castle, and I didn't plan on revealing that to her. Telling her would give away that I knew more than I let on, that I may not be the person she believed me to be. So, I kept that small detail to myself and gave a response I had a feeling would pleasantly irritate her. Pleasant for me, anyway.

"Oh, Little Star, the only person who will be miserable in my company will be you. I find myself to be quite the conversationalist and very entertaining company. If you refuse to participate, that is your own choice, but I assure you, you'll be missing out." I shot her a wink and a smile as I clicked my tongue at Odin to pick up the pace slightly. I began to sing a cheery melody as I moved along past her, her annoyance nearly palpable in the air between us.

Evening came quickly as we stopped to rest near the foothills of the Singing Mountains. We found a spot with good tree coverage, far enough off the trails that we wouldn't attract the attention of passersby. We worked together to set up a small campsite, clear the forest floor, gather kindling and firewood, and prepare our bed rolls. I proposed that we have our rolls next to each other for warmth, but the Princess insisted on opposite sides of the fire. I decided against continuing that argument as night began to fall, taking with it most small game as they sought shelter and sleep. With no desire to have another helping of bread and fruit, I reached for my bow and quiver to find some meat for dinner.

"Are you able to get the fire going?" I asked her as I strapped my quiver to my back over my cloak.

"Do I look like I am completely helpless and inept?" She was obviously offended by my inquiry.

"I don't know, Princess. How much fire-starting experience did you get in etiquette class?" She shot me a seething glare, angered at my statement, which had my cock twitching in my pants. "Woah, easy there, tiger. Try aiming that heated gaze at the kindling unless you want to start a different type of fire." She did not seem amused. "It was a joke; no need to get so murderous over there. I'm going to find something aside from fruit for dinner." I turned to leave when I heard her speak behind me.

"You're going to leave me here alone?" Fear laced her voice.

"I'm not going far," I reassured her. "I'll stay within ear shot. If anything happens, just yell out, and I'll be back." My statement didn't seem to do much to assuage her nerves. "We're far enough off the trail that we should not have any visitors or encounters tonight. If for some reason we do, yell for me, use that fancy dagger, and then run."

I looked up at the sky, the last bit of the sun's light fading quickly. "I won't be gone long, but we need food. Substantial food. Just work on getting that fire going, and I'll be back before you know it." She hesitantly nodded and turned back to the pile of kindling.

I crept off into the brush, narrowing my eyes to try and spot any game that may be nearby. As I slowly and silently ventured a little further away from the camp, I felt a small twinge of guilt for leaving her there. *She is going to be fine*, I told myself, and I knew that she would be. The chances of anyone stumbling upon us tonight were nearly nonexistent.

I heard the rustling of leaves behind me so I crouched down and turned slowly on the balls of my feet, removing an arrow from my quiver and reading my bow. I pulled back on the string, prepared to release my arrow as soon as the creature broke through the brush. The rustling grew louder—whatever it was would be here soon. Its footfalls cracked the twigs underneath it; whatever it was, it was larger than I had originally anticipated.

I leaned back, planting my back foot into the ground, knowing that if I missed my mark, I may have to go at it with my dagger. The leaves in front of me shifted, and I started to release my arrow when at the last minute, Asteria emerged from the brush, and I quickly shifted my aim, narrowly missing her.

"Fuck, Asteria! What were you thinking?" Adrenaline coursed

through me. "Do you know how close I just came to killing you?" I panted as I walked over to rip out my arrow from where it had impaled the ground. "Why are you out here?" She looked shocked and hurt at my sudden outburst, but I was too worked up to care at the moment.

"I got the fire started, and I thought I might be able to help find something to eat." She held out the front of her clothing that she had gathered into a makeshift basket. "I've found some wild garlic and root vegetables. I noticed them as we set up the camp; I thought we could use them."

I looked at her collection of foraged provisions, and I felt the anger drain from my body.

"I understand your intention, but please, next time I tell you to stay at the camp, *stay at the camp*." I made sure to emphasize the last part. "You do not know these woods, and it is not safe to venture off in the dark. Not to mention, you almost became some predator's kabob dinner." I pointed the arrow that had almost been her demise, waving it around in a playful manner as I spoke.

"I'm sorry," she apologized, "but I am not going to sit around twiddling my thumbs while I wait for you to return. And for you to-"

"Shh," I cut her off, holding up my hand and then slowly bringing my finger to my lips, signaling for her to be silent. I heard the rustling of leaves to my right. I listened another moment longer, tracking the creature's movements before I knocked an arrow and sent it flying through the dense tangle of limbs and dying leaves. A shrill tore through the air, indicating that it had found its mark. The sound startled Astra, causing her to drop the vegetables she had gathered, "What was that?!" she asked.

I disappeared behind the bush momentarily before returning, fowl in hand. I raised the bird up by its feet, dangling it in front of her with a shit-eating grin across my face. "Dinner."

She stumbled back, disgusted by the dead animal swaying in

front of her. "You're an absolute heathen," she sneered as she began to pick up the root vegetables and place them back into the folds of her skirt.

"Oh, Little Star." I leaned over and whispered in her ear, "You have no idea." The startled gasp she let out gave me all the satisfaction I needed. I snickered as I picked up the last of the produce and handed it to her before walking back in the direction of the small camp. I could hear her muttering obscenities under her breath, and the fire she emanated sent sparks across my skin.

This woman was going to be the absolute death of me, and I could not wait for my demise.

CHAPTER 13
ASTRAEUS

We spent most of the rest of the evening in silence as I prepared the fowl and she prepared the vegetables. Because of her knowledge of herbology and healing, she actually had quite a few herbs that made for a much more pleasant meal than I had grown accustomed to while traveling.

When we had finished up and packed away the remaining items we could travel with, we sat across the fire from each other. I watched her keenly as she reorganized and fussed with her herbs. She was obviously trying to avoid conversation by busying herself with something. I leaned back against a stump, one leg outstretched, the other hitched at the knee, upon which I rested an arm. Using a twig I had swiped earlier and whittled down with my knife, I cleaned the remnants of dinner from my teeth. I continued to stare, my eyes boring holes into the side of her face as I tried to unravel her story.

How did the princess of one of the most powerful kingdoms end up forcefully betrothed to one of the vilest humans I had ever encountered? What had Stefan so enraptured with her that he would propose a marriage to his cousin? I mean, I saw why he was obsessed with her— she was beyond beautiful. Her long black hair fell over her shoulder as she leaned over her things, obscuring my view of her face. The bruises and injuries from our first encounter had all but faded—the only remaining evidence was a small scar near her hairline on the side of her temple. Her steel grey eyes were so intense that she could send even the strongest of men to their knees with just a look. They were framed by the thickest, darkest lashes, which just further intensified her gaze. Her skin was smooth and pale, with just a flush of rose on the apples of her full cheeks. Her lips were soft and pillowy, with a shade that mimicked the flush of her cheeks.

My eyes slid down her frame, slowly drinking in every curve of her full breasts and hips. The trousers she wore seemed more like a second skin, showing off the swell of her ass, which, despite having just had dinner, I found myself desperately wanting to take a bite of it. But even more than that, I wanted to bury my face between her thick thighs. *Yup,* I thought to myself, *that's how I want to die. Blissfully buried between them.*

"Can I help you?" Her curt tone pulled my focus back to reality. She was visibly irritated by my staring, and fuck, did I love it.

"*Actually,*" I exaggerated my tone, "you can. Can I ask you a question?"

"I don't know," she replied flatly. "Can you keep your eyes off my ass long enough to ask?"

"If you insist." I leaned forward slightly, my eyes drifting from her face to her cleavage.

"Are you kidding me?" she asked, her face starting to flush with anger.

"When it comes to those," I shot a glance back at her breasts, "absolutely not. I would never dream of kidding about those."

"Fuck you. No, you cannot ask me a question." She pulled the furs back on her bed roll and tucked herself beneath them as she turned away from me.

"Come on, Little Star. I would much rather look at your face." The only evidence that she heard me was the obscene gesture she made over the fire with her hand. "In all seriousness, why Stefan? I'm sure there were plenty of other perfectly admirable suitors over the years. Why him?"

"I don't know, Rae," she snapped, utterly done with my antics. "I don't know why my parents chose to sell me off like cattle to the most horrendous of heirs, but they did. And now, as an added bonus, I'm in the middle of the woods, sleeping on the ground, with you incessantly annoying me with your pointless questions. Now, if you don't mind, I would like to try and sleep."

I just laughed quietly and shook my head as I leaned it back against the stump. "Goodnight, Princess," I whispered so that only the air could hear.

I stayed awake for some time longer, listening to the sounds of the forest at night: the breeze rattling the dying leaves, the symphony of chirps and clicks of the insects that sang out to each other. I thought back to my home, to my family and people. I wondered how they were fairing, if the news of the fleeing princess had reached our scouts and informants. I couldn't risk trying to get a message to my father yet, not this far from the mountains.

The scent of the cool fall air pulled me back in time to when I was child. Asphodel had been a place of magic growing up, at least through my eyes it was. People were happy, our crops yielded more than enough food, and game was plentiful. Fall had always been my favorite season. The crisp scent of the fires and the cider filled the air, and the town baker always made the most delicious apple bread, and our kitchen always ensured there was a loaf for us to have with evening tea. It had been my favorite part of the day as a kid. I would sit alongside my sister in my fathers' studies we gathered as a family, sipping on steaming hot apple astra cider with apple bread. That was before the cursed winter decimated our crops and so much of the wild game perished. It had been a horrible season. Our people did well rallying together to take care of each other, but when spring came and the crops failed to produce, our people began to panic. Despite my father's efforts and the endless work of the farmers and hunters, we never recovered.

People began to leave in droves, eventually it slowed to just a few small families or individuals over the years. My family placed themselves side by side with our people, working the land and hunting game. Our family evenings began to consist of tea and no chatter, the exhaustion evident in the deepening lines in both of my parents' faces. Even those small moments began to dwindle down to only a few nights a week, until eventually they stopped. As I got older, and I understood the struggle my parents were going through to keep our people alive, I decided that I would be the one to end our kingdom's suffering.

I had dedicated my life to successfully bringing Asphodel back into the folds of Leethe. The biggest challenge had been trying to decide how to deal with Pyrus and Solaria. They had been at the forefront of the War that sent my people into hiding. We assumed they had kept tabs on us when they told the rest of the kingdoms that our had perished and that Asphodel was no more. They told the rest of the kingdoms long ago that our people had perished, that the kingdom was no more than ruins. When the opportunity of infiltrating both kingdoms as they united under one crown presented itself, I knew it was now or never.

I rolled my shoulders and exhaled as I crawled into my bed roll, feeling the weight of my responsibilities beginning to crush me. I heard Asteria's breathing even out, the rhythmic pattern of her breath along with the subtle rise and fall of her chest were the last things I sensed before I closed my eyes and found sleep.

I was jarred awake by panicked cries coming from the direction of Asteria's bed roll. I shot up, reaching for my sword at my side, as my eyes volleyed around the camp, looking for the danger while the distressed cries and pleas for help continued from where she lay next to the fire.

A nightmare. She was having a nightmare. My fists clenched at the sounds of her pain, of the scenes her cries conjured in my mind. I wiped the sleep from my eyes and sheathed my sword as I readied to try and wake her, but before I had the chance to remove the furs on top of me, the cries stopped, and her breathing evened back out. I looked over at her, waiting for her to sit up, to do something, to say something, but she never did.

I removed the furs anyways and walked to my belongings, pulling a handkerchief from the bag. Her face was just visible in the dark, the flickers of the dying flame illuminating her features. She was crying, or at least, she had been. I cracked my neck in an attempt to tamper down the anger that began to rise inside me. I retrieved my water bladder and poured some of the cool water on the cloth. I kept light on my feet, making sure not to wake her as I dropped to one knee beside her. Strands of her onyx hair were plastered to her face, her tears mixing with the beads of sweat that coated her skin. I took the dampened cloth and gently dabbed it across her forehead and cheeks, cleaning the sweat and tears from her skin. I'm not sure what compelled the desire to comfort her, but I chose not to shy away from it at this moment.

She stirred and turned onto her back, startling me slightly. I stared down at her—she really was something unique, in the most intoxicating way. I carefully pushed the stray hairs out of her face and wiped away the remaining tears from her cheeks. I pulled her furs up, covering her from the cold air that began to whip around us.

I returned to my own bedroll after stoking the fire and feeding it more wood before finally examining the instinctual anger that reared its head at the sounds of her distress. I wouldn't say that it was an abnormal reaction; I absolutely do not tolerate the mistreatment of women. No, it was the visceral anger that began to well up inside me at the thought of *her* specifically being harmed. I didn't understand the spell this woman had on me, but she was most definitely going to make my plans difficult if I couldn't control this pull. I could not fail in my task.

The wind continued to pick up, swirling the leaves across the camp. The air was uncharacteristically cold, dropping in temperature rapidly. I burrowed beneath my own furs, laying on my side and facing the fire. I could see Asteria through the dancing flames, and for a moment, I swore I saw her staring back at me. I blinked, and through the next sway of the flames, her eyes were closed. I yawned, taking one last look through the fire to see if those beautiful grey eyes were looking back, they weren't. I closed my eyes and slipped into darkness as well.

CHAPTER 14
ASTERIA

Nightmares plagued my sleep once again, flashes of Stefan's face as he so greedily took what did not belong to him. I begged him to stop, but my pleas went unheard and unanswered. I could almost feel the tears, like little droplets of ice traveling across my heated skin. I fought and I fought until the nightmare subsided, only to have the strangest dream, so vivid that I questioned if it was a dream at all. Rae was at my side, his hands gently cleaning the sweat and tears from my skin. I could feel the ghost of a cool damp cloth swiping across my skin, his warm fingers brushing along my cheek as he pushed my hair from my face. It all seemed so...intimate.

I shook myself out of my dream state, quickly opening my eyes, meeting Rae's stare through the fire between us. He was laying on his side beneath his furs, his eyes piercing through the flames in my direction. I must have woken him during my nightmare. I can only imagine what he might have heard, what I might have said. My face flushed with both embarrassment and a feeling I could not quite name as I pictured him kneeling beside, caring for me as he had in my dream. A dream, that's all it was, all it would ever be.

This man drove me to sanity's edge; something about his sunny and sarcastic disposition edged its way to the end of every single nerve, and he knew it. He enjoyed pushing me to the brink of anger. The thought of ever feeling more than annoying repugnance towards him was laughable. At least that's what I told myself. Embarrassed at my own thoughts, I snapped my eyes shut, not wanting to endure any of his small talk.

The sun broke through the trees the next morning, stirring me from my sleep as the morning birds and animals began to wake. I sat up and stretched out my tense, sore muscles, the cool air sending a shiver down my spine. The night of restless sleep left me feeling drained.

"Good morning, sunshine," Rae's too-cheery voice sounded from near the horses. I rolled my eyes—how can someone who slept on the ground in the middle of woods wake with so much energy and be in such a good mood? I was most definitely not prepared to handle him this early in the morning. I lazily waved a hand in his direction, acknowledging his greeting.

"Are you ready to get started?" he asked as he stalked towards me with a steaming mug of what I was desperately hoping was some derivative of coffee. I glared up at him; Goddess, I was most definitely not a morning person.

"The only thing I'm ready for is a cup of coffee," I grumbled as I began to untuck myself from the furs I had become entwined in throughout the night.

"Coffee, huh?" he asked as he knelt before me, a knowing smirk tugging at his lips. "You mean like this?"

He kneeled before me, swaying the steaming mug in front of my face. The scent of coffee hit my senses like a ton of bricks making my mouth water, and my spirits instinctively felt lifted. I inhaled deeply, relishing the effect that even the smell had on me. I knew he was watching me closely, studying my reaction, trying to figure out anything he could about me. Suddenly, the smirk morphed into a mischievous grin as he drew the cup away from my face and took a long drink.

"You want some? Earn it." His face lit up as he stood and he strode back to the horses. My face instantly soured, one once again he had succeeded in his task of irritating the fuck out of me. I let out a growl of frustration as I stood and grabbed the small roll of cloth I had used as a pillow, channeling all of my frustration and anger from the last few months into my arm as I reared back, aiming for the back of his head. The bundle flew straight towards its intended target, and a small bit of satisfaction blossomed in my chest. At the last second, though, as if he knew exactly what I had planned, he turned towards me, the bundle flying past his head. It was close enough that I saw his hair shift from the breeze it had created, but he did not flinch.

"Did that make you feel better, Princess?" he asked as he lifted his mug to mouth again, this time dramatizing the whole thing by moaning in pleasure as he drank, leaving me standing there flabbergasted.

"How did you? I mean, what? How?" I stumbled over my words as he walked back towards me.

I looked up at him as he towered over me, and again, he smirked as he sipped from that damned mug. I tried to match his intensity, but my attention caught on his lips as he lowered the mug and lightly swiped his tongue across his bottom lip before biting it. The act was so small, but that electric feeling that sparked whenever we touched lit up my skin at the sight. I quickly pulled my focus back up to his eyes, only for his lips to tighten slightly as he fought back a smile. The fucking bastard knew exactly where my attention had drifted.

He leaned forward, his tousled curls brushing against my face and his breath warming my ear as he lowered his voice. "Princess, you're not exactly mysterious. You wear your intentions all over your face. You might want to work on that."

I stepped back from him, needing the space to breathe. Something about him overwhelmed me—with frustration, irritation, anger, but also with something completely new to me...Desire? Is that what these fiery sparks were every time our skin touched? Every time I saw how unrealistically handsome he was? Every time he made some small gesture, like biting his lower lip and made me feel like I was melting and freezing at the same time?

"Maybe that can be your first lesson," he huffed as he held his position in front of me.

"Maybe learning to piss off and stop being a sarcastic ass can be yours," I snipped, trying to collect myself.

He turned his back. "We're losing daylight, Princess, so I suggest you get yourself together and get ready to start moving. It's going to be a long day."

With a sigh, I hastily shoved my feet into my boots and began lacing them before quickly gathering up my bed roll and throwing my cloak over my shoulders. Rae was gathering food left over from the night before to prepare breakfast before we left, placing them into a small cast iron bowl over the fire. The fragrant herbs we had used the night before began to fill the air, and my stomach began to rumble, reminding me that I was much hungrier than I had realized.

While Rae finished up the food, I began to load my bed roll and saddle the horses for the day's journey. I had set aside a small stash of root vegetables as treats for the horses, and I felt this was as good a time as any to treat them. I pulled out two carrots from the stash and moved so that I was face to face with them as they both pawed at the ground and bowed their heads.

"Oh, there is no need for such formalities," I joked as I used my free hand to give them each a gentle rub down their snouts. "Here," I whispered as I handed them each a carrot. "No reason for you to be left out over here."

I stepped back into Rae's line of sight to find him looking in my direction, raising his bowl to indicate that it was time to eat. He handed me my bowl and sat down on a small rock across from me. Slowly, I brought the bowl to my mouth and sipped at the broth, testing its temperature. The soup was warm, but not too hot, but as I drank it down, I could feel the warmth spreading throughout my body.

"Thank you." Rae looked surprised at my thanks. "I am a princess, I do have manners," Rolling my eyes, I swallowed down another mouthful of soup.

"I never said you didn't have manners." He placed his empty bowl down in front of him. "I'm just surprised to hear something so docile coming from your mouth while directed at me."

"Ah, well, my mistake. I'll try to remember not to thank you in the future."

His shoulders rose and fell with a laugh I could not hear. "Don't worry, Princess. I'm sure that after today, you won't be wanting to thank me anytime soon."

His comment caught me off guard, and I found myself almost choking on the piece of chicken I had been attempting to eat. "What is that supposed to mean?"

"You'll find out soon enough." As if his first statement wasn't ominous enough. He stood and stomped out the rest of the dying embers as I choked down the rest of the soup in my bowl.

"Rae! What do you mean?" I asked him again. He kept moving, walking off towards the horses, not answering me. "Dammit, Rae, answer me!"

He got to the horses and stopped. "Your training starts today. You asked me to train you, so I'm going to train you." He mounted his horse gracefully, "Ready to go?"

"Was that really so hard?" I gripped the saddle and placed my foot in the stirrup, readying myself to mount my own horse.

"What do you think you're doing?" he asked, as if I had done some idiotic thing. I turned to look at him, utterly confused as to what he was implying.

"I'm trying to get onto my horse and into the saddle so we can leave, or did you forget that was what we were trying to do?"

"Oh, I know what *we're* doing, but I'm asking what you think *you're* doing. You're not riding today. You're walking." The amusement that flashed across his face lit a fire in my core, but this time, that fire was strictly out of anger.

"Excuse me?" My mouth gaped, my eyes wide in disbelief. "I am going to do what?"

"Walk," he shrugged nonchalantly.

"You're joking right?" I gaped at him, unable to believe that he was serious. "There is no way I'm going to walk while you sit, quite literally, on your high horse!"

"Well, we're not going anywhere with your ass in that saddle, so I suggest you think about what's more important to you: putting distance between you and the Royal Guards or sitting in this saddle here." He motioned to where I stood, two hands till on the leather.

I dropped my hands from their place on the saddle and turned to face him, my head arched back to find his eyes from where he sat atop his own horse.

He let out a devilishly charming laugh that matched the smile he wore as I looked at him incredulously. He leaned forward in his saddle, resting his arm across the horn as he lowered himself closer to me. The leather groaned under him as he shifted. "Be a good girl, and you won't have to walk the whole day."

I shuffled back, unsure of what to say. I wasn't sure where this man got the audacity to try and boss me around like that. In fact, being told I had to do something made me want to do the exact opposite. Telling me I couldn't do something essentially guaranteed that I was going to try and do exactly that. "What makes you think that you have any authority to order me around, to tell me what it is I can and cannot do? What I will or will not be doing?"

"Oh, Princess, don't think that I've forgotten who you are. But let us not forget who saved you, and who you asked to train you. Unless you would prefer to remain the damsel in distress. Actually, you know what?" He lowered his voice so that the next part was barely more than a whisper. "I think you quite enjoy it when I save you, Princess. Maybe you're just trying to keep me close by."

"I am not even going to dignify that comment with a response." I cocked my hip and folded my arms over my chest. "Would you like to tell me what walking is supposed to accomplish?"

"Endurance, strength, stamina. If it makes you feel any better, this is me taking it easy on you." He said it like he had offered me some huge favor, like I should be thanking him for his kindness and consideration.

"Oh," I clasped my hands together and brought them to my chest, "my hero! My knight in shining armor, how will I ever repay your kindness?" My tone was sarcastic, but it quickly flattened out, losing any trace of amusement.

He smiled, and I knew he was intentionally trying to rile me up. It fanned that flame building in my core, causing it to burn hotter with anger, but with small sparks of a feeling that had me clenching my thighs together. Something about our banter excited me just as much as it angered me, and that only angered me more. I did not want to feel anything even somewhat resembling desire and attraction towards him, towards anyone right now, maybe ever. I rolled my shoulders and twisted my head from side to side, trying to relieve some of the tension that had built there. I could feel his eyes on me, waiting to see what I said or did next, but I did nothing.

"Well, whatever way you decide, you better decide soon, because we're wasting daylight. You have two choices. You can start walking, or we can stand here and wait for your pursuers to escort you back to your wedding."

I let out a groan of frustration and ripped my cloak from the back of my saddle, quickly fastening it around my shoulders. "Fine." I turned towards my horse and grabbed the reins to hand them Rae. "Lead the way."

CHAPTER 15
ASTERIA

It couldn't have been more than two hours into the journey before I was removing the cloak. Despite the cool fall air that had begun to settle into the lands and the shade from the trees that towered above us, I had broken out into a sweat. The terrain wasn't particularly treacherous or difficult, but I didn't think I had ever kept my body in motion for so long before. It wasn't allowed for women to train back home, so my time was spent in studies, in the gardens, or on horseback. Walking for hours a day was something my body was not accustomed to, and I was *not* a fan. My feet were protesting, carrying my weight for this much time across the forest floor caused them to cramp in places I didn't even realize had muscles. My thighs burned, and my calves felt like razor blades sliced through them with each step.

My breaths were heavy and uneven, and I did not dare to even try and speak with the man who had spent this entire morning riding either just in front of or behind me. He remained perched on his horse, singing shanties and tunes like he were a songbird sent from the depths of the underworld specifically to torture me.

I focused on the sounds of my breathing to drone Rae out as I kept my eyes down, focused on where I was stepping—so much so that I had failed to realize Rae had stopped ahead of me, he was no longer on his horse but walking in my direction. I slammed into him with enough force that I stumbled back and crashed into the ground, rattling my already aching bones. I traced the line from the toes of his boots to the striking green of his eyes.

"Lesson number two: be aware of your surroundings." His smartass tone just made the situation worse. He stretched out his hand as a gesture to help me up, but I swatted it away, glaring up at him through the locks of long black hair that obscured my vision.

"I can get myself up, so no, thank you." I shifted so that I was unintentionally on my knees in front of him.

"Well, Princess, that is one way to thank me." He raised a brow at me as a smile spread across his face—a full one this time, his near perfect teeth a stark contrast to the dark shadow his facial hair created.

"Oh fuck off," I scoffed, shoving him as I stood. "You would find yourself missing a very valuable body part if you ever tried anything with me."

"What foul words that pretty little mouth speaks. Tell me, what part of your etiquette training taught you such language?"

I rolled my eyes. "The same part that taught me men like you have more balls than they do brain cells."

I wasn't sure if I had moved closer to him or if he had moved closer to me, but either way, I found myself acutely aware of our proximity. Even standing, he towered over me, the top of my head barely meeting the base of his chin. I had to tilt my head back to meet his gaze.

"Careful, Princess. With such charming words, I may mistake your bite for interest."

His warm breath moved the stray strands of hair that still lingered in my face, and I swallowed deeply as we stood there, chest to chest, breathing the same air. I followed the lines of his sharp features, and it was then I noticed the scar on his lips. I didn't know how I hadn't noticed it before; it was such a unique feature. It was older, the pink coloring of a fresh scar having faded to match the pallor of his skin. It was straight, indicating it had been an intentional cut as opposed to an accident, beginning at the lower portion of his right nostril and traveling down across both lips, stopping less than a finger's width from his bottom one. I wanted to ask him what it was from, but as I inhaled, I felt his fingers grazing my skin as he went to push the hair out of my face. I could feel him watching as I flinched from the contact.

I stepped back, clearing my throat. "So is there a reason for our stopping?" I asked as I gathered myself, dusting off my palms on my pants, looking at anything but him.

"I figured you would like a break." He walked back towards where he had dismounted and tied the horses just off the road. "There's a small clearing just through these trees, perfect for a short rest before training."

"Training? Isn't that what I have been doing all morning? I thought that all the walking was training?"

"That was part of it, yes. That was conditioning. You didn't really think that training was going to just consist of walking, did you?

"No," I lied, but I honestly hadn't given it much thought. All I knew was that I was tired, sore, and still pissed that he refused to let me have any coffee this morning. "I just didn't think that there was going to be more today." Only a partial lie this time.

"You do lie so prettily, don't you, Little Star?"

I rolled my eyes as I followed him, muttering under my breath. "I'll show you what I can do prettily. I'll prettily kick your ass."

"What was that?" He whipped around at my comment. "You'll prettily do what?"

Nervous and regretting my comment, I hesitated as he prowled towards me, backing me into a tree. "I was just talking to myself; it wasn't important." I could feel my pulse quickening as he caged me in, his arms on either side of my head as he leaned down.

"No, no. Tell me what you said."

I looked from side to side, trying to find some quick escape from this situation. Suddenly, I felt as if I were ripped from the present and dropped into the nightmare that plagued me when I slept. I no longer saw Rae's face looking down at me. Instead, it was Stefan who stood before me. The arms that trapped me were the same ones that had held me down while he violated me, forcing me to give him what I didn't want to give. Nausea rolled through me as the ground moved beneath me. I couldn't be back, not after everything I had done to escape. This couldn't be real. I began to shake violently—no, someone was shaking me. A voice grew louder as it cut through the thick haze of fog that separated me from the present.

"Asteria! Asteria, open your eyes!" Rae fervently repeated my name, slowly pulling me through the heavy black that surrounded me. My eyes fluttered open, sun beams cutting through the dying leaves above me, casting a near ethereal halo around the man cradling me in his arms.

Staring up at him, I tried to reconcile how I had ended up on the forest floor in his arms. Shaking my head, I sat up and backed out of Rae's embrace until I was able to relax into the tree. "What happened?" I asked, still trying to remember what led to the memory lapse.

"I was going to ask you the same thing." His brows furrowed in concern while those piercing eyes seemed to map my every move-ment, as if trying to read my thoughts through my reactions. How could I explain what happened when I wasn't exactly sure myself? I was still trying to regain my bearings when he spoke again, inter-preting my silence as a cue for him to answer my question.

"You were standing against the tree when you suddenly went

pale, and your eyes became distant..." He looked down at the ground, plucking a piece of grass and twirling it in his fingers, a simple action that seemed to help him to relax. "Your eyes, you looked terrified. I stepped back to give you space and tried to reassure you that you were safe, but you weren't there. You were frozen in place, but your mind was somewhere else." He threw the now-shredded blade of grass to the side and replaced it with a new one. "Then, you just collapsed. I was able to break your fall, which is when I started trying to bring you back from wherever you were, and then here we are." He looked back up at, still twisting the blade of grass. "What happened to you before we met?"

I couldn't tell him where I had been, where his actions had sent me back to, because then I would have to tell him everything that happened with Stefan, and that was something I was not going to do. Nausea rolled through me, sending me stumbling into the brush near the tree to empty my breakfast. The echoes of Stefans words seemed to be getting louder. Fuck, how was I going to get rid of his lingering hold on me? Even with all this distance between us, I still felt as though he was breathing down my neck, waiting for an opportunity to take me back and use me as he pleased.

The shadows of that night caressed my skin, sending an eruption of goosebumps down my arms as I shivered. I felt dirty, and not from the dry sweat that left a film along my skin, and not from the vomit I was still hunched over. No, this kind of dirty wasn't something I was going to be able to wash away—it was embedded in every corner of my mind. I was tainted, dirty, and ashamed of it. To divulge the events of that night to Rae would bring the shame to light, making it real. It would illuminate these dark parts I wanted, *needed*, to keep hidden. Steadying myself and breathing deeply, I shoved the demons back into their cage, willing them to remain there and let me get through this day. Turning to face Rae, I found him standing, propped up against the tree I had just been leaning against myself. His posture seemed rigid, and I didn't know if it was out of anger and frustration at my weakness, or if it was out of fear and concern.

"Are you okay?" His voice was stern and demanding, making his remark seem less like a question and more like an order to report on my status like I was a soldier.

I swiped my hand across my forehead, wiping at the cold sweat that had broken out during my emesis episode. "I'm fine; just fatigued from this morning's travels. Some food and ginger tea, and I will be good as new." I made to walk past him, but he reached out, grabbing my hand softly, an action that stopped me in my tracks.

"What just happened was more than just fatigue. Something scared you."

"I'm sorry to disappoint, but maybe your intuition isn't as accurate as you think it is. There was nothing scaring me, aside from your poor attempts to be a smart ass. Now, if you will please release me, I would like to prepare some lunch so that this feeling will pass." Reluctantly, he dropped my hand, seeming to see straight through the façade I was attempting to put on. His intuition was on point, but I wasn't going to let *him* know that.

Another meal in awkward silence. Rae didn't push anymore about what had happened, and I didn't volunteer any more information. Finishing my ginger tea, I looked up at Rae, who had begun to ready the horses to continue. "I thought we were going to train more?"

"We'll pick up tomorrow," he said, sighing as he tightened the straps on his saddle and stroked Odin's mane. "We should get moving anyway. I would like for us to make it out of these woods before nightfall. There is a small town just beyond the tree line near the base of the Singing Mountains. If we leave now, we should be able to rest there for the night."

I went to protest, but I honestly had no effort to give, and if I was being honest with myself, the instinct to protest was more of a desire to argue with him, to engage in quippy taunting like we had been before the memory of that night tried to drag me down into that dark abyss. Inhaling deeply, I followed his lead, mounting Freya for the next leg of the journey. We headed off, back onto the trail that would eventually lead us out of these woods. The silence continued between us as we rode, the only sounds steady hoof-beats and the rustling of the golden leaves as the wind blew them from the trees around us. There was no singing of birds, as they had already flown south for the colder weather, the absence of their songs set a heavy tone in the air around us.

I couldn't stop the never-ending string of thoughts that wove their way through my mind. I began wondering if I had done something to anger Rae. He hadn't been silent this long since we had met. I wanted to ask him if he was okay, or if he was irritated, but I feared that if he wasn't, my asking might cause him to be. Surely he wasn't upset with me—I hadn't done anything to anger him, had I?

I began to go over the afternoon, analyzing what happened. No, he wouldn't be angered by my episode, but annoyed? How could he not be? My attitude and argumentative statements must have aggravated him. Then, I had fainted from basically nothing. Goddess he probably thought that I was pathetic. I swallowed back the ball of hurt and emotion welling in my throat. If I felt I was disgusting and pathetic, then there was no way that he didn't feel the same. I began to fear he was regretting his offer to help me, that he was contemplating the best way to be released from the arrangement. My nerves began to get the best of me, my thoughts berating me until I began to panic. I needed to know what was wrong, why he was being so silent, so out of character. Clearing my throat, I worked up the courage to ask. "Rae? Is everything okay?"

"Of course, Princess. Why wouldn't it be?" He turned his face towards mine as I trotted up beside him.

"You've been awfully silent." I tried to interpret his facial expression. His brows were drawn together as though he had been deep in thought, trying to work out a problem of some sort. His body was tense, his grip on the reins tight, and his jaw seemed to clench and unclench repeatedly. His posturing could be mistaken for being angry, but yet, his eyes seemed to be filled with ghosts and teaming with sadness. Something about him just didn't feel angry, I couldn't explain how I knew, but I did. He was upset by something, something that seemed to be haunting him from the past.

He looked at me, his face relaxing slightly. "Just got lost in my thoughts."

"So you're not upset with me?" I felt stupid for even asking, but at the same time, I wasn't able to stop myself.

"Upset with you?" He seemed caught off guard and shocked by my question. "Why would you think I was upset with you?"

"I don't know," I answered, shifting in my saddle uncomfortably. "I ruined your plans for training this afternoon."

He let out a small laugh, and his expression softened completely then. "You didn't ruin anything, Princess. I shouldn't have tried to push you so hard right out of the gate, so if anyone ruined anything, it was me. Plus, there is no way I could ever be upset with you, Little Star." He tilted the corner of his mouth into a soft grin, and I returned the gesture with a smile of my own.

He dropped his head momentarily before returning his gaze to the trail ahead. I began to slow my pace, returning to where I had been before. I glanced at Rae as I fell behind, and as quickly as he had banished them, the ghosts of whatever was plaguing him returned, his expression hardening again.

CHAPTER 16
ASTRAEUS

She thought I was upset with her—it was the most asinine thing that had come out of her pretty little mouth yet. I meant what I said: I didn't think there was anything she could do that would cause me to be upset with her. Yes, I *was* upset—but not with her: with myself, with whoever caused the fear I saw blossom in her eyes. I knew exactly what had happened; I had seen the same expression on my sister's face. I had seen the same terror in her eyes nearly every time she was pinned once we had begun training together. For months afterwards, almost any contact from a male sent her into a panic. It was like she couldn't separate it, like every touch sent her back to the attack. Each time I saw her struggle, it ignited a rage in me so potent, I eventually found the men responsible and eviscerated them. It hadn't cured my sister's trauma, but it felt so fucking good to see the same fear instilled in their eyes. It felt even better to watch that fear flicker away as they bled out at my feet. I wouldn't typically consider myself a vengeful man, but there were certain acts that humans deserved to be punished for. Being the reason for the fear in an innocent person's eyes was one of those things.

I internally beat myself up for triggering that fear in Asteria. I knew I was not the reason it was there, but I had been careless and sent her back to that moment. I knew something had happened the night she fled. I had wanted to ask her what it was, but I hadn't. I needed to keep my feelings towards her impartial if I was to follow through with my plans.

The problem was, I was failing epically. This woman had me enthralled. Everything about her excited me. She had the figure of a goddess and the heart of a saint. She should have entire temples dedicated to her. She had the face of an angel and the personality of a devil, her tongue quick and her words deliciously clever. She was caring, but she had a fire in her that needed to be stoked. I had a feeling she had been smothered her entire life, and I wanted to set her free. I'd only seen a tiny spark of her true self, and I was starving for more.

She had also been hurt, and I should have been more cautious. I should have backed off, given her space to work through whatever happened. But fuck me, something about her just made me want to play; I couldn't stop myself from pushing. This afternoon, I pushed too far, I crossed a boundary, and I fucked up. I had heard her cries in her sleep, had seen her face that night in the castle, in the tavern with the merchant. I was careless; I didn't respect her trauma, and I felt like shit about it.

It was because of all these things that tonight, I planned to give us both some much needed space. Perfectly timed with my thoughts, the small village came into view through the thinning tree line. "There's the village. Pull the hood of your cloak up; we need to make sure you're not recognized."

"Are you sure we shouldn't just find a small clearing here in the woods?" Fear and uneasiness were clear in her tone.

"We could, but it's going to rain, and I would prefer to sleep in a bed, with a roof over my head and a fire keeping me warm. Plus, this is the last town we will be passing through before the Dead

Mountains. We should take advantage of the opportunity." Her apprehension was written clearly in her expression—she was worried she would be caught or turned in. "It's going to be okay. I promise I won't let anything happen to you, Little Star. Come on, let's get you a hot bath and some dinner."

We got to the inn as night fell upon us, the days growing shorter already. "Stay here with the horses, keep your hood up, and speak to nobody. I'm going to settle things with the Innkeeper and I'll be back soon."

She nodded as she dismounted her horse, grabbing the reins out of my hand and taking control of my horse as well. I tipped my head as I twisted under Odin's neck and headed inside. It was a shit inn, but it would also be the last place anyone would think to find the Princess of Pyrus. Plus, it was cheap, which meant we could stock up on supplies before leaving. "Two rooms, please."

"That will be fifteen gold pieces," the innkeeper crowed. She was a elderly woman with unruly silver locks hanging in front of her eyes. Despite her age and slightly unkempt appearance, she still radiated a comforting aura.

I reached into my pocket and pulled out twenty gold pieces. "Have hot water sent to both rooms, please." I gave her a charming wink, and her cheeks flushed a rose pink.

I returned outside to find Asteria feeding both horses carrots. "Where did you manage to find those?" I asked.

"I stashed some from the ones I found in the forest." She sounded proud of herself, like she'd pulled off some clever trick.

"Well, I'm sure you've just become Odin's new favorite person." I gathered our things from the horses, readying them for the night. "Would you like any help getting your things to your room?" I asked, not making the mistake of assuming she would accept or want help again.

Much to my surprise, she accepted, so I gathered her things, not leaving anything for her to carry. I opened the door to her room, setting her things on the floor near the small, dilapidated bed in the corner. I walked over to the fireplace, striking a match to get it started. The fire roared to life, the heat instantly filling the small room.

"They should be on their way up with hot water. I'm going to go take care of the horses and get us some dinner. That should give you time to bathe." She stood in the center of the room, her eyes tracing over every detail of the dingy space. "I know it's not much, but it's the last place anyone will come looking for you, and it's nicer than the forest floor."

"It's perfect."

Just then, a knock on the door signaled the arrival of hot water, and I took it as my cue to leave. I finished unloading the horses and walked them to the small stable at the back of the inn, nestling them in for the evening as a loud crack of lightning followed by the deep rumble of thunder signaled the oncoming storm.

As I rounded the corner, the first drops of rain began to fall. I inhaled, drinking in the smell of fresh fall rain, the scent taking me back to falls spent with my family. The memory pulled at my heartstrings, reminding me of a simpler time, when my kingdom wasn't on the verge of eradication. My kingdom: that was why I was here. I needed to remember why I had agreed to escort Asteria in the first place. Whatever this complicated desire I had to protect her, to know her, to want her was, I needed to get it under control.

Fuck, I was so conflicted. I knew what I had to do. As the future King of Asphodel my people would always come first, but she was making it very hard.

I refused to send her back to her doom defenseless. I would supply her with the skills necessary to protect herself, and my people would flourish once again. It was a good plan, and it would all work out. At least, that was what I kept telling myself as I returned to her room with a large bowl of stew, a platter of cheese and bread, and a pitcher of fresh water. I had taken my time settling my things into my room and retrieving food from the tavern, giving Asteria ample time to soak in the hot bath and relax. I steadied my breathing as I knocked and waited for her door to open.

Time seemed to have slowed, and it felt like an eternity had passed before she twisted the knob. There she stood, hair dripping wet over her shoulders onto her shockingly sheer chemise. I could very plainly see the shadow of her nipples and the shape of her breasts through the fabric, and my cock responded instantly, twitching in my trousers as blood rushed to it.

I stared down at the woman in front of me, unable to think anything coherent as the water continued to soak into the sheer fabric. Fuck, fuck, fuck. If she would let me, I would bury my face between her thighs while my hands explored the curves of her ass, her hips, her stomach, her breasts. I would lick and suck and taste with my name on her lips—my cock strained further against my waistband at the thought.

My mind continued to wander, and I wasn't sure how long I stood there in the doorway, dreaming of the ways I would glorify every inch of her, but it was more than long enough. I cleared my throat, wrenching my thoughts back to reality. "I brought you some dinner. It's not much, but it's hot and fresh, and it's probably better than what I could make."

"Oh," she chirped as she took the tray of food from me. "Thank you." She turned, walking to set the tray on a table near the fireplace, and I almost fell to my knees.

The light from the fire shined through her chemise, illuminating a perfect silhouette of her body. I watched the sway of her hips as she walked, and I felt my balance falter with each step she took. When she got to the table, she leaned over to set the tray down, and I could see her impeccable ass clear as day in the glow of the fire. My cock was so hard, it was aching, and I fought every urge I had to palm it through my pants. I needed to get back to my room soon, because all I could think about was how exhilarating it would feel to keep her bent over that table while I pressed my cock deep into her ass. I might have unintentionally let out a pained moan as I shifted my stance, trying to lessen the throbbing in my pants.

"Aren't you coming in?" she asked, completely unaware of the way my body was responding to seeing her in that goddess damned wet gown that was now... Fuck, that was now clinging to the sides of her breasts. I could see her nipples, and my tongue ran across the back of my teeth as I imagined biting them.

"Uhh, no, I'm going to head over to my room and bathe." I shifted my stance again, and the friction nearly caused my hips to buck. "My dinner is already in my room."

I didn't miss the flash of disappointment that crossed her face. "So you're not staying with me?" Fuck, did she want me to? Because I wanted to, but I was trying to give her space, respect her privacy, be the gentleman I so badly did not want to be.

"Not tonight, Little Star." I began to reach out to cup her chin, but quickly diverted my hand, crossing my arms across my chest instead instead. "I thought you would enjoy the privacy and space. There won't be much of that for the rest of the journey, so enjoy it while you have it." I stood straight, careful to not bring attention to my fully erect cock straining to escape my pants. "Get some rest. Goodnight, Princess."

She stared into my eyes, and I wasn't sure what she was looking for. Whatever it was, she offered up a polite smile and sweetly said, "Goodnight Rae" as she closed the door.

I marched back to my room, each step more excruciating than the last as my imagination ran rampant with images of Asteria and all the things I was desperate to do to her. I didn't think I'd ever been this hard before, and I needed release as soon as possible.

I barely had the door closed before I was unlacing my trousers and freeing my swollen cock. Beads of precum had already moistened the tip, and I envisioned it was her sweet arousal coating the head of my dick. I didn't waste time making it to the bed; instead, I leaned back against the door and slid my fist down my shaft.

I closed my eyes, picturing my Little Star bent over that table, her supple ass on display for me. I wanted to brand that ass with my teeth, to drag my dick through her folds, drenching me with her liquid heat before sliding it up between her cheeks and stopping right at the hollow of her ass. My pulse thrummed in my ears, and the sounds of my own breathing began to drown out any other noise.

I increased the speed and pressure, gripping my cock tighter as I fantasized about grasping her hips and pressing into her slowly, pulling her back onto me. I tried to imagine the noises she would make as I sunk into her, stretching her around me, what her breathy moans might sound like as I withdrew to the tip before pushing back in, deeper than before. I was feral at the images, heat dipping lower in my belly as my balls tightened. I kicked my head back, letting out a deep moan as my hips began to jerk as my orgasm crested. My breath stuttered as my cock began to pulse, ribbons of cum spilling from me. I was blind with pleasure, losing control of my body, her name leaving my lips on a growl.

This was the second time I had gone delirious with desire at the thought of her, this time more intense than the last. I was consumed by the way my body craved to feel her, to taste her, to smell her. I wanted her imprinted on all my senses, to be consumed by her. I wanted her to want me as badly as I wanted her. Fuck, I *needed* her to need me as badly as I needed her. I would do anything for that woman. I would give her the sun, the moon, the stars, the oceans, whatever she desired. The realization incited a fear stronger than anything I had felt before—I was starting to viscerally understand that I may not be able to give her up to save my people. And risking my kingdom for her? That was something I couldn't do, something I wouldn't do, even if it killed me.

CHAPTER 17
ASTERIA

The journey was slow, and our days became a blur of routine. Mornings consisted of breakfast and traveling on foot. Rae had taken to walking with me instead of riding, an act that stirred some unnamed emotion within me. Early afternoon, we would stop for lunch and a short rest, and Rae would share stories of his travels through the different kingdoms while I listened, absorbing his stories like dried soil soaked up the rain. He had seen so much and been to so many places, living a life I couldn't have even dreamed of.

He would talk about the difference in politics between each kingdom, asking me to weigh in with my perspective as a Royal who had grown up knowing the other kings and queens. We would discuss the contrasts and similarities in the royal families and their approaches to governing their people. I would share stories of the heirs and our time growing up together, how different we all turned out to be. The heirs in the more distant kingdoms of Nyxtas and Dalia believed in a more modern approach to ruling, sharing power. Believing that the power of the crown should be shared equally between the monarchs. They believed in working together to build a kingdom, with a daily presence in the lives of their people.

Solaria and Pyrus believed in tradition. The king and his advisors made the decisions, while the queen bore his children and practiced needlepoint in the library. They didn't believe in meandering with the lower classes, creating a disconnect between them and their people. I had always thought it was a disgusting way of leading. How can you do what's best for your people if you never understand their needs? 'What's best for the people' translated to what is best for the crown. Rae seemed just as captivated by my stories and opinions as I was by his.

After lunch, we would continue on horseback to cover more ground. In the evenings, after setting up our camp, we would spend a few hours training—strength training, agility, stamina, all things that I turned out to be severely lacking in. We started with hand-to-hand combat, and he taught me how to utilize my dagger. Each day, I felt stronger and more confident in my skills. I started to notice changes in the way my clothing fit; my body was changing. I was still curvy, but my arms had become more defined, my legs sturdier, my ass firmer. I hadn't seen myself in a mirror, but I began to feel like I wouldn't hate what I saw if I did.

Things had changed since my nightmare. I didn't know what happened, but the dynamic was different. It wasn't a bad change, but Rae's demeanor had changed. He was still the unrelentingly sarcastic asshole, but he had stopped making the sexual jokes and remarks. Things had become very platonic—we were becoming friends. We laughed at each other's stories, he celebrated my successes during training, and we would stay up past when we should just talking about everything and nothing. I was beginning to feel very comfortable around him, and it was disconcerting. I had never had a male friend before, or any friend, to be frank. Nor had I thought that I would find myself feeling safe and comfortable in the company of a man.

It had been a little over three weeks since our stay at the inn, the last civilized lodging we would have on this journey. As we crested over the Singing Mountains into the northern territories, fall had just about given way to winter, and it caused our pace to slow even more. We had preemptively obtained heavier clothes and more furs before we started our journey over the mountains, and it was a very wise choice. We'd found shelter from the elements in small caves or alcoves in the stone, but now, the full exposure to the weather reminded me how difficult the rest of the journey would be.

"We will find cover and set up camp in the forest just beyond here." Rae pointed to the barely visible outcropping of trees beyond the horizon. "We may be more exposed to the weather, but the forest should have plenty of wood for a fire and more game. We should get there before night falls."

I nodded at him, too tired and cold to carry on any sort of conversation. The dramatic change in my lifestyle, despite strengthening me in many ways, also exhausted me. The cold wind whipped around us, blowing strands of my dark hair loose from my braid and flushing my cheeks red. I shivered and pulled my cloak tighter, trying to conceal how intolerant I was to the cold. I had been struggling enough with feeling weak over the last few weeks with all that had happened—or maybe I had felt that way my whole life; I just hadn't stepped outside of my sheltered life to realize it. Either way, I had been working too hard to expel those appearances and feelings with Rae, with myself, through our training, and I wasn't about to be brought down by nature's frigid touch.

I took a deep, stuttering breath; *mind over matter*, I thought to myself. I could overcome anything if I just breathed, even the cold. I rode behind Rae, my eyes closed as I tried to focus. Unfortunately, my body did not agree with my thoughts, and my teeth began to chatter.

"What are you doing?" Rae's unexpected voice startled me, and with my uncontrollable chattering, I bit my tongue, and the tang of iron filled my mouth.

"Ouch," I exclaimed as I reached up, wiping some of the blood from where it drained from my tongue. "I was just trying to focus."

He slowed, bringing Odin and himself to my side. He reached up, running his thumb along the corner of my mouth, where a small bit of blood had escaped.

"What were you so focused on that you injured yourself?" His tone was half sarcastic, half concerned as his eyes scanned my features, his hand remaining on my face.

I suddenly realized I was no longer shivering—in fact, I felt warm. *Very* warm. It seemed to radiate from his touch, flowing through every fiber of my being, heating me from the inside out in the most pleasurable of ways. I suddenly felt a fluttering in my core, and I wanted to take his thumb into my mouth and suck on it. I stared back at him, still silent, as I tried to will my thoughts to stop wherever it was they were trying to go. Any further down this line of thinking, and whatever this feeling was would very quickly fade into something much less pleasurable. I couldn't think intimately of another man's touch without my stomach dropping and ice flooding my veins. Without realizing I had even moved, my hand was clasped over his, a rush of fear and insecurities making me push his hand away with more force than intended.

"I was trying to focus on the drills we went over last night. I guess I just got a little lost in my head. You startled me, and I bit my tongue." The chill of the wind began to creep back into my bones, and I once again began to shiver.

"You're cold." He stated flatly. "Why didn't you say anything?"

"I'm fine," I protested. "I'm just not used to true autumns or winters. The seasons are more mild in Pyrus. It's just going to take some adjusting." Trying to prove my point, I shifted so my cloak loosened around me slightly. "See? I'm fine." He rolled his eyes at me and reached for the clasp on his cloak to remove it. "I'm fine Rae, I don't need you baby me. I can handle a little bit of cold weather. Let's just get moving so we can get to camp for the night."

He looked at me and paused, his hand on the clasp of his cloak, his expression fell flat as he turned Odin back towards the trail. "Whatever you say, Princess, but there is no shame in admitting you are uncomfortable or need help." His tone was bitter, but he chose not to continue the conversation and picked up the pace, moving us along into a trot. We forged on that way for a few hours, keeping silent as we rode.

Why was I like this? What harm was there in admitting I was cold? Because in all honesty, I would have loved to have taken his cloak. It was a genuine and kind offer, but my instinct to refuse help from others, to acknowledge that I may need help, reared its ugly head, and I was unnecessarily rude. A flaw I needed to work on. I looked up, with all my internal fretting, I failed to notice the deepening hues of the sky as twilight began to settle upon us.

"Are we nearing our resting spot for the night?"

Without even turning over his shoulder to face me, he answered, "Almost, Princess."

A well of anxiety filled my chest as I worried I had set us back in our whatever this was developing between us. I fought the intrusive thoughts by forcing myself to focus on training, going over the drills I had learned in my head. The distraction began to pay off, the well of anxiety emptying as we slowed, breaking past the tree line.

Rae dismounted his horse, and I stopped Freya, following his lead and climbing out of my saddle. I gathered wood, starting a fire and setting up our bed rolls—opposite sides of the fire, as usual— and began to gather supplies needed to cook whatever game it was that Rae returned with.

"Why, Princess, you may just become a professional hand maid yet." Rae rounded the trees on the side of the camp nearest to the trail. Slung across his shoulder were two rabbits, and my mouth began salivating at the sight. Our food had been mostly composed of dried meat and breads, the game small and scarce, usually not worth the effort it would have taken to prepare them. "What, no snarky retort? Are you feeling okay over there?" He walked over to the opposite edge of the camp, preparing the rabbits.

"I'm just processing the fact that we have actual meat to eat. Fresh meat. Hot, freshly cooked meat."

"Well, I'm glad I could impress you, but the fact that you even doubted my ability to provide for you wounds my heart." He grabbed his chest dramatically, as if he were genuinely hurt. I couldn't help but let out a small laugh, dipping my head so that he couldn't see the smile blossoming on my face.

Stoking the fire for a few minutes, I tried working up the courage to do the thing I had been wanting to do all day. "Rae?" My voice was soft and timid as I stood and took a few hesitant steps in his direction.

He stopped, turning to face me, one prepped rabbit in his grasp. His face had become scruffy with hair, and his black mane of curls had become wild and unruly, with clumps of curls tumbling down into his face. I was always taken back by the stark brightness of his green eyes as they peered through the black veil. His cheeks and nose were blushed red from the winter air, and it gave him this ruggedly innocent appearance. When I looked at him, I had this strange sensation of not wanting to live a life without him in it, which was insane. I hadn't known him for long, but he had taught me more and showed me more kindness and affection than anyone else ever had. Which is why, despite the pounding in my chest and the instinct to run the other way, I had to do this.

"What is it, Princess? You look like you're about to be sick." He stepped forward, reaching out to me but stopping when he remembered the blood on his hands.

"I'm fine. It's just..." I swallowed hard and took a step back from him, needing the air between us thinned. "I didn't mean to upset you earlier. You were being kind, and I snapped at you when I shouldn't have. I'm sorry —"

"Woah there," he cut me off, his face a combination of confusion and amusement as he let out a laugh. "Do you think you upset me when you refused my cloak?" He tossed the rabbit back onto a tree stump, where the other waited for the same treatment. He quickly cleaned the blood from his hands and approached me, but I stepped back, apprehensive.

"I just didn't mean to disrespect you by refusing your offer." I knew it could be viewed as offensive for a woman to deny a man's direct aid, and I wasn't sure if things were different in his world. In Pyrus and Solaria, we were to ensure the man felt like the leader, the provider, the one in charge at all times.

He cautiously closed the distance between us and cupped my face with his hands. "Asteria, I grew up with a very strong willed and hardheaded sister. It is going to take so much more than the occasional sharp tone to offend or upset me. You are your own person, and you make your own choices. You should never let a man dictate your life, Princess. You deserve better than that, and anyone who tells you otherwise wants something from you."

I felt the heat of a tear flow down my cheek at his words—words that had never been spoken to me in my entire life. I was raised to be the perfect lady, to be seen and not heard, to make whatever prince I married happy, no matter what it cost me. Yet here, not only did Rae offer me freedom, he supported it.

The pad of his thumb swiped across my face, wiping the tear from my skin as he tilted my head up so that our eyes met. "What happened to you, Princess? What made you run?"

Shaking my head, I closed my eyes, not able to stand the intensity of his stare, as if he were looking straight into my most shameful parts. "We should get the rabbits on the fire before they begin to spoil."

Stepping back, I dragged my palms down my face, inhaling deeply and resealing the box of shame he'd almost pried open. He seemed to understand what I needed, and that was to move on and not dwell on this emotional moment any longer. He scooped up the prepped rabbit and handed it to me so I could season it and place it over the fire while he went back to prepping the second one. While we waited for them to cook, we sat on our bedrolls facing each other, sharing stories of our childhoods.

"I remember deciding it would be a good idea to play a prank on my sister," he started, laughing at his own story already. "I knew we were going to train with swords that day, and she had taken the last slice of my favorite cake the night before, so I thought it would be a great opportunity to get her back. Early the next morning, I went to the kitchen and asked the cook to prepare a massive vat of just purple pudding."

He was laughing so hard, he was almost rolling onto his back. His laugh was deep but so full of joy, the sounds reverberated through the woods like a call into the universe, summoning happiness to fill the souls of anyone blessed enough to hear it. It took him a few moments to compose himself so that he could go on.

"So," he continued to giggle. "Okay, so I took the bowl of pudding and rigged it up above the weapons in the training area, anchoring it with a rope tied to her sword." I could already see where this was going, and I could feel laughter beginning to bubble up inside me. "I waited patiently, trying to keep from seeming suspicious. The training arena was full of others by the time she showed up, and everyone was waiting for the show. She didn't notice the silence as we all waited for her to reach for her sword. The tension was so high, and then it happened: she grabbed her sword and went to pull it from the rack, and splat! She was completely covered in purple pudding!"

This time, he really was rolling on his back, and I couldn't stop myself from joining. We both sat there, laughing uncontrollably, until we couldn't breathe. Panting and heaving, trying to compose ourselves, we couldn't help but smile through the flames.

"How mad was she?" I finally managed to get out, though it was still strangled from my effort to stifle more laughter.

"Oh, mad doesn't even begin to describe it!" He roared with laughter once again. "The cook had used so much purple dye in the pudding that it stained her skin! She was purple for like two weeks. Fuck, she didn't forgive me for weeks. I started to think she was never going to."

"All that because she took the last slice of cake?" I asked incredulously.

"It was my favorite cake!" he barked, like that explained everything.

"How did you finally get her to forgive you?"

"Oh man." He sat with one knee pulled to his chest while his other leg crossed under him, resting his elbow on his raised knee. He dropped his head, shoulders bobbing as he laughed. "This is going haunt me for the rest of my life," he said apprehensively. "She made me wear a dress to training..." He flushed red in embarrassment, and I threw my head back, howling at the image of him in a dress.

"Yea, yea, yea, get your kicks," he said as he checked the rabbits and stoked the fire. "It's never going to happen again." I just eyed him, taking him in.

"So, your sister," I began as he handed me my food. "She was allowed to train?"

"Of course," he said, as if it was common practice. "Any of our women who wish to be taught defense are allowed to train. Our women also hunt, and we even have women in our Kingdom's Royal Guard." I couldn't believe what I was hearing—women acting as guards? Hunting? Fighting? Such things would never be tolerated in my Kingdom, and especially not Stefan's.

"Where are you from?" I needed to know what kingdom he

hailed from, because none of the ones in Leethe allowed such things, at least not as far as I knew.

"Oh, a land far from your Kingdom, Princess. A place much different than yours."

"I bet it's amazing." I leaned back, taking a bite of my food, trying to imagine how different my life could have been if I had been born in a place like that. "Can royals pursue other occupations? Could a princess be a healer?"

"A princess could be a healer, an advisor. They could lead troops into battle if they so desired. We don't believe in putting constraints on anyone based on their gender. Women can be just as valuable as a man in any aspect. In fact, they usually are able to offer a new perspective to problem solving. Is that really so shocking to hear?"

"It is in Pyrus or Solaria." I picked at my food, having devoured most of it already.

"Well, I think that is a damned shame and a waste of potential," he said, picking his teeth with one of his knives.

I couldn't help but agree with him—there was so much potential being squandered by the overly dominant patriarchal structure back home.

"I'd have to concur with that statement. Women back home are meant to act as silent property unless spoken to, expected to fulfill some maternal or marital duty."

"That is..." He paused, as if trying to sort through his vocabulary, looking for the correct word to describe his feelings. "I don't think there's a word to describe what that is, aside from wrong. I can see why you wanted to leave."

If you only knew, I thought as I watched him through the flames. "So, what are we working on tonight?" I said through a yawn, not realizing how tired I was, how much the warm food had relaxed me.

He echoed my yawn while he stretched his arms high above his head, getting up and adding more wood to the fire. "No training tonight. Just resting."

I wasn't going to argue with him—my eyes were getting heavier every minute. I crawled into my bedroll, removing the cloak I had been wearing and laying it on top of the furs already covering me. I hadn't prepared for how cold the ground was going to be; despite all my covers, I couldn't stop shivering. I tried to inch closer to the fire without bringing too much attention to myself, still not wanting to admit I was too weak to tolerate the cold. I sank deeper under the furs and closed my eyes, hoping that, with enough time, the shaking would stop.

Against my efforts, my teeth began to chatter, and I squeezed my eyes tighter, as if I could force the cold out of my bones. I was startled at the sound of a large thump behind me. My eyes flew open, and through the fire, I looked for Rae, only to find him missing. Where had he gone? I took a deep breath, reaching for the dagger that rested under my head, preparing to face whatever was behind me. I closed my eyes and took a deep breath, but before I could move, I felt a body lay behind me. I froze, every muscle in my body turning to stone as an arm weaved its way around my waist, and I was pulled back into someone's hard chest.

"Don't worry, Princess. It's just me." Rae's breath brushed the shell of my ear as he laid behind me.

"What are you doing?"

"Don't get your hopes up. It's cold, and the best way for us to avoid freezing to death in our sleep is to share body heat. You were shivering, and you can't tell me you're not already warmer, because guess what?" His voice dropped to a whisper. "You stopped shivering."

"I don't know if I'm comfortable with this, Rae." This felt strange to me. His body next to mine definitely felt good, and I was warmer already, but this wasn't appropriate.

"I promise you, I am not going to touch or harm you in any way you don't want. We're just going to sleep, Princess, sharing covers and heat so we survive. Nothing inappropriate or scandalous." He added the covers from his bedroll on top of mine, and the combination of his body head, the fire, and the extra covers felt so comfortable and warm. "I can go back to the other side of the fire if you want. I don't want you to feel as if you're not safe with me."

"I do," I replied quickly, "feel safe with you. It's just... I've never slept next to a man before."

"Just say the word, and I'm back over there."

I sat there for a few moments, trying to work through my feelings and separate my fear from the person who was behind me, who had done nothing but keep me safe. He took my lack of a reply as his answer and shifted to get up, but I grabbed his hand before he could.

"Stay," I whispered, partially shocked I had said it. "Please... Stay."

"Are you sure?" He hesitated, not moving to leave or to return to his spot next to me.

"I'm sure." I pulled slightly at his hand, reinforcing my decision, and he obliged, nestling his body against mine again.

He pulled me close, and his leather and amber scent flooded my senses. He snaked his arm over my waist, his hand resting on my lower stomach, just above the waistband of my trousers. The touch was so intimate but so innocent at the same time. I melted into him, the soft curves of my body molding to the hard, muscular planes of his. We laid there in silence, listening to the crackling of the fire, the rusting of the leaves, the songs of the nocturnal animals that called the surrounding trees home.

I closed my eyes as my body warmed, both inside and out. The feeling of him sent a frenzy of heat and butterflies swirling in my stomach, quickly followed by a wave of fear and anxiety at the feeling of him, a man, touching me in such an intimate way. The things that Stefan did to me were hateful, evil. There was no intimacy in what Stefan did—it was primal dominance with him, and this felt safe and caring, the juxtaposition filled me with conflict.

His breathing began to deepen and slow, and I didn't know if it was the feeling of safety or the darkness that did it, but I suddenly wanted to tell him everything.

"Rae, are you still awake?" My voice was hushed, scared to speak these things too loudly, to become too exposed.

"Mmmhmmm," he mumbled, the sound vibrating through his chest.

"Earlier, you asked me what happened to me, what made me run." My palms began to sweat, scared to unlock this trauma, but also feeling like I needed to. His breathing picked up—he was definitely awake now.

"You don't have to tell me, Princess." His voice was low and careful as he spoke.

"I want to. I need to." He shifted, propping his head up in his hand, trying to angle my body so I faced him. "No," I said, refusing to move. "I won't be able to say it if I can see you looking at me, if I have to look at you."

"Asteria..." He was concerned; I could feel it in the tension in his muscles and the worry in his voice.

"It's okay, I promise. It's time." I swallowed. "It's time to talk about it."

And, I did. I told him everything. I told him about the day under the willow when Stefan and I were younger, about the marriage arrangement, about the journey there and the incident with the guard, Valdin. I told him about the two months of taunting and harassment I endured at Stefan's hands, how there was nothing I could do to stop the marriage. I told him how I had begged my Father to reconsider, and how he'd refused.

I told him about the night in the maze, how Stefan had touched me, about the disgusting things he said to me, how he left me there crying once he had his fun. I could feel Rae's body stiffen the further I got, the increase in his breathing and the rapid pounding of his heart in his chest. Still, he stayed silent, listening to every word with full attention, not daring to cut me off. The closer I got to the night of the ball, the night before the wedding, the night I ran, the harder it became to speak. My eyes burned with tears as I stared into the flames that danced in front of me, burning away the nightmarish memories as I spoke them. I stopped as my ability to hold back the tears came crashing down.

"Asteria." He went to cup my face, but if I let him comfort me now, I would never be able to finish. It was time to acknowledge what happened, to accept it, to let myself heal.

"I'm okay," I reassured him. "The night before the wedding, we made our official presentation at our engagement ball. Stefan drank, and the more he drank, the more possessive he became until he finally retired for the night. I slipped off to my room, needing to be alone before I was committed to sharing a life with the monster down the hall." I let out a sob as the memory flooded me, everything feeling as prominent as it had the night it happened.

"There was a loud banging on my door." My body shook as I spoke. "It was so late, I was worried there was an emergency. I went to open the door, but before I could, he forced his way into my room. He was angry with me—he said I had embarrassed him, that I had been looking at other men at the ball like I was going to get on my knees for them. He…" I swallowed back another sob. "He told me I was his, and he forced me against the wall, and he touched me. When I tried to fight back or scream for help, he threatened to break my fingers. He forced himself on me – in me." I could feel Rae's hands forming into fists against me. "He took me for himself that night. He made me tell him that I was his, that I belonged to him, and when he finished, he told me if I tried to accuse him of anything, no one would care or believe me. I was his betrothed—I was expected to please him, and he said that I would pleasure him, whether he took it for himself, or I gave it willingly."

"He told me I was ruined, that no man would ever touch me again, that I was his and forever would be." Curling in on myself, I cried, remembering the fear he had instilled in me. "I couldn't chain myself to him. I couldn't live through that again and again and again. I knew if I stayed, that night would be my reality every day until I died, and I couldn't endure it. So, I ran. I ran while his words shred every fiber of my self-worth and self-love. Most days, I don't know who I hate more: him or myself."

I hadn't even admitted that last part to myself. The last thread I had on my emotions snapped and I fell apart. Right there, in the dark of the night, in the middle of the woods, in the presence of only nature and the man who laid silently beside me, I broke. Rae never spoke; he never uttered a single word. He only wrapped his arm around me, pulling me close and holding me tight, doing his best to hold together what was left of me.

He held me like that until I had cried myself to sleep. It wasn't until after he thought I had fallen asleep that he spoke, whispering softly.

"He didn't ruin you, Princess. You are perfect in every way." Then, he brushed a soft kiss to my temple before he drifted off to sleep beside me.

CHAPTER 18
ASTRAEUS

Lying there, listening to her bare her soul, was one of the most difficult things I'd done, second only to hearing what happened to my sister. The chasm of rage that broke open inside me was deep enough to swallow entire kingdoms.

At the same time, all I had wanted to do was to pull her into my arms and kiss away her anguish, reassuring her she was safe, that she was free. I needed to make sure she knew absolutely everything that piss poor excuse for a man said to her was false. She was gorgeous, talented, intelligent, strong, kind, and far from being ruined. What happened to her was not her fault—his actions don't make her less of woman, less desirable, less worthy of love and affection.

The last thing she said truly broke my heart. For her to hate herself for what she endured was wrong. I had a new mission for the rest of our journey: to make sure she knew how worthy and desirable she was. She deserved to be loved by a man who would worship the ground she walked on, to be treated like the goddess she was. To know her was a blessing, and I considered myself lucky, even if my time with her was temporary.

Fuck... I was feeling things for her I could *not* be feeling. But, every day I spent getting to know her, seeing her let down her walls and become strong and free in her own skin, was like watching the first astra flower bloom every season. It was such a momentous and thrilling thing for our Kingdom. We used the flower for so much, and it was such an important part of our lives —just like she was now such an integral part of mine.

I laid there holding her as she cried herself to sleep, spilling all of the trauma she had been keeping inside, and I knew my plans were going to hurt. If I followed through with trading her back to Stefan for a treaty, it would be the end of whatever this was. She would never forgive me—and I began to wonder if I would ever forgive myself.

Stick to the plan Astraeus, I told myself. *Your duty is to your Kingdom first and foremost. Don't let them down.* I held her a little bit tighter, knowing that, in the end, it didn't matter how I felt: I would have to let her go.

MORNING CAME QUICKLY, but I couldn't find it in myself to wake the beautiful woman next to me. Her face was puffy and raw from crying, and she looked so at peace sleeping. I knew we should continue our travels, but I felt we could take things a little bit slower this morning.

I quietly slipped from the covers, careful not to wake my Little Star, stretching to try to work the morning chill from my stiff muscles. I looked around the camp, taking in the morning silence. The world was still, a light layer of frosted dew coating the ground, the trees twinkling in the early morning sun.

I inhaled deeply, taking in the scent of the frost and dampened leaves, accentuated by the smell of burning wood from the fire that was no more than embers. Walking over to the fire, I grabbed some kindling and added it to the pit, stoking it back to life. The wave of heat graced my skin as the flames grew, fighting back the cold. I donned my cloak and laced up my boots, slinging the bow and arrows I used to hunt across my back. I made sure the fire had enough fuel to last until I returned, and then I knelt beside Asteria, gently tucking the furs to make sure she was warm before I crept out of camp to find breakfast.

I returned within the hour to find the camp unchanged. Asteria was still sleeping peacefully, and the horses grazed on the scarce patches of grass that remained. I moved to the fire to prepare the eggs I had scavenged, cooking them alongside some toasted bread. In a small pot, I had water heating for the remaining coffee grounds, knowing coffee was her favorite part of mornings. It didn't take long for the scent of toasted bread and steeping coffee to arouse the sleeping beauty across the fire.

"Good morning, Princess." I smiled at her as I poured two cups of weak coffee. "Sleep well?" She sat up slowly, wiping the sleep from her eyes with the palms of her hands.

"Actually," she yawned, "I slept very well. Probably the best I've slept in weeks." Her attention shifted to the cups in my hands. "Is that coffee?"

"It's not very strong." I walked over to her and handed her a mug. "That's the last of it. I may be able to slip into a nearby town and get us some more." I sat down next to her near the fire so I could finish cooking. "Are you hungry?" I asked her as I stirred the eggs. "I hope you don't mind, but I helped myself to your herbs and spices."

She cupped her mug tightly in her hands, holding it just below her chin, breathing in the aromatic vapors that floated across her face. Sitting there with her eyes closed, newly awakened, wrapped in furs up to her chin, simply enjoying the simple pleasure of her favorite beverage, was such a simple and beautiful thing, that caused my heart to skip a beat. She really was the most celestial being I had ever seen. She had to have been handcrafted by the Goddess in her own image, because I couldn't imagine anything out there comparing to her. I was lost in her beauty, staring at every perfectly sculpted detail of her face when she cleared her throat.

"Do you see something you like?"

"You have no idea, Princess." I handed her a serving of eggs and toast while she looked up at me in surprise. "Did the cold freeze your sharp tongue?"

"No," she scoffed. "I'm just trying to figure out why you're acting so strange this morning."

She was obviously suspicious of my shift in behavior. It wasn't that I wasn't kind and playful with her normally, but something had changed in my feelings towards her, and I didn't want to keep it to myself.

"Am I not allowed to appreciate your beauty?"

Her mouth nearly gaped as her eyes widened at my direct truth. "I don't—what are you playing at? Is there something you want from me?"

"Why would you assume I want something from you just because I stated a fact?"

She shrugged. "Because kindness and sugared statements rarely come without expectations of something in return, especially when the statement is obviously false."

This time, it was my mouth that gaped. "Do you honestly believe me to be lying?"

"I don't honestly believe you find me beautiful. So yes, I guess I believe you are lying and are searching for something from me." Her tone was a combination of hurt and defeat.

"Princess." I turned to face her, placing my own food to the side. "I don't know what you have been told or what you think of yourself, but honestly," I reached for her, resting my hand on her knee, "you are absolutely and undoubtedly beautiful."

She pulled back slightly, turning her face as if hearing my words pained her, and I squeezed her knee lightly.

"Someday, you're going to see the same beauty I see." A rosy tint rose along her face as she shook her head, the conversation obviously made her uncomfortable. Huffing a light laugh, I removed my hand from her knee and used the toast to scoop up a mouthful of eggs. "Eat up. We'll need to get moving soon."

The mornings carried on like usual: we walked side by side with our horses behind us for the first half of the day, and during lunch, we trained harder, since I was determined to make sure she was able to defend herself when I was no longer with her.

"Keep your arm up and protect your head!" I reminded her sternly. "Arm up!" I stepped into her space, moving her arm up. "Don't let that arm drop."

Turning around, I stalked back to my place to spar with her again. I rolled my head from side to side, cracking my neck and relieving the pressure building there. I wiped the sweat from my brow as I faced her.

"Dagger out," I instructed, and she obliged by removing the obsidian dagger from her side.

The dagger had come from Asphodel, the metal mined from the Dead Mountains that bordered the Kingdom. Weapons forged from the metal were used by magic wielders, the Umbra Siderum, to harness their powers. The purple veins that ran through the onyx metal amplified their powers and imbued the weapons with their strength and abilities. During the Great War, most of the soldiers were stripped of any weapons made from it. Houses were raided by Solaria and Pryus, anything resembling the metal was confiscated. To possess such a thing outside of Asphodel was extremely rare—no doubt the merchant she had purchased it from had stolen it from one of the old armories.

Sweat beaded along my neck before rolling down my back and chest. I removed the light overcoat I had been wearing, leaving me in a fitted tunic and leather trousers. I dragged my arm across my forehead before rolling up the sleeve, exposing my muscled fore-arm. I watched as her eyes drifted down to where I grasped my forearm, pushing up the other, following the movements of her gaze.

"Eyes up here, Princess." I gave her a devilish smirk and met her stare, the stunning grey swallowed by darkness as her eyes lit with desire.

A red flush crept up her neck at the realization that I had caught her staring. Little did she know, I didn't mind the attention in the least bit. I had worked hard to build my body—years of training, hand to hand combat, with swords, spears, archery; you name it, I'd probably trained with it. In addition to that, years of helping our farmers harvest their crops, tend to their fields, and repair the structures throughout the town.

All of this had given me strength, yes, but also taught me how to use that strength to my advantage. Combat wasn't about who could dole out the most brute force—no, it was about strategy. Knowing when to use that force and when not to use it. Combat was strategy, endurance, and grace, as much it was about force and strength. The person who can assess their opponent and identify their weaknesses has to exude much less force to defeat them than the person who just goes in swinging. These are things that I had spent my entire life learning and perfecting, and I was trying to teach Asteria as much as I could in the little time we had together. She was incredibly smart and perceptive; she picked up the moves quickly and she had great instincts, but she lacked confidence in herself and continually second-guessed her decisions. It was something that could get her killed, and that was something I was not willing to accept.

"Are you ready?" I questioned as I positioned myself in a predatory stance.

I watched as she visibly tensed, lowering herself slightly and placing her foot behind her, twisting her hips into a fighting stance. She raised her front arm, balling her hand into a fist and keeping it up.

Good girl, I thought to myself. *Protect your head.*

Her other hand was hitched at the elbow and tucked into her side, protecting her core. In that same hand, she gripped her dagger, the hilt a stark contrast to the blanched white of her knuckles. She rolled her shoulders and inhaled deeply before locking her eyes with mine and nodding.

I lunged forward, striking out with my fist and barely grazing her cheek as she side stepped me. I quickly followed with a jab that found its mark, knocking the air from her lungs, and she lurched forward, gasping for air. I grabbed her shoulder, holding her there as I prepared to follow up with a knee, but I was stopped short when she halted my leg mid-strike, using her entire body to push me back.

The act threw me back slightly, and I recovered quickly, but she was already lunging towards me, her dagger aimed for my shoulder. I shifted to the side just enough for the dagger to move past me before grabbing her wrist and stepping forward, turning so I stood behind her, her wrist still in my grasp. She folded as her arm was twisted behind her. I adjusted my grip and leaned over her, whispering in her ear.

"Too slow, Princess." She grunted in frustration as she tried to force herself back up. "Think. What's your next move?"

"I don't know." The tension in her muscles and tightness of her voice made her frustration evident.

"Then you better learn to like this position, because I'm not letting you up until you tell me your next move."

She struggled against my hold again, but I refused to let her up. She needed to learn to think, to assess, to get herself out of it. She continued to fight, and I steeled my grip, squeezing her wrist so she released the dagger. I heard a soft thud as it landed on the ground beside us.

"What now? You're weaponless and pinned. What are you going to do?" My voice was tense, my frustration beginning to rise. She had to learn. She groaned and struggled but made no move, aside from pushing against my hold. "Think, Princess!" My tone edged on anger. "What are you going to do?"

She let out a scream of frustration. "I don't fucking know, Rae!"

"Go with your first instinct. Quit second guessing yourself!" We were both yelling now. "Goddess dammit, Asteria, fight back!"

Without warning, she kicked out with force, sweeping my feet from underneath me and sending us both to our backs. Before I could recover, she had rolled to straddle me, and she retrieved the dagger from beside us. Panting and angered, her eyes brimming with tears, she leaned over me, the sharp blade pressed against my neck. I stared up at her in shock, not daring to move while she fought whatever emotions were swirling in her eyes, as she held the dagger to my throat.

"When I say I don't know, I mean I don't fucking know." Her jaw was tense, her voice rough. "I don't know what my next move is. I don't know what the fuck I'm doing." She seemed to be fighting something in her mind, her gaze distant. "You can't just fucking do whatever you want with me. You don't get to fucking control me."

Slowly and gently, I wrapped a hand around hers holding the dagger and another gently around her elbow. She flinched, pressing the blade harder into my skin, causing me to hiss from the sting as the metal broke flesh, drawing beads of blood to the surface. I tightened my grip slightly as I tried to break her from the trance she seemed to be stuck in.

"Asteria..." My voice was calm and steady. "Look at me. It's me. It's Rae. I am not going to hurt you." The weight of the blade began to lift from my throat, and I released her elbow, reaching up to cup her cheek. "Asteria, are you with me?" A tear rolled down her face, and I caught it with my thumb, swiping it away as I coaxed her back to the moment, pulling her back from the darkness. "You're okay, Princess. You're safe with me. You're safe."

She inhaled sharply as she blinked the memory away. She looked down at me, her face draining of color when she saw the trails of blood that flowed down the side of my neck from where her blade had broken the skin. She dropped the blade and rolled off me, pulling her knees into her chest and shivering. Sitting up, I ran the back of my hand across my neck—the cut was superficial, and it would heal quickly.

"Rae, I am so sorry." She dipped her head from my eye line, the guilt heavy in her tone.

"For what?" I questioned as I stood. "Knocking me on my ass? Because if I'm 100% honest, I liked it, and I would like to see you do it more often. The view from beneath you is quite enjoyable." I reached out my hand to help her up, and to my surprise, she took it.

She wiped the dust from her legs and began to pace. "How am I supposed to learn to defend myself if I keep freezing? How am I supposed to keep going if I keep getting stuck in memories of the past?" She tugged at her hair, pacing faster, and I stepped forward, cutting off her path and placing my hands on her shoulders to anchor her in place.

"You're going to because you have to, because you can, and because you will."

"I'm serious, Rae. I can't do this. I'm not good enough. I'm a princess, for fuck's sake, and not even a good one at that! I abandoned my people, fled from my responsibilities. I left my family! I'm a terrible princess and a terrible daughter." Her chest heaved rapidly. "I have never been the one people had faith in. I couldn't even look the part of a beautiful princess, much less execute the role. If I can't do the one thing I was born to do, how do you ever expect me to learn how to do what is expected of men when I fail daily as a woman?"

Her eyes were red and rimmed with tears that threatened to fall with each statement she made, like a wound torn open and salted. The pain and anguish in her words filled the open space, and the forest fell silent. I pulled her into my chest, wrapping her into my arms, my hand threading into the hair at the base of her neck as I cradled her head into my shoulder. She shook in my arms as she sobbed, as her words wedged their way into each corner of her soul.

"You are the farthest thing from a failure," I whispered into her hair. "Running was not a thing of cowardice. Leaving your life, all you knew, took more courage and bravery than most people could ever muster. You chose freedom over a life of condemnation, over a life of abuse and misery. Sacrificing your own well-being helps no one. Leaving your Kingdom saved them—saved *you*—from the rule of that monster. You have failed no one. No, you saved them." I released her, stepping back and cupping her face, tilting her chin up so I could look into her eyes.

"You, Asteria, are more capable, stronger, caring and powerful than you give yourself credit for. You shame the stars with your radiance, and when you smile, the cosmos quake in jealousy. I have yet to see another being hold a candle to your beauty. Do not ever feel you are not enough—you are more than enough. I will do everything in my power to ensure you see yourself as the astounding woman you are."

She stared back at me silently, her eyes seeming to light from within at my words.

"I mean every word I say." I leaned forward and placed a kiss on her forehead, soft and gentle. She shuddered at the touch but didn't move. I squeezed her shoulders, and before she could say anything, I suggested that we prepare the camp for the night and get some rest. We would continue on in the morning.

CHAPTER 19
ASTERIA

I had done it again: I had slipped into the past and gotten lost in the pain of my trauma, and it caused me to fail. Again. I have been working so hard at my training, but today was different. Rae went harder than usual, and the minute I felt trapped and out-maneuvered, I froze.

Then, it wasn't Rae who was restraining me anymore: it was Stefan. The fear and adrenaline that pumped through my veins alongside the deep-seated rage had me seeing red. I wanted to hurt him, to *kill* him. Stefan, not Rae. But it wasn't Stefan's neck that my blade met—it was Rae's. I didn't know why I stopped when the blade met his flesh, but I was thankful it did. Every time I looked at him and saw the scabbed line that ran along the base of his throat, a pang of guilt hit me, quickly followed by shame and embarrassment for my behavior. I lost control, not only of my actions, but my words and emotions. The insecurities I spewed at him, the faults and damage I exposed...

After I fell apart in his arms for a second time, he picked up my sorrows and shame and tried to burn them away with words of comfort and praise. He showered me with beautiful words and sentiments that I had never heard uttered alongside my name—for the first time, I felt as though the trenches of anguish in my soul were bandaged. The wounds were still there, deep and cavernous, but Rae had made them feel a little smaller, like maybe, just maybe, they could be healed. He had pulled me in tight, and in his arms, I felt I was safe. That day under the willow, Stefan fractured something in me, and that fracture only grew until he split it wide the night he forced himself upon me. So no, safety was never a feeling I associated with men. Not until now, not until Rae. When he brushed his lips across my forehead, electricity tore through my body, lighting my nerves like a comet lit the night sky, and I shuddered in his hold.

If he noticed, he didn't let it be known.

We returned to the warmth of fire, preparing our dinner in silence. I don't know if he was trying to give me space and time to process what had happened, or if we were both waiting for the other to speak first. Either way, the silence was comfortable, with no pressure to fill the void with words just for the sake of hearing our own voices. At this point, our evening ritual was pretty automatic—I would stoke the fire and prepare the bed roll while he scavenged the area for something of substance for us to eat.

The further north we traveled, the more difficult it was to find animals that provided any amount of meat. Most nights, it was small game like small birds or squirrels. We had nearly run out of supplies; tonight, we would finish off the rest of the bread. We had consumed the last of the vegetables a few days ago, and even my herbs were dwindling. Rae would use the rest of the salve I had made for healing the injury from my blade. Over the weeks, there had been mishaps and small injuries to both of us, along with the horses. Many nights, I brewed my sleeping draught to help silence the nightmares. I wasn't sure how we were going to complete the last leg of the journey as depleted as we were.

"How much further until we reach the Dead Mountains?" I

turned to look at Rae from where I sat next to him, stoking the fire and adding what I could to the weak excuse of soup trying to make it as palatable as I could.

"Two or three weeks, depending on the weather," he replied while he tried to fashion a pair of gloves for each of us from the squirrels we had caught for dinner the previous week.

"We are running too low on supplies," I stated. "We won't have enough for that long."

"Are these living circumstances not up to your expectations, Princess?" The intense green of his eyes cut through the tangled mess of black curls that obscured his view as he peered at me, his lips pulling back into a flippant grin as he raised his brow.

"Have I not told you I've always dreamed of a life where I survive off poorly seasoned, boiled squirrel meat, freezing my ass off and sharing furs with a man who seems to think sarcasm and an arrogant personality are an acceptable replacement for hygiene?"

His jaw went slack at my comment. "Well, Princess," he chortled. "That is quite the accusation from someone who has dirt smeared across her forehead."

My hand flew to my head trying to wipe it clean. "Does it happen to match the shape of your lips?"

This time, *my* brow rose sardonically. We stared at each other, the flames dancing alongside us, lighting our faces as we wait for the other to make some sort of retort. After a few moments, Rae fell back onto the bed roll, a deep laugh tearing from his chest. He laid there, trying to catch his breath, but failing as he continued to howl in amusement. The sound of joy that erupted from him broke me as well, and I shortly joined him, giggling uncontrollably. Each time one of us composed ourselves, it took just a glance at the other to begin roaring again.

After what felt like an eternity, we laid side by side, panting as we calmed our breathing, the stars twinkling brightly above us. I inhaled deeply, the brisk air filling my lungs and freezing my nose. "Thank you, by the way."

I turned my head to the side to face him, to my surprise he was already looking at me. His face was soft, the curve of his lips accentuated by the firelight; I was captivated by them, remembering how soft they felt as he swept them across my forehead earlier. I wanted to brush my thumb across them, to feel how supple they were, to imagine how they would feel if he were to press them against mine. The muscles tensed in my arm as I prepared to move my hand, but before I could, Rae spoke.

"And what are you thanking me for, Little Star?"

I returned my gaze to his. "For earlier. For what you said—for training me, for helping me, for everything."

I searched his expression for any sign of pity or regret, but all I saw when he looked at me was compassion, understanding, and something that seemed like... longing? He turned to face me, bringing his hand up and gently tucking a strand of hair behind my ear before cupping my face.

"There is nothing I've done that I haven't wanted to do, nothing I've said that I didn't mean. You do not need to thank me for doing or saying those things." His thumb traced along the top of my cheek, and I closed my eyes, turning my head further to the side, away from his touch. "I'm serious." He lightly tucked his thumb under my chin and brought my eyes back to his. "You..." He sighed deeply, his face tilting towards mine.

I stared up at him, my pulse thrumming as my heart flipped in my chest. His touch felt electric, awaking every cell in my body, and I shuddered in a breath as he touched his forehead to mine.

"I am thankful our paths crossed, Asteria. I will always be thankful to have been blessed to know you."

Tears welled in my eyes, and I struggled to breathe as his words entwined themselves into the fibers of my heart. I felt weak, my heartbeat unsteady, my breathing uneven as he looked down at me. His eyes were bright and warm as his breath hitched, and I swore that his hand shook as he angled my face up to his. Time seemed to slow, and I felt my body vibrate in anticipation. I closed my eyes, anxiety and excitement pulsing through my veins, and I took a deep breath, readying myself, when suddenly I felt frozen, fear crawling up my spine. Panic replaced the excitement I had felt moments ago. I instantly felt every word Stefan had said to me shoot through me like a spear aimed to kill. *Ruined. Dirty. Unlovable. Damaged goods.*

I exhaled sharply and pulled back, sitting up quickly. "The soup is ready."

I stood quickly, leaving Rae on the furs as I hurried to fetch the mugs we would use for the soup and filled them. I returned to sit next to him, making sure to put extra distance between us as I handed him his mug. He remained on his side as he took the mug, staring at me, tracing my every move, trying to understand what had just happened. I brought the steaming mug to my lips, not bothering to let it cool before drinking the scalding broth—it was weak, barely more flavorful than the water it was cooked in. I brought my knees to my chest, resting the mug on one knee while I ran my finger around the lip of it. I kept my eyes downward, unable to bear seeing the expression on Rae's face.

Clearing my throat, I spoke softly. "I'm sorry."

He dropped his gaze, looking at his mug. "There's no need to apologize." His voice was low and strained, and I slid my gaze to him, his brows furrowed as he avoided my gaze. "I shouldn't have..."

"No," I interjected as I looked at the fire, unable to look at him as I spoke. "You didn't do anything wrong. It's me. I'm just not... I'm damaged, Rae. I'm not whole, and I don't know if I ever will be. You deserve someone who is, someone who isn't paralyzed with fear each time she feels any sort of intimacy. You deserve someone ready for you. I am broken..."

I jolted at the feel of his hand on mine; I hadn't realized he had moved, now sitting up facing me.

"We are all broken, Asteria, in our own way, and we all heal at our own pace. Don't rush yours, and do not ever apologize for not being ready or not being 'whole'. You are where you need to be, and you are perfect just as you are. Don't ever think otherwise. You deserve to be cherished, no matter what stage of healing you're in." He grabbed my hand, turning it over as he brought it to his lips to place a kiss on my palm. "You have nothing to apologize for."

We finished up our soup, talking about the plans for the rest of our journey. "The next three days will be long days of travel," he started. "We won't have much time for training, but there are some ruins where we can spend a day or two resting. We're not too far from a town, so I will be able to get more supplies."

"I'll go with you so I can stop by an apothecary and get more herbs."

"No," he argued. "It's too risky. Solaria and Pyrus will have guards crawling throughout the villages looking for you. It's too dangerous."

"I can take care of myself, Rae," I deadpanned, annoyed that he wanted me to stay back.

"Can you, Princess? You've come a long way in your training, yes, but these are Royal Guards. If one of them identifies you, do you think you will be able to fight him off? Two or three guards at one time?"

"We have successfully evaded them before."

"Yes, because I had spent time planning multiple outs and paid off multiple people. We won't have that luxury."

"But..."

"But nothing, Asteria. There are too many variables. It is a risk that I—that we—cannot afford. I'm sorry, Princess, I really am, but please trust me. It will be much safer and faster if it is just me.

Make me a list of herbs you need, and I promise I will bring you buckets of them."

I huffed at him, annoyed at his insistence that I stay. "Fine," I frustratedly agreed. "But I don't think that *buckets* of herbs are necessary. Just an ounce or so of each will be fine."

He smiled at me, shaking his head. "Okay. No buckets, and you'll stay at camp?"

I just waved a hand at him as he stood, adding fuel to the fire for the night. I crawled into the furs, exhausted and ready for rest. After stoking the flames, Rae slid under the furs behind me, pulling me tight to his chest, just as he had the previous nights.

"Rae," I whispered his name.

"Mmmhmmm," he replied as he adjusted the furs to make sure I was adequately covered.

"I really am sorry," I said, my eyes watching the flames swirl as they illuminated the night.

"Shhhhhh." His breath warmed my neck as he nestled into me. "Go to sleep, Little Star." I closed my eyes and did as he said, drifting off into sleep.

For the first time in weeks, I had no nightmares.

CHAPTER 20
ASTERIA

Rae hadn't lied when he said the next few days were going to be long. The temperature continued to drop as the sky turned a deep grey, the clouds blocking out the sun. The wind whipped relentlessly, driving the cold deep into my bones. The thick trousers and tunic I wore, layered with a sweater and fur cloaks, kept me just warm enough to function. The gloves that Rae had made kept my fingers from turning blue, and the fabric around my neck and face covered all but my eyes and forehead. The icy wind stung my eyes, but I pushed through. In the mornings, I would fill our water bladders with boiling water, and we would wear them across our chest to help keep us warm, but the heat only lasted a few hours.

We would set up camp in the most sheltered area we could find to help stave off the wind, but even then, we could not escape winter's frigid touch. In the evenings, we huddled together as we sipped on hot, flavorless water.

The furs, combined with placing hot water bladders in them and our closeness, managed to provide enough warmth that we were able to get decent rest. We didn't talk much, both too cold and miserable to muster up any real conversation. I would dream of hot baths and warm beds, trying to remember what it was like to live inside the comforts of a castle. It seemed so long ago now, like another lifetime. I guessed in many ways, it was. I had been through so much and changed so much—I was no longer the same person I was a few months ago. In some ways, I mourned the person I had lost, the person I spent the majority of my life being, but she was gone. The person I was now would have never recognized the old me. She was weak, quiet, useless. She sat quietly while her family made every decision for her. She sat there quietly while a monster took advantage of her, while he abused her, and while he ruined her. Why? Because, she feared upsetting the family balance.

I should have told my parents what happened the day Stefan first touched me as a child, but no. I protected him, thinking that what happened had been my fault, and that if I tried to tell someone, I would be the one punished. Not anymore. I would not return to that life, to that girl.

No. I may be broken now, but I refused to allow anyone to choose my path for me from. I was taking control of my own life, where I could choose to be, to do, to love who I want. Someday, I told myself. Someday, I will find love.

THE NEXT MORNING, we awoke to a surprisingly clear day. The sun beamed through the withering canopy of leaves, slowly shed by the trees they once called home. The breeze was gentle, and the ground glistened as it reflected the light of the waking sun. I exhaled the crisp air, my breath a fleeting cloud above me. The ground was frozen beneath me, my body aching from the long night of sleep. I shifted my hips trying to relieve some of the pain and pressed myself further into the man behind me, seeking his warmth. A low groan echoed in my ear from behind me.

"Keep moving like that, Princess, and you're going to cause problems for both of us." Rae's voice was low and graveled with sleep, and I could feel his chest rumble against my back as he spoke.

Heat rushed to my cheeks as his words were quickly punctuated by the fully erect cock pressing into my ass. My eyes widened, and I frantically apologized as I tried to move my body away. To my surprise, the hand resting on my side quickly tightened its grip, holding me tightly.

"Don't even think about it," he grumbled as he wrapped his arm tightly around me. "I'm enjoying this too much, and I'm not ready for it to end."

"Rae," I argued, "we need to get moving."

"Not yet," he yawned. "It's cold and I'm comfortable."

"It's been cold, and there is no way you're actually comfortable."

"I have you in my arms, and that is all the comfort I need." His words caught me off guard; I fumbled my thoughts and couldn't think of anything to say back, so I gave in, relaxing into his hold. "See," he murmured sleepily, "isn't this nice?"

I smiled, not saying anything back to him as we both fell back asleep.

The sun wasn't very high in the sky when we awoke the second time, meaning we had not slept much longer. Rae rolled onto his back, stretching his arms high above his head as he let out a loud and overly-dramatic yawn. I looked back over my shoulder at him, rolling my eyes.

"Sleep well, Princess?" I mocked him.

"Oh, delightfully so. Didn't you?" He smirked devilishly at me as he sat up, looking down at where I still laid.

"Mmmmmm," I jokingly contemplated. "I've had better."

He drastically gasped, mimicking a dagger being plunged into his chest. "You wound me, Princess. I don't think I'll ever recover."

Laughing, I rolled onto my knees. "Something tells me you'll be just fine."

I placed my hand over where he had plunged the invisible dagger and shoved him back onto the bed roll. I moved to stand when he rolled, kicking and sweeping my legs out from under me, causing me to fall back onto the furs. I landed firmly on my ass, letting out a small grunt as I hit the ground.

"Are you serious?" I asked, dumbfounded at what had just happened.

"Always expect the unexpected."

He smiled smugly as he stood, offering me his hand. I glared up at him, reaching out to accept his helping hand. I grasped his hand, but before he could pull me up, I latched onto his arm with my other hand and pulled. He stumbled forward, losing his balance, and I used the opportunity to hook my leg around his, forcing him to the ground. I pulled one of the maneuvers he taught me, using the momentum from his fall to direct him onto his back, rolling with him so that I straddled his hips. I leaned forward, pinning his arms above his head.

"Always expect the unexpected," I snarked, my hair falling over my shoulders like a curtain as I looked down at him, shielding our faces from the outside world. I smiled at the shocked and impressed expression on his face.

"One thing you should know, Princess." His eyes lit with mischief, and an impish smile pulled at his mouth. Suddenly, his foot was hooked with mine, and he bucked his hips, rolling us off the furs, landing on top of me. His hips rested between my legs as he trapped my arms beside my head. "With you, it's all unexpected, and I relish in every unexpected moment."

His eyes darkened, and his smile softened, his expression almost hungry. My gaze flicked from his eyes to his mouth, and suddenly, I was biting at my own lip. I looked back to his eyes, and they were lit with a fiery desire. Our hearts pounded in the silent woods, beating so hard that I could hear them as they beat in tandem. *Thump thump, thump thump, thump thump.*

"Rae..." I echoed his name on an unsteady breath.

"Asteria." My name was a gentle caress as it passed his lips—his sultry, full, perfect lips.

All I could think about was those lips—how they would feel on mine, how they would taste, what it would be like to have them trail along my skin. My face flushed and heat pooled between my legs as our gazes locked. Our faces drifted closer to each other; our breath mingled between us. Our faces were merely inches apart when the horses started to snort and pull at the leads tying them to a tree—something had alarmed them.

Rae sprang into action, his demeanor instantly changing. He tried calming the horses when his attention shifted to what had alarmed them: a small group of royal soldiers riding down the path less than a quarter of a mile from where we had made camp.

Terror tore through me, and the brisk morning suddenly felt warm compared to the frigid ice coursing through my veins. Consumed by panic, I was unable to speak, to move, to think. Tears pricked my eyes as I tried to breathe. What were we going to do? Rae was in front of me in an instant, his hands grasping my face as he forced me to look at him.

"Breathe, Princess," he said fervently. "You have to breathe." I looked at him as I closed my mouth and took in a deep and shaky breath through my nose. "Good girl. Now out, nice and slow. One, two, three, four, five. Good. Again for me."

Closing my eyes, I repeated the steps. In. *One, two, three, four, five.* Hold. *One, two, three, four, five.* Out. *One, two, three, four, five.* Feeling my blood thaw, I opened my eyes and placed my hands on top of his. "I told you we should have moved earlier."

"Really?" he whispered, "Now? Right now is when you want to say I told you so?"

"No time like the present," I whispered back. "What are we going to do?"

He tightened his grip on my face as he brought his head to mine. "We are going to do nothing."

I opened my mouth to protest, but he stopped me, covering my mouth with a hand. "*We* are going to *nothing*, because *I* am going to get the horses ready, and *you* are going to hide." I shook my head, but he didn't release his hand from my mouth. "Yes, you are going to hide, and you are to stay absolutely silent. We cannot risk you being found, you are too close to freedom to be caught now. Do you trust me? Nod if you understand."

I stared at him as I nodded, because I did—I trusted him completely.

"Good," he whispered. "See that small grouping of trees just up that bank?" I bowed my head in acknowledgment. "I want you to stay low and, as silently as possible, I want you to go up there and make yourself invisible. Stay there until I come and get you. Stay invisible, okay?" I signaled my understanding and he let out a sigh of relief before pulling me in and kissing my temple. "Go."

And I did.

CHAPTER 21
ASTRAEUS

I couldn't fucking believe what was happening. A group of about ten guards were nearing our camp, and though it was set back a small way from the road, the dying trees did not offer as much coverage as I wanted. If they spotted the horses, I had no idea what would happen. Solarian and Pyrusian guards weren't known for their kind and understanding disposition. They had a reputation for causing trouble, and I'd be fucking damned if this wasn't a pristine opportunity for them to fuck with me.

They could fuck with me all they wanted, just as long as they didn't find Asteria. I prayed she was hidden in the small grove of trees up the bank by now, that she would stay there and stay silent.

I quickly broke down the camp, packing away the furs, and smothering the remaining embers of the morning fire with dirt. I was doing my best to not attract attention to this small clearing, and dousing the fire with water would have ensured their full attention. They were close enough that I could hear their muffled voices and the clopping of hooves on the packed and frozen ground. I looked over at the horses when I realized Asteria's saddles bore the Solarian insignia.

"Fuck," I muttered to myself as I hurried to unfasten the saddle and remove it from Freya.

I ripped the saddle off the horse's back and jogged into the brush to dump it somewhere it wouldn't be seen. As I emerged, the guards were passing the clearing, and I held my breath as I carefully stalked up to the horses, hoping we had managed to remain unnoticed.

The road curved shortly after the clearing, and I slowly exhaled as the last few guards rounded the bend. I felt my muscles relax as we avoided discovery, but as the last guard disappeared from view, a branch fell from a nearby tree and startled the horses, their frenzied cries and stomping caught the attention of the guard.

"Hold!" he yelled at the squadron as he whipped his head in my direction. "We've got company here!" He turned his horse and trotted back up the road into the clearing, followed by the other nine riders. I cursed under my breath as I turned to meet them.

"Well," the commanding officer said as he made his way to the front of the group, "what's going on here?" He surveyed the clearing, eyeing the horses and then me. "And who might you be?" he sneered.

I bowed my head as a sign of respect and subservience. "My name is Rae, sir."

"Rae." He spat my name like it was a bitter taste in his mouth. "What would a commoner like yourself be doing with such well-bred steeds?" His tone dripped with condescension.

Keeping my eyes down, I replied with the best lie I could think of. "My family breeds them, sir."

"Is that so?" His disbelief was evident. "I don't know of any breeders from this kingdom. You wouldn't be lying to me, would you?"

"No, sir. My family is not from here." Not exactly a lie. "We traveled here from one of the other realms. We are trying to establish a trade deal with the Kingdoms of Leethe. These horses are gifts to the royal family of Dalia."

"Taking the scenic route, are we?" He circled me on his horse, trying to make me feel trapped.

"Our ship docked at the port in Harmonia to meet with the king there, and then separated for differing courts. I received correspondence to travel to Dalia and Nyxtas."

He stopped in front of me, while the rest of his men slowly surrounded me. "This correspondence, do you have it?"

Shit. "I..." I fumbled my words as I tried to think of how to get out of this. "I do not, sir."

"Interesting. How am I to believe that you, a man from none of our Kingdoms, has managed to be granted an audience with *all* our royal families? Can you not produce them because you are, in fact, lying to me?" The group chortled behind him, enjoying the interrogation and prospect of getting to dole out punishment to a liar.

"No, sir." I stepped back, giving myself some space. "I lost the letters, along with much of my supplies, as we crossed the Singing Mountains. What supplies you see now were gracious gifts from the King and Queen of Nyxtas, a debt and a kindness I hope to repay."

He dismounted and stalked towards me, inspecting my face for anything that may give away my lies. He looked over at the supplies I had loaded onto the horses. "Tell me, do you travel alone?"

I swallowed and lifted my gaze to his. "I do." He turned his back, and I took the opportunity to shoot a look over at the trees, ensuring she was still hidden. *Please stay hidden.*

"Well, *Rae*," he said with disgust as he swung his leg over his horse, seating himself back into his saddle. "I do hope you enjoy the rest of your journey. I wish you the best of luck."

He turned his horse to face his men, giving them a curt nod before he rode out of the clearing. The men didn't move to follow, and I knew what was about to happen. As if connected, they all dismounted in unison. I glanced up at the trees one more time, hoping she could see me and read my thoughts.

Do not move. Stay hidden. Stay silent. Please. I closed my eyes and braced myself for what was about to happen.

The first blow landed on my stomach, and I folded, the air rushing out of my lungs. The second was an uppercut to the chin, sending me stumbling back into the hold of two soldiers who restrained me, keeping me upright for the one delivering the punches. I would not fight back; I knew that if I did, it would more than likely end in my death. So, I stood here, taking every hit, absorbing the pain, refusing to let it show. I would not give them the satisfaction of crying, shouting, grunting, or begging for them to stop. They would get nothing from me except the blood that coated their fists.

While three of them continued to use me as a punching bag, the others took to looting our supplies and destroying whatever they could. Once they were satisfied with their destruction, they untied the horses and whipped them until they ran. I was tossed onto the cold ground as they laughed, mounting their horses and turning to leave.

I laid there, coughing and wheezing as I tried to catch my breath. They had delivered quite the beating, but I'd had worse. The last guard was just out of view when I heard Asteria crashing through the brush. I sat myself up to face her as she entered the clearing, her cheeks glistening with tears, her eyes bloodshot.

"Are you okay?" she asked, dropping to her knees with force. "Oh my. Rae, your face..." Her voice quivered as she spoke. She gently pushed aside the hair that fell into my eyes, gasping when she saw my swollen and bloodied eye. "Your...They...I am so sorry." She began crying as she inspected my face, noting every cut, scrape, bruise. "This is all my fault." Her brows creased and her chin trembled as she looked at me.

I went to stand, wincing with the movement. "I'm fine," I hissed. "This is nothing." I gave her a half smile as I struggled to straighten, pain lancing my side as I realized he had probably fractured a rib.

"You are not fine! You need to sit down!" Looping my arm over her shoulder, she led me to the tree where the horses had been tied. "Sit down and let me take a look at your injuries."

"Look, Princess..." I removed my arm from her support. "I don't know if you've noticed, but there are bigger issues at the moment." Wincing, I gestured to the ground littered with our ruined supplies. "Like the fact that we have next to no usable supplies and our horses are gone." I moved to step forward, but she halted me.

"The horses are well trained, and they will return. If not, I will go find them myself." She tried to force me back, but I refused to budge. "Look..." She sounded exasperated. "You may have had the upper hand this morning, but from the looks of it, I have the upper hand now. So you can do this the easy way and sit down so I can assess your injuries."

"And the hard way?" I jested through the pain.

"I add a few more injuries I'll need to assess."

My brow raised at the thought of her manhandling me onto the ground. I contemplated momentarily, but I knew the better option was to just shut my trap and listen to the woman.

"As tempting as the thought of you kicking my ass is," I leaned back into the tree and slowly lowered myself into a sitting position, "I think I'll save that treat for another day." I shut my eyes and blew out a breath, leaning my head back. "They either bruised or fractured a rib," I admitted to her as I struggled, each breath causing a stabbing pain in my side.

"I need you to take off your shirt and lay back," she said as she manipulated my arm, assessing my reaction to each movement.

"Woah, slow down there, Little Star. I think we're skipping a few steps." I stifled a laugh at her wide eyes and slackened jaw. "Ouch!" I yelped as she prodded my side roughly.

"Oops," she said blandly. "My bad."

Inhaling through gritted teeth, I pulled my shirt over my head. "It was a joke, Princess."

Using her hands to support me while I laid back onto the cold ground, she smiled wickedly. "It was an accident."

"Yeah, I bet." Balling up the shirt, I just removed, I placed it beneath my head as a makeshift pillow.

She shook her head slightly, her eyes still rimmed with redness and her face flushed from tears. She began her assessment, palpating my side and looking for the source of the pain. When she found it, I resisted the urge to yell out.

"Mmmmmm." A growl rumbled in the back of my throat. "Yea, that's the spot," I groaned.

"Feels like it's your seventh rib." She laid her palm over the point of pain. "The tissue is heated and swollen. It's going to bruise. Badly." Her hand began to circle the area, seeing how far the inflammation spread. "How far above your head can you move your arm?"

I went to lift my left arm above my head and got about halfway before the pain became excruciating.

"It's definitely a fracture, if not a more serious break." She cradled my head and shoulders as she helped me sit back up. "I hope you're proficient at functioning with your right hand, because this arm is going to need a sling."

"Yeah, that's not going to work, Princess." I struggled to replace my shirt with the restrictions from my injury. "There is no way I can get us where we need to be with only one functioning arm. I need to hunt, to carry things, to fight if needed. I've had worse injuries; it's just a little pain. I'll be fine. Just help me up so I can start salvaging what I can of our supplies and hunt down the horses."

"It wasn't a suggestion." She eyed me seriously. "Take it easy and let your rib heal. I can clean this mess and get the horses. Your only job is to keep your ass planted." Standing, she surveyed the disaster that was our supplies. "I don't think we're going anywhere today. I'll track down the horses after I get the fire going and make sure you're settled." She stalked into the trees, emerging a short time later with her arms stacked full of kindling.

"Well damn, Princess. Someone's been working out," I remarked, eyeing her figure while she knelt beside the cold remnants of the evening's fire.

"Someone insists on me performing the lighter and more feminine duties, so someone has little idea of what this *Princess* is capable of." Within minutes, with very little effort from her, the fire was blazing. "You don't think I observe as much as I do." Standing, she began to collect the furs and place them near the fire. "In reality, I have been observing you, and I have learned quite a lot." She walked over and held out her hand to me. "Come on. Time to rest." She nodded her head towards the pallet of furs she had made.

I decided there would be no point in fighting her, because as much as I hated to admit it, she was right. I wasn't going to be able to do the things I needed to, which meant I couldn't take care of her the way she deserved. The longer it took me to heal, the longer it would take to get home.

I looked over at the sound of fabric ripping, only to see her shredding one of her blouses. "What are you doing?" I questioned.

"Making a sling for your arm." She knelt beside me. "Hold your arm like this across your chest." She bent my arm at the elbow, laying my forearm over my chest before cradling it in the scrap of fabric, tying it up behind my neck so my arm was nestled into my side and chest, restricting its movement.

"Well, aren't you just full of surprises, Little Star?" Looking up at her, I lifted my free arm and caressed her face. "Thank you." She looked down at me, her eyes seemed as though they were phosphorescent with light from within.

"It's the least I could do," she said, touching my cheek in return. After a moment, she cleared her throat. "I'd better go find our horses." She stood, pulling a small satchel out of her waist band and mixing it with a mug of water, "This should help with the pain." She smiled down at me as she handed me the mug of tea. "Drink it, you'll feel better." I obliged, bringing the mug to my lips and drinking in the sweet, floral mixture.

With that, she stood and went off on her own. Slowly, I laid back onto the furs, inhaling the crisp air. *She really is something magnificent,* I thought to myself.

A smile tugged at the corners of my mouth as I thought back to the first time I laid eyes on her, to that night in the castle corridor. I knew she was different then—something about her just pulled at my soul, like hers was calling to mine. She was broken that night, but still, her beauty eclipsed that of any woman I had ever seen.

When I saw her the second time in that pub, her eyes full of fear as that worthless merchant tried to hurt her, I knew then that I had to help. Our paths crossing again was not a coincidence—no, it was something that had been mapped out in the stars by the Goddess. I don't know if our meeting was so I could save my people, or so I could save her, but either way, I no longer cared. She was with me, and each day I spent with her, it got harder to imagine spending a day without her.

I closed my eyes, and between the heat from the fire and the fiery passion that flooded my body with each beat of my heart, I soon drifted off to sleep.

CHAPTER 22
ASTERIA

Much to my surprise and my relief, the horses had not gone more than a half a mile from the clearing, so it did not take long to find them. They had stopped at a small stream and were drinking from it when I found them. They were a beautiful set of horses, Odin darker than night, standing tall and packed with muscle, a true warhorse. Next to him stood Freya, her coat a nearly pristine white, even her hooves paler than most. She wasn't as tall as Odin, nor as muscular, but she was every bit as swift and loyal.

I let out a soft whistle, and she halted, turning to face me. She snorted and swiped her front hoof at the ground before dipping her head slightly, and I lowered mine in mutual respect. I approached, reaching out and running my hand down her snout as I neared her.

"I knew you wouldn't have wandered far." I reached over, running my hand down the length of Odin's back. "Are you two ready to get back?"

When we got back to the clearing, the fire was still blazing, and

Rae had fallen asleep where I left him. I tied the horses back up and began to gather the supplies littering the ground. There wasn't much that was usable, which put us even further into trouble. I had no herbs left to make anything that may help speed Rae's healing. Half the furs had been stolen by the guards, and most everything else had been broken, including the bow that Rae used to hunt.

"Fuck," I muttered to myself. I knew what needed to be done, and I knew that Rae was not going to agree to it at all—I had to go into town.

I paced the perimeter of the clearing, fighting with myself over what I should do. I knew what *needed* to be done, I just didn't know if it *should* be done. Sitting down next to him while he slept so peacefully, I thought to myself, *this man has risked so much to help me. He has saved my life more than once, and in more ways than one.*

He may not know it, but he had saved me from my own self-loathing, and he deserved to be saved too, to receive some of the selflessness he had given me. I leaned down and placed a kiss on his cheek, hoping that the sleeping caught I had given kept him out for a few hours.

"I am so sorry for this." Standing up and looking down at him, I felt my heart skip a beat. "Please don't hate me too much for this."

I quickly threw on extra layers of clothing and a large cloak so I could put the hood up and hide my face. I couldn't ride into town with Freya wearing the Solarian saddle, so I knew what I had to do, and it would most definitely anger Rae.

I untied Freya first, then Odin. Checking that Rae was still sleeping, I hurriedly stepped into the stirrup of Odin's saddle and threw my other leg over before lashing Freya's lead to the saddle horn. I whispered another apology into the wind as I rode out, both horses in tow. I knew if I left either horse, Rae would have come after me, and I couldn't let him do that. I left a quickly scrawled note on a piece of parchment with some charcoal left from the morning's fire.

> *I know what you're going to want to do, but you cannot follow me. I am going to fetch supplies, and I will return as quickly as possible. Please trust me. I will be safe. Rest well, and I'll see you soon.*
> *~Princess*

I SET A SWIFT PACE, following the road and praying the town was close. The sun was already approaching the highest point in the sky, and I knew I only had a handful of hours before night would fall. After a few hours, I crested a hill, breathing a sigh of relief as I saw the town below.

Thank you, Goddess. I looked up at the sky and closed my eyes in thanks. I made my way down the hill, making a mental list of all the things I needed to find. As we approached the village, I got a sinking feeling in the pit of my stomach—something wasn't right.

The guards, I thought to myself. *They must have been heading here.* My nerves made my stomach uneasy, and I knew I needed a plan. I made my way along the edge of the town until I found a secluded area that would be easy for me to get back to in a hurry.

I quickly dismounted and tied Odin loosely to a stump. "Stay here and be ready to go, okay?" I murmured to him, as if he could understand me.

Always have an alternate escape route, Raes' voice echoed in my head.

Yeah, yeah, yeah, I thought. *I don't plan on needing one.* I pulled my hood up over my head, making sure to keep track of the route so I could find my way back. The town became busier and more crowded the closer to the market I got, and while it made maneuvering more difficult, it made me feel like I was less likely to be recognized. I pushed my way through the throngs of people as I searched for my first stop: the herbalist apothecary. If I were to only get one thing, it was going to be the herbs I needed to help heal Rae. It didn't take too long before I was able to spot it across the square, I headed straight for it. I kept my head down and spurned solicitations from other vendors.

The tinkling of a bell announced my entrance, and a charming old man stepped from behind a curtain at the back.

"Ah, good day, my lady!" His brittle voice was a perfect complement to his fragile appearance. "How could I help you with today?"

"Good day to you, sir. You seem to have quite the collection." My kind words pulled at the wrinkles in his face as he smiled. "I have few needs. Do you think you could help me?"

"I would be honored," he graciously agreed. "Just tell me what it is you need, and I'll hunt it down for you."

I began to rattle off the list of herbs and flowers I was looking for, and as I expected, he had everything I needed. I had him add a few tins and other things to help me store my herbal mixtures, and he began to tally up my total. I rifled through the large satchel I had brought with me and paid the man what he was owed before leaving the shop.

When I stepped out back into the market, the scent of warm, sweet bread flooded my senses, and my mouth salivated instantly. I followed my nose, searching for the source. I spotted it a few doors down, the Bakery, I turned my feet and headed in that direction.

Before the bakery, there was a tavern, lively music and conversation drifting out the door as it swung open, and a Royal Guard stepped out into the early evening air. I stalled, transfixed on him, watching his every move to see if he would recognize me. I pulled my hood forward, gripping my cloak tightly around my chest, my breath coming out in visible puffs. He stood just before the door, staring out into the market, his eyes raking back and forth over the crowd. The door to the tavern swung open again, and the hollers from his fellow guards inside spilled out.

"Hey, hurry it up out there. We've not got all night!"

"Oh, piss off!" he yelled back over his shoulder. "I'm coming, I'm coming." He waved them off as he stepped forward and began walking in my direction. My breathing seized as he approached.

"Good evening," he muttered as he walked past, his breath coated with the scent of ale.

I tipped my head at him, refusing to speak, and I watched as he approached a group of horses tied along the alley behind the tavern. He reached into the pack of one saddle and pulled out a pouch before stalking back my way. I hurried out of his path, stepping into the doorway of the bakery as he threw the door of the pub open.

"Here you are, you great pussy!" he yelled at someone. "There's your smoke. Now quit your bitching. You're giving me a headache."

My body relaxed as I stepped inside the bakery. I had managed to not be seen by the guard, which hopefully was my one and only encounter with one. The heat of the brick ovens and the smell of sweet pastries and savory breads invoked a strong feeling of warmth and comfort. I inhaled deeply and smiled at the plump lady behind the counter.

She smiled back at me. "What can I get for you today?"

I looked around at the variety of loaves and sweets, drinking in the aromas that made my stomach churn with hunger. I knew I needed to be practical, but the temptation was overwhelming.

"I'll take four loaves of these ones here." I pointed to a batch of simple white bread that would be versatile and easy to eat.

"Of course. Anything else?" She began pulling the loaves out and wrapping them in a simple linen cloth.

"Actually," my heart began to flutter at the sight of the small apple loaves that sat behind the counter, "could I also have two of those apple loaves?" I smiled at the thought of surprising Rae with the apple loaves, something I knew he missed about home.

"Oh of course!" She excitedly plucked them down. "These are the last of them for the season, so you came just in time!" She began packing them up when she stopped. "Here," she grabbed the last two off the shelf, "these two are on the house." She beamed as she turned to hand me my things.

"Oh no!" I startled, "you don't have to do that!" I tried arguing.

"No," she insisted, "you take them. Here are your things, you have a wonderful evening!" I handed her the coins and packed away the bread before rushing out the door.

Stepping into the cool air, I looked around at the lively market. I hadn't fully observed the crowds before, but now, looking around, I saw the abundance of flowers and banners. People dressed in varying shades of blue and white, flowers weaved into the hair of women and children, the large pole with rainbow strips of fabric that children would hold onto as they skipped and danced in circles around it—a festival. They were preparing for a festival. Soon, the market would be full of families and guards celebrating the new winter season.

Shit. I still hadn't gotten everything, I had wanted to get more furs, and possibly some dried meats and a few vegetables. I looked around, trying to see if there were any shops still open. I started to feel defeated when, suddenly, a wicked idea came to me. I made my way back to the tavern, taking my time so I could assess my surroundings before I tried my plan. I needed to get through the back to the alley where the horses were being kept, but my options were limited.

I could try to pay off the stable boy and hope he didn't turn around and rat me out for a bigger payout. I could go through the tavern to the back alley and get to the horses that way, or—I didn't want to even think of the other option.

None of them were exactly ideal. I took a look inside the tavern as someone from the market made their way in. It was busy, and the Royal Guards had made themselves comfortable inside. Going inside was definitely risky. The other option depended on a person, and I didn't trust people. I didn't think a hooded woman trying to pay off a stable hand to gain access to the horses of the Royal Guard would go over well. It would more than likely end in me getting caught.

Taking my cloak off posed way too much risk, but trying to get through the tavern inconspicuously in a large cloak might draw more attention. I looked through one of the windows, but it was difficult to see through the condensation coating it. It looked like guards were closer to the center of the room, so if I stuck to the edges, it should be okay, right? This was such a stupid plan, but it was my plan, and I was going to do it. I took a deep, steadying breath, pursing my lips before I blew out the air slowly, trying to steady the pounding in my chest. I stretched my neck from side to side, flexing my hands at my side. *You can do this.*

I turned as the door opened, a male exited; I avoided him as I slipped into the tavern before the door closed. I dipped into a shadowy alcove near the door as I surveyed the room. It was definitely crowded, but that was probably for the better. I locked my eyes on the large table of guards that sat near the center. Ten—there were ten of them currently sitting there, the same ten from this morning.

My fists clenched involuntarily as I remembered them beating Rae and destroying all our things. I wanted nothing more than to see their arms ripped from their bodies and shoved down their throats. My skin heated as my rage began to cloud my vision with a burning white light, but just then, the door flew open, missing me by only inches. The fire in my veins was instantly replaced with shards of ice as the person who entered the pub came into view.

His bronze Solarian armor was accented with a velveteen sunset orange cape that cascaded from one shoulder. I stepped back further into the alcove, trying to disappear completely as the man joined the table of guards, sitting in the center, facing directly towards me. Terror seized me at the monster sitting across the room, his grim and tense expression accentuated by his thinned lips and furrowed brow, his chiseled jaw clenched. He was frustrated and angered, a look I had seen aimed at me before. His sun-kissed skin only brightened his golden blonde hair that reflected the warm glow of the lanterns lighting the room, his eyes a deep honey color. He was tall, and though he wore his armor, you knew his body was well sculpted. He looked like sunshine incarnate.

Most would find him unbelievably attractive, but all I saw when I looked at him was the vile human who lived beneath the gorgeous mask. The guard dog of my 'betrothed', Stefan's head of the Solarian Guard, Valdin, was here, and I was prey, hiding in the shadows. After the time I had spent with Valdin on the journey to Solaria, I saw exactly why he held his position: he was Stefan's mirror. Not only were they both varied incarnations of the sun, but they also both thrived off dwelling in darkness. They thrived off inflicting pain, relishing in the misery they caused others. On the other side of the coin, they could both hide their deviance, convincing others they were every bit the charming gentleman they presented themselves to be. Only those unlucky enough to fall on the dark side of their personalities ever knew who they really were. Staring at Valdin now, I saw so much of Stefan in him, his mannerisms, his appearance, his rage.

I steeled my spine despite every instinct in me telling me to run. I couldn't run—as much as I wanted to run, to flee, to put as much distance between this man and me, I couldn't. We needed the supplies, and unless I spent the night in this village, this was the only way I would get them tonight. Rae needed me, and I needed to get back to him. I swallowed hard; *stick to the plan*. I adjusted my hood, keeping my face shadowed as I stepped out into the light of the tavern. I immediately turned my back to the table of guards as they spoke.

"We're just about dry over here. I'll go get us a fresh pitcher of ale." The scraping of the wooden chair legs against the wooden floor sent needles down my spine. "Valdin, you want anything special? Maybe one of these pretty ladies?"

"Maybe you should plant your ass back in your chair." The voice made my skin crawl. "Before you become anymore of an embarrassment to the Royal Guard."

"Settle your dick, Valdin," the drunk guard argued back. "We've searched the city; she's not here. Now sit back, relax, have a pint... or some pussy."

Raucous laughter from the other guards echoed through the bar. I jumped at the clattering of a chair hitting the ground as someone stood forcefully, the gasps of other patrons quickly following the commotion. I carefully turned my head from where I stood at the counter to see what was happening.

Valdin had the drunk guard by the throat, pulling him across the table so their faces were mere inches from each other. The guard struggled to breathe as Valdin's grip on his windpipe increased.

"Do not speak to me with such casual regard, soldier. I am your commanding officer, and you will respect me as such. So, unless you want to speak with the prince yourself and tell him you weren't able to find his princess because you were too busy with pints and pussy—" the guard began pulling at Valdin's arm, his face turning blue from lack of oxygen and blood flow, "—you will sit your fucking ass down, or I will remove your fucking cock right here." He threw the guard back, and he fell back onto the ground, rubbing at his neck, gasping for air.

Valdin straightened and glanced around the room before sitting back in his chair and propping his boots on the table. "Another pitcher of ale here!"

Everyone went back to their conversations, and the music continued as if he hadn't just threatened to cut off someone's dick in the middle of the tavern. I felt his eyes fall on me, and I quickly turned my head back to the barkeep. With his eyes burning into me, I knew I had caught his attention, and I needed to act quickly.

I looked towards the door leading out to the back; it was close, but it was in Valdin's direct sight. He was already tracking my movements—I could feel it, his gaze a heavy weight on my back. If I went out the back, he would follow, and I would be trapped. I rolled my eyes, knowing it was the last option I wanted to go with, but it was rapidly becoming the only one left.

"Excuse me, sir, do you have any rooms available tonight?" I asked the barkeep, who just nodded his head in reply. "I'll take one please, preferably with a bath. Could you have hot water sent up?" I asked sweetly.

He just huffed a little before handing me a key with a room number and directed me towards the stairs with a wave of his hand. I made my way to the stairs, careful to keep my face hidden, weaving behind people or bumping into them so my back was aimed towards Valdin's gaze. As I climbed the stairs, I looked back to see Valdin walking to the barkeep before they both looked towards the stairs.

Fuck. I didn't have much time. I hurried to the room that matched the number of the key and quickly let myself in. I locked the door behind me and looked around the room—it was bare, like most tavern rooms. There was a small bed, a writing desk and chair, a shallow tub, and a dresser. There was a window on the far wall, and I rushed over to it, looking down to see that it did indeed face the alleyway. I heard voices and boots coming up the stairs, and I knew I needed to act. I grabbed the chair, wedging it under the door handle—it wouldn't keep them out, but it would at least slow them down. I walked over to the window and unlatched it, and—*bam bam bam*. Three loud knocks filled the small room.

"Royal Guard, open up." I didn't reply, and another three knocks rang through the room. "Royal Guard. Open the door now." I still didn't reply as I threw one leg out the window, straddling the window ledge. "If you don't open the door, we will force our way in."

I pulled my other leg through the window, balancing on the edge that ran along the building. It was wide enough to fit the balls of my feet comfortably, and the thatching of the roof came down far enough that I could hold on to the supports for balance. I leaned in and pulled the window shut as the doorknob began to rattle. The rocks of the stone wall were just uneven enough that I could climb down without much difficulty.

I reminded myself to breathe as I adjusted the satchel across my body so it was resting behind me as I began to descend. The stones were cold, biting into my skin as I gripped them with all the strength I could muster. I was about halfway down when I heard the repeated banging of them trying to break into the room. It wouldn't be long before they were in, which meant I was just about out of time. Looking down, the drop seemed to be about eight feet, which wasn't that high, but landing wrong could mean a fractured bone at least, a broken one at the most.

"Time to prove you're not a princess," I muttered to myself I prepared to make the jump. *Inhale. One two three four five. Exhale. One two three four five.* I pushed off slightly and braced myself for the landing.

To my surprise, the ground was softer than expected, a layer of scattered hay cushioned my landing. I heard a crash from above and then yelling: they were in the room, and it wouldn't take long before they figured out I had climbed from the window.

I needed to move fast. I walked along the wall down the alley to where the horses were. I wasn't sure which ones belonged to the guards and which belonged to other patrons of the tavern, but I didn't exactly have the luxury of asking. I weaved in and out of them until I spotted what I was looking for. One of the horses was strapped down with the furs stolen from us. Using my dagger, I cut the strap holding them to the back of the saddle and gathered as many as I could feasibly carry. The rest, I left on the ground—they didn't deserve them. I tried to look into the other bags for more supplies when I heard someone yell from above.

"There look! By the horses!" *Shit.* It was time to go. I turned to leave when I was cut off by a man not much younger than me.

"What the hell do you think you're doing?"

He charged at me, and I looked around—there wasn't anywhere for me to run. He was barreling at me as I backed up, hitting the railing the horses were tied to. Placing both hands on the rail, I leaned back, bracing myself, and with all the strength I had, I pushed off the ground, slamming both feet into the chest of the man as he ran full speed into them. He collapsed to the ground, out of breath and unconscious.

"I'm sorry," I whispered as I stepped over him to leave.

I paused, flashes of what the guards had done earlier to Rae playing through my mind. Without hesitation, I turned to the leads and quickly unsheathed my dagger, slicing through the horses' leads one by one, freeing them. I rushed at them, smacking their backsides until they began to flee into the square, straight into the festivities.

I heard the commotion from inside the tavern, realizing the guards were coming through the back door. At the same time, screaming echoed from the market center as festival participants were surprised by a stampede of horses. I heard the thundering of boots pause as the yelling from the square grew louder.

"You five, go see what all that screaming is about! The rest of you are with me!"

I started sprinting the opposite way I had come, cutting down the alley on the other side of the building and heading for the outer edge of town. The satchel and furs were weighing me down, and I wasn't able to move as quickly as I wanted. I stopped for a moment, leaning back against a small home as I tried to catch my breath. I waited a few moments, listening for any signs of being followed, but I heard nothing outside of the normal household symphony of families talking, children laughing and crying, and the crackling of warm fires.

It seemed the distraction of freeing the horses had worked, leading the soldiers away from me while I disappeared in the other direction. I needed to get back to Odin and Freya, but they were on the northern edge of the city, and I was on the western side. I debated if I should cut through the city, but with the guards on alert and hunting, I risked running into them. I decided on skirting around the outer edge of the city, sticking to the shadows and prayed the search stayed more centralized.

I began skulking my way around the perimeter of the city, sticking to dimly lit alleys and weaving through the small outcroppings of homes that surrounded the city center. I kept my eyes peeled for any signs of the guards; the commotion had seemed to have settled at the center of the market, and the music from the celebration echoed through the city, a joyful symphony of laughter and singing. The outer rim was mostly silent and dark, aside from the occasional clattering and scurrying of animals searching for scraps of food.

I neared the western border of the town, relieved and exhausted, ready to be out of this city. It was cold, the stress and exertion of my escape had coated my skin in sweat, which felt like needles as the brisk winter air froze it. My pace slowed, and I found myself short of breath.

You're almost in the clear. Just keep going. I whispered the phrase to myself over and over again as I tried to locate the horses, but I couldn't find them. They should have been right there. I could have sworn I had left them right over there—I could see the small area and the stump I had tied Odin's reigns to. I began to frantically look around, searching the darkness for any sign of the horses.

"Fuck, fuck, fuck..." I paced back and forth, each step timed with the thrumming of my pulse as panic began to take over. My mind raced through different scenarios, different ways to get back to him. Back to Rae.

My focus was torn from my thoughts at the sound of hooves growing louder behind me. I turned around to see a mounted guard, and to my dismay, he saw me as well.

"You there!" he shouted from the shadows. "What are you doing? Identify yourself!" I turned my head from the silver moonlight that cut through the clouds, hoping to conceal my features.

"I... um..."

Fuck, I didn't know what to say, how to explain what I was doing lurking in the back alley. My instinct to flee took over, and I began sprinting towards the maze of homes and alleys that surrounded the town. I could hear him yelling after me, the sounds drowned out by the rapid thudding hooves as he launched into motion after me.

I hung a left down a side street, trying to continue towards the edge of the city so I could make a break for the woods. The echoes of the guard's pursuit grew louder as he began closing in. I refused to look behind me, keeping my focus on the route ahead. I saw the entry to a small throughway coming up to my right, and I began bracing myself for the sharp redirection. My lungs hurt, a sharp stabbing pain with each panting breath I took. My legs were weak, screaming at me with each step, each slight movement. Tears began pricking my eyes from the fear and the sting of the frigid air.

You just need to lose him, I thought to myself. *Lose him and get to the woods. You can regroup your thoughts there.* I inhaled a deep and agonizing breath as I changed directions at the last second heading down the throughway. Except, it wasn't a throughway—it was a dead end. I came face to face with the large stone wall that encapsulated half the city. How had I not seen that, how had I not remembered?

I turned on my heel to find another way out, but it was too late. At the mouth of the path was a Solarian guard on his horse.

"That didn't go as planned, did it?" he mocked as he dismounted and began stalking towards me. I didn't speak. "I asked you a question, thief."

His anger was palpable. In the time I had spent with Rae, I had forgotten how short tempered and cruel Solarian men were. Still, I refused to speak. I slowly began stepping backwards, trying to maintain distance between me and this guard.

"Who the fuck do you think you are?" he spat. "Refusing to identify yourself to a Royal Guard is a crime worthy of severe punishment."

It wasn't though—refusal to identify yourself to a guard was a minor offense, deserving of no more than a slap on the wrist. Unfortunately, the guards' egos were generally too fragile to handle a refusal, feeling as though their position of dominance of was being threatened. I had run out of space as my back hit the cold stone wall. I was trapped, and the guard continued his advancement—I knew that once he reached me, he would inflict whatever malicious punishment he felt was appropriate.

The pain in my lungs began to spread to my chest as my heart pounded against my ribcage. The puffs of vapor visible from my quickened breathing nearly clouded my vision as the guard came toe to toe with me.

"I'll teach you to show some respect, you little cunt." He snarled as he reached up, clasping his frozen hand around my throat.

Color drained from my face as the guard's features were lit by the moon. I knew him. He was one of the guards who escorted me from Pyrus to Solaria. He had been one I had seen spending ample time at Valdin's side. I felt my stomach drop as the action caused my hood to fall back, and I saw his eyes widen in excitement as he took in my face.

"Well, well, well..." he preened, "if it isn't the traitorous little bitch from Pyrus." His gaze traced over my body before landing back on my face. "You know, I never understood why Stefan put so much effort into finding you." He leaned in, pressing his weight against my body. "But now that I've gotten a closer look..." He paused, his grip on my neck tightening. "I can see why he would want to sink his cock into that pretty little pussy of yours."

My hand drifted beneath my cloak, stopping when it found the cold metal of my dagger. "Fuck you," I spat in his face.

He pulled back momentarily, shocked at my action, I used that moment to make my move, pushing off the wall and bringing my knee to his groin with every ounce of strength I had. He doubled over, cupping his dick as he groaned in pain.

"You're going to pay for that, you stupid bitch," he seethed through clenched teeth.

He raised up, his jaw set angrily as he charged at me, his hand raised. He brought his hand down, aiming to drag it across my face, but I quickly stepped out of the way, catching his arm as it came down. Gripping his wrist tightly, I stepped under his arm, twisting it behind him as I did. I grasped his hand, forcing it forward at the wrist as he cried out in pain. I kicked the back of his knee, causing him to buckle, falling to his knee.

"You stupid bitch!" He groaned in pain.

Leaning forward, I applied more pressure to his wrist. "Call me a bitch again, and I'm going to break your wrist."

A dark laugh rumbled through his chest. "You're going to have to do more than break my wrist to change my vocabulary."

He inhaled deeply, quickly pivoting on his knee and causing me to lose my grasp on his arm. I hardly processed what had happened before his fist landed firmly in my stomach, knocking the air from my lungs and knocking me to the ground. I tried to roll to my knees and get up, but he moved faster. I had just made it to my stomach to push myself up before he was there, standing over me. He grabbed my hair and pulled me up to my knees. It took everything in me to not scream—fearing it would attract the attention of more guards. I gripped his arm, trying to relieve the tension on my scalp and figure out how to get out of this. I had dropped my dagger when he had punched me—it was laying a few feet from me, and I had no idea how to get my hands on it. I struggled against his grip, letting out a whine of frustration.

"I'd like to see you break my wrist now," he laughed, "you dumb bitch."

Anger boiled inside me. Anger at him. Anger at my choices. Anger for getting caught.

"She may not be able to break your wrist, but I can." I froze at the sound of Rae's voice behind me.

"And who the fuck are you?" the guard asked indignantly, looking over his shoulder at the man who had intervened in his fun.

"The man who is about to plunge this dagger into your neck if you don't take your fucking hands off her." I could hear the gravel of anger in Rae's voice.

"Is that so?" he asked as he swung us around, dragging me by my hair so that we were facing Rae. He pulled back on my hair, forcing my head back so I was looking up at him. "Hear that your Highness? He's going to put that dagger into my neck if I don't let you go."

The sarcasm in the guard's tone sent chills through my body—he had no plans of letting me go. I looked at Rae to find his face contorted in rage, and I swore the shadows deepened behind him as his eyes grew darker. He was fully prepared to fight this guard for my freedom, bruised and battered from earlier, and without the sling I had placed him in.

"I could put it through your heart if you would prefer, though it may take you longer to bleed out that way." Rae's voice was so void of remorse or sympathy, it was unsettling.

The guard threw his head back in laughter. "What do you think?" he asked, looking down at me. "Kill him and then we can finish our little game before we return to you to your betrothed?" Gripping my hair tighter, he strained my head so far back, I struggled to breathe. "I can't fucking wait to see what punishment Stefan has planned for you." He pulled his lips back into a disturbing grin as he slid his free hand around my contorted neck. "I may ask if I can watch."

The sky darkened, deeper than the inky black it already was, and I could feel Rae's anger filling the ally, icy and hard. The guard looked up, his malicious smile aimed at Rae, and when their eyes met, the temperature dropped a few degrees.

"Get. Your. Fucking. Hands. Off. Her." Each word was short and filled with rage.

"Whatever you say," the guard said with nonchalance as he tightened his grip on my neck and threw me to the side.

I landed hard on the ground, rubbing at my neck and gasping for air. Before I could even look up, Rae was running at the guard. The darkness shifted as though it followed him, keeping his movements hidden from the guard. I had seen him more like a shadow before, but this was something else.

The guard hadn't even taken a step forward before Rae plunged the dagger deep into the man's chest. He had gone for the heart, driving the blade with such force that the hilt was flush with the wound. Rae followed the guard to the ground, keeping a firm grip on the weapon. The guard coughed, blood spewing from his mouth as he tried to speak, but Rae twisted the dagger, cutting off the words and wrenching a drowned scream instead.

"I told you to get your fucking hands off her." Another twist of the dagger in the man's chest followed. "But you didn't listen." Another twist. "Instead, you thought it wise to place your hand on her throat. Big mistake." Another twist.

The guard struggled to breath as his airway flooded with blood, unable to fight back against the man twisting the blade in his heart. "Now you get to lay here alone, choking on the consequences of your own dumb fucking choices. I hope it's a slow and agonizing death." Rae pulled the blade from his chest, and the guard flinched but made no attempt to move. Rae stood looking down at the guard and spat on his body, "Bitch.".

I stared at him from my spot on the ground, in complete shock. I had seen him kill someone before, but not like that... Not with that cruelty. And he had done it because of me, because the guard had tried to hurt me. I watched him closely as he walked beside me, reaching out to help me stand. I placed my hand in his and stood, unable to speak, staring at him in bewilderment.

"Are you okay?" he asked, his tone more cold than caring. Unable to answer him I nodded my head. "Good. We need to leave." He dropped my hand and turned to the entrance of the alley.

I watched him as he walked away, the shock beginning to wear off. "Rae!" I yelled after him, but he didn't stop. "Rae!" I repeated. "Are you okay? How did you get here?" I chased after him, a million questions racing through my mind. "How did you find me?" I got no response. "Rae!" I yelled this time. "Stop! What is wrong with you?" I snapped, my frustration and adrenaline getting the better of me.

He froze, and I saw his shoulder tense as he slowly turned towards me. "Is that a joke?" he asked in disbelief. "What is wrong with me?" He stalked towards me, his brows furrowed and clenching his jaw. "You lied to me. You lied to me, and then you took the horses and left me in the middle of the woods. With no more than a note, none the less, telling me that you were doing the *one* thing you promised me you wouldn't do. You left me stranded with no way to get to you! No way to know if you were okay, if you had been hurt or captured. You…" He stopped, his chest heaving as his anger grew. "What the fuck were you thinking? How could you be so stupid and reckless? How could you be so careless?"

"Careless?" Now I was mad. "Why do you think I left in the first place? To get the things you needed to get better, to get the supplies we needed so you didn't have to further injure yourself. I left because I *do* care!"

"Oh really? And how did that work out for you?"

"It worked out fine! I got the supplies, didn't I?

"Fine?" he scoffed. "Is that what that was just now? You being held up by your hair in the custody of a Solarian Guard? That was fine?"

"I was handling it!" I yelled back.

"Obviously. You didn't need my help at all." He turned and started to pace in front of me. "What do you think would have happened if I hadn't gotten here when I did? That he would have just let you go? That you have taken him down and escaped?"

"Maybe! I don't know, Rae, but I would have figured it out!"

"No you wouldn't have! Don't you understand? If he had taken you back to his commanding officer, you would have been done for —hauled off back to Stefan, not let out of his sight. You would have been right back where you worked so hard to leave, or worse—you would be dead! Is that what you want? Because if so, why am I helping you?"

"I never asked you to help me! You offered. You came to me, not the other way around."

"And you accepted! You said you wanted help, so here I am, helping *you* instead of my family. You have *no* idea what I am risking by helping you, what I've sacrificed!"

"You? What *you've* risked? I'm the one who abandoned their

kingdom, who committed treason, gave up their home. Gave up their *life*! What exactly have you risked?"

"Everything!" he yelled back at me. "I have risked *everything* for you!"

I stared at him in disbelief, unsure of how to respond. Everything? What did he mean, *everything?* I opened my mouth to question him, but he cut me off before I had the chance.

"We need to get out of here—now." He turned, silently heading for the street, and I ran after him, trying to keep up with the brisk pace he set.

"How are we supposed to get out of here? When I went to get the horses, they weren't where I had left them." As I rounded the corner into the street, there stood Rae with the horses. "How did you find them?"

"You left them in the same place I would have." He handed Freya's reins over to me, and without another word, he mounted his horse, motioning for me to do the same.

I did as instructed, and we took off, weaving through the streets without a sound as he led us out, unnoticed by any other guards.

The tension between us was palpable as we rode in silence through the night. I had asked Rae where we were heading as he led us in the opposite direction I had come from that morning.

"We need to move forward; they'll be looking for us, for the person who stole back his supplies from the guards and killed one of them in the process. That person is heading towards Dalia. *We* are heading towards Nyxtas."

"I'm sorry," I said to him, "for making you kill that guard."

"You didn't *make* me do anything. I gave him a choice, and he chose death."

"You shouldn't have had to give him a choice. I shouldn't have been in that situation in the first place," I admitted solemnly.

"You're right," he stated, "you shouldn't have. But you were, and now, we have to take extra precautions to make sure we are not tracked and caught. If we are, then we're both dead."

I looked over at him, his jaw tense and his brows furrowed. He was angry with me. I turned my head back to the road, dropping my shoulders as the weight of his disappointment set in.

CHAPTER 23
ASTERIA

It was mid-morning before we stopped, allowing the horses to rest and drink from a nearby stream. It was the first time we had spoken since my apology.

"Are you hungry?" he asked as he led the horses to the water.

Neither of us had eaten since, well, I wasn't sure. Yesterday morning? I hadn't even realized how hungry I was; I had been so focused on my thoughts and emotions while we rode, the hunger pains didn't register until now.

"Very." My stomach echoed that sentiment right on cue. "I have some bread."

Sitting on the ground, I dug through the heavy satchel that still hung over my shoulder. I removed the furs and herbs and found the four small loaves of the apple bread I had gotten for Rae. I started to smile, excited to see his reaction, but when I looked at him, I knew this wasn't the time. I quickly wrapped them back up, pulling out only a loaf of the white bread.

"Here," I said, breaking off a moderate sized piece for him. "I got four loaves. I know it's not much, but we should be able to make it last most of the journey." He grabbed the bread before handing me the last of the meat. "What about you?" I asked.

"I'm not that hungry," he lied. "I'll be good with just the bread for now." He winced and inhaled sharply as he moved to sit down near me, favoring his uninjured side.

"You took off the sling." I took a bite of the bread waiting for his response. I didn't get one. "I have the herbs I need now; you should let me make a salve for you."

"I'm fine," he stated, avoiding my gaze. Another lie.

"No." My response was sharp. "You are not *fine*. You're mad at me, I get that, but we are not going to do this."

"Do what?" he asked.

"This." I motioned between us. "Pushing each other away. You can be upset with me, but we are still in this together, and we have to be able to rely on each other. I broke my promise, and I have apologized, but I broke my promise for you, Rae. Why can't you understand that? I couldn't sit there and do nothing when I have the skills to help you. You needed a healer. You still do. And while I may be a princess, I am also a well-trained healer, and for fuck's sake, you're going to let me help you. Don't make my broken promise useless."

"Fine..." he relented, finishing off the bread in his hand. "We'll rest here for a bit, try and get some sleep before we continue on."

I stood, frustrated that he insisted on harboring his anger. "Fine. I need to get a fire going then." I turned and stalked off into the nearby trees to gather kindling and fuel for a fire.

Within an hour, I had managed to make a small batch of an herbal salve to apply to his wounds, after he let me place his arm back into a sling to keep him from further displacing his rib. While I had been working on the ointment, he had prepared the furs so we could try and get a short rest in. He had nestled them back under a large tree out of sight of the road.

"Here." I handed him a mug of steaming tea I'd made while the salve set.

"What's this?" He looked up at me suspiciously. "Another one of your teas to put me to sleep? Trying to run off again?"

I rolled my eyes, setting the mug down in front of him.

"It's elderberry tea, you ass."

Exhausted and so very drained from everything that had happened, I no longer had the energy to continue this argument with him. Fetching the aids I had made, I came back to where he sat and kneeled in front of him.

"Here, let me."

I cleaned and treated the wounds and bruises from the previous day. He flinched at my touch, and I wasn't sure if it was because it hurt or because it was me. Reaching out with my free hand I cupped his face gently, his skin warmed in the palm of my hand and his eyes fluttered shut momentarily. When he opened them again, the world around us was brighter as I gazed into the vibrant emerald eyes of the man who had done so much for me. I wondered if the heat that flowed through me at the feel of his skin against mine, the warmth that flooded my soul each time I looked into those pools of green, the immense care I had for him—I wondered if he felt any of it too.

Just as quickly as the moment started, it was over. He pulled his face from my hand, inhaling deeply before he cleared his throat.

"Think I'm going to make it, Princess?" His sarcasm fell flat, his frustration with me still saturating his tone.

"I think you're going to survive." I dropped my hand and reached for a bowl of herbal paste. "Lift your shirt. This is for your side." He eyed the bowl, grimacing at the concoction inside it and looking at me with a face of disapproval.

"Do I even want to know what that is?" he sneered.

"Can you be quiet and lift your damn shirt so I can be done."

My attitude soured the longer this took, and he huffed a sigh of annoyance, doing as I instructed. I took the paste and applied a thick layer of it over the badly bruised and swollen area of his side before using scraps of cloth to bind his chest and stomach, better immobilizing his rib and ensuring the medicine stayed in place.

"The paste had analgesic properties, so it should help with the pain."

"Thank you." It was the first genuine and sincere sounding statement he had uttered since we left the town.

"You're welcome."

I rose and walked to the fire where I had left the warmed water, transferring the past into a tin before washing my hands. I yawned deeply as I stoked the fire, adding logs to it so that it continued burning. Sitting down near the crackling flames, I pulled my knees to my chest and rested my head on them. I was so tired. Closing my eyes, I tried to allow myself to drift off to sleep, but before I could, Rae's voice softly called out to me.

"What are you doing?" He looked at me, his face scrunched in confusion.

"I figured you wanted space," I answered sleepily, "so I was giving you space."

"I'm upset, not inhumane." He pulled back the furs next to him as an invitation to join him. "You're going to freeze to death if you try to sleep like that. Plus, I'd prefer to have to next to me so you can't try sneaking off on some suicide mission again."

Without a word, I laid down next to him under the furs, and despite his anger, he pulled me tightly into his chest. Closing my eyes, I quickly fell asleep.

Screams. Blood curdling screams. They came from everywhere.

I opened my eyes and saw only chaos. I stood in the middle of a town square, around me the mangled bodies of women, men, and children. Some were still alive, screaming in anguish for someone to either save them or finish the job. The metallic stench of iron filled the air, and the steel clanging of swords and the screams of the dying flooded my senses.

Where was I? I screamed out for Rae, but I received no answer. The sky was cloaked in a darkness that moved as if it were sentient, following some sort of trail. I looked around at the buildings, most only half standing while the rest had fallen completely.

I ran, looking for someone I knew, anyone who could explain to me what happened. I turned a corner and that's when I saw it: the Solarian castle. Its walls were lined with archers firing at will at a mass of soldiers clad in black armor. The soldiers below fought back with arrows of their own, except they weren't arrows—they were...shadows? Black wisps of shadows that took the form of an arrow, becoming corporeal at the last second before tearing through the armor and flesh of the Solarian guards. Black tendrils snaked up the stone, grabbing soldiers by their legs and throwing them off wall to their death.

I had heard whispers of shadow wielders, but I always thought they were a myth. Was this a vision of the past? Was it a manifestation of stories told at bedtime?

"No!" I heard a voice from somewhere behind me, a voice I recognized.

I searched for its source, turning in circles looking for him before I stopped, the blood leaving my body as I spotted him. Rae was on his knees, beaten and bloody, staring up at a man in golden armor. The man brought his knee to Rae's chest, knocking the breath from his lungs.

I screamed out, but he did not look my way as I ran towards him, tripping over the bodies that littered the ground and avoiding the men who fought around me. I lost sight of them for a moment, but when I found them again, I stopped dead in my tracks. The man in the golden armor had removed his helmet, his honey brown hair and tanned skin sent chills down my spine.

"Beg for your life." My stomach turned at the voice that had haunted me for so long.

He held Rae's head up by his hair, smiling that vile and malicious grin. He was enjoying what he was doing to Rae, hurting him, making him beg. Rae opened his mouth like he was about to speak, but instead, he pursed his lips and spat in Stefan's face. He had hit his target, and I saw the rage churning beneath Stefan's skin as he wiped the bloody spit from his face with the back of his hand before bringing it down across Rae's cheek. Blood spewed from his mouth as he took the impact of the hit before Stefan roughly grabbed him by his hair again.

"I said to beg for your fucking life, you coward."

Again, Rae did not speak. I saw Stefan's hand move as he reached for the dagger he kept in his boot. I screamed for him to stop, trying to get to him before he could do anything; I was close, so close, but I couldn't seem to get there, to save him. The dagger plunged into Rae's chest, blood coating Stefan's hand as he twisted the dagger sharply. I fell to my knees as I released a visceral scream.

Slowly, Stefan's head turned in my direction as his rage filled eyes met mine and a wicked, sadistic smile spread across his face.

"I told you: you are mine."

He laughed as he pulled the blade from Rae's chest, his body falling limply to the ground. I crawled to him, pulling him into my arms, tears flooding my eyes as I begged him to come back to me. I felt Stefan kneeling beside me before he grabbed my chin, forcing me to face him.

"Have you learned your lesson yet?" he whispered to me, bringing the dagger coated in Rae's blood to his mouth and running the flat side of the blade along his tongue. "Next time you run, it will be your blood I taste from my dagger."

Anger began to rise within me, a white hot, burning rage that pressed against my skin, begging to be released. I looked at him, my vision clouding with a blinding light as the bough broke and I let my fury consume me.

"I will never be yours."

A blast of scalding sunlight blinded me as I screamed, nearly thirty years of resentment and pain finally freeing itself from its cage. The world disappeared as I shook with fury.

"Wake up! Asteria, wake up!"

I opened my eyes, only to find it was dark and cold. I was struggling to place where I was.

"Hey, you're okay, you're safe."

I turned my head towards the voice, and the dying firelight danced across his features, illuminating his green eyes as he looked down at me. I felt a tear trail down my cheek as I reached for him, needing to know he was real.

"It was a bad dream, that's all. It wasn't real. I'm here."

I held onto him as the visions of my dream consumed my consciousness. It had felt all too real to be a dream. Maybe it wasn't a dream. Maybe it was a vision.

CHAPTER 24

ASTRAEUS

Asteria was terrified by whatever nightmare she had. The fear in her eyes when she woke and the way she reached to me for comfort pushed out every ounce of anger I harbored.

What was supposed to be a quick rest turned into an unplanned overnight stay. We were both incredibly depleted, not only from the events and lack of sleep from the previous day, but from the entire journey. Winter had landed, and we had been traveling for weeks with no beds, no roof over our heads, and not enough food in our stomachs. Our bodies were weary, and the stress had begun to drain us. After her episode during the night, I had pulled her close and held her tight, reminding her she was safe. Eventually, we both fell asleep, but morning light burst through the barren trees earlier than we were ready for. Her eyes fluttered open, the morning sunlight reflecting off her irises, shifting the color to a piercing, icy grey. Those eyes had captivated me the moment I saw them. Slowly but surely, she was pulling me into her depths, and I didn't feel like fighting. I would gladly drown if it meant waking up beside her every day until I die.

She turned her face to mine, her eyes widening in shock as she took in the details.

"Your face." She sat up in a frenzy, tracing over the wounds she had tended to the day before. "What happened?"

Confused and alarmed by her question, I placed my hand on her shoulder, my attempt at trying to ground her. "You don't remember?"

"I remember that you were beaten, that you were badly injured." Her hands were still roving over my face. "I want to know what happened to the wounds."

I began to worry; I wasn't sure what she meant. Were they infected? All I had done since treating them yesterday was sleep— how could I have made things worse? "What do you mean?"

"They're..." She paused, her voice hushed in disbelief. "Gone."

"What do you mean?" Sitting up, I braced myself for the shooting pain of my fractured rib, but it never came. Looking down, I grabbed my side instinctively, pressing on it, checking for the pain I knew I should be experiencing. "How is that even possible?"

I removed the sling, lifting my arm, moving it back and forth and around in circles. I had full mobility back. I had nursed many injuries in my time, and while I did consider myself a quick healer, I had never mended a fracture overnight before. Lifting my shirt, Asteria began to remove the bandaging from my chest, exposing where she had applied the paste. Using the scraps of fabric, she wiped away the dried remnants of the medicine. The bruise was no more than a faint yellow shadow along my skin.

"What did you put in that stuff?"

"Nothing," she said, her mind still flustered from the situation. "I mean, nothing that I haven't used before. I've never seen anything like this. To mend a fracture like that overnight is like... Well, like..."

"Magic?" I interjected, and her eyes shot to mine. "Maybe

you've got magic running through those skilled hands of yours." I smiled at her, hoping she would mirror my amusement, but instead, her stare turned distant. "Hey," I brushed her hair off her shoulder, "are you okay?"

She shook her head, as if shaking off whatever had taken her from the moment. "Yeah, I'm fine. I'm just still tired." She turned her head, looking towards the horses to avoid my gaze. "We should probably get going."

We slowly pulled ourselves up from the frozen ground, having a small breakfast before loading our things and getting back to our travels. I had tried to get her to speak about her dream and whatever had her so disturbed this morning, but she refused, shutting down and withdrawing into herself. Not wanting to drive her further into her isolation, I chose to drop it, and we spent the day in the solemn isolation of our own thoughts.

As evening approached and we neared our next stop for the night, I slowed to a stop near a small forest.

"Are we stopping for the night?" she asked, slowing her horse to a stop next to me.

"No, this is just a stopover." Lowering myself out of the saddle, I stretched my arms over my head, still astonished that my side had healed so quickly.

"A stopover?" she questioned as she followed my lead, stepping out of her saddle and stretching.

"Mmmhmm," I hummed. "We need to find dinner before we go any further. There isn't anywhere to hunt where we're staying tonight." I removed the quiver and bow Asteria had snatched for me from one of the guards. "Do you want to be the hunter or the gatherer today?" I smirked at her while I extended the bow in her direction—her face said everything she was thinking. "Right, well..." Chuckling, I placed the bow and arrows over my shoulder.

"I wouldn't know what to pick anyways. I would probably end

up killing us." She rolled her eyes as she turned and headed off into the trees, a slight tilt at the corner of her mouth.

It wasn't a smile, but it was close enough, and I would take it as a win... for now.

I returned an hour later with two small rabbits in hand. Asteria was standing by the horses running her hands down the side of Freya and Odins snouts; they nuzzled into her touch as she whispered. I tried to read her lips as she spoke, but she was too far away.

"Telling secrets, are we?" She startled at the sound of my voice, jumping back and almost tripping over her own feet.

"Fuck, Rae!" she exclaimed. "Next time, try making a little more noise as you approach. That way, you don't stop my heart."

"Oh, we both know all I have to do is look into your eyes and your heart stops." A devilish grin spread across my face.

"You're right." Turning her attention back to the horses, her face was serious. "The sheer horror and atrocity that is your face stops my heart out of pure terror each time you look at me."

"Ouch, Princess. That one hurt."

"Good." Grinning at herself, she continued. "Your ego probably needed to be checked."

I threw my head back and let out a howling laugh. The last few days had been so full of tension and anger, it felt like such a relief to laugh.

"Well if anyone is able to do that, it would be you."

Catching my breath, I looked at her, expecting a smile mirroring mine, but her expression was pained. She met my gaze, her eyes glossy with tears as she swallowed down whatever momentary breath of relief we had shared, replacing it with the same silent hurt as before. My smile dropped as I stepped towards her, reaching out and brushing a tear from her rosy cheek. Inhaling sharply, she took a step back, breaking the contact between us.

"Asteria..."

"I'm fine, Rae." Sniffling, she wiped her eyes clear of the tears threatening to escape. "We should get to our resting place for the night." With that, she mounted her horse, looking down at me. "Well, come on. You're the one leading the way here."

Letting out a soft sigh, I threw the rabbits over the saddle bag and settled myself into the seat. I gave her a quick glance—she had pulled her hood up over her face so I couldn't see her. Dropping my shoulders in defeat, I clicked my tongue, digging my heel into Odin's side as we set off.

THE SUN WAS DIPPING below the horizon as we approached the ruins of an old Dalian watchtower near the coast. It had been abandoned after the Great War, left to decay, a remnant of a time before the desolation of my people. The stone monument rose from the ground, dark and haunting as it cast its shadow over the barren land.

"Where are we?" she asked, her eyes wide in awe.

"This is one of the last watchtowers from before the Great War." Lifting her head, she followed the walls stretching into the sky above us. "It was used to monitor the coast for enemy ships, and then for armies of the Forgotten Kingdom, the 'magic wielders'. You've heard the stories, right?" I looked at her, her mouth gaping as she continued inspecting the structure.

"It's so tall," she whispered. Tearing her focus from the ruins, she turned to me. "Did people live here?"

"They did. Soldiers." Her attention drifted back to the tower, and I brought myself closer to her. "How would you like to sleep under a roof tonight?"

Her head shot in my direction. "This is where we're staying?"

she questioned, her eyes shimmering at the prospect of sleeping within four walls.

"It is," I answered her. "It's no castle or tavern, but it has a roof and walls."

The tower had withstood the sands of time, remaining in near-working condition. Despite the ruin of the grounds around it, its walls stood strong, refusing to let the Earth reclaim it. It stretched nearly one hundred and fifty feet high, spiraling stairs framing its inner walls, and barren rooms sat at its center all the way to the roof. Surrounding it were walls littered with small openings and archways, creating a courtyard. These walls had not resisted the weathering of time as the tower itself had, many of them half fallen, and, in some places, no more than a few boulders remained.

"Shall we?" I ushered us forward through the desolate court-yard, weaving through the remnants of walls until we rounded the tower to where the entrance stood.

We began unloading our supplies and carrying them inside before settling the horses into what would have been a small stable once upon a time. By the time I returned to Asteria, she had unrolled the furs and began preparing the rabbits to be cooked.

"I don't know how we're going to prepare these." She lifted one of them as she looked over at me. "We have no fire."

I smiled at her as I walked past her into a small room tucked behind a tattered curtain, only to return moments later with one arm full of wood and the other holding a bottle of wine.

"How?" She was at a loss for words, her eyes shifting between mine, the wood, and the wine.

"I have stayed here many times on my travels," I said, carrying the wood to the fireplace built into the wall. "Over time, I began to store things. You know, just in case." I set the bottle down at her feet before I arranged the logs and worked on kindling the fire. "That there," I motioned to the bottle, "is the finest wine you will find in this realm." She picked up the bottle, eyeing it warily. "I'm serious—it's damned near impossible to find and only produced in small batches once a year. Go on, try it."

"If it's so rare, why do you have a bottle stashed in an abandoned watchtower?"

"Because, Princess." The flames roared to life in front of me, and I sat back on my heels. "Aside from home, this is my safe place. I come here when I need to clear my head and ground myself. Sometimes, having a few drinks of that," I pointed to the wine in her hand, "helps me remember who I am and why I do what I do." Her brows knitted together in confusion, and she opened her mouth to speak, but she said nothing. "That wine is an old family recipe. My family's, and having a drink makes me feel close to them, even when I'm hundreds of miles away."

"Oh," she breathed before uncorking the bottle and bringing it to her mouth to sample.

She wiped her lips gently with her thumb as she swallowed the wine, and my gaze fixated on her mouth. I fought the desire to taste her lips as she brought the bottle to them and took a second drink.

"It's amazing," she said after her second taste.

"I know," I said smugly. "The only thing that makes it better is pairing it with a slice of spiced apple loaf."

Taking the bottle from her hands, I helped myself to a large sampling of the rich, sweet wine. The taste always took me back home to winter celebrations and cozy nights. I took another drink, the nostalgia of better days filling my senses.

"Rae." I hadn't even noticed that she had gotten up and was now standing behind me. I turned my head looking up at her. "This is for you."

She held out an offering to me wrapped in cloth, and I nodded my head as I took it, assuming it was more bread to go with dinner.

"Thank you," I said, setting it aside so I could put the meat over the fire.

Her gentle touch on my shoulder stopped me before I could reach for the rabbits. "Unwrap it," she insisted. "Please."

"Only because you asked so nicely." Teasing her, I picked up the cloth, gently unwrapping the contents.

My breath caught when it revealed four small, spiced apple loaves, with the scent of cinnamon, clove, and the crisp apple filling my nose. She had remembered the story I had told her one night, about how my favorite memories consisted of sharing this with my family in the evenings. I looked up at her.

"Asteria." I grabbed her hand, placing a gentle kiss in her palm. "Thank you. This..." I struggled to find the exact words, failing to come up with anything that would convey the emotions writhing inside me. "Thank you."

"I know it's not exactly like what you had when you were younger, but I saw them and I thought about you, and I thought you might like it, so..." She had started rambling, and I couldn't help but smile as she tried explaining herself to me.

"You don't have to explain. It's perfect." Breaking off a corner of one of the loaves, I popped it into my mouth, sighing deeply as the wave of familiar flavors flooded my tongue. "Absolutely perfect." Her eyes lit with joy as she smiled. "Here." I handed her a loaf, insisting she try it with the wine.

"No," she pushed it back towards me, "it's yours."

"You're right. It is." I placed it in her hand. "Therefore, it is mine to give. Plus, you almost died getting it, so the least you should be able to do is enjoy it."

She dropped her hand, her expression dropping with it. "Really?" she asked, her frustration evident in her stance. "I really don't want to have this fight again, Rae."

I raised my hand in defense. "Hey, I am not trying to start a fight. I was just stating the obvious. I understand why you did what you did. I don't like that you did it, that you almost got hurt and captured doing it, but.."

Her eyebrow raised. "But what?"

"But," I rolled my eyes, admitting that I was wrong, "you did the right thing." I turned back to the fire, skewering the rabbits and placing them next to the fire to roast. "I was too badly injured and needed your help. I just wish I didn't have to put you in that position."

Kneeling next to me, she spoke softly. "You have done so much for me, Rae. You taught me to defend myself, to hunt, to trust myself... to believe in myself. If risking my well-being returned a fraction of the help you've given me, then I would do it ten times over."

She leaned her head on my shoulder, and I rested my head on hers. "Thank you, Princess."

"You're welcome."

We sat down across from each other in front of the fireplace, taking turns drinking from the bottle of wine as she told me about her adventure into the village. She laughed as she reminisced, and I joined in, amused by her quick thinking and interesting choices. As the warmth of the fire filled the room, her smile warmed my heart. She finished her story just as the last drop of wine was drunk and the food finished cooking.

I looked up at her, my face serious. "Can we talk about last night?"

She froze, her eyes widening at the mention of the night terrors that had woken us both. "No." Her tone was short.

"Please talk to me," I tried urging her. "It was a nightmare, and something about it has obviously disturbed you. Just tell me about it. Maybe I can help work out what it meant."

"I said no, Rae." Her voice rose. "I don't want to talk about it." Standing, she began to pace the length of the small room.

"I just want to help you." I placed myself in front of her, stopping her in tracks and placing a hand on her arm.

"I don't want your help with this, Rae!" She pulled her arm

from my grasp. "I don't want to talk about it, so just stop! Leave it alone." She turned to walk outside.

"Princess…"

"Please, Rae." She stopped in the doorway, ending the conversation without turning to me. "I need you to leave it alone." Walking outside without another word or glance in my direction, she disappeared as she rounded the side of the tower.

I stood there for a few moments, unsure of what to do. I hadn't meant to upset her. I just wanted to help her work through whatever nightmare she had and help her see that it was just that: a nightmare. My soul ached at not being able to take those from her, to banish the darkness that plagued her, even in sleep. I ran my hand through my hair as I blew out a deep breath. Faint music echoed in the background through the windows of the tower, drawing my attention from my thoughts. I looked out to see white flakes slowly drifting from the sky—the first snow of the year. I took my plate and headed out the door, turning in the direction Asteria had gone.

I turned around the corner of the building, and there she was, sitting on the remnants of a half wall, staring up at the snowfall. She looked so defeated, and it tore at my core. Her pain had become my pain, her worries my own, her fears now entwined in my very being. I wanted to share it all with her, to lighten the burdens that weighed on her heart, mind, and soul. Slowly, I approached her, taking a seat beside her. Keeping her focus on the night sky, she closed her eyes, inhaling the icy air as the snow caught on her thick lashes.

"The first snow was always my favorite day of the year." She dropped her head, facing me. "It's winter solstice, you know."

I nodded my head. "I do." I angled my head towards the distant lights at the bottom of the hill. "They're having their celebration." A joyful melody carried on the wind as the people below danced and laughed.

"I have been through so much," she admitted, dropping her shoulders and watching the ground. "So fucking much." She sniffled, her voice breaking as she spoke. "I have had to fight to hold on to myself. Every chance someone got, they took a part of me. Whether it be telling me I wasn't good enough, I wasn't pretty enough, I needed to be skinner, quieter, more compliant, more ladylike, or more intelligent. My parents forced me into a union with a monster who found joy in breaking me. He found joy in shredding my soul, piece by piece, in watching me disintegrate into a fraction of myself. And they just let it happen; they just agreed to it, no hesitation, no qualms. They just handed me over like I was their property, not their daughter. Stefan took the one thing that was mine to give. He stole it from me, knowing that was the last part of myself I controlled. He stole it, and I lost all of me. I broke." She took in a shaky breath, tears falling from the corners of her eyes. "I left, not having any idea what I was going to do, how I was going to survive, or if I even wanted to. Then, you came along, this mysterious stranger, swooping in and saving me from the monsters in the world, helping to put me back together, teaching me to save myself from my own demons. I have no idea how I will ever be able to repay you."

I sat there as silent as the snow that fell around us, listening to her. I didn't know if she was breaking or healing in this moment, but I knew she needed to be heard, so that's what I was going to do. I was going to hear her.

"You are my first friend; did you know that?" She paused, glancing at me before continuing. "My parents kept me isolated the majority of the time. The only time I felt like I had friends was when we attended events with the other royal families. But in reality, none of them were my friends, we were all just acquaintances of circumstance. That's all I've ever had, people filtering in and out of my life, never developing lasting relationships, never getting close to anyone. Not until you. I don't know why you decided to help me, and quite frankly, I don't care. I'm just thankful that you did. I don't know what I would do without you in my life. I know you want to help me, and I want to let you, but I need more time. I need to work through my own feelings before I'm ready to share them with you. I need you to understand."

I did understand. There were things I wished I could share with her, but I wasn't ready either. I looked away, back down at the lights, and smiled at the melody that surrounded us, cutting through the white flakes that swirled and blanketed the ground at our feet. I stood and turned to her, holding out my hand.

"What are you doing?" she asked.

"Understanding," I said as I reached down, grabbing the plate from her hand and placing it on the wall beside her before I extended my arm again. "Dance with me?"

"What?" She laughed at the proposition, shaking her head at me. "Are you serious?"

"Princess, please don't make me have to ask again." I lowered my voice, "It's a little embarrassing to have to ask more than once."

A smile blossomed across her face as she obliged, accepting my hand and standing. I pulled her in, twirling her as I did. The tune was quick and exciting, and I matched the tempo as we danced around the courtyard, the fresh snow crushing beneath our feet. The beat increased, and we spun, faster and faster, our heads tilted back in laughter. The sound of her giggling innocently caused my heart to skip—she sounded so light in this moment, like every-thing else had melted away and it was just this, just us, just joy.

The tempo slowed slightly as it transitioned into another song, slower and sweeter. Our turns became more leisurely as we matched the rhythm of the new music. Our bodies moved closer, swaying as my hand drifted softly to the middle of her back, my other hand holding hers to the side. Her free hand was on my shoulder as we began to waltz, the world around us melting away. The only thing that existed in the moment was *her*. I didn't know when we stopped moving, but we stood there, her hand drifting off my shoulder to my chest next to where she rested her face. I held her, scared that if we moved, this moment would dissipate like it was nothing more than a dream. I breathed her in deeply, surrounded by the intoxicating scent of lavender and pomegranate.

"Thank you for understanding," she muttered softly against my chest.

I pulled back, curing my finger beneath her chin and lifting her face so I could look into her eyes. They mirrored the light of the moon above us, glowing silver beneath her lashes. I leaned in, resting my forehead to hers.

"You never have to go a day without me if you don't want to. I will *always* be here for you." She shifted, wrapping her arms around me and squeezing like she might lose me if she let go. I laughed as I ran my hand down her back. "Come here—I want to show you something." Taking her hand, I led her back inside the tower.

"Where are we going?"

"To my favorite place away from home," I said as we began ascending the stairs.

As we reached the top, I pushed open the wooden hatch that led to the roof. Climbing up first, I turned to help pull her through the opening before closing the hatch. It was a relatively still night, and the snow had stopped falling, leaving a small glistening blanket of white over the world. The clouds had parted, and the night sky was showered with shimmering stars, as the full moon illuminated the world beneath us. Asteria stopped, looking out over the parapets at the view before us as she gasped in wonder.

"Let me show you my favorite part." I walked to the opposite side and I inclined my head for her to look out. "The Dead Mountains."

Along the horizon, rising from the ground, stood the magnificent mountains that bordered my home. Their peaks were snow-capped, and I felt like if you looked close enough, you could see the snow glimmer in the starlight. I liked to come here when I was homesick and look out at the mountain range protecting my family and kingdom. They were beautiful and powerful, and, if you believed the stories, imbibed with ancient magic. I felt her step up next to me, shivering.

"Here," I said, stepping back and moving her in front of me. I wrapped my arms around her, shielding her from the cold. We stood there for a few minutes, just taking in the beauty.

"It's a breathtaking view," she whispered.

Looking down and admiring her, I agreed. "It really is..."

My heart ached; I wanted to tell her everything at that moment: who I was, where I was from, why I was there, why I had helped her, what happened to my people and why I had done what I had. More than anything, I wanted to tell her that none of it mattered anymore, because she was the only thing that mattered. But as soon as I opened my mouth to tell her, I knew I couldn't. What if I told her and she left, telling the first guard she saw? That would put my entire kingdom at risk. I couldn't do that, couldn't risk it. I had already risked everything with my original plan, which didn't include me falling for her. I had no idea what I was going to do now, but I was going to figure that out before I told her. I had to have a plan in place for my kingdom before I told her the truth.

"I don't know what I'm going to do," she said, still staring at the mountains.

"What do you mean?" I asked her.

"Once you get me to the Dead Mountains." She paused for a moment, sighing before she elaborated. "I haven't thought about what my plans are after. I get there and then, what? I live in the forest? Continue running? Leave the realm? I just... I don't know what I'm going to do."

I turned her around to face me. "Just stay with me."

Her eyes grew wide. "What?"

"Stay with me," I repeated. "You said you don't want to lose me. I don't want to lose you either, Princess. Stay with me. I will keep you safe. I promise."

"Rae, I don't know. Where would we go? Where would we stay?"

"We can go anywhere you want." Cupping her, face I stared into her eyes. "Please. Stay with me."

She stared at me, and I could feel her breathing quicken slightly, her gaze shifting between my eyes and my lips. My heart pounded in anticipation of her response, my lungs stilling, unable to breathe until she answered. Time seemed to stand still, the air frozen around us, as if it also awaited her answer.

She exhaled nervously. "Yes."

That was all she said, and it was all I needed before I pulled her in, bringing my mouth to her and kissing her deeply. I drank her in, savoring the feel of her lips on mine, the taste of her against my tongue, the feel of her body as she melted into me and wrapped her arms around my neck. The Earth seemed to respond, the wind picking up and the snow that had rested at our feet swirled around us. The stars shining brighter as we fell further into each other's embrace. I knew it then: it was her. It had always been her. We were two stars set on course to collide—becoming one, we belonged together. She was my light, and I would protect her no matter the darkness I had to walk through.

I broke our kiss, pulling away slightly and looking down at her with a very serious expression. "Slow down, Princess. You're moving a little fast. I might get the idea that you actually like me."

She glared up at me, unamused by my sarcasm. "Really?"

"Really. You've been sharing a bed with me for a while now. You can't imagine the scandalous gossip." I said, lowering my voice and whispering into her ear. "And to be honest, you're kind of a fur thief." She slammed her fist into my chest. "Ouch!" I exclaimed. "I was just being honest!"

She reached up, grabbing both sides of my face. "Rae, would you stop talking and kiss me?"

So, I did. Picking her up, I carried her back down the stairs of the tower to the furs in the lower room. Gently setting her down, I laid down next to her, pulling her tightly to me. Then, she rolled over onto her back, looking up at me with a shy smile, her eyes tense. I brushed the hair from her face before running my thumb across the worry lines creasing her forehead.

"What's wrong?" I asked, gently running my fingers through her hair.

"I don't think I'm ready..." she averted her gaze from mine, "to..." She paused, unable to finish her thought.

"Not ready for what?" I looked at her, studying her expression —the worry, the fear and anxiety, and I immediately understood what she meant. "Not ready to have sex with me?"

She nodded her head. "I'm sorry. I don't mean to upset you or disappoint you. I want you to be happy, but..." I leaned in, kissing her and cutting her off.

"Don't ever apologize for saying no. I know you're not ready, and that wasn't even on my mind. I am not upset, nor am I disappointed. There is no reason to feel sorry or worried. I am just happy to be able to hold you like this." I flipped her and pulled her in close to face me.

"I will never ask you to do something you are not ready to do. Not when it comes to this, anyways." I tilted her lips to mine, placing a soft kiss there. "Let's get some sleep. It's been too long since we've had the luxury of a roof and walls and adequate warmth."

I released her so that she could turn over and make herself comfortable. Kissing her shoulder, I whispered into her ear.

"Goodnight, my Little Star."

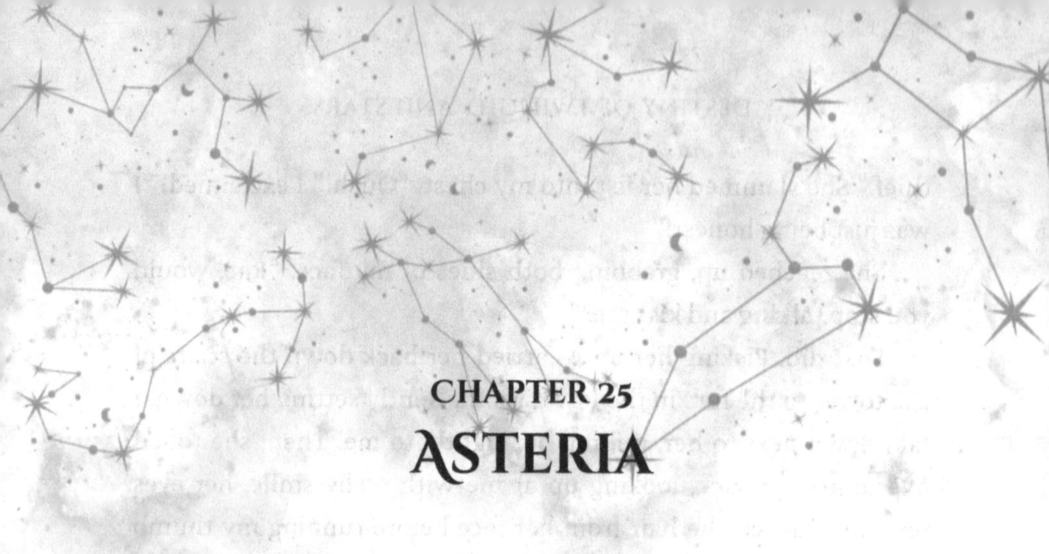

CHAPTER 25
ASTERIA

His breath warmed my ear as he whispered goodnight. *Little Star.* He had called me that before, but it felt different tonight. My skin flushed as I replayed the kiss in my head. I reached up, placing my fingers over my lips. *Was this real?* His kiss was gentle yet deep, passionate yet caring, the complete antithesis of anytime Stefan had tried to claim me with a kiss. Is that what a kiss was supposed to be like? Was I supposed to be feeling every nerve ending excited by his touch? My heart felt as though it was going to fly out of my chest, my lungs weak, my knees nearly buckling beneath me. It felt like I was falling, a new thrilling sensation gracing every inch of my body.

He asked me to stay with him, promising to keep me safe, and I believed him completely. So, I followed the tugging in my chest and said yes. His eyes had brightened at my response, his entire expression softening and filling with joy as he pulled my mouth to his. It felt like a dream, like I was finally finding where I belonged: with Rae.

I closed my eyes, feeling the rise and fall of his chest against my back as his breathing slowed, signaling that he had drifted off to sleep. His hand slipped down my arm and rested in the curve of my waist. I wrapped his hand in mine and brought it to my lips. Turning it over, I spread his fingers and kissed his palm as he had done to mine. I had been worried that he would become upset when I admitted I wasn't ready to be intimate with him, but he hadn't even batted an eye. It wasn't that I hadn't wanted to—part of me did, to know what it would be like to give yourself to someone willingly, someone who was gentle and caring like Rae— but I was scared.

When I thought about the pain of Stefan forcing himself upon me, the tearing as he pushed into me over and over again, it made my blood run cold. What if it isn't any different with Rae? What if it hurt, if I didn't enjoy it? What if he didn't enjoy it? I was scared Stefan had accomplished what he had set out to do. I was scared that he ruined me for anyone else. What if I let Rae in, took this step with him, and it wasn't what he wanted, what he expected: I couldn't bear the thought of losing him because of this, because of Stefan. It killed me that, even after all this time and distance away, there he was, his claws still digging into me and shredding the one good thing in my life.

When would I finally be able to leech the last remnants of his presence from my life? Even in my sleep, he found ways to torment me. I laid there, unable to will myself to close my eyes, knowing that as soon as I did, I would have to watch him drive his blade into Rae's chest again, just as I had anytime I closed my eyes. After tonight, after his kiss and his promise... The agony in my chest at the thought of losing him, of seeing the light drain from his eyes again, ripped apart my soul. I couldn't go to sleep. I couldn't close my eyes. I couldn't lose him. I stayed up tracing the lines of his palm until my eyelids were too heavy to hold open any longer.

The sweet caressing of my side and the brush of Rae's lips along my shoulder and neck roused me from my sleep. Inhaling his scent—deep amber and rugged leather—I moaned as I cataloged that scent in my mind.

"Good morning, Little Star." Pushing away the hair that had fallen over my face, he leaned over a softly kissed my temple. "How did you sleep?"

I refused to open my eyes to the morning light that warmed my face through the tower windows. "Better when you weren't waking me up," I said with a smile.

It was true: once I had finally given in to the exhaustion, I had a warm, peaceful sleep, void of nightmares or ghosts. He wrapped his arm around my waist and, with a swift movement, had flipped me onto my back so he was propped on his elbow, leaning over me.

"Oh, is that so, Princess?" he teased. "Did I disturb your beauty rest?" He began showering my face with kisses while badgering me with teasing questions.

I laughed uncontrollably as he pinched at my sides, tickling me as he moved his lips to my neck, nibbling at the base of it. "Stop!" I hollered as I tried to push his hands away, struggling to catch my breath. "Please, I can't breathe!"

He stopped. "Taking your breath away so soon, am I?"

I pushed at his chest and snorted at him. "More like suffocating me."

He feigned offense as he brought his hand to my chin. "Well then," he lowered his face, his mouth hovering just above mine, "I guess I better apologize."

My unsteady breathing caused my voice to waver. "I guess so," I whispered.

The corners of his mouth pulled back in a slight smile as he closed the short distance between us, kissing me. That same electric feeling shot through my body, heating my blood, releasing a swarm of butterflies in my chest. I wanted more of him.

Snaking my hand around the back of his neck and weaving my fingers into his hair, I pulled him further into me as he lowered his body, running his tongue along the seam of my lips, parting them as he deepened the kiss, moaning as he tasted me further. He removed his hand from where it had rested beneath my chin and began running it down my side. His thumb grazed my breast, the touch sending a burst of pleasure through my core as my nipple hardened, and it was I who moaned this time.

He drank in the sound, letting it fuel his kiss as he pressed himself further into my body. I could feel the hardened length of him pressing against my thigh, causing a molten heat to pool between my legs. I squirmed beneath him, shifting so I could squeeze my thighs together to try and relieve the tension building at my center. I tightened my hold on his hair and groaned, his grasp squeezing my hip. I was flushed from head to toe, the heat overwhelming me as I yearned for his touch. His hand shifted, drifting across my stomach, his thumb just under the band of pants. The touch startled me, and I flinched.

Rae immediately broke the kiss, removing his hand from me. "I'm sorry," he panted. "I got carried away. Are you okay?" I couldn't catch my breath to reply, pulling my lower lip into my mouth as I nodded my head. He rolled onto his back, his arms flopping down above his head. "I shouldn't have done that. I am sorry."

His chest rose and fell rapidly as he tried to collect himself. Sitting up, I found his face flushed from desire, his bare chest was covered in a thin layer of sweat.

I placed my hand on his chest. "It's okay," I tried assuring him. "I'm okay. I promise you." Leaning in, I placed a gentle kiss on his head. "You didn't do anything wrong."

Climbing off the bed roll, I stood, stretching out my heavy muscles. The cold wind blew in through the windows, carrying small traces of the fresh snow from outside. A small shiver echoed through my body, and I huffed lightly before asking, "Breakfast?"

Rolling onto his side, he looked at me longingly and whined.

"Do we have to?" He stuck out his lower lip into a pout and knitted his brows together. "Can't we just lay down and spend the day in the warmth? I don't think I'm ready to leave the comforts of this tower and brave the snow yet." Reaching out, he tried to grab at my ankle and pull me back down to him.

I stepped out of his reach, rolling my eyes at him. "As someone said yesterday, the guards will be looking for us. So, as tempting as a day snuggled up here sounds, avoiding capture sounds like the more logical option." He sighed and drew his hand down his face in defeat before dramatically pulling himself from the ground to stand beside me.

"Fine." Grabbing my hand, he spun me into him. "You make a good point. But in the future, you should tell *that* someone to keep their mouth shut."

"I do believe I've been telling that *someone*," I dug my finger into his chest to drive my point home, "to keep their mouth shut since I met him."

He looked up, as if trying to remember if what I said was true. "Well, he enjoys seeing you flustered too much to keep his mouth shut."

He leaned in as if to give me a kiss, but instead, he blew into my mouth, puffing up my cheeks. I pulled back, coughing and staring at him confused. He let out a cackle, amused with himself.

I shoved him back, both annoyed and amused. "I need breakfast and coffee before I deal with you."

After breakfast, we packed up our belongings, preparing for the frigid journey that laid before us. We had loaded the majority of the supplies onto Freya because of Rae's insistence that we ride together.

'It will help keep us from getting hypothermia if we keep our bodies close.'

While that may be true, from the sinister smile that crossed his face as he said it, I knew there were ulterior motives. He had settled behind me in the saddle, wrapping his arm around my waist and yanking me back so I was snug against his chest. The act had sent my heart into a frenzy, and I could feel my skin heating.

"You're feeling a little warm, Princess." His breath caressed the back of my neck, brushing the shell of my ear, and I could hear the smile in his voice. "Are you feeling okay?"

I swallowed down my embarrassment, willing my body to stop reacting to his touch and failing. "I'm fine." I shifted in the saddle, trying to put a modicum of space between us, but his grip held me in place.

"Uh-uh Little Star—we're sharing body heat, remember?" I wanted to smack the smug tone out of his mouth. "I promise I'll behave."

I scoffed, lightly nudging his side with my elbow, my silent way of saying *'I'll believe it when I see it.'*

The wind was relentless this morning, and it wasn't more than thirty minutes into our ride that I knew he had been right. Taking one of the fur pelts, he wrapped it around us, handing me the ends, which I grasped tightly in my gloved hands. Rae kept his arm firmly wrapped around me, his thumb occasionally trailing up and down my side just under the hem of my tunic. Each pass sent my hair standing on end, a fiery desire building and receding in my core as he started and stopped. I leaned my head back, resting it on his chest, and he responded by resting his chin lightly on the top of my head. We rode most of the morning like that, leaning against each other, sharing our warmth in solace.

As the sun peaked in the sky and the wind rested, my thoughts began to shift, wandering back to the night before, to the fears I had about intimacy with Rae.

"What's on your mind, Little Star?"

His question surprised me. "What do you mean?"

"I can feel tension in your muscles that wasn't there just a few moments ago." He squeezed my waist. "So tell me: what's on your mind?"

His attention to detail and intuition both amazed and irritated me. I really didn't know how to broach the subject with him, but I also didn't want to lie to him. "I was thinking about last night."

"Hmmm." He took a moment, considering my statement. "What about last night is causing you to feel so tense?"

"I..." Groaning in frustration, I bowed my head. "I'm worried that I disappointed you and failed to meet an expectation you might have had."

"Expectations about us?" He let out a long sigh. "Do you mean about sex?" I didn't answer, which was an answer in its own right. "Princess, you did not disappoint me. I told you that I did not expect that from you."

"I know," I cut him off before he could go any further, "but eventually, you will. A time will come where it will be an inevitable expectation, and I don't want to upset you. Eventually, there will come a time when you are going to want more, or maybe you already do, and you're too polite to pressure me. Either way, I don't want to be a disappointment. I want to be able to do this with you. All of it." I paused, taking a moment to collect my thoughts and calm myself. "It's just that... Fuck, this is not easy to say."

He pulled me closer and kissed the top of my head. "You don't have to tell me."

"I want to. I need to." I adjusted myself so his grip on me loosened. "I want to be able to do these things with you, to experience it all with you, but I am scared. I'm scared that it will hurt. I know that it's supposed to be this special thing, but I only know it to be painful. That's all I remember from that night—the pain. The thought of that pain sends ice down my spine, despite what I feel about you or what my body is feeling. What if that's how it is again? What if you hurt me?" My voice was unsteady as I spoke my fears to him.

"Asteria, I would never do anything to hurt you," he tried to assure me and calm me, "and it shouldn't have been like that. It's not supposed to hurt, not like that. It's not how it would be for us. I would make sure that it wasn't."

"But what if it does? Isn't that going to disappoint you? Wouldn't that make you not want me? I feel like he was right." A tear tried rolling down my cheek, but it froze before it had the chance. "He ruined me. No one will truly want me because of what he did. It made me undesirable and ruined me for any other man. He found a way to stay with me forever, to keep me broken." I breathed in a shuddering breath, and Rae stopped the horse. He wrapped both of his hands around my waist, pulling me tightly into his embrace as he rested his head on my shoulder.

"You are not ruined. You are not undesirable. What he did to you was the lowest and most vile thing a man can do. He took away your sense of power and control. He violated you and made you feel disgusted in your own flesh. It will take time and effort for that to be healed, and as much as I wish that I could be the one who heals that wound, I cannot. That is something only you can mend. I can sit here and tell you how beautiful, desirable, unique, breathtaking, and alluring I find every curve of your body, but it means nothing if you don't feel that way about yourself. You must remember that your worth is not determined or diminished by the things that happened to you. You cannot be ruined for another man; at least, not one who sees you for who you are and not for what you've suffered, what you've survived. Because that's what you did, Princess: you survived, and that makes you all the more desirable and powerful in my eyes. It's the thought of waking up next to you every day that excites me. You," he turned my face to the side and tilted it towards his, pressing his lips to mine in a sweet and gentle kiss, "are enough for me."

His words filled my soul with light, and I couldn't help from smiling against his lips. I began to flush; while he had begun to assuage my biggest fear, there was still another reservation I had.

"There's still one more thing." Pulling back, I looked into his eyes, full of compassion and longing, his brows furrowed slightly at my statement. "I..." Not able to stand the embarrassment that washed over me, I turned, facing forward. "I don't know how to... what to... What if I do it wrong?"

I could hear the smile in his voice as it dropped low. "Oh, Princess, you leave that part up to me." He nipped at my ear as he rocked forward, pressing himself against me while driving the horse into motion. "You'll learn what you do and don't like, and I am more than happy to help you learn exactly what those things are, whenever you are ready." He placed a quick kiss on my temple as we set off, leaving me with racing thoughts.

I wasn't ruined? *I wasn't ruined.* He was right. Stefan's actions were no fault of my own. I hadn't done anything to ask for his persistent advances, I hadn't asked for the marriage, I hadn't asked for mental, emotional, physical torture. I hadn't asked for him to force himself on me. Those were all things that happened to me, not things that I chose for myself. In the past few weeks, I had become stronger, more fit, more confident, more in love with my skin and the woman beneath the clothing. So what was holding me back from being ready? Was I ready? The things holding me back were things I could only get over by moving forward. I needed to decide, the first real choice I would ever make for myself. I chose this. I chose him. I chose Rae.

THE FIRE CRACKLED as the flames danced in the night, melting the snow that coated the ground around it. The weather improved as we rode through the day, snow falling intermittently, but the harsh winds had ceased and remained gone. We had made it to camp just as night had fallen, and I was quickly setting up the furs while Rae scouted the area to ensure it was safe.

We had ended up on the edge of a small forest on the north-eastern border of The Barrens, just under two days from the Dead Mountains, according to Rae. We had settled between the trees and a large pond that was fed by an underground heated stream. A thin layer of steam rested along the surface, the sun and stars just barely reflected in the still waters. I had begun to boil water for a quick vegetable soup, prepping it so that it would be ready shortly after Rae returned. I hoped he was able to find some sort of small animal, but with the snow on the ground, I wasn't too hopeful of success. My head spun to the trees at the sound of cracking twigs, only to find Rae emerging empty handed from the desolate forest.

"I see you've returned with nothing in hand," I teased him while I dropped a handful of chopped vegetables into the water, following with herbs for flavor. "You're lucky I'm such a grand cook and can make something out of nearly nothing."

Chuckling, he dropped to one knee beside me and kissed my head. I couldn't help but lean into him, needing to feel his closeness, his protective presence. I felt safe with him—not just from physical harm, but with my emotions, my thoughts, my fears. I was overwhelmed with feelings when I thought about him, a tangled web I very much so looking forward to deconstructing and learning.

"There's time before dinner is done. Why don't you take advantage of the warm water?"

I looked at him before glancing at the water behind us. "That sounds like a perfect idea."

I unlaced my boots, removing them and setting them by the fire. I stood, preparing to walk to the water's edge, when I got the most devilish of ideas. Reaching up, I undid the clasp of my cloak, dropping it to the ground where I stood, followed by my trousers, allowing them to fall to my ankles. Rae stared up at me in bewilderment as I began to walk to the steaming water. I slowly began to unbraid my long raven hair, allowing it to fall down my back. In the next step, I pulled the hem of my tunic over my head, dropping it on the ground before fingering the laces of my stay. Looking over my shoulder, I gave him a sly smile.

"Well, aren't you going to join me?"

I dropped the last article of clothing to the ground and stepped up to the edge of the bank. The warm water lapped gently against my feet, and I inhaled deeply as I stepped in, the warm waters easing my tired muscles and weary body. As I moved further into the pond, I turned, looking back at the shore where Rae was stepping out of his trousers, bare and naked to the world.

Instinctively, I averted my gaze, shying away from the man in front of me as I took a deep breath, filling myself with confidence and exhaling my insecurities. I looked back to Rae, at his immaculately sculpted form. The dips and curves of his muscled chest and arms were accentuated in the silver moonlight, his abs flexing with each step he took. My eyes followed the narrowing of his waist and the lines that drew my attention to his erection. The sight of him made my cheeks turn rosy as a wave of heat, much warmer than the water surrounding me, flooded my center.

"Why, Princess, you seem flustered," he taunted as he strode towards me through the water. "Something got you worked up?"

My words failed me as I tried to summon a quippy remark. He was right; I *was* flustered and worked up, and I couldn't force my brain to focus on anything except for him.

"Relax, Little Star." He was in front of me now, his form below his shoulders covered by the water. "You're in charge here."

He grabbed my waist and pulled me into him, wrapping my legs around his waist and my arms around his neck. The feeling of his bare flesh against mine sent my body into a frenzy. I could feel him, his rigid length resting between us, pressing against the sensitive flesh between my legs. My breath hitched as he moved, adjusting his hold, causing him to grind against me, sending a shock of pleasure down my spine.

"You really are the most breathtakingly beautiful person I have ever laid eyes on." His green eyes, luminescent in the glow of the night, traced over my face, drinking me in.

I tipped my head, avoiding his gaze. His words, as loving as they were, did not feel truthful to me—not because he wasn't telling me the truth, but because I couldn't believe that he felt that way about me.

"Look at me," he whispered as he hooked his finger beneath my chin. "You are magnificent, Asteria. Someday, you will learn to accept that fact about yourself, but until then, I will believe it enough for the both of us." He brushed his nose against mine, an act so innocently sweet and wholesome, I couldn't stop smiling.

"Thank you for everything you've done for me Rae," I said softly. "I wouldn't have survived without you."

"Oh, I'm sure you would have charmed another poor soul to help you. Although, they probably wouldn't have been as handsome or as strong and alluring as I am."

"You're ridiculous." Pushing off him, I swam back, laying my head back and dipping it into the water.

This swim was the closest thing to an actual bath I'd had in weeks. Warm water and wet rags were all that I'd been able to use to clean myself. I exhaled as I floated weightlessly on the surface, listening to the still of the night and staring into the star-laden blackness above me. The only thing that would have made this moment better was if I had my soaps and oils, but, considering the situation, I was just thankful to soak in the heated pool. I heard light splashing behind me as Rae swam to me.

"May I?" He stood behind me as he ran his hands up and down the length of my arms.

"May you what?" I asked, looking up at him as he towered over me.

"Relax you." The corner of his mouth lifted as he massaged my neck and shoulders. It felt so fucking good.

I wasn't able to muster any actual words, so I just groaned a long hum.

He slowly and thoroughly worked the muscles of my body, starting with my neck and shoulders before he worked his way down my arms to my hands. He took my hand in his, rubbing my palm with his fingers.

"I'm glad you spoke to me, that you shared your fears with me." He released my hand and reached for the other. "I don't want you to ever feel like you can't be open and honest with me."

He kissed my hand before returning it to the water, moving around me so he was at my feet. Tenderly, he moved his hands up my legs, making just enough contact to send fire and ice through my body. When he reached my knees, he moved his hands to push my legs apart, stepping between them as he continued his path upwards. As he reached the apex of my thighs, he trailed his hands around my hips, gripping them and pulling me to him, his thumbs tracing back and forth over the bony prominences there. He made no moves to further his advances, though; he just stood there holding me, my legs wrapped around him, my torso laying back in the water.

My heart was racing, a fluttering sensation circling my chest and heat pooling in my core as I tilted my head back, the desire for him to touch me more overwhelmed my entire being.

"Rae," I whispered his name on an exhale.

He dipped down into the water, pulling me up, my flesh pebbling despite the warmth surrounding us. I slid my hands into his hair and pressed my legs into him, leveling our faces. Tightening my grip around his hair, I pulled him in, crushing our lips together in a passionate kiss. Without hesitation, I opened my mouth, tasting him while he pulled me selfishly closer. My bare chest pressed into his, the sensation puckering my nipples, a groan rolled through his chest as he wrapped his hands around my ass and ground me into his cock. I wanted to feel more of this pleasure as it continued to heighten, building a gnawing sensation in my center, begging to be relieved. I mimicked his motions, moving my hips in the same rocking movement, pressing against his straining erection. Our breaths mingled as he pulled away, gripping me hard to still my hips.

"We need to take it easy, Princess," he panted as he struggled to control himself. I knew he wanted me; I could feel his desire throbbing against my sensitive flesh, just begging to be touched.

I nipped at his lip and shook my head. "I don't want to."

He looked down at me, eyes dark and swirling with both lust and concern. "I don't want you to feel like you have to. You don't need to rush this. I want you to be sure. I *need* you to be sure."

"I am," I answered. "I want to do this. For the first time in my life, I am choosing something for me. I am choosing to do this with you. I'm ready, and please, don't make me say it again." Without hesitation, he lifted me up out of the water, and I laughed. "What are you doing?"

He began walking towards the camp. "Showing you what this is supposed to be like."

We emerged from the water, the cold breeze battling the warmth from the water still on our skin. He laid me down on the furs before covering me with another and adding logs to the fire. He crawled under the pelt with me, laying on his side he dragged his fingertips up the center of my bare stomach.

"There are many ways to be intimate, Little Star, so many ways to give and receive pleasure without having my cock inside you." He nipped my lip and brushed his thumb over my nipple; it responded to his touch, immediately hardening. "I plan on showing you many of those ways tonight." He brushed his thumb over the other nipple, eliciting the same response. "I want you to experience pure bliss at my hands. Tonight is all about you, Princess."

I opened my mouth to argue, but before I could, Rae's mouth was on mine. He pulled my lower lip between his teeth, sucking on it while his hand traced circles around my nipples, just barely caressing the edges. My body responded intensely, and I arched into his touch, needing more.

He released my lip, and I groaned at the loss. "I want to learn what spots make you cry out my name, what spots make you beg for more." He ran his mouth along the edge of my jaw, inhaling as he moved from the base of my neck to my ear, his words heating my neck. "I want to know what makes you come for me, Princess." My lungs stuttered as he spoke, his words melting into me like molten lava, heating all of me. "So tell me," he began to slowly kiss down the side of neck, "do you like it when I do this?"

He bared his teeth, sinking them into the curve of my shoulder at the base of my neck, sending a sharp wave of pain down my spine that had me hissing sharply, but before I could truly process the pain, he was dragging his tongue over the bite, kissing it. The pain dissipated as quickly as it came, his touch feeling even more intense than it had before when he brushed his lips over the mark. A strangle moan escaped my mouth.

"Good girl," he whispered against my skin as he continued to kiss down my body.

He worked his way down the center of my chest, stopping when he got to my breasts. He gently rolled them in his hands, stopping to flick his tongue across my nipple before he blew a gentle stream of air over it. I was shocked at the tremor of pleasure it sent to my core, shifting slightly and squirming as I tried to offer the pressure building between my legs some sort of relief. Rae smirked as he watched me suffer, repeating the same treatment to the other breast.

"Rae." His name came out strangled as he took my breast into his mouth, tongue circling my nipple as he sucked at it.

The other one was being worked in his hand, and the feeling made my head kick back, pushing my chest forward, further into his mouth. His chest rumbled, an answer to my pleasure as his hips jerked forward, pressing his hardened cock into my leg. His body's response to mine was an intoxicating wave of confidence. I reached for him, wanting to feel him, to offer him something, but he caught my wrist, pinning my wrist above my head with ease. I groaned in frustration, and he lifted his head.

"Tonight is for your pleasure."

"I want to do something for you. I don't want you to be unsatisfied." I tried to force my wrist from his grip but failed.

"You have no idea how pleasurable this is. All the satisfaction I need is you being taken care of so well, that you're begging me to stop." His eyes were heavy with desire as a sultry expression formed on his face. "Fucking you would be selfish, and I, Princess, am a very giving man."

He winked as he released my wrist, grabbing my hips and flipping me onto my side, his chest pressing into my back. I turned my head so that I could see him as he looked down at me, pressing his erection into my ass.

"You do drive me wild, Little Star," he ground his hips forward to accentuate his point, "and I can't wait to hear you screaming my fucking name."

He captured my mouth with his, his kiss aggressive and passionate, his hand groping my breast desperately. I could feel the liquid heat between my legs begin to drip, and I tensed my thighs, trying to stop it. The movement ground me back into Rae, and he growled at the friction.

"Are you ready for more?" he asked against my mouth. I hesitated to answer, unsure of how he would respond to the wetness between my legs. "Do you want to stop?" he asked, concerned he may have pushed too far.

"No," I answered quickly. "No, I don't want to stop." My words were breathy, my body aching for him to touch me more.

"Do you trust me?" he asked.

"With my entire being," I responded, and he pulled me back into a passionate kiss as he moved his hand down around my leg, hitching it at the knee, opening me to him.

His hand drifted down my thigh, leaving a trail of electricity in its wake. Slowly and gingerly, he ran his finger around the edge of my lips, nearing my entrance. The sensation and building pressure felt like it was clawing to get out, needing—no, *demanding*—release.

"Fuck," he moaned into my mouth. "You're so fucking wet." He brushed his fingers between my folds, touching my sensitive flesh, and I inhaled sharply at the feel of him spreading my desire around, teasing me lightly.

"Oh my goddess," I exhaled. "Please, don't stop."

"Do you like that?" His voice was husky and low. "Do you like when I play with you while you're all wet and ready for me?"

I didn't know how to answer, or if I even could answer. All I could focus on was his touch as he began to work the bundle of nerves at my apex. I reached back, gripping the back of his neck, trying to ground myself.

"That's my good fucking girl," he growled in my ear. I started to cry out his name as the pressure built and it felt like I couldn't handle it anymore, but I was cut off as he stopped his movements. "Not yet, Princess."

I wanted to yell in frustration, but he pressed his lips to mine as he began to trace his finger around my entrance. My breathing stilled at the new sensation, similar to the last but yet, different. Slowly, he dipped a finger inside me, and I tensed in surprise at the unexpected feel of him inside me.

"Breathe, Little Star," he whispered into my ear as he pulled his finger out and pressed in again, further this time.

Each movement sent shocks of euphoria through my core. Soon, he had buried himself to the knuckle, and he began to move, curling it, working it inside me. Suddenly, something happened— he moved it against a spot that elicited a cry of pleasure from deep in my chest.

"There she is," he groaned as he suddenly removed his finger.

"What are you doing?" I asked on a whine.

"Patience, Princess." He brought his hand to his mouth, sucking his finger into his mouth, and my eyes widened in shock— that finger had just been inside of me. "You're fucking delectable." He smiled as he reached back down, running two fingers through my wetness. "Remember to breathe."

He slid his other arm under my waist, circling my clit as he began to work those two fingers into me. I couldn't think straight with the sensation of his fingers entering me, the feeling of him working my sensitive flesh. He moved his fingers faster and faster, hitting that sensitive spot from before as he continued to rub circles into my clit. I gripped his hair as I tried to breathe, the pleasure building and cresting, overwhelming my being, making me lose sight of everything except for this—the feeling of him inside me, touching me, kissing me. My hips rocked, matching the rhythm and pace his fingers had set, working them deeper, chasing that release my body was craving.

Behind me, Rae groaned. "Fuck, Asteria, yes. Come for me, Princess."

His desire laden voice pushed me over the edge, and suddenly, I was falling, my body tensed as unmeasurable pleasure washed over me, causing me to cry out. Rae's fingers continued to move inside me, seeing the orgasm through as I tightened around him. I came down slowly, my senses clearing, my body and mind trying to put itself back together after an explosion of euphoria. My muscles shook, and I continued to tense around Rae's fingers. Without warning, an animalistic noise rumbled in his chest as he withdrew his fingers and moved, flipping me onto my back.

"What's wrong?" I asked. "What are you..."

I gasped as he kneeled between my legs, spreading them and lowering his head, dragging his tongue through the orgasm that dripped from my cunt. My head rolled back from the sensation, and I didn't have time to collect myself before Rae began feasting on me, the intense pleasure building again. He spread me, tracing his tongue before flicking it over my clit and sucking it into his mouth. He worked his mouth over me, sucking, licking, and devouring me like a man starved. I cried out, unable to stop myself as I was consumed by bliss, every movement of his tongue euphoric.

I arched back, my hips lifting and pressing into his mouth, searching for more. As if he could read my mind, he wrapped his arms around my waist roughly, holding me to the ground, holding me still. I searched for something to hold onto, anything to anchor myself to reality. Reaching out, I fisted the furs, closing my eyes and calling out into the night. Rae lowered his mouth, circling my entrance with his tongue before slipping it inside me, tasting me, drinking me in.

The pressure built to the point of breaking again, and I tried to pull away, but he kept me locked in place as he worked me through the orgasm. I cried his name as I broke, the only name I ever wanted to say again. He gave me no time to recover, removing his tongue and replacing it with his fingers, working them into me, curling them in and out. He looked up at me then, the devil in his eyes as he lowered his head again, pulling my clit into his mouth. The mix of sensations had me climbing that wave for a third time, my body shaking and tensing as I reached the top.

I did not fall off the ledge this time. No, I flew, my back arching off the ground, my screams strangled as I shattered into a thousand different pieces. I fell back onto the furs exhausted, with a feeling of satisfaction I had never experienced nor knew was possible. Rae sat up on his knees, licking his lips before wiping his face with the back of his hand, a sultry and pleased smile on his face.

When he stood, his erection dripped with the milky evidence that he did indeed find pleasure in the act of pleasuring me. Reaching for a bathing cloth warmed with water from near the fire, he cleaned himself before gently and thoroughly cleaning me. He returned to my side in the furs, pulling me into a snug hold.

"You are magnificent," he whispered as he kissed my temple.

"I..." I didn't know what to say. I didn't even know how I felt, aside from being completely and wholly exhausted. My eyes fought to stay open as I spoke, my body relaxing into his as my mind drifted into the dark.

"Shhhh," he pulled the furs up over us, "sleep."

I mumbled, the realization hitting me. "We didn't eat dinner."

He chuckled. "I'm not particularly hungry. I've already eaten."

The meaning of his words didn't come to me until after sleep took me. I fell into the deepest and most restful sleep I could remember ever having.

And it was all thanks to him.

CHAPTER 26
ASTRAEUS

She laid beside me, her breathing deep and steady. She had slept more peacefully than I had ever seen. Usually, she spoke, cried, or moved around restlessly at night, but not last night—no, last night, she drifted off with a smile on her face, and I swear there were still traces of it now as she slept beside me.

We crossed a line last night, taking a huge step in this relationship, if that was what we were calling this. We hadn't really discussed it, but I knew she was all I wanted. She trusted me, gave herself to me in a way I would forever cherish. I felt a joy and comfort I had never experienced before, but cutting through it was a blade of guilt.

She had been so open and honest with me, and I was still hiding so much from her. Regardless of who I really was, my feelings were truer than anything I knew. I had to tell her; I knew I did, but I needed more time to come up with a failsafe, in case telling her the truth backfires, putting my kingdom and its people in danger, and I was quickly running out of time. We had less than a two-day journey to the Dead Mountains, which would inevitably lead us to my Kingdom, and everything would come out, whether I was prepared or not.

She stirred next to me, her eyes struggling to open, still heavy with sleep.

"Good morning, Little Star." I pulled her into my chest, her head resting on my shoulder. "How did you sleep?" She mumbled something unintelligible, and I couldn't help but snicker at her. "That well, huh?"

"Mmmmhmmm," she hummed under her breath.

"Do you want to be my breakfast?" I whispered in her ear, and she mumbled in agreement as before her eyes shot open.

"What?" she questioned, her surprise and alarm evident.

"Ahhhh," I sang, "Now she's awake. I said, do you want breakfast?"

"That is not what you said," she argued, pulling her head back so she could get a clearer view of my face.

"Isn't it?" I raised my brow at her in feigned confusion.

"Most definitely not."

"Well, regardless of what I might or might not have said, would you like breakfast?"

She eyed me suspiciously before agreeing. I reached for the clothes I had collected after she fell asleep last night, putting them on before crawling out of the warmth of the bed roll and into the frigid air. The sun was hidden behind a grey sky, casting a dull hue over the already-dying lands. I gathered some water from the pond and placed it over the fire to boil, adding coffee grounds to it.

As soon as the aroma wafted to her nose, she sat up. "Is that coffee?"

I shook my head. "Is that really a question? Like you couldn't sniff this stuff out from a mile away?" She just smiled as she pulled the furs up, trying to block the cold. "Your clothes are there." I pointed to the neatly folded pile between her and the fire. "They should be warm."

She smiled as she reached out for them, a smile that could have parted the clouds and outshone the sun. She disappeared beneath the covers, emerging a few moments later fully clothed.

"What's for breakfast?" she asked, taking the mug of steaming coffee I held out for her.

"I thought we would finish off the apple loaves." I reached into the satchel and pulled out the remaining two loaves. "There are not exactly a lot of options for foraging or hunting."

She looked around at the barren landscape of decaying trees and frozen ground. "And here I thought we were in the dead of spring." The corner of her lips tilted up.

"Well, feel free to take a look around, Princess." I sat back, taking a bite of the bread I held in my hand. "I, on the other hand, will be sitting here, enjoying what little comforts I have before we have to start our day." Walking over to me, she snatched the bread out of my hand, biting into it. I was stunned by her actions and even more so by the grin that crossed her face when she looked down at me. "What are you doing?" I questioned.

She just laughed, handing the rest of the loaf back. "Consider it a finder's fee."

I reached out, grabbing her behind the knee and pulling her down, catching her in my lap. She let out a small scream as she landed, her reflexes going to save her drink.

"You really are trouble. You know that, right?" I questioned her as I took the mug from her hand and set it aside. I pulled her in, wrapping my arms around her waist and resting my chin on her shoulder. "How are you feeling this morning?" I wanted to check in on her, to make sure she still felt okay about her decision.

"I feel..." She sighed heavily. "Confident in my choices."

"You promise?" I asked, needing to confirm she didn't feel her boundaries had been crossed.

"I promise," she said, twisting her torso so she could see me better. "Last night was incredible, and I don't regret a single thing."

"Good." I said as I gave her a soft kiss. "Here." I handed her the coffee and other loaf of spiced apple bread. "I'll start loading the horses."

A few hours into our ride, the weather had taken a turn for the worse, temperatures dropping as the wind howled around us, biting at our exposed skin. We did our best to cover ourselves, wrapping our bodies tightly in furs and pulling our hoods over our faces, but the relentless gusts continued to rip them off. We had been pushing through, trying to keep to the easternmost side of the forest, following the river as a guide, but the dying trees offered little relief.

"How much longer do we have?" she yelled ahead of me. I scrunched my eyes, trying to see through the stinging tears that welled in them, looking around to see if I could recognize where we were.

"A few more hours at least," I spoke into her ear.

"It's safer for us and the horses if we walk from here." I held out my hand, helping Asteria from the saddle.

The wind whipped and whistled around us, making the narrow trail leading up to the cave we would be staying in treacherous to take. I wrapped her in extra furs, trying to keep her warm and protected. I was in the lead, Asteria following, and the two horses behind her, all in a single file line, pressing ourselves against the side of the mountain. Some called it the Desolate Mountain, but most gave it no name, avoiding it due to its proximity to the Dead Mountains. That fear meant it remained vacant of passersby, making it the perfect stop on the long journey to and from Asphodel. There was a large cave just short of halfway up the mountain, one I had spent many nights alone in. The trail from this side of the mountain was significantly more tedious and riskier, and the weather we traveled in made it that much more dangerous.

"Where exactly are we going?" she asked, her head down tracking her steps, plotting where the next foot should go.

"Somewhere safe and guarded from the weather," I said, looking back at her.

"So a cave?" she deadpanned, unimpressed with my response.

"Yes, a cave," I grinned, "but a nice cave." She just rolled her eyes at me. "We're climbing the side of mountain, Princess. What were you expecting? An extravagant bed chamber?"

"No," she said indignantly, "but maybe something less likely to home to a bear or bats."

"Trust me, those are not things you are going to have to worry about up here."

"And what exactly are the things I have to worry about up here?"

A strong gust of wind swept off the side of the mountain, causing Asteria to lose her footing. A scream sounded behind me as she mis-stepped and fell forward, nearly going over the steep ledge. Quickly, I reached out, grabbing her hand as she went down, half her body hanging over the edge. She screamed, fighting to gain her footing as I grasped her tightly and fought to pull her up. I grunted as I used all my strength to haul her over the edge and into my arms. We fell back, slamming into the stone wall, both struggling to calm our breathing. I held her tightly, thankful I caught her. "That," I murmured to her.

"What?"

"That is what you have to worry about up here," I answered her. "That and me. Because if you do something like that again, you will have me to contend with either in this life or the next. Is that understood, Princess?"

Nodding her head, she nestled into my chest as she agreed. "Understood."

I kissed the top of her head before releasing her. "Come on, let's keep going. Please, be careful and watch your step."

We forged on, making our way to the entrance of the cave that revealed itself as we crested a false peak. "Wait here," I instructed. "Let me make sure it's vacant."

"Vacant of what?" she alarmed. "You said there wouldn't be bats or bears up here."

"Right," I said, looking back at her as I stepped into the cave, "but wolves are definitely a possibility."

"Wolves?" she exclaimed.

I smiled as I disappeared from her view. I hadn't seen wolves in the area for years, but her reaction was every bit worth the lie. I entered the cave, making my way to the center, where the remnants of a fire pit remained. Looking to the back, I found the stockpile of kindling and logs and quickly got to building a roaring fire, heating the space.

I sauntered out back to where she stood with the horses. "We are in the clear. No creatures to be seen." I bowed, flourishing my arm and directing her into the cave. I followed her, leading the horses in and leaving them near the entrance, out of the elements.

She stopped when she saw the crackling fire. "You didn't come in here to check for wolves, did you?"

"That would be a no." I walked up behind her, unclasping her cloak and removing it from her shoulders. "Why don't you relax and warm up while I set up for the night?" Turning to protest, I placed a finger over her mouth before she could speak. "It would be my pleasure. Please, I insist."

Dropping my hand, I turned her back towards the fire. I slowly began to layer the pelts and remove our supplies. There wasn't an active source of water within a short distance from here, so I opted for roasting some vegetables over the fire and serving them with the last of the white bread we had.

"Are you defrosted yet, Little Star?" I asked her as we finished our dinner.

"I'm getting there," she smiled. "Little by little."

"Good." I leaned in to tease her. "If there's anything I can do to help, just let me know."

Raising her brows at me, she muttered. "Oh? Is that so? What did you have in mind?"

"Little Star, what don't I have in mind?" I stared at her, her eyes growing dark as she listened intently. "For starters," I grabbed her hands and pulled her into my lap, her thighs straddling mine, "it would be imperative that we remove these constraining clothes. Body heat is better shared skin to skin."

Running my hands up her legs, I slid them under her tunic, slowly lifting it over her head. I kissed at the curves of her breasts as I began to slowly unlace the front of her stay.

"Is this helping?" I asked as I pushed the straps off her shoulders, exposing her bare chest to me.

Beneath her, my cock began to strain against my pants, and she moaned breathlessly at my touch. Her skin was like silk beneath my rough hands as I ran my hand up her stomach, between her full breasts, wrapping around her neck, lightly gripping and pulling her in to taste her. Her hands entangled themselves into my hair as she opened her mouth, deepening our kiss. Her hips rocked into me, causing my cock to twitch from the friction. It felt so fucking good—I gipped her hips, grinding her into me, each movement sending more blood rushing to my already steeled erection.

She took over her movements, slowly rocking back and forth. My chest rumbled in pleasure as I slid my hand up her back, fisting a handful of hair at the base of her neck and pulling her head to the side, exposing her neck. There was a small yellow bruise from where I had marked her the night before, and it sent a jolt of pleasure down my spine seeing it there. I kissed her neck, starting at the top and working my back down, stopping to pay extra attention to the shadowed imprint of my teeth, pulling my lips back and biting down on the now-sensitive flesh, harder this time. She gasped at the sharp pain, but that gasp quickly turned into a moan as I released her skin and dragged my tongue across the spot.

She whispered into my ear. "Please, Rae. I need more."

Goddess fucking dammit if that didn't make me nearly come undone right then. Without hesitation, I flipped us, laying her onto her back as I straddled her. I pulled my shirt off before I looked down at her flushed skin and swollen lips, her eyes dark with desire.

"Fuck," I muttered, knowing damn well this woman was going to be my downfall. I leaned down, circling the shell of her ear with the tip of my tongue. "Tell me what you want, Princess."

Her voice was unsteady and weak. "Everything. I want all of it. I want you."

My cock was begging to be freed, pressing harder into the waistband of my pants. I growled darkly as I tried to hold myself together; I wanted so badly to rip the rest of her clothes off and claim her, to fuck her until she knew only me.

But I wouldn't do that with her, not tonight. She needed this to be done right, and I was going to give her right. I dipped my head, working my way down her torso, stopping to take her breast into my mouth, sucking and licking until she arched into me.

"Do you want more, Princess?" I asked.

"Yes," she groaned, pressing into me.

"Good girl," I whispered as I kissed down her stomach until I reached the hem of her trousers. I looked up at her as I began to undo the laces, loosening the waist. "Lift your hips for me, Princess."

She did, lifting them as I removed her pants, pulling them

down over her hips and slipping them off. I sat on my knees before her bare form, taking in the beauty that was her. Her curves, her full breasts and thighs—every part of her was art. Her pale, rosy skin was flushed in arousal, making it brighter than usual, a light glint of sweat coating her skin. I lifted one of her legs, hitching over my shoulder as I kissed her ankle, following the line down to her center, glistening with arousal. I dragged my thumb from her entrance to the apex of her clit, circling the sensitive bundle, feeling how wet she was for me. I moved my hand down, sliding my finger into her, moaning at how tight she was. My balls tightened at the thought of sliding into her, of feeling her come around my cock.

"Did you like it when I tasted you last night, Little Star?"

She panted as I moved my finger in and out of her wet pussy. "Yes," she moaned. "Yes, yes, yes."

I smiled, enjoying every twitch of her hip, every flex of her cunt around my finger, the arch of her back, each moan on her breath, the sounds of her pleasure were enough to drive me to completion. Keeping her leg over my shoulder, I leaned down, removing my finger and burying my face between her legs. I ran my tongue up her in one, long stroke, relishing in the sweet taste on my tongue. It was a meal I could enjoy every day.

"You taste so fucking delectable," I groaned into her sensitive flesh, sending shivers through her body.

I worked her with my tongue, drowning myself in her pleasure as her cry for more cut through the dark of the cave, echoing off the walls, a symphony of bliss. I dipped my fingers back into her as I licked and sucked at her clit, working her until she was breathless, beginning to clench around my fingers. I growled into her as I feasted, pushing her over the edge, drinking her in, working her through her orgasm.

Desperate to feel her drenching my cock, I sat back on my heels, untying the laces of my pants and pulling them down, releasing my throbbing erection. Her eyes widened at the sight of me, and I smirked.

"Like what you see?" She blushed in embarrassment, and I leaned over to kiss her. As badly as I fucking wanted her, I needed to make sure she felt the same. "Are you sure about this?"

She stared deeply into my eyes. "I'm sure."

I kissed her gently. "If you change your mind, just say so and we will stop, okay? Just say the word."

She inhaled deeply and nodded her head in understanding. I positioned myself between her legs, grabbing my cock and running it through her folds, coating myself in her arousal. Leaning down, I rested my forehead on hers as I lined myself up with her entrance.

"I'm going to take it slow. Just remember to breathe."

"I will." She kissed me lightly. "I trust you, Rae."

I slowly pressed into her with a deep inhale, and she gasped at the intrusion, wincing slightly.

I stopped my efforts, letting her body adjust to me for a few moments. "Breathe," I reminded her as I pulled back before pressing into her further. Little by little, I worked myself into her until at last, I was fully seated. "Are you okay?" I was afraid to move and cause her pain.

Her breath hitched. "It's good, it's okay, I'm okay." She lifted her chin and dragged her tongue across my lips, nipping at the bottom one. "Don't stop."

I felt her rock her hips, and my cock twitched inside her before I pulled out to the tip and slid back inside her. "Fuck," I moaned into her ear. "You feel fucking unbelievable."

I breathed heavily as I began to work in and out of her, setting a gentle pace and rhythm. Her head kicked back. as she let out a cry of pleasure.

"More," she begged, digging her nails into my back.

Unable to resist her plea, I drove into her faster and harder, her cries growing louder. She began rocking her hips, matching my pace, driving me further into her. It felt better than anything I had ever experienced, and her sounds became more desperate as we picked up our pace, needing to fill her completely. I took her legs, keeping them wrapped around me as I sat up, straightening my back. I gripped her hips and pulled her into me, forcing my cock deeper. I felt the pressure building as my balls began to draw up, each stroke more intense than the last. I was preparing to slow, not wanting to finish without her, when she fell silent, her body tensing as her pussy clenched around me.

"Fucking yes," I growled as I picked up my thrusts, not stopping until I felt her coming around me.

I filled her as she clenched and spasmed around me. I collapsed on top of her, unable to breathe, speak, or even think. That had been everything I had imagined it would be and more. I pulled out of her, grabbing the warm, wet cloth we had used to clean up for dinner, wiping away the cum that coated her skin. Flopping onto my back, I cleaned myself before I turned my head to her.

"Asteria?" I asked, her silence worrying me. She faced me, her eyes brimming with tears. I sat up, concerned. "What's wrong? Are you hurt? Are you okay?" I began to panic.

She sniffled and closed her eyes. "I am... perfect." She smiled. "Rae, that was... I never thought it could be like that. I don't know what to say other than thank you."

I laughed under my breath. "Little Star, you don't have to thank me." I leaned down and kissed her. "It was perfect. You were perfect. I should be thanking you."

She giggled as she pulled me down, forcing me onto my back as she laid her head on my chest. I trailed my hand up and down her back, content with having her in my arms. We laid there for a while in silence, just happy being in each other's presence. Suddenly, I felt her shift, moving to climb on top of me.

"What are you—"

She cut me off in a kiss, positioning herself over my cock that was growing under her. She ran her hand under my chin, forcing my head to the side. She trailed her tongue from the base of my neck to my ear, pulling the lobe into her mouth and sucking.

"Mmmmmmm," I moaned as she took the initiative.

I let her take her time exploring my body, discovering what made me tick, what made me yearn for more. When I couldn't handle it anymore, I took control, doing the things I knew made her weak, and I spent the rest of the evening doing just that.

I fucked and pleased her until both our bodies gave out.

CHAPTER 27
ASTERIA

Morning light filtered through the entrance to the cave we had stayed in last night. Laying flat on my stomach with my arms crossed beneath my head, I smiled as the heat from the sun warmed my face. Blinking my eyes open, I looked around; from the brightness of the sun, it had to be close to mid-morning.

It was dawn before we finally laid down to sleep, and as I shifted slightly, the aching between my thighs was a reminder of why. We had spent the entire night exploring each other's bodies, spiraling in and out of pure bliss. I stretched, trying my best not to disturb the sleeping man next to me. I turned my head to face him, admiring him as he laid on his back, tilting his face towards me.

His features were soft from sleep, his breath slow and steady as I memorized the curves of his face. I lay there with a small smile on my face; I had given myself to him completely last night, something I never believed I would be able to do. But he pulled me over the edge, and I fell freely and deeply into the pools of him, his touch like a tether keeping me anchored, and safe.

I think I could do this with him for eternity. I couldn't fathom ever feeling another man's touch. Stefan thought he had ruined me for other men, but he couldn't have been more wrong. What Stefan took from me, what he ripped out by force, leaving me an empty shell full of despair, shame, and hate, Rae had begun to fill with kindness, pleasure, and love. Love... I didn't know if what I fele for Rae was love or infatuation, but it was intoxicating either way. I would explore those feelings later; right now, I was enjoying feeling his bare body so close to mine.

He shifted slightly, turning onto his side, his arm draping across the small of my back, the touch sending sparks coursing through my veins. I imagined spending the rest of my life drowning in his touch. His eyes fluttered open, still heavy from sleep, and the corners of his lips tilted up into a sweet smile. He leaned forward, placing a soft kiss to my lips, and I smiled shyly, my heart fluttering in my chest.

"Good morning, Little Star." He inhaled deeply, pulling me closer to his chest as he exhaled. "Your smile is warmer than the sun. You should wear it more often. It's a gift."

"You jest, sir," I said, moving to cover my face, but he caught my chin before I could bury myself into my arms, tilting my lips to his.

"I never joke when it comes to your beauty, Asteria." His lips brushed mine as he spoke. "You will learn to see yourself for the breathtaking goddess you are. Yours is an altar I would happily kneel before, worshiping you for the rest of my days."

He closed the distance, kissing me gently at first, but it deepened as he began to trace up and down my spine with his hand. The action sent shivers across my body, and heat began pooling in my core. I parted my lips, dragging my tongue across his, urging him to open, allowing me to explore his mouth, to taste him. His hand drifted lower down my back, grazing my ass before he reached between my thighs, running his finger through my wetness, a moan escaping from my throat.

He began slowly working me, running his fingers along my slit, spreading my arousal over my entrance. He slid his finger back up, finding that glorious bundle of nerves at my apex, lightly circling it. He wasn't quick; no, he took his time applying just enough pressure to cause my breath to hitch and have me wanting more. I deepened the kiss, desire driving my actions. I needed more. This wasn't enough. I began to grind against his hand, seeking more—more pleasure, more touch, just...more. He laughed into my mouth, knowing what he was doing, dragging out the pleasure, torturing me, withholding my reward. He was wholly in control, and he knew it. He stopped his ministrations, leaving his hand where it was but refusing to move it. It had me whimpering for more.

"Tell me what you want, Little Star." His voice was deep with sleep and desire.

Goddess he was beautiful. His eyes had darkened, deepening to a green rivaling the darkest forest. He was looking at me so intently, I was unable to think. His fingers moved now, lightly circling my entrance, and all I could think was how badly I wanted to feel them inside me.

"What do you want, Little Star?" he said again, more dominance in his tone this time.

"You," I whispered. "You. I want you."

Before I could even inhale, he plunged a finger deep inside me, curling it so that it reached that blissful spot, and I couldn't do more than gasp from the sensation. Capturing my mouth in a hungry kiss, he bit my lower lip, eliciting a moan of both pain and pleasure from me. The tang of copper flooded my mouth – he had broken the skin. I moved to pull away, but he stopped me, sucking at my lip before he pulled back, licking at the blood.

Holy fuck, that was unbearably arousing. I looked up at him, my face a mixture of pleasure and awe. Pulling his lower lip between his teeth, he bit down with enough force to break his own skin, allowing the blood to pool in his mouth. He had two fingers working inside me as he leaned down, his gaze burning with desire, and kissed me. His blood tasted like cinnamon, and it was an incredibly mind-bending sensation to have him working me, pulling at my lip, tasting me, and allowing me to taste him. The act had me racing towards climax, and I tightened around his fingers. He paused, pulling his face back, his eyes almost black now.

"Don't you fucking come yet," he commanded, his tone almost making me come undone right then.

He removed his fingers and quickly shifted, kneeling behind me, my body aching for the feel of him again. He grabbed my hips, hitching my lower body up so I was on my knees.

"Keep your head down," he commanded, and I more than gladly obeyed. I was unable to see what he was doing, but when I felt his mouth on me, I cried out as he licked my center slowly and languidly. "You, my goddess, taste like nectar and I want to drown in you."

He wasted no time devouring me, lapping at my entrance while working my clit. I was fisting the furs beneath me like they were my lifeline as he stroked his tongue through my folds before halting at my entrance, his hand still circling my clit.

"Tell me, Princess, how do you feel this morning?" He dipped his tongue into my entrance just once to indicate what he was really asking.

Am I hurting from last night? Am I okay? I couldn't think straight with his fingers doing what they were, his tongue gently dancing where it was.

"I... I feel," I tried to say between breaths when he drew his tongue up past my folds and higher still, circling over the puckered skin of my ass. Shivers erupted through my body as he stopped circling, dipping his tongue into the hole I wasn't even aware could be used for pleasure.

"Fuck me," I moaned, and I could feel him smiling against me.

He laughed lightly at my command. "I asked you a question, Princess. How are you feeling this morning?"

His voice vibrated against me, which had me trembling from the sensation. He didn't wait for me to answer before he dipped his finger inside my dripping entrance and returned to dancing his tongue around that newly revealed pleasure spot. *How does he expect me to answer him when I can barely think straight? This is all too much. It feels too good.*

"Great, I feel great," I said between thrusts of his fingers.

"That's my good girl," he growled against my ass.

His praise sent me careening over the edge, and I screamed out in pleasure as he continued, fucking me with his fingers and licking my ass until I came down from my high. It took me a moment to remember who I was, but the feeling of him move behind me brought me out of the haze of bliss.

I looked over my shoulder, locking eyes with the man who just tasted parts of me no one else had. He pulled his fingers out of me and brought them to his mouth, drawing his fingers through his lips, my arousal coating them. He slowly licked them clean with a moan that should have been outlawed.

"You are the best tasting treat to grace my mouth," he groaned.

I traced his chiseled body slowly, admiring the sculpted muscles of his arms, moving to his tanned and steeled chest. This was a man who had been training with weapons and fighting most of his life. He had a mosaic of scars across his chest, but I found they made him even more attractive. I needed to remember to learn the stories behind them. I followed that glorious chest further down to where his obliques crested into a perfect v.

It was just below that where he held his cock in his hand, gripping it and working himself. It was a visual reminder of why I was sore. He was...well endowed—that would be the lady-like way to say it. His fingers didn't meet as he held himself, and, if the girth wasn't enough to make a lady blush, the length most definitely would. I couldn't say I'd seen many males naked, so I didn't really have much to compare it to, but surely, that wasn't the average male size. He had to be eight inches in length easily, maybe more, and right now, all I could think about was feeling him inside me.

He followed my gaze, and a cocky smile graced his already charming face. "Is this not enough for you?" he asked mockingly.

I blushed, stumbling over my words before deciding against speaking and pressing myself back, grinding my ass along his length. He exhaled sharply, gripping my hips and pulling me roughly into him, pumping his cock between us, wetting himself with my arousal. He pulled back, aligning himself against my entrance, teasingly pressing into me without actually penetrating —just deep enough for me to feel how hard he was for me, how wet I was for him.

The anticipation and the promise of pleasure had me whimpering. "Please, Rae...please."

He leaned forward, rubbing his thumb across my lips, pressing at them for me to open. He dipped his thumb into my mouth, and I sucked at it. He pulled it back, running it along my backside, stopping to press lightly at my entrance, just enough to have me incredibly curious what more would feel like.

"Little Star." His voice sounded as if he was fighting to restrain himself. "Please tell me I can have you. All of you."

I looked back, staring deep into his eyes. "For eternity."

That was all it took: his restraint came crashing down as he thrust into me deeply, fully. I moaned loudly at the intrusion; the feel of him filling me was a painfully blissful sensation. He was still for a moment, his entire length inside me, allowing my body to adjust to his size. It was overwhelming, coupled with those that came with the movements of his thumb around my ass.

"You are going to be my most pleasurable demise," he moaned.

I inhaled to reply, but before I could form any words, he pulled out to the tip and thrust back in, and this time, he dipped his thumb into my ass, and I yelped in both pleasure and pain. That didn't slow him, though; he pounded into me fervently, his thumb working a deliciously evil spot, sending me spiraling into a new height of bliss. Our moans reverberated off the cave walls, filling the air with a symphony of pleasure. The sensations were overwhelming, and I found myself pleading, but I honestly didn't know if I was pleading for him to stop or if I was pleading for more.

His hand held my hip, using it to pull me into him before tracing its way up my back to fist my hair, pulling me upright so my back was against his chest. He slid his hand from my ass around to my front, sliding his fingers through my wet pussy. He explored the planes of my stomach and chest with his free hand, his other fisted in my hair, arching my head back and exposing my neck to him. He licked up the curve of my neck before the sting of his bite pulled an animalistic noise from my chest, which seemed to only urge him on. I snaked my hands around his hips and reached back, grabbing his ass and pulling him deeper into me.

He growled in my ear. "Fuck, Asteria, you feel better than I could have ever imagined."

The comment had me twisting my head to nip at his jaw, and he pulled my hair tighter as he worked my clit harder. I screamed out in pleasure, and he echoed the sentiment.

He released his grip on my hair and snaked his hand around my neck. "Do you trust me?" he whispered in my ear.

I looked up at him, my eyes heavy-lidded from the pleasure. "Yes."

He tilted my head up and kissed me like I was the finest wine he had ever tasted. He thrust harder and faster, and my head knocked back onto his shoulder as I gave into the sensations of his body against mine, the feel of him thrusting inside me, hitting every right spot, the swirl of his fingers across my clit. He was either heaven or pure sin, but either way, he was mine. His hand resting on my neck strengthened its grip, and momentarily, panic flooded my system before he released, sensing my distress.

"Trust me, Princess."

I nodded, giving him my trust. His grip tightened again, the blood supply to my head slowing, and all the sensations seemed to heighten and fade at the same time. I was falling, falling into blackness, a pool of nothing and everything.

I didn't know how long I swam in the black nothing, but when I came back to reality, I was screaming out an orgasm so intense, that my vision filled with stars. The noises coming from Rae were animalistic and pleasure-filled as he came just as hard. We rode the tidal wave of stars and pleasure together, and when we came back down, I questioned who I was, what my life had been, what had brought me to this, to him.

Because now that I had him, I was never going to let him go.

CHAPTER 28
ASTRAEUS

I laid on the floor of the cave, the soft furs I had thrown down as a bed for us sticking to our sweat-slicked skin. I turned my head to look at Asteria, only to find her eyes were closed and her breathing was slowing—she had fallen asleep. I watched her for a moment, awe struck by her beauty; my Little Star, my beacon of light in a world of darkness and trials. She had ruined me, completely shattered me, and every broken part of my soul now belonged to her. I loved her, and I would go to any lengths to keep her safe. I dragged my hand over my face, my stomach churning from anxiety and stress, because everything had changed. Everything.

When I made the decision to use Asteria, the Princess of Pyrus, future Queen of Solaria, fiancée of Prince Stefan, I had only one concern: my kingdom. Sacrifice the life of one to save the life of my people. This girl was nothing more than a bargaining tool to ensure my kingdom could be reunited with the trade routes it needed to survive.

Prince Stefan had a reputation for being cruel and selfish, and my sources had told me he had been obsessed with the princess for years. No one knew why exactly, but the assumption was that he wanted to unite Pyrus and Solaria under one rule, taking control of the two largest and richest Kingdoms in the realm of Leethe. Whatever the reason, he wouldn't get the chance.

I heaved a sigh, not sure how I was going to fix the problems with my kingdom, but they wouldn't include trading her. I pulled her into my chest, placing a kiss to her exposed shoulder. She moaned lightly in her sleep, as if even asleep the act comforted her. We wouldn't be able to rest here much longer; we needed to get to our next destination before dark, and we'd already lost most of the morning. We would skip training today and ride hard to reach the base of the Dead Mountains, her destination and the entrance to my home, Asphodel.

I would have to tell her the truth of who I was soon. I feared she would be angry with me, so for now, I would allow us another day of this, of just being together and enjoying each other without the cares and stresses that clouded our future.

I brushed her hair off her shoulder and neck, caressing her arm with the lightest touch of my fingers. I breathed her in; pomegranates and lavender, a scent I would never tire of. I spent time memorizing the curves of her body, mapping the small patch of freckles gracing her right left shoulder. I imagined taking a quill and connecting the dots, seeing what shapes I could create. My gaze drifted to her chest, watching it rise and fall with each breath she took, then back to the freckles. Mapping them in my mind, I began to drift off to sleep, and as my eyes gave in to the weight of exhaustion, I heard my father's voice in my head, repeating the words I'd heard so many times before, passed down for generations.

"Change comes on two moons bearing the belt of Orion.
When the falling star is enraptured by twilight,
darkness will fall upon the kingdoms.
Out of the dark, a star will rise to remake the realm.

Beneath shadow and light, a new era will emerge, and power once lost will be returned.
For theirs is a destiny written in twilight and stars."

My eyes flew open, and my breath stalled in my chest. Suddenly it was as if I was being ripped out of my body and out of time. Flashes of scenes and images surrounded me—I was spiraling as I realized it was all her. A mosaic of her bright grey eyes, the way they seemed to be lit from within, her midnight hair, the constellation of freckles... They were the Orion constellation. It all began to fall into place; it all made sense: why she was kept so secluded from the other kingdoms, why Stefan was so intent on the marriage, why her father had agreed to it. It felt as if all the heat had been leeched from my body, my skin pebbled as a cold sweat slicked my skin. I stared at her as she slept, so still, so peaceful. My Asteria, my Little Star. She was the key, the one who would bring magic back to Asphodel, and I had the sinking feeling she had no idea.

I sat up, not able to lay there any longer. I needed air, to process, to think. I reached for my shirt and pants, the motions waking Asteria.

"Sleep, Little Star. I'll be back shortly," I said, forcing my tone to be soft and calming, concealing the turmoil of anxiety, excitement, and fear that swirled within me.

"Where are you going?" she mumbled, still in that space between wake and sleep.

"To catch breakfast." Fastening my boots, I stood. "Something other than bread and fruit today."

She nodded and whispered something incoherent as she rolled over and went back to sleep. I headed towards the cave entrance, retrieving the bow and quiver of arrows from where they sat against the wall.

Trekking through the woods, I headed towards the stream,

hoping to find small game drinking from it. The wind nipped at my exposed skin; usually, that would irritate me, but I found it therapeutic and grounding today. I came across what seemed to be a game trail crossing the riverbed, and looking around, I found a tree downwind of the trail. I climbed up, settling onto a sturdy branch, adjusting so I had a clear view of the river but was concealed from any possible prey. I reached down, grabbing an arrow from the quiver at my side, readying for a shot. Now, I just had to wait for a creature to cross my path. I shrugged deeper into my cloak, using the quiet and space to sort through everything.

I lost myself in my thoughts. I don't know how, but I had to assume Stefan was aware that Asteria was the key. What I don't know was how long he had known and who else was aware. Her father had to know—did her mother know as well? Stefan's parents? Had all the Kingdoms known? No, they couldn't have. They would have called for her death to prevent the chance of the prophecy being fulfilled. So why didn't Stefan have the same instinct? If Asteria was the key, and she was alive and well, why hadn't the magic returned? Something was missing, a part of the prophecy.

I went over the lines of the prophecy again and again in my head. What was I not seeing? *"Change comes on two moons bearing the belt of Orion."* The birth of Asteria. *"When the falling star is enraptured by twilight, darkness will fall upon the kingdoms."* Something had to happen to trigger the prophecy. *The falling star*, again, Asteria, but what did it mean when she *'becomes enraptured by twilight'?* I couldn't decipher it, but I had a sickening sense that it meant something bad for my star. The rest seemed pretty clear: *darkness will fall upon the kingdoms. Out of the dark a star will rise to remake the realm. Beneath shadow and light, a new era will emerge, and power once lost will be returned. A destiny written in twilight and stars.*

Once the prophecy was triggered, a dark time would be ahead

as the magic wielders regained their power. I could only assume another war would be on the horizon. The kingdoms had almost decimated our people in the last one, and I worried my people did not have the strength or numbers to survive another one. I was going to have to tell her the truth today. We had to discuss this. I had to know if she knew anything, if she knew who she was.

The snapping of twig jerked me from my thoughts, and as I looked up to see what had made the noise, I froze. A small group of Royal Guards bearing the crests of Solaria and Pyrus were crossing the river on horseback. Adrenaline flooded my system as I thought of Asteria asleep in the cave, not more than twenty minutes from my position. I remained in my spot, hidden from view, holding my breath until I knew I was out of earshot of the search party. Then, I dropped from the branch, landing with a light thud before I took off in a sprint. I raced through the trees, branches whipping at my face, the cuts and welts stinging from the cold air. I didn't care, the pounding of my heart echoing in my ears as I begged and prayed to the Goddess that she had not been found, that she was safe.

I rushed through the entrance to the cave, panic overtaking my senses. "Asteria!" I screamed.

I halted instantly, my blood turning to ice when I saw the pallet of furs vacant. She was gone. I spun around, inspecting the items left in the cave to see if anything was disturbed, if there was any sign of a struggle. Everything was how I had left it— everything except the furs that no longer contained my Little Star. I yelled, kicking the pile of supplies near the edge of the makeshift bed, sending things flying and ricocheting off the cave wall. I dropped to my knees, fisting my hair. I needed to feel pain, to be grounded. I needed to pull myself together, because I was barely holding on. Something suddenly glinted in the sunlight, catching my eye—sticking out of the furs was the handle of her dagger, the amethyst stone reflecting the sun. The last thread of control I had was cut, that dagger sliced right through it. I let out a scream that had the horses outside the cave shifting nervously.

"Rae," a soft voice sounded behind me, followed by the light touch of a hand on my shoulder. I stood, turning and grabbing her wrist as I pulled her into me. I held her like she was the air I needed to survive, because as far I was concerned, she was. With her free hand, she reached up, cupping my face and tracing her thumb along my cheek. I shut my eyes and leaned into her touch, dipping my head until our foreheads met.

"What happened?" she asked, concern deepening her tone. I pulled back and looked down at her, her forehead was creased with worry as her breathing quickened.

"We have to go. Now." My tone was serious. "I came across a group of Royal Guards from your kingdom and Solaria. They're searching for you; it's the only reason for them to be this far north, this close to the Dead Mountains."

She was already in motion, lacing her boots and shrugging on her cloak. I reached down to gather the furs, but I stopped when I felt the cold metal of her dagger. I turned to face her, stepping forward, backing her into the wall. For a moment, fear seemed to cross her features as she held my stare.

I hardened my tone. "And Asteria, do not ever, and I mean ever," I placed the dagger in her grip, closing my hand over hers, squeezing tightly to emphasize my point, "leave your dagger behind again. Do not ever wander without protection. It stays on you at all times. Do you understand?"

She swallowed, beads of sweat forming on her brow as she nodded carefully. I released her hand, moving to clench her jaw in my grasp as I pulled her in for a deep and hungry kiss. I released her, leaving her face flushed and her wanting.

"We can't stay here any longer. Saddle your horse and prepare to ride hard. We have to get into the mountains before sundown." As we saddled the horses and secured our supplies, I told her the plan. "We will ride until we reach the base of the mountains, and then we take only what we need and proceed on foot. It will be easier to navigate the mountains and cover our tracks without the horses. There are old trade routes through the mountains, and very few know of their existence. From there, we will enter the lands of Asphodel."

She threw her leg over Freya, seating herself in her saddle. "Asphodel? The Forgotten Kingdom?"

"Yes. There are still small villages there. Once we reach the passage, we will be safe. I will get you to safety, Princess. I need you to trust me. All will be explained once we're safe."

She just stared at me. I could tell she wanted to ask more questions, but instead, she tipped her head and kicked off, sending her horse into a sprint. I followed suit, picking up speed quickly to take the lead. We rode, putting the small cave where both our lives changed behind us. There was so much that had happened in the last twelve hours, and yet so much she didn't know. My stomach lurched at the thought of everything I had to tell her, but it would have to wait. I had to make sure she was safe first, and then I would tell her everything. I would answer all her questions, help her understand. Together, we would figure out what was next, what the future held for us.

As long as we were together, we could handle whatever was thrown our way.

CHAPTER 29
ASTERIA

We rode fast, pushing our horses to their limits. The wind whipped wildly around me, stinging my eyes and pulling my hair out of the quick and messy braid I had done before we left. My body pumped with adrenaline and fear; the sounds of hooves were almost drowned out by the thrumming of my pulse.

Rae led us through the forest expertly, avoiding game trails and areas where we were likely to encounter the Royal Guards. Every few minutes, he looked back over his shoulder at me, checking that I was keeping pace, his face marred with welts and scratches from his sprint through the woods earlier. Some of the scratches were superficial, while others had cut deep enough to draw blood. None of them should leave any lasting marks with proper care, and I planned to properly nurse every one of them once we got to safety.

I had so many questions for him, but now was not the time. He promised he would answer them all once we got through the borders of Asphodel. The discovery that there were still people inhabiting the lands shocked me. We had been told that the lands were desolate, that no one survived the aftermath of the Great

War. Maybe the inhabitants were deserters of their own kingdoms, though that thought didn't exactly calm my nerves. The only reason someone deserted their kingdom was to avoid criminal charges and punishment. Was I headed into a den of criminals? Had I run from one monster only to fall into the hands of many?

I pushed the thoughts out of my head and focused on the task at hand. Rae had promised me safety, and I trusted him with my life. After everything, after last night, after this morning, I was beginning to believe I could even trust him with my heart, which seemed like an unfathomable notion. Then again, until very recently, I'd never believed I would trust someone enough to willingly give them my body, and my body now belonged to Rae.

The sun began to dip below the horizon as the forest thinned and the Dead Mountains stood before us. I gasped, taken aback by the size of the mountain range.

It dwarfed the mountains that spread across the horizon bordering the sea near Solaria. I had spent many hours dreaming of a life beyond those mountains, a life without royalty and titles, without the duties and expectations that had been plaguing me since I was old enough to comprehend them. A life where I was free to be me, to explore, to love who I wanted, to be what I wanted. A healer, an artist, a writer? It didn't matter, so long as it was my decision to make. There were times when I had all but convinced myself to go, to abandon reason and responsibility, to take what I could carry and run, but the guilt of abandoning my family, my responsibilities to my kingdom—but mostly fear—kept me from leaving.

Now, though, that seemed such a silly excuse to remain caged. Because that's what I was: a caged bird, trained to sit pretty while the men ruled the kingdoms. I couldn't even do that right. I couldn't be the pretty little bird I was expected to be. I was never enough, yet too much, all at the same time. I wasn't pretty enough. I wasn't skinny enough. I wasn't smart enough. I couldn't execute my duties well enough. I was never good enough. Yet, in the same breath, I was too much. I was too loud. I was too odd, my hobbies too strange. My personality was too different. I had never been chosen because of who I was. I had never been loved for who I was. Love came with expectations. Until now.

Rae chose me. He chose me knowing who I was. He didn't care about the title. He cared that I was kind, loyal, fierce. He showed me the worst parts of myself and twisted them into something beautiful and bright. To him, I wasn't too loud; I was powerful. I wasn't odd, I was unique. My interests weren't strange—they made me an asset. Rae chose me. He chose my curves, my quirks, my scars, my flaws. Every broken piece of me, he chose. To him, I was enough, just as I was.

Becoming caught up in my thoughts, I hadn't realized that the horses had slowed. I surveyed our surroundings, realizing we were approaching the base of the mountains. The air was still, and the forest that climbed the mountain side was eerily quiet.

"Dead Mountains, indeed," I said, my voice barely above a whisper. Rae slid out of his saddle, and I quickly followed.

"It's said that when the Great War pushed the magic wielders over the mountains back into Asphodel, the magic abandoned its people and laid itself to rest in these mountains, awaiting the prophecy. When that happens, the magic will return to its people and help them return to power."

I stared at Rae, my jaw slackened. Prophecy? Magic returning to the people? What was he talking about? I shook my head, trying to process his words. "What are you talking about? I've never heard of a prophecy. And how can magic return to its people when the magic wielders died out ages ago after the Great War?"

He scoffed. "They really don't teach you anything about the history of the realm, do they?"

I wasn't going to dignify that comment with a response. I opened my mouth to ask him another question when something moved behind him—not something: someone. Before I could utter a warning, Rae was on the ground, a crack echoing through the trees from the impact of a guard's hilt to the back of his head.

I screamed, rushing to his side. "Rae, please look at me."

He groaned in pain, and I released a breath. I rolled him over, helping him up to his feet as his hand massaged where the sword's hilt had met his skull. He winced at the touch, but when he removed his hand, there was no blood. He might end up with a concussion, but the impact had not seriously injured him.

We stopped, noticing the hoard of Royal Guards that had us encircled. I felt the color drain from my face—I was going to be sick. We had gotten close, so fucking close, to freedom. There was no way we would win; we were outnumbered. I looked at Rae, his face set in determination as he tried to work out a plan. He would try to fight. I could see it in his stony expression, and I couldn't allow that to happen. I stepped close to him, placing my hands on the sides of his face and pulling his attention to me.

"Rae." I spoke softly so that only he could hear me. "This is not a fight we will win. I will not risk you. I can't."

My eyes began to sting as I stared into those breathtaking green eyes. I saw my future with him fading away, fading into blackness as I held back my tears. He moved, one hand lacing into the hair at the nape of my neck, the other grazing the small of my back. He held me, and I could see him warring within himself with the desire to protect me, to fight, and the knowledge that we would both lose if we tried.

His voice quivered slightly as he spoke. "I promised you. I promised that I would free you from this life, from him. I will not let you go." His grip on me tightened. "I love you, Asteria. I can't let you go back to him." He pressed a kiss to my forehead, his eyes trained on the guards around us. "When I say the word, you will run. You will run, and you will not stop. Do you understand me?

Keep going east until you cross the mountains. From there, you go south."

I jerked my head back, looking at him. He was going to sacrifice himself to give me the chance to run, to save me. I shook my head at him, the tears threatening to spill over.

"No." It sounded more like a plea than a statement. "I am not leaving without you. If you fight, then I fight with you." I leaned, kissing him like it was the last time, because there was a very good chance that it was.

Behind me, someone began clapping. "Well isn't this sweet?"

The voice sent ice shooting through my veins. I froze, knowing who owned that voice. I turned to see the guards parting as Valdin rode forward on his horse. My heart dropped.

"Tell me, Prince Astraeus, is the Kingdom of Asphodel so barren of women that you had travel across the realm to steal our princess here?"

What? I looked up at Rae, and his pale face and thinned lips answered the question before it left my mouth. I stepped back, releasing myself from Rae's hold. It suddenly felt as if the ground had shifted beneath me, the world around me spinning, and I couldn't breathe. I folded at the waist, feeling as if I was going to be sick. *He was a prince. No, not just a prince. The Prince of Asphodel. The Forgotten Kingdom. The prince of the magic wielders. He had lied to me—about everything.*

"Asteria," Rae's voice was barely more than a whisper as he stepped towards me, his hand reaching for mine.

I took another step away from him. "No," was all I could manage to say, my arms still wrapped around my center as I kept my gaze down.

"Please, Asteria," he pleaded. "Look at me. Let me explain."

Valdin let out a dark laugh. "Let you explain what? That you've spent months infiltrating the kingdoms and their courts, trying to dig up information so you could blackmail them into helping your pathetic excuse of a kingdom? Did you really think we didn't know of your existence? That we haven't been keeping an eye on you? Tell me, Prince Astraeus, was your intention always to kidnap the princess and bargain her life for aid? Or was it just luck that you came across our little Asteria here when she decided to stand Prince Stefan up at the altar? Naughty little bitch, isn't she?"

How could I have been so naive? It was then when something inside me fractured. My heart broke into a million pieces, shattering so violently that it was almost audible. My knees buckled under the weight of his betrayal, and I slammed into the ground. I thought I heard Rae scream my name, but I couldn't hear anything over the buzzing of anger and hurt overwhelming my senses. I couldn't feel anything, and yet I felt everything. I felt the hurt, the sadness, the betrayal, the shame, the embarrassment, the anger. Anger at Rae for lying to me, anger at my parents for agreeing to marry me off to Stefan, anger at Stefan for spending months breaking me, and above all, I was angry at myself. I was angry for allowing myself to be so easily manipulated, for allowing this man to heal me, to make me feel loved, to make me feel whole, just so he could break me into even smaller pieces. I felt it all, and it was excruciating.

When I looked up, I saw Rae being restrained by two guards, blood trickling from a fresh wound above his brow. He was pleading with me to listen to him, to hear him out, to believe him, but I drowned it all out, replacing it with the fury raging inside me.

I got to my feet and walked to where he was being held, stopping in front of him. I looked at his face, covered in scrapes, fresh blood dripping into his eye as he looked up at me. His eyes were red and glassed over with tears, and if I had known better, I would have said it was hurt behind them. No. I didn't believe that this bastard was capable of hurt and remorse.

"Asteria." I pulled my arm back, balling my hand into a fist, and swinging before he could finish the next word. His head flew back from the impact, the punch landing in the middle of his face, and I felt the cracking of his nose as it broke beneath my fist. A perfect punch—it seemed like all his training paid off. He struggled to keep his head up as he looked at me.

"You lied to me. You used me. You made me trust you, want you. You made me lo..." I stopped myself before I uttered that last word and lowered my voice, struggling to keep it steady. "Was I just another one of your missions? Was this all some sick twisted game of yours? Did I play my part right? The naïve, broken princess —did I give everything you needed? Was fucking me how you rewarded yourself?" I paused as a sob wretched its way out of my throat. "Well, you won! I hope the prize was worth it." I turned and began to walk away.

Behind me, Astraeus coughed, spewing blood across the ground. He tried to break free of the guards, yelling my name but he failed. I stopped and turned, raking my eyes over him as I fixed my face and sneered at him in disgust.

"No, fuck you, *Prince Astraeus.*"

I turned back towards where Valdin sat atop his horse, laughing. The bastard was laughing. I should cut him down now and save us all from his worthless existence.

Between fits of laughter, Valdin managed to speak. "You fucked her?" He aimed the question at Astraeus. "Oh, that's great. Stefan is going to love this. Tell me, was her cunt as tight and warm as the prince says it is?"

The question had me reaching for my dagger and aiming for his side. The blade barely caught the fabric of his tunic before my wrist was in his grip and he was wrenching the dagger from my hand. I let out a pained scream as he twisted my wrist just slightly further than it was meant to.

Astraeus let loose an animalistic roar. "Don't you fucking touch her, you piece of shit!" One of the guards restraining him planted a punch to his midsection, sending him barreling over.

Tsk tsk tsk, Valdin clicked his tongue. "Now, now, Prince. There is no need to feign affection for your little whore any longer." His gaze shifted to where he still clenched my wrist, causing me to writhe in pain. "Princess, need I to remind you of what happened the last time you lashed out at me?" He twisted my wrist just a little further, eliciting another cry from my lips. "Let's not give Prince Stefan another reason to be upset. I'm sure the news that the Forgotten Prince over here defiled his favorite possession will be more than adequate fuel for his fire." He released me, flipping the dagger in the air, catching it by the blade and handing it back to me. "It was an adorable effort, I assure you, but try something like that again, and last time will feel like child's play."

I yanked the dagger from his hold, my temper fuming. "I am not a possession. Stefan does not own me." I sheathed my dagger at my side and locked eyes with him, spearing him with a look which promised pain. "Threaten me again, and I promise you it will be me who slits your throat and watches you choke on your own blood. I will have you praying to the Goddess for reprieve, but she will not answer. The only Goddess who will hear your cries will be me, for I will be your Goddess of Death."

He leaned forward with a sneer and grabbed the front of my cloak, pulling me up so I was barely balancing on my toes. He pressed his lips to my ear. "I can't wait to see you try, Princess." Valdin released his hold, shoving me back into the grasp of another guard. "Get on her horse and bind her hands. If she mouths off, gag her."

The guard pushed me forward, urging me to move. His focus was now on Prince Astraeus, who was kneeling, slumped forward, his forearms resting on the ground. Valdin sat there, pinching his chin, a sarcastic gesture to imply he was thinking, which was something I found preposterous—as it required more than one brain cell to produce thoughts. Finally, he heaved a dramatic sigh.

"Tie him and do the same. Prince Stefan will want to perform the execution himself."

I halted in my tracks. "What?" I snapped, whipping around to face the pompous ass with a shit-eating grin on his face.

"Why, the execution of your dear lover here." He gestured to where Astraeus was being hauled to his feet.

"Absolutely not," I argued. "I will not allow him to be killed." As furious as I was at him, I did not want to be the reason he died. I did not want his blood on my hands.

"Still harboring feelings, are we?" he chortled, as if this were friendly banter between mates.

Every passing second in this guard's presence fueled my desire to flay the skin from his bones.

"No." Anger and frustration laced my voice. "Still, I will not have him killed. Killing him would be a mercy, allowing him to escape the guilt and shame of his failure. No, I would have him released, forced to return home to his kingdom knowing he has failed them, living the rest of days knowing he was so close to victory, but in the end, he could not provide." There was a wave of guilt that washed over me as I uttered the statement, because some small part of me didn't believe a word of it. That part wanted him to live, for him to be safe.

An eerie glint in the guard's eyes had me thinking that Rae's psychological torture was a gift to him. He seemed to mull the idea over, weighing the pros and cons of setting him free to live a life racked with guilt or taking him to Stefan to have him killed.

I steeled my spine and infused authority into my voice as I spoke. "As the Princess of Pyrus, the future Queen of Solaria, and your superior, I order you to free him."

Malice, pure hatred and malice, is what I saw in Valdin's eyes, knowing he had no choice but to obey a direct order or risk punishment. He growled angrily as he ordered the guards to let Prince

Astraeus go, and I had a sick feeling I would be paying for this somehow.

With a nod of Valdin's chin, the guards began urging me back to my horse, and as I mounted Freya, Valdin snatched the ropes from the lesser guards' grasps. He motioned for me to hold my wrists together so he could bind them, and when I did, he forcefully shoved them down to the saddle horn. He roughly bound my hands together and then to the saddle; the binding was tight, too tight. Any movement had it digging into my skin, causing abrasions around the circumference of my wrist.

"Comfortable?" he asked, reaching into his pocket to retrieve a kerchief that he dabbed his brow with.

I opened my mouth to tell him the bindings were too tight, but it was a trick. The moment I parted my lips, he took the kerchief and gagged me, cutting off anything I had planned on saying. He called for one of the guards, ordering him to take my horse's reins and charging him with leading Freya to camp. He ordered another to take the reins of Rae's steed, claiming he would make a fine addition to the calvary.

With a few more orders from Valdin, the guards mounted their horses and closed ranks, placing me in the center of the group. By some miracle, if I did escape these bindings, I had no chance of running. Valdin rode to where Astraeus knelt on the ground, hands bound, bleeding and barely conscious. He looked down at him, and with a swift movement, he kicked Rae in the head, sending him sprawled back onto the ground. I watched in shock, unable to do or say anything staring at his lifeless body before a whistle sounded and the horses started forward.

Move, move, move. I silently pleaded. *Move. Let me know you're alive.* As the sun finally dipped below the horizon, extinguishing the flicker of the day's light, we were gone, and I had no idea if Astraeus—*Rae*—was alive or dead.

CHAPTER 30
ASTERIA

I had no idea how long we rode. Eventually, I gave into the exhaustion, wanting to disappear and forget the day's events. When I finally awoke, I was no longer bound to a saddle, but in a tent. I looked around, trying to discern my surroundings, but it was dark, and the only source of light were the quickly-dying embers of a fire near the center. I moved to sit up, bringing my arms up from over my head, but I was abruptly stopped when cold metal bit into the already-torn skin on my wrist. Shackles. I had been shackled to something. *Wonderful.* I rolled, testing to see how much leeway I had, and it wasn't much. I froze when I sensed movement from the other side of the tent.

"Evening, Princess." *Valdin, great.* "That little prince of yours must have really worked you hard and wore you out. You've been asleep for a day and half."

A day and a half? There's no telling where we were or how far we could have gotten in that time. That was going to make escaping exponentially harder, and *much* harder for Rae.

Rae. Was he alive? If he was, would he find me? Did I want him to? It was no secret that I was furious with him, and I most definitely planned on kicking his ass when I saw him again...*if* I saw him again. My stomach rolled; I still had so much to process, and I didn't even know where to start. That was a lie—I did know where to start, and I began plotting out my steps:

1. Figure out our location
2. Escape
3. Get back to the Dead Mountains and find Asphodel
4. Find out if Rae was alive
5. Kick Rae's ass if he was alive
6. Learn about this prophecy and all the things Rae had promised to tell me
7. Return to Solaria, kick Stefan's ass, and kill the jackass sitting in the dark watching me like some kind of fucking pervert.

"I hope you don't mind." He leaned forward so the embers illuminated his face just enough to make him look more manic than usual. "I took it upon myself to help you get more comfortable by getting you out of those filthy clothes."

It was at that moment I realized I was naked under the furs.

"You fucking beast," I spat at him, attempting to wriggle deeper into the furs despite already being concealed.

"Don't worry," he chuckled. "I didn't do anything your betrothed wouldn't approve of. He's made it very clear that to try anything of that nature ensures we lose a hand or two."

"Where are we?"

He cracked his knuckles and sat back in the chair. "We've almost crossed the barrens of Nyxtas."

That was promising; we were far, but not so far that I couldn't find my way back to the Dead Mountains. I shifted, wincing at the sting of the metal rubbing my raw skin.

"Do you think you could unshackle me? Possibly give me clean clothing, food, water?"

He stood from his spot and stalked over to me, the faint light distorting his features. Instead of leaning down to unlock the shackles, he straddled me, shifting in a way that ground himself over my sensitive flesh. Even with the furs acting as a barrier, the act sent a vile chill through my body. He leaned down, coming face to face with me as he slid the key into the lock without turning it.

"If you try anything, Princess, I will not be responsible for the actions I take to keep you from running. Understood?" He waited for a response, and I stared at him, contemplating my options.

I could try and run, but with no clothes, no weapons, and no idea where in the barrens we were, much less where in the camp I was, I knew my time to escape was not tonight.

I answered him with a curt nod of my head, and he turned the key. The shackles emitted an audible click, and the cool metal fell from my wrists. He lingered on top of me, as if he was waiting to see if I had lied about my understanding.

"Clothing, food, water?" I reminded him with a sneer, and he roughly pushed off the makeshift bed.

"There are clothes at the foot of the bed. Breakfast will be served in two hours when the sun begins to rise. Water is to your right." He returned to his spot in the chair in the opposite corner of the tent.

"Privacy?" I sat up, hugging the furs close to my body as I brought my wrists to my chest, massaging them. They would need ointment, and I had some in my satchel. "Where are my belongings? I have a satchel of salves and ointments." I could just barely make out his form in the dark, pointing to a small pile of belongings near the water.

"If you think you're getting any privacy, you are mistaken. I plan to keep you in eyesight at all times until I hand you off to your precious betrothed."

Pulling the tunic from the pile of clothing, I shrugged it over my head, making sure to keep myself covered. Not that it mattered; he had seen me when he stripped me bare and shackled me to the bed, but the thought of him watching me dress made me nauseous.

"When will that be?" I questioned, thinking it would give me an idea of how many more days of travel I had before reaching Solaira, how many days I had to plan my escape.

"This evening."

I halted my dressing. "What do you mean, this evening?"

He chuckled lowly. "He is awaiting our arrival at the main camp this evening. I hear he has quite the homecoming planned for you."

Shit. Tonight. Once I was back in Stefan's hands, my chances of escaping were very, very slim—as if they weren't already.

I felt the panic start to creep in, but I kept my face neutral as I finished dressing under the cover of the furs. When I was clothed, I fetched my satchel and poured myself a cup of water, guzzling it down. I hadn't realized how parched I was, and I quickly poured myself another one, drinking it down quicker than the first. I poured myself a third glass, but I set it aside for later.

I dug through my satchel until I found what I was looking for: another tin of the same healing ointment I had given to Rae the day we escaped the guard in Harmonia. Opening the tin, I rubbed some between my palms, warming it before massaging it into my wrists. The smell of the herbs had an instant calming effect on my nerves, and the camphor quickly got to work relieving the pain. I breathed a sigh of contentment when the pain subsided, and I could move my hands without wincing. I looked up at the corner of the tent, feeling Valdin's eyes tracking my movements.

"Don't you sleep?" I asked sarcastically.

I heard him shift in his spot. "Only if you're asleep and restrained."

That was a comforting thought. I glanced towards the entrance of the tent, but I couldn't detect any fragments of light peeking through the flaps to indicate dawn was here. Not sure what to do, seeing as I wasn't going anywhere without my watchdog and I had no interest in making small talk with him, I settled on trying to get some more sleep. I knew I would need to be well rested if I planned on trying to make it back to Asphodel.

I laid on my side turning so my back was facing the lurker in the corner. A cool breeze blew through the tent, the flaps snapping in the wind. I shivered and pulled the furs up, tucking them under my chin. I clenched my eyes shut, pushing away the feeling of dread trying to suffocate me. I had twelve hours, probably less, until Stefan's talons were back under my skin, and I had a feeling that he had no plans of allowing me to escape them this time. How was I going to get out of this? My mind raced through every possible plan, and all of them ended with me back in his possession. Despite my efforts, tears began to break past my tightly-closed lids, rolling down my cheeks, wetting the pillow beneath my head.

I must have eventually fallen back asleep, because I was awoken by the rough nudging of a boot on my back.

"Up, Princess." If I never heard his voice again, it would be a blessing. "Eat quickly. Camp is packed, and it's time to move."

I sat up, wiping the sleep from my puffy eyes. When I opened them, there Valdin stood, holding out a tin of room temperature oatmeal for me.

"You have ten minutes to prepare to leave. I suggest you move quickly. Anything not loaded by then is left behind."

"What?" I questioned, my brain still groggy from sleep.

"If you can't carry it, you can't take it. It's not a difficult concept to grasp, Princess. Now, move." He dropped the tin of food on the ground, its contents splattering in my face and all over the furs still covering me.

The sound jarred me from my half-asleep state, and I began

absorbing his words. I threw back the covers, searching the tent for my boots. When I found them, I shoved them on quickly and went straight to the pile of belongings. I threw my satchel of medicine across my body and donned my cloak, knowing how chilly the ride would be. I sifted through the pile, looking for my dagger and the thigh sheath that had come with it. When I couldn't find it, I began frantically tearing apart the tent while Valdin just stood there, watching with amusement.

"Where is my dagger?" I shouted angrily as I stalked over to him, straightening my spine and locking eyes with him, refusing to cower.

"Hmmm," he hummed deeply, the sound vibrating in his chest. "Dagger? What dagger?"

"Do not play games with me, guard," I refused to use his name, instead calling him by his post: a royal guard, sworn to protect the crown and its descendants, reminding him that he answered to me.

"Oh, right." He reached under his cloak, unsheathing my dagger from the bandolier across his chest. "This dagger. I didn't think it would be wise allowing you to be reunited with your intended while armed."

A growl of frustration and anger rumbled in my throat as I reached to reclaim my dagger. Predicting my reaction, he raised his arm, holding the dagger just out of my reach.

I hardened my tone, refusing to cower. "Return it to me. Now."

He stepped back, returning the dagger to its place across his chest. "Our little traitor developed a bite during her time away." Patting the dagger he smirked, "No, I think not. I think I will let Prince Stefan decide if you deserve it."

The sound that escaped from my mouth was unlike any sound I had made before. I launched forward, bringing my knee up with brutal force that I aimed for his dick. He shifted, taking the hit to his thigh instead as he laughed. A sinister smile spread across his face as he grabbed my wrist, holding me in place while he brought his knee to my midsection.

I fell to the ground with a loud thud as the air left my lungs, and I leaned forward on my knees, a hand cradling my stomach. I wheezed, trying to breathe, but my lungs would not work as I fought for air. My vision began to tunnel and my fingers began to tingle, my body starving for oxygen. My forehead fell forward, resting on the cold ground, when the heel of a boot crashed into my ribs, causing me to lose what little balance I had. It was as if that impact reset my system, and I gasped, taking in a deep, raspy breath. I stayed there on the ground, curling into myself and panting as I caught my breath.

"I warned you what would happen if you tried me again, Princess." I had pinched my eyes closed, stopping me from seeing him as he leaned forward, grabbing the nape of my neck and hauling me up to my feet. His grip was unrelenting, and I whimpered in pain. "Do not fuck with me again, or it will be the last thing you do." He released his hold and stalked out of the tent. "Your ten minutes are up. We're leaving."

I followed silently behind him, my breath shaky and uneven. We joined the rest of the guard mounting their horses to leave, and I found Freya, her reins tied to the saddle horn of the same guard from the previous day. I put my right foot into the stirrup and hauled myself up, throwing my left leg over and seating myself in the saddle. The guard manning Freya's reins cleared his throat to gain my attention. When I shot him a disgusted look, he motioned for me to place my hands on the saddle horn so he could bind them again. I complied silently, not looking to give him or anyone else a reason to injure me today.

He tightly bound my hands, albeit not as tightly as Valdin had, and thankfully, he decided to forgo the gag. I heard a command shouted from the front of the ranks, and the horses began moving. I attempted to swallow the lump that had formed in the back of my throat as fear and dread washed over me; every part of me knew how this was the end. I might as well have been a criminal climbing the stairs to the gallows. I knew there was no getting out of this.

Whatever Stefan had planned for me would have me begging for death.

CHAPTER 31
ASTERIA

Twilight was just starting to fall as we reached the camp. We had ridden through the day, stopping only a handful of times so the horses could drink and rest before continuing on. I hadn't been able to eat, my stomach was in knots and my throat choked with fear. When we crested the final hilltop and the glowing lights from the fires below signaled we had reached our destination, I was swallowed with a sense of impending doom.

This is it, I thought. *This is my demise.* I tilted my head back, staring at the dim purple sky above us. *Please Goddess, if you're there, please help me*, I prayed to the stars that shone in the sky. They twinkled lightly as if to say, *I hear you.* Even so, I knew that there would be no help for me. The only person who would be able to help me was me, and I had no idea how I was going to do that. The horses began down the hill, the downward slope almost toppling me out of the saddle had it not been for the bindings around my wrist.

We approached the camp, rows of tents with soldiers sitting outside, chattering and eating. They stopped to look up at us as we navigated our way around them, as the soldiers with us began to break off and head in the direction of their own tents until it was just Valdin who accompanied me.

With each step closer to the tent I knew housed Stefan, the sense of doom grew, burrowing its way deeper beneath my skin, coupling with my icy fear. My breathing became erratic, and tears threatened to fall. How had I gotten here? How had I gotten so close to freedom to end up right where I had started, under Stefan's merciless thumb? The muscles in my body tensed as the horses slowed to a halt at the front of the tent. Moments later, the flaps of the tent were pushed open, and Stefan emerged, standing tall as he looked at me. I tried to decipher the look in his eyes, in his pleasant smile, like he was the concerned fiancé who had just gotten his lover back. It was his eyes, though—they held something dark, something swirling beneath them that I couldn't place, and that was utterly terrifying.

"Asteria, my love, you've returned to me," he said joyfully as we walked to stand beside my horse. He reached up to caress my face, and I flinched, withdrawing from his touch.

He placed a hand on my leg, and in that moment, it was as if his touch erased everything I had spent the last few months learning, and I was that same helpless victim. The upward twitch at the corner of his mouth told me he knew exactly how I felt.

"Let's get you inside and cleaned up." He began to loosen my bindings, just enough to remove my hands from the saddle horn. "Surely you must be famished and in need of a warm wash. Don't worry, my wife, I'll take care of you." His honeyed tone was laced with something evil that sent my hair standing on end.

He lifted me out of my saddle, helping me to dismount before placing his hand at my lower back, his other hand holding the rope that bound my hands as he led me into the tent.

The tent was larger than any tent I had stayed in before, lavishly decorated in golds and oranges, a large pallet of furs rested in the corner with a large wooden chest at the foot. A writing desk covered in correspondence sat on the opposite corner while a fire blazed in the center, casting a ballet of shadows and lights dancing along the sides of the tent. But it was what sat just beyond the flames that had my heart pounding in alarm: in the center of the tent, just a few feet from the fire, stood two towering wooden posts. Near the tops of the posts hung shackles—they were bolted into the wood, ensuring no amount of struggling or fighting would free them. Beside them was a table; I couldn't make out what was laid out atop it, but I had a sinking feeling I didn't want to know.

My voice trembled as I spoke. "What is that?"

"Oh, no need to worry about that now. I think it's time we had some dinner, wouldn't you agree?" he asked, as if to try and placate me, though it sounded more condescending than anything.

He pulled out the chair to a small table and motioned for me to sit. I did as he wanted, not able to tear my eyes from the spot beyond the flames. The sound of Stefan clearing his throat as he seated himself broke my attention, and I looked over the table at him. I realized there were two covered plates, one in front of each of us.

He leaned over, removing the cover from my plate, and I was instantly greeted with the scent of chicken and roasted vegetables. The smells had my mouth watering; I couldn't remember the last time I had a meal like this. He leaned back, removing the cover from his own plate before he picked up his silver cutlery and began to eat. I looked around and realized I had no cutlery of my own. Confused, I looked up to find Stefan watching me while silently chewing his food. He must have sensed my thoughts because he swallowed his food.

"Until we've talked and I can feel confident you're not going to try anything stupid, like try to kill me or escape, I am keeping away all things you might think to use as a weapon. Now eat—we have much to discuss."

I decided it would be pointless to argue, so I wasted no time lifting my still-bound hands to my plate and picking up the chicken leg. I tore into the meat, moaning from the flavor; it had been at least two months since I had anything this flavorful. I was ravenous, shoveling food into my mouth as quickly as my body would allow. Stefan just sat there, staring indifferently. He either did not care, or he had mastered the art of keeping all his emotions separate from his expression. The manipulative bastard.

When I finished, I picked up the napkin next to my plate and wiped the grease and oils from my mouth. I had not realized how badly I was starving, and now that I had eaten so much, I felt bloated and uncomfortable. Stefan's plate had been cleaned, but he ate with the decorum and manners expected of nobility. He sat back, his hands crossed over his chest while his gaze traced over me, inspecting me. Suddenly he stopped, focusing on the base of my neck, his eyes locked on something. My heart began to race as I realized he was staring at the mark left by Raes teeth, the yellow shadow of his claim on me from that morning. He said nothing, but I could see the emotions boiling behind his eyes.

Fury, rage, malice, jealousy. The silence was deafening. It was then that I noticed his hands were balled into fists, his knuckles drained of color from the force he was putting into restraining himself. I examined his face, the tension that set his features. His jaw was clenched, his lips pulled into a thin line, and his brows were slightly furrowed.

He moved then, striking me across the face with enough brutality that it knocked me out of my chair. I had been so distracted examining the fine details of his rage that I hadn't seen him move. He was on me seconds later, standing over me like a monster.

His form was large thanks to his broad shoulders and tall stature. He was built of pure muscle, fueled by his desire to inflict pain. He bent down, grabbing me by the hair at the crown of my head, dragging me across the ground. I yelled out in pain, kicking out and flailing, screaming for help, but with my hands still tied, there was not much I could do.

He dragged me to the space between the posts and released my hair, but before I had time to react, he kicked, his boot colliding with my ribs. I hollered, curling in on myself to trying protect my ribs and head from another blow. With my face covered, I did not see him lean down, grabbing my wrists, hauling me so that I sat on my knees.

Pain shot through my side from the kick, and I felt the warmth of blood dripping from my nose. I tried to fight back, but that just earned me a knee to my spine that sent my head flying back. He took hold of my bound hands, raising them above my head before removing a dagger and slicing through the bonds in a single, swift motion. My hands free, he grabbed one, quickly slapping the manacle from one post around it before moving to do the same to the other.

From there, I knew the night would only get worse. My head was spinning as it fell forward. My shoulders ached from the distance and stress the chains put on them, pulling them just more than they could go. My thoughts were racing, but none of them were a solution to the situation. Instead, they were focused on the pain Stefan had inflicted. I could feel Stefan shifting behind me, and then his head was behind mine as he leaned forward, his hot breath heating the side of my face.

"I told you: you belong to me." He traced the shell of my ear with his tongue, sending a wave of nausea through me. "I will teach you what happens when you disobey, Asteria. You will learn your place. You will learn to fall in line, or you will suffer."

His threat made me rage inside. I did not belong to him, and I never would. I dropped my head slightly more, and then, with all my strength, I threw it back, the loud crack confirming I had made contact.

"You fucking bitch!" he seethed. Walking in front of me, he clutched his nose—I had broken it. For a moment, a small part of me smiled, but when he looked at me, I knew all I had done was feed the fire of his anger.

I dropped my head as he stomped towards me, stopping when I was looking at the toes of his boots. He squatted, roughly grasping my jaw and forcing my head up. Blood trickled down his face from his nose, but the expression on his face wasn't one of anger. No, it was much, much worse. His smile stretched from ear to ear, his teeth coated in his own blood, and his eyes seemed to light with something sinister. He had seen my action as a challenge, a refusal to obey him, and that just made him more determined to break me.

"You really are a stupid little cunt, aren't you?" he asked through the gritted teeth of his smile. "Tell me, did you give it up to that bastard prince willingly, or did he have to force it from you like I did?"

"Fuck you!" I spat at him; he was not going to get any information out of me.

He crushed his bloody mouth to mine, clenching my jaw tighter so that I opened my mouth to cry out in pain, and he took the opportunity to drive his tongue in. The taste of him was acrid and bitter, like a poison, and I fought to pull back, to free myself from his touch, but the chains held me in place. As I began to fight for air, he released me, and I inhaled before spitting Stefan's blood from my mouth, the bitter taste lingering.

"So," he said with a smile, but I could see the muscles in his jaw tensing, holding in his rage. "Did you let him fuck you?"

I refused to look up at him, refused to answer his question. It was not his business what I chose to do with my own body. I remained silent, and he stood, pacing a trail in front of me. I focused on my breathing. Inhale, *pain is temporary,* exhale, *you will survive.* Inhale, *Stefan is just a man, not a god.* Exhale, *you will rip him limb from limb if you survive this. No, not if—when.*

The thought brought me a little peace, and the pain seemed to improve slightly, but it was then I realized he had stopped pacing and was standing over me now. I looked up at him as he reached down, cupping my face gently, like he hadn't nearly just broken my jaw. He brushed his thumb along my cheek as he kneeled before me. I wanted to pull away from his touch, but for a moment, the tenderness was comforting, and I stupidly allowed myself to fall into his trap.

"Tell me, love: did he forcefully take what's mine, or did you stupidly give it away?" His voice was calm, but in no way was it hiding the anger filling his eyes.

I looked up at him through narrowed eyes. "I am not yours."

I pulled my face from the hand he used to cradle it, refusing to allow him to think I would break after a few gentle touches and softened tones. His eyes went dark, and as quickly as he had deigned to offer false kindness, he unleashed. His hand reared back, and all I could do was flinch as the back of his hand and knuckles cracked against my face, splitting my lip. He reached up with a sneer, grasping my clothing at the neck and ripping straight down, exposing me to him.

"Did he have to restrain you like this?" he questioned as he cupped my breast, tracing kisses along my shoulders. He stopped when he reached the mark on my neck, and growl of carnal rage rumbled though his chest before he bit down. Breaking the skin he replaced the mark with his own, erasing Raes claim. My skin paled at his touch, and tears rolled down my face like the tide crashing upon the beach as I cried out, pleading with him to stop.

"Please," I sobbed. "Don't do this. I'm begging you Stefan, please."

He continued his exploration of my body, running his hands down my sides and gripping me, pulling my lower half closer to him so I could feel his arousal through his pants. The tears flooded my vision, and I choked on my own sobs, snot coating my upper lip.

"Please, don't do this. Don't make me do this again." The words were uneven and barely above a whisper as he traced his fingers along the hem of my pants.

My pulse swelled, pounding so hard, I thought my heart may beat out of my own chest. I couldn't hear anything, couldn't feel anything. My body had gone numb; my *mind* had gone numb. I turned my head to the side, repeating my pleas in a low voice as he tore at the opening of my pants, sliding his hand down to feel my center.

"I bet you got wet for *his* fucking cock, didn't you?" He began rubbing at my entrance, trying to elicit a response from my body, but it refused to give him what he wanted. "Stupid fucking slut." Removing his hand he stood and spat, "It's fine—I want to make sure you remember what happens if you try to run, incase you think of trying again. I want the pain of your disobedience to forever be etched into the fiber of your being," he said in a low voice before disappearing behind me.

The sound of what was left of my shirts being torn from my body brought on a new round of sobs. I was bare to him, tied up and on display for his viewing pleasure. I could do nothing—I was at his mercy. But Stefan had no mercy; he was every bit as cruel and wicked as he was rumored to be. I thought his redeeming quality was that he kept his hands clean, having his guard dog dole out punishments for him, but I was wrong. He was equally sadistic as Valdin. They really did make the perfect pair.

"I am going to ask you again, Princess: did you fuck him? And before you speak, know that for each lie that escapes your mouth, you will be punished." His voice didn't sound like his own; no, it was dark, excited. He was getting off on the thought of punishing me. "So, what is your answer?"

I remained silent. I would not speak. Moments later, I screamed out in pain as the lash of a cat o' nine tails lanced down my back. Pain like I had never experienced wrecked every nerve in my body as I arched back from the impact. I couldn't breathe, my lungs seizing from the pure agony.

Over the sound of my cries, I heard Stefan yelling, "Did you fuck him?"

I had forgotten how to speak. I couldn't remember how to form words, and before I could remember, he delivered another lash. I screamed again, this time louder than the last. The pain was like fire invading my body, burning the skin on my back.

"Yes!" I screamed. "Yes!" I pulled at my restraints despite knowing it was pointless. I pulled and pulled, the movement sending new shockwaves of pain down my back.

"Did you like it?" he questioned. I knew the answer he wanted to hear, so it was the answer I offered.

Between sobs, I shook my head. "No."

Crack. The whip came down, twice this time.

"Don't lie to me!" Stefan screamed, loud enough to drown out my own. "Did you like it when he fucked you?"

I shook my head again, not wanting to admit how good it had felt to have Rae inside me, how badly I had desired to have him for the rest of my life. Two more lashings came; my back burned, and the skin split beneath the tails of the whip. My screams were so loud, I questioned if it was just I who was screaming. There was a long pause before Stefan spoke again, the silence filled with my pointless cries, mixed with the sounds of my tears and blood dripping onto the cold, firm ground. My body was trembling from the cold, mixing with the warmth of the blood that flowed from the injuries and the icy stabs of the air on the open wounds.

Stefan stood behind me, and I could feel his presence looming, soaking in the sight of me bleeding on my knees before him, memorizing every detail. He yanked my head back by my hair and stared down at me with black eyes. I whimpered in his grasp, my face red and wet from my tears. His jaw was tense, and his lips pressed into a thin line as he forced my head back even further, straining my neck to the point of pain. He leaned down, dragging his tongue across my cheek, lapping up the tears and blood before he smiled.

"Did you like it," he paused as he trailed his tongue across my lips, sucking on the split before biting it, "when he fucked you?"

I nodded my head, not daring to speak the words.

"Say it," he demanded. When I remained silent, he dug his knee into my injured back and forced my head back so far, I thought he may break my neck.

I whimpered. "Please, Stefan, please, stop."

He cocked his head to the side slightly, as if he were pondering my request. His hold on my hair lessened slightly, and he removed his knee from my back. Relieved, I sighed deeply, allowing the air to fill my unrestricted lungs. Stefan waited behind me, watching me, waiting for the moment when I breathed a deep breath before he kicked, forcing all the air I just inhaled out of my lungs. He struck again and I barreled forward as far as the chains would allow me. The agony was so unbearable, I couldn't even scream as I felt the bone snap. My rib had broken and the pain was indescribable. I struggled for air, wheezing and rasping as my chest heaved. Behind me, I heard Stefan laughing, the sound growing louder as he approached me from behind.

"When I ask you a question, you answer it with your words. Understood?"

I was barely able to get the word *yes* out before his thumb was in one of the wounds on my back, pressing into the flesh, wrenching a scream from my throat. His breath brushed against my ear again.

"Did you like it?"

"Yes," I mumbled.

The answer was true, but that didn't stop the next round of punishment. He stood, quickly and forcefully landing a cession of kicks to my side, each one more brutal than the last. When he finally stopped, I couldn't cry anymore, couldn't scream. I was choking and coughing up my own blood. My mind tried to shut it all out, but he wouldn't let me shut down, wouldn't let me escape. If he saw me drifting out of consciousness, he delivered another lashing. I began to wonder if there was any flesh left covering my spine. I hung lifelessly, blood, saliva, and tears falling to the ground and mixing with the soil.

I thought of the events that led me here. It was always here, no matter what choices I had made, could have made, would have made. They all ended here. Maybe not in this tent, maybe not these questions, but it was always going to be by Stefan's hand that I met my demise. I knew that now. I wanted to give up, to slip into the twilight and let the Goddess claim me, to take my place among the stars, but he wouldn't let me. He had plans for me. For now, I was a toy for him to torture, and later, a womb for his child. Eventually, I would escape him by way of death.

It just wouldn't be tonight.

CHAPTER 32
ASTRAEUS

I awoke to the sound of my sister's voice as she stood above me, shaking me. "Rae? Rae? Open your eyes!"

When I did, I stared up at the star-laden sky. I did not know how long I had been out, but it was already too long. I looked at the body now kneeling beside me, holding a lit torch that illuminated her soft face. My younger sister, eyes shining a bright jade green, as she stared at me, her face tight with concern.

"Ardisia." I sat up, my head throbbing from the repeated impacts. "What are you doing here?" I asked, looking at her young features. She would always look so young to me. I surveyed the clearing I had been laying in, trying to remember what all had happened. Then, it came flooding back to me: Asteria and I had been readying to head into the Dead Mountains to cross over into Asphodel when the Solaria and Pyrus royal guards ambushed us. I began to try to stand, swaying slightly as my sister grabbed my arm to steady me.

"I think it's me who should be asking that," she said, her tone hard. "A scout came bursting into Father's office, telling us that you had been ambushed, injured, and left for dead. We gathered a search parties immediately. What happened?"

I leaned forward, my world spinning as I began to quickly recount the events.

"They told her who I was, and she left with them." My stomach turned at the memory of Asteria learning my true identity. The betrayal and hurt in her expression had felt like my own heart had been ripped from my chest and ground into pulp. "I have to go to her. I have to find her." I straightened, noticing the small group of Asphodel soldiers on the edge of the clearing.

"Are you mad?" Isa argued back. "You need to be taken to a healer. You need to come home. Father needs you to come home. He needs to know what happened, and I need to know that you are okay."

"No." I shoved her hand from my shoulder. "I have to find her. I have to save her. I promised her I wouldn't let her fall back into his hands." I laced my fingers, locking them behind my head and staring up at the stars as I began to slowly walk in a small circle, trying to make a plan.

"You can find her after you've come home and healed." She moved to place her hand on my shoulder, but I stepped away.

"No," I yelled, terror and panic filling my senses. "You don't understand. She won't survive him, and I.." I paused as the deep realization of what I felt hit me. "I won't survive without her."

Isa stepped slowly towards me, grasping my hand gently as she caught my gaze. "What do you need me to do?" she asked. It was all I needed to spring into action.

"I need a horse. Go back to Father and tell him I need more men. I am going to ride ahead to find her. They will be headed back towards Solaria. I just pray they haven't gained too much ground and that I can still catch them before they cross the border of Nyxtas. Gather forces and meet me at the northernmost end of the barrens. Tell the healers to prepare for our arrival and tell Father...

tell him I found her. Tell him we will get our magic back, that our people will survive." I mounted one of the soldiers' horses and looked down at my sister who stood there, handing me the reins.

"Please be careful, Rae. Our people need you," she said before she stepped back, allowing me room to kick off.

"No," I said. "Our people need a miracle, and I intended to bring her back no matter the cost. Without her, our kingdom is doomed anyways."

I yelled, my heel kicking into the horse's side, setting it into a sprint as I rode off into the night to find her. My Little Star. My miracle. My love.

CHAPTER 33
ASTERIA

Stefan was again kneeling before me, reaching out to grab my jaw and force my gaze to his. He reached into his boot and pulled out the dagger he had used to cut my binding earlier—the dagger he held was mine. He wielded my dagger, the one I had grown attached to, the one I learned to fight with, the one I had imagined slitting his very throat with. He held it in front of my face, and I stared at it, tracking its movements as he taunted me.

"Such a marvelous dagger," he started. "Very rare, but not quite one of a kind. Do you know where this dagger came from?"

I coughed, my blood spattering his face, but he didn't seem to notice. "The market in Harmonia." I managed to form the words despite his hold on my face.

"Ahhh," he said as if realizing something. "No, you see that is where you got the dagger, but it is not where it was made, where it was forged. This," he said, twirling it by the handle, "is from Asphodel, the kingdom of your bastard prince. I assumed he had given it to you, but apparently, I was wrong. You see, the metal this dagger is forged from can only be mined from the Dead Mountains.

"Even were we to successfully find and mine the metal, we would not be able to use it. This is gifted from the Goddess to her precious race of magic folk. To forge and use this metal, you must be a descendent of that race. Their magic was able to flow into and combine with the little purple veins you see running through the blade. It helped them to focus their powers, to magnify them, making them nearly unbeatable. It's said to never dull, no matter its age or use, a theory I would like to test."

His eyes shifted to mine. "We're going to play a little game. Here are the rules: I am going to start counting, and when I get to the number of times you let that fucking heathen defile you, that will be how many times I test this little theory."

He dropped my head and stood, walking behind me to the table housing his tools he laid out to torture me with. I hadn't been able to make it out earlier, but it was obvious now.

"Now, since I know you have a compulsion to lie to me, I will ask you once without aid. Then, I will ask you a second time. The third time, though, we have assistance to ensure your honesty." He kneeled back down, holding something strange in his hand. "Now, I'm going to start counting, and you say stop when we get to that magic number. One."

"Stop," I said weakly, and he lifted my head and stared into my eyes, as if searching for the lie.

"No." He dropped my head. "You're lying. Try again. One, two."

"Stop." This time, it came out more like a plea than a statement. He lifted my face, examining my expression again.

"No. You just can't help but lie, can you?" *Tsk, tsk, tsk,* he clicked his tongue, his hand revealing a syringe. "I spent some time working with the healers on this little concoction. It took a long time, but eventually we perfected it. I have been using it for years to interrogate prisoners. Truth serum; ever heard of it?" Before I could protest, the needle was sliding into my neck, and the burn of the serum entering my bloodstream cause me to thrash.

"It is incredibly painful, working its way through your entire body, your nerves feel like they're burning. Then, you feel like your limbs are going rigid, and before you know it, you have no control over your tongue. You will tell me anything and everything, no matter how badly you fight to stop it."

My body ignited in pain. It was exactly as Stefan said: every nerve in my body began to feel as though it was dipped into scorching coals. I cried out for relief, but none came. It felt like it was going to last forever, but after a few moments, the burning began to subside as my limbs locked up. It was as if I had been paralyzed. I could not move my arms or legs, and I began to panic. It felt as though I was locked into my own body; I willed my extremities to work, but they would not listen, would not even try.

"Last try, Asteria." He brushed the tears from my face. "How many times did you let him fuck you? One, two, three..."

My jaw was locked. I couldn't form words, so a strangled noise escaped my throat, and a fresh wave of tears poured down my face.

"That wasn't so hard, was it? Feels good to tell the truth, does it not?"

He stood, turning to the entrance of the tent, but instead of leaving, he went to the writing desk. He retrieved a small mirror and pulled one of the chairs from the dining table over to where I sat on my knees, unable to move, restrained and still paralyzed from the serum. I tried to crane my head up at him as he sat, my neck still stiff—but it was wearing off.

Reading the confusion in my expression, he leaned forward. "I'm waiting until the physical effects wear off. I want to hear every sound you make during this next part."

His lips pulled back into an evil smile, and a renewed sense of panic and dread washed over me. When he sat back, spreading his legs wide, I saw the evidence of just how much he enjoyed my torture. His erection strained against the seams of his trousers, and the sight of it disgusted me. He used the tip of his boot to lift my chin to his eyeline.

"Don't worry, love. You'll learn to enjoy the pleasure I offer as well." I shuddered at the thought, and he leaned forward, holding the mirror in front of my face. "Take a look at yourself."

My face was bruised and swollen, my right eye discolored from the broken blood vessels, turning the white of it red. My lower lip was split, blood still oozing from the wound. I cringed at my own appearance, hardly able to recognize the face that stared back at me. I dropped my head, unable to muster the strength to hold it up any longer.

I was weak, I was tired, and the amount of blood I had lost had drained the color from my skin. I both felt like and resembled a corpse, a hollowed out and empty shell of the person I had been only three days before. My muscles began to release, and I felt everything—every cut, every broken bone, every bruise. It overwhelmed my senses, and all I could do was cry. I slumped forward, my arms holding the weight of my body as they stretched out behind me, the metal of the manacles cutting into my wrists, the blood flowing down my forearms. A low rumble came from Stefan's chest; it started deep before turning into laughter, a laugh sinister enough to blanch even the devil's flesh.

"I think it's time to finish up, don't you?" he asked, his voice soft, sweet, the fabricated concern rolling off him like a bead of water on a window. I wouldn't be fooled by his honeyed words.

"Tell me, my wife," his tone still honeyed, "have you learned your lesson? Do you see now what happens when you disobey me? What your disobedience forces me to do?"

I shook my head. He didn't have to do this. He didn't have do these things, to punish me, to torture me. No, he did this because he wanted to.

"Ah, ah, ah." The tip of my dagger dug into the underside of my chin, digging just deep enough to draw blood and force me to lift my head. I felt every muscle in my body strain to keep my head from pushing into the blade that rested beneath it. "Do you need another lesson?" he asked, sweat rolling down my temple, mixing with the blood and tears that already saturated my skin.

"No," I whimpered, my voice hoarse and weak from my screams. My body shook as I shut my eyes tightly. "No, please. I won't leave. I won't disobey you again."

"That's a good girl," he cooed, replacing the point of the blade with his hand. "Open your eyes, Asteria." His face was a mockery of sympathy and compassion, one he had spent years perfecting.

"I don't want to hurt you," he lied. "I don't want to have to do these things to you, but you have to learn, and you have to remember." He rested his elbow on his knee, holding the dagger in front of me, his eyes tracing the blade as he spoke. "I need to make sure you never forget the lessons you learned here tonight."

He shifted his gaze to my face, and I began to plead and beg as he continued, bringing the tip of the blade to my face above my right eyebrow, just past the inner corner of my eye . I began to cry out as he forced the blade into my skin, and drug it in a line down my face, through the skin below my eye and down by cheek, stopping just above where his thumb rested on my face. I let out a screeching sob, the pain unfathomable, the salt from my tears adding to the fire burning in the gash now marking my face.

"I need to make sure others know they cannot cross me." He clenched my jaw tighter as he brought the blade just right of the cut and began slicing another line down my face. "I can't have people thinking their actions have no repercussions."

I refused to scream, to offer him that satisfaction as he removed the blade just below my cheekbone. My body was trembling uncontrollably now, my blood coating his hands as he held me in place. Placing the dagger at the highest point of my brow, he used enough force that I felt the metal scrape the bone. His tone was more aggressive, more anger filled as he nearly shouted now.

"I can't have people thinking they can touch what belongs to me and get away with it!" The third and last cut was the deepest as he poured his dominance and fury into it.

He panted as he looked at the dagger now coated in my blood, smiling as he brought it to his mouth and licked the blade, tasting my blood. He sheathed the dagger back in his boot and held up the mirror to my face once again.

"Look at yourself," he commanded, but I refused to open my eyes. "Look at yourself," he raged, jerking my head towards the mirror.

I opened my eyes slowly, my right eye swelling and obscuring my vision. The left eye could still see mostly normal—it could see the hideous monster now reflected in the mirror. There were three cuts along my face, side by side like tally marks, marring my flesh.

"Three," Stefan said, admiring his work. "Three reminders for each time you let him stick his filthy cock in you and defile what didn't belong to him."

I turned my head, unable to look at my own reflection. He had made sure he had broken my spirit, stripped me of my self-worth, forced me to feel shame in every corner of my being, taking from me the one thing I had never had the chance to willingly give. Now, he had taken all that hate, that shame, that self-loathing and painted it on my skin for all to see. I felt everything then—every physical ailment, every insult I'd ever received, every reprimand, every dirty look, every disappointment, every betrayal. I felt it all. It came crashing down on me, and I shattered. He had won, and he knew it. I stopped then—stopped fighting, stopped feeling. I hung there, lifeless and content to die, when in the back of my mind, I heard a voice.

"Don't give up yet, Little Star," Rae's voice echoed. "Don't you stop fighting. You can't give into the darkness. You have to keep fighting." It was as if my heart shattered all over again.

"I can't," I cried softly. "I can't do it. I can't fight. Please, Rae, just let me die."

The mention of Rae's name caught Stefan's attention from where he stood on the other side of the tent, pouring himself a glass of bourbon. He lifted the glass to his lips, tilting it back and swallowing its contents in one gulp before he slammed the glass on the table. Wiping his mouth with the back of his hand, he prowled towards me, a hungry, predatory look in his eyes.

Rae's voice continued to urge me to fight, to survive, to live, but I shook my head, too tired to fight. Stefan reached me, his anger and arousal palpable as he removed the chains from the post, keeping my wrists shackled. He yanked me back, pulling me off my knees and throwing me onto my shredded back. I screamed out in pain, the agony almost causing me to fade into unconsciousness.

"You worthless bitch," he spat as he continued to drag me back towards the pallet of furs. "You will learn to keep his fucking name from crossing your lips again."

I thrashed, my back searing from the friction as he forced me onto the furs. Keeping the chains in his hands, he climbed on top of me and forced my hands above my head.

"You don't have to do this. Please, Stefan, you can stop. Please stop," I sobbed as he took my dagger from his boot and raised it above his head.

My eyes went wide with fear before I turned my head, not wanting to see the dagger plunging into my flesh. His arm fell with brutality and found its mark, landing between the links in the chain and pinning my hands above my head. I breathed a sigh, and in the moment, I didn't know if it was of relief or disappointment that it had not landed in my chest. My pleas continued, though I knew they would have no impact on my fate; they were empty pleas made to a soulless monster.

Stefan forced my head to the side, displaying the fresh cuts that still bled onto the fur beneath us.

"Do you really think your prince is going to save you? Do you think he would touch you now? You're fucking hideous. Only a monster would want you now." He leaned in, whispering in my ear as he moved to force his free hand beneath the waistband of my pants. "Lucky for you, I am the worst monster of them all."

He plunged a finger inside of me, and I screamed from the viscous force he used to spread my legs. He had removed my bottoms, tossing them aside as he kneeled over me, pumping himself till he was fully and fiercely aroused. He swiped his hand over the wounds on my face, eliciting a pained cry from me, and coated his cock in my blood before he shifted, hovering above my entrance.

"When I'm done with you, the only thing you'll feel when you think of him is fucking pain." Then, he thrusted forward, forcing himself inside me. He began to move, working to find his own pleasure despite my cries of agony. I was about to give over to the darkness, to allow myself to slip into a place where I could feel no more pain, no more hurt, no more of him.

Then, I heard it: his voice calling to me through the veil of shadows. "Little Star, you have to fight like your life depends on it, because it does. You are a goddess. Rise up and take your throne. Fight. Come home to me." The sound of Rae's voice brought me back from the edge, and a wave of determination and strength fortified me. I opened my eyes and glared at the monster on top of me. I would be a victim no more.

"No." My voice cut through his own moans of pleasure. He slowed, caught off guard by my protest.

"What?" he asked, irritated and confused. I kept my eyes locked on his as I reached back, searching for the hilt of my dagger. When I found it, I gripped it tight with both hands, steeled my strength, and repeated myself.

"No."

I used the moment of distraction to my advantage and pulled

the dagger hard, ripping it from the ground and bringing it crashing down on Stefan's head. He grunted in pain, shocked from the sudden impact. I raised my hands, bringing the hilt down once again, this time where his skull met his neck. The hit sent him barreling over onto his side, and I scrambled to my feet. I turned to face him, dagger at the ready, but he did not move. He laid there, seemingly lifeless, his chest barely rising. For a moment, I thought to gut him, leaving his entrails spread out for the guards to find later, but no, the risk of being caught was too high. I had to move fast. I grabbed the tunic Stefan had worn and pulled it over my head. I inhaled sharply at the pain in my back; I did not know the full extent of my injuries, but I knew the adrenaline coursing through my system would only last for so long, and I needed to take advantage of it.

I grabbed a cloak from the back of a chair and threw it on, pulling the hood over my head to conceal my face. I knew the front of the tent would be guarded, and I imagined it would not be long before the silence attracted attention. I crept to the back of the tent, glancing over my shoulder to take one last look at Stefan, ensuring he had not yet moved, and I noticed the blood wetting his hair. I smiled to myself and slipped out of the back of the tent.

Stefan's tent had been placed at the back of the camp, away from the others so his activities would not be disturbed. Luckily for me, it also meant there were less eyes to avoid. I silently crept along the back, peering around the corner, noticing two guards stationed about fifteen feet from the entrance. They seemed to be deep in conversation and unaware of my presence. There were woods that surrounded the encampment, and they would have to be my cover as I made the journey back to the barrens—assuming I made it that far without collapsing.

I was weak, the food I had eaten with Stefan had long been thrown up, and the blood loss and cold weather had my bones rattling. I didn't know how long I had before my body gave up, but

I would rather it give in to the elements and die escaping than be shackled to that sadistic beast. I surveyed my surroundings once more, ensuring my passage into the forest was clear. The snap of a twig from the other side of the tent had me jumping, and I moved quickly, keeping my steps light as I headed straight for the tree line.

Once I was under cover of the forest, I headed north towards the barrens of Nyxtas. I knew the encampment was on the southernmost portion, so heading north would take me back to familiar territory. I shivered in the frigid night air as I trudged through the woods that neighbored the camp. I stayed just far enough inside them to remain concealed, but close enough that I could monitor the activities of camp. The night was still and quiet, making my attempt to stay silent and avoid leaving a trail even more difficult. The wounds wore heavily on my body, weighing down my steps and hunching my shoulders.

I neared the north edge of the camp, approaching the base of the hill we had rode down the previous evening. It looked so much more daunting now that I was drained. I turned my head towards the tents at the sound of yells and alarm—they had found Stefan. I don't know if he was breathing, but the discovery set the entire camp in motion. The yells of the guards and the sounds of the horses being readied sent a new wave of adrenaline coursing through my muscles, pushing me to continue. I wasted no time, using every ounce of my strength to run, crashing through the brush and colliding with the low hanging branches of the trees in my path. I ran, slipping on the cold, wet ground that inclined beneath my feet, the sounds of the chaos growing louder behind me. I clawed at the ground, dirt lodging beneath my nails as I grappled for any assistance. I couldn't risk a backwards glance, not until I had reached the top, and I was so close.

I was fading. I could feel my muscles giving up on me. Tears stung my eyes as I begged my body not to quit, not yet, not now.

My breaths came in rapid succession as I worked to crest the top of the hill, my body slowing with each strained step. I couldn't quit yet. I was close, so close to the top. I could taste the salty wind that whipped across the barrens, feeling its daunting gusts as I looked ahead, seeing the top just there. I dug deep within myself and let out a ragged cry as I pushed off a rock and threw myself into a mockery of a run. It was all I needed to get to the top. Cresting the hill to freedom my body out, and I fell forward. The gravity of the earth pulling me close to its bosom, and holding me there as the lights below flared to life. Fires raged to light the paths through and around the camp, shining brightest at the southern end, where most of the commotion remained. He was alive, then. I should have raged, but I didn't care. I had done what I had wanted: I had escaped, and if this was my last look at the world, then at least it was a free one.

I heard the impact of hooves in the distance behind me, moving quickly towards me. I worried it was a scout from the troops below, so I pushed myself to my feet, gripping my dagger tight. I would not go back there. I would not return to him. I would die fighting. I turned, ready to die battling this foe, but when I faced the stranger, my heart stopped.

In front of me, dismounting a new steed, was Rae. He was here. Tears clouded my vision, and his voice cut through the winds like the sweetest song I had ever heard.

"Asteria?"

"Rae." My reply was lost in the howls of the wind, but it didn't matter—he was here. I ran towards him, crashing into his arms as my legs gave out beneath me. I slumped to the ground as he pulled my in tightly to his chest, and I could hear his heart pounding as loudly as a war drum. I pulled my head back, looking up at him as tears began to flood my bruised and beaten face.

"You found me," I managed to say between sobs, my voice raspy and hoarse from my tortured screams. He cupped my chin, looking down at me, his own eyes brimming with tears. He gently ran his thumb across my jaw, examining the deep cuts that now marked my skin.

"Oh, Little Star." He inhaled deeply, shoving down a sob as he leaned down, placing a soft kiss to my forehead. "You are my true north, and I will always find you." His voice cracked, a mixture of both relief and rage. "My love will always tie me to you, and the stars themselves will burn out before I lose my way to you."

I opened my mouth to reply, but as I struggled to tell him how I felt, darkness swallowed me, and I fell limp in his hold.

CHAPTER 34
ASTRAEUS

I held her in my arms as she struggled to speak, her body broken and weak. She was so cold as I brushed my thumb across her jaw just below her mangled cheek, and as I spoke, her eyes began to flutter, rolling back as she went limp.

Panic surged through me as I cradled her lifeless body and desperately searched for a pulse. I pressed my hand to her chest, feeling and praying for something, any sign of life. I held my breath as I waited for the thrum of her heart beating, and I exhaled when I felt a thumping so faint and weak, it was barely perceptible.

I looked down at her ashen, colorless skin riddled with bruises and cuts, the slices down her cheek and the warmth of her blood saturated the back of her clothing as rage boiled within me. I wanted to gut every single person responsible for her pain, to bleed dry every witness who refused to step in. But now was not the time; she was fading fast, and she needed help.

I lifted her into my arms and returned to my horse. I placed her in the saddle before I settled in behind her. I wrapped my own cloak around her, pulling her tightly into my chest as I looked down the hill at the camp below, a small group of torches moved up the hill towards us. I turned the horse quickly and set off at full speed, racing to meet the soldiers hopefully arriving at the other side of the barrens shortly.

"Hold on, Little Star," I whispered into her ear. "Hold onto my voice. Don't give in; don't leave me. I've got you, Princess. You're safe now." I looked up at the stars above us and begged them to save her. "Goddess, if you have any blessings left to bestow, bestow them to her and give her life. Let her live. Let me love her, let me show her what it is to be loved unconditionally."

Her head fell back, resting on my shoulder as a small groan escaped her lips. The sound was like a breath of air after almost drowning, and I dug my heel deeper into the horse's ribs, telling him to pick up speed. The whistle of an arrow flying past my face startled me, breaking my concentration as I turned my head to look behind us. A small group of mounted royal archers raced behind us, their arrows flying, nearly missing us. I yelled out, pulling on the reins and forcing the horse to change directions. Switchbacks would slow our speed, but it would be the easiest way to ensure we would be missed by the archers. We weaved back and forth unpredictably across the salt barren, keeping as quick a pace as we could. The archers were gaining on us, and sweat coated my palms, causing my leather reins to slip in my grip. I clenched them harder as I tried to shield Asterias body from any incoming arrows.

Her head rolled side to side as we quickly changed directions, but the movement elicited a groan, ensuring me she still lived. We neared the northern border of the barren, and I began to fear my father had refused to send troops to our aid. Maybe Isa hadn't gotten home in time. A sinking feeling began to take hold as I worried we would not make it. I leaned in and brushed a kiss to Asteria's temple.

"I love you, Little Star, and I'm sorry for everything. I hope that in the next life, you find it in your heart to forgive me."

Just as I gave up hope, one after another, a line of lights flared to life along the horizon. My lips pulled back into a smile as a volley of torched arrows launched into the air, aimed at the guards who tailed us.

I sat up tall in my saddle and yelled out the cry of our kingdom. "Donec Tenebris!"

The answering cry rang through the barren like a boom of thunder: "in Astra!"

The shouts were followed by another wave of arrows that lit up the night sky. I looked behind me as the arrows searched for their targets, finding their homes in the chests of two of the guards. The rest of the mounted guards screeched to a halt as the third wave of arrows were released, turning their horses as they fled back towards the camp in the south.

I let out a holler as an arrow struck me from behind, and I could hear the scream of horror escape my sister's mouth as she rode towards us. The arrow had torn into my left shoulder, causing me to drop the reins I held in my hands. I lurched forwards, almost falling out of the saddle and taking Asteria with me. I managed to reach for the saddle horn, holding it with enough strength to keep us from crashing to the ground. I groaned in pain as I righted myself and Asteria back in the saddle, leaning her against my chest.

Ardisia reached our side soon after, reaching to grab the reins and return them to my hold.

"We have to get her to the healers," I grunted through my gritted teeth.

"We need to get *you* to the healers," she insisted as she examined the arrow protruding from my shoulder. "Can you ride?"

"Do I have a choice?" I huffed. The pain intensified with each movement, but it didn't matter. We must forge on. We had to get Asteria to Asphodel. I tried to adjust in the saddle and nearly fell sideways, the arrow hindering my movement. "Pull it," I said to my sister.

"What?" She was clearly shocked at my request.

"Pull it. I cannot ride with it in," I told her.

"I can't pull it. We don't know how deep it is, nor do we know if it is occluding any vessels, stopping you from bleeding out," she argued.

"Damn it, Ardisia! Pull the fucking arrow out!" I screamed at her. "We don't have time to argue, and quite frankly, I don't give a fuck if I bleed out if it means we get Asteria to the healers. So pull the goddess damned arrow out, or I will fucking do it myself!"

She looked at me, stunned at my admission. At the moment, though, I didn't care; she could look at me however she wanted, but this arrow was coming out one way or another, and it was happening now. She hesitated a moment longer, so I began to reach for it with my other hand.

"Stop!" she snapped. "Goddess fucking hell, Rae. If you bleed to death, I'm having the Goddess bring you back so I can fucking kill you again myself. Got it?"

"It's a deal," I grunted.

She rested one hand flat against my spine and wrapped the other at the base of the arrow where it met my flesh.

"Ready?" she asked.

"Just do it." I grimaced and braced for the pain, and with a hard and swift pull, she ripped the arrow from my body. I let out a deep, low growl of pain before reaching up and unclasping my cloak. I hung it around Asteria's shoulders before reaching to rip my sleeve off for my sister to tie up the wound. She tied the makeshift bandage, giving a solid and unnecessary yank to ensure it was tight, eliciting a groan and a nasty look from me.

"Maybe next time, you'll think twice before asking me to do something so fucking idiotic, like risk you bleeding out for a girl," she sneered before she turned and rode off towards the line of guards awaiting us.

My jaw tensed, and I rolled my head, cracking my neck to

relieve the stress there before I started after her. When we reached the line of guards, they bowed their heads in respect, and I returned the gesture.

"We will move fast," I began. "Make for the throughway at the base of the Dead Mountains. We do not stop, no matter what. Your orders are to ensure that this woman in my arms, makes it to Asphodel and to the healers—alive."

Ardisia began arguing, but I quickly cut her off. "That is my final order. She is to take priority over me and anyone else. She is my heart, and the key to our kingdom's survival. Understood?"

In unison, the guards responded, "In Astra," and placed their fists over their hearts. I mimicked their gesture as I echoed them.

We took off, Asteria and me leading the way, the guards following behind in a v formation. We rode without stopping until we reached the base of the Dead Mountains, just as the sun began to light the sky in a deep, fiery orange-red.

"A blood sunrise," Ardisia gasped. "That can't be good."

A blood sunrise only shone on the fields of battle or as an omen to coming war. She was right—it couldn't be good. It meant war was coming to us, and I had a feeling I was holding the key to victory in my arms. We slowed as we breached the forest.

"Be on guard," I ordered as we approached the clearing. The guards drew their swords and others readied arrows on their bows. We proceeded forwards, all on edge as the mountains seemed to hum with a strange and unfamiliar energy.

"Something's changed," I said under my breath to my sister. The hair on my arms stood on end; the Dead Mountains felt as if they had awakened, an ominous energy shifting in the breeze towards us. I looked towards my sister, who met my gaze, her eyes a more piercing green than I had ever seen them. Something was happening. The woods were silent, more silent than normal, as if all wildlife had left, leaving only the plants that seemed talk to one another.

We stayed quiet as we approached the secret throughway under the mountain into Asphodel. As the entrance came into view and I knew we were safe, it was as if my body relaxed, and whatever adrenaline had kept me going diminished.

My grip on Asteria and the reins loosened, and I fell back, unable to muster the strength to hold myself upright any longer. I called out for Asteria as I tumbled off the horse and towards the ground. I landed with a heaviness that knocked the air from my lungs, and the sight of Asteria following me out of the saddle with no one to catch her was the last thing I saw as my vision narrowed and the world went dark.

CHAPTER 35
ASTRAEUS

I awoke to the sterile aroma of the healing wing, hints of the astra flower and healing herbs on the breeze. The morning light filtered through the sheer linen that hung between the beds housing the sick and healing. I moved to raise up, but the stabbing pain in my shoulder had me hissing through my teeth as I fell back onto the mattress.

"I told you to leave it in," Ardisia's voice was soft, bringing my attention to where she sat reading near the head of the bed. "They said pulling the arrow out caused more damage than had you waited and removed it here." She closed her book and leaned forward, resting her hand on my arm. She looked at me, her face was soft but the dark circles under her eyes and the lines that traveled along her forehead told me she had not rested much since we got back.

"I wouldn't have been able to ride if you hadn't pulled it out," I sighed, still feeling weak. "Asteria?" I asked.

"She was in really bad shape, Rae." Her tone was solemn, her eyes dipped, and it felt as if my world had stalled. The color drained from my skin, and ice flooded my veins; she couldn't be telling me that I had failed. I wouldn't believe it. I had lost her, and my world shattered around me as my feelings swiftly shifted from despair and agony to rage.

The ice in my veins quickly melted as fire roared beneath my skin. I shot up, the pain dissolving as adrenaline fueled my movements. Isa stood with me, moving to stand in front of me. She placed her hands on my shoulders, and I stumbled into her, my body too weak to support my weight. She guided me back onto the hospital bed, trying to recenter my focus.

"Rae!" Her voice seemed distant as she tried to speak to me, her hands on my face as she forced me to look at her. "Look at me. She is alive. Asteria is alive."

Everything came back into focus as I inhaled deeply, not realizing I had been panting during my panic. I looked at my sister, her eyes mirroring the panic in mine, and suddenly, I felt guilty for the stress and pain I had put her through I had no idea how long I had been unconscious; I had vague memories of people in white linen working over me, the sounds of my mother crying, my father shouting, but it was all so vague, as if it had all been a bad dream.

"How long have we been back in Asphodel?" I asked.

"Four very long, very stressful days," she answered. "Between you and Asteria, the healers have been running at full steam for four straight days."

I sighed, dropping my head. Four days. I had been back for four days. I had no clue what kind of chaos I had brought back to my kingdom by returning half alive with Asteria, the Princess of Pyrus, future Queen of Solaria, nearly dead herself. I needed to see her, to find out how she was doing, but I also needed to see my father, to report to him, to ask him to help me make a plan. As of right now, I had no idea what to do.

"Where is she?" I asked. "I need to see her."

Isa stood, nodding to one the healers who stood nearby waiting, just in case I lost my wits again. She looped her arm beneath mine so she was supporting me. "She's in bad shape, Rae. You need to prepare yourself. She's made it so far, but she was barely breathing when we got her here." She dipped her head low, as if trying to decide how or if she should deliver her next thought.

"What she's been through... The injuries she sustained, there's no knowing if she's going to wake up, if she *wants* to wake up. What he did to her, Rae, the things he put her through—it was sadistic. She's had fits, like she's stuck in the memory of what happened. Her body is..." Isa took in a sharp breath, her eyes glistening with tears that threatened to escape as her voice softened. "If her mind is nearly as damaged as her body, she may never be the same."

A tear flowed down her cheek, and I knew that thinking of what Asteria suffered had brought back memories of her own trauma. I pulled her into my side, trying to offer her a bit of comfort, but I knew that, despite the time and healing, she was never going to be able to get rid of those nightmares.

We began walking through the corridor lined with small beds dressed in white, gauze like curtains separating them. Most of the beds remained empty, but a few were occupied by villagers who had been brought by family or sought aid themselves. Most of our people were healthy, but as the resources dwindled, those who had suffered ailments before found themselves weaker and more susceptible to illness. There is a good chance we would have been wiped out completely by now were it not for the astra flower, the flower of Asphodel. It had always grown bountiful in our lands; they only grew near the homes of descendants of the Umbra Siderum, or the shadows of the stars, the race of shadow wielders who had long inhabited this land. The healing properties of the astra flower were unmatched by any other herb or medicine available. Our people used it daily, in their teas, salves, medicines, everything. Thank the goddess that the flower had not died out when our magic had.

We reached the end of the corridor and stopped before the door to the intensive corridor of the healing wing. Our most skilled healers worked there, taking care of our most ill and near dying. I shuddered out a breath as I readied myself. I had not been able to assess her damage when she collapsed in my arms. I knew she was hurt, but I had not seen the gravity of her injuries amidst all the chaos that followed. I reached for the door but stopped before the icy cold of the metal handle touched my skin. I didn't know why I was suddenly fearful of seeing her; all I wanted was to see her, to touch her, to let her know that she was safe.

"Are you okay?" The soft and tenuous voice of my sister startled me. "Rae?" she questioned.

I looked down at her, meeting her concerned gaze. Her eyes mirrored mine, only a few shades lighter, and were brimmed with tears. She was worried, and I understood her concern and fears. I had been gravely injured when we returned, and I knew she feared that I wasn't strong enough to handle what lay beyond that door. Maybe she knew that part of me felt the same. Still, I had to go. I had to see her. She deserved to know that she was away from Stefan, that she was free of him, that she survived him. That she was finally safe.

"I'm okay," I said in a not-so-steady breath. "I have to do this. I have to see her, to feel her heart beating and know she's alive. That I didn't put our people in harm's way for nothing."

Ardisia tilted her head in a nod, signaling that she understood. I returned the gesture and turned back towards the door, steeling my spine as I reached for the handle. I looked back at the healer who had been following along.

"Room five, Your Highness." he said with a slight bow of his head.

"I need to do this alone," I said to them both, my eyes fixed on the door in front of me.

"Rae," my sister placed her hand on my shoulder, "I don't think that's a good idea."

I shook my head. "No, I need to be alone for this. I am fine. I was injured, but I am not made of glass. I do not need to be supervised like a child. I am doing this alone. End of story."

Isa withdrew her hand like a viper had just struck her. I knew that my tone had been harsher than necessary, but I could not handle the coddling. I needed some space, and I did not want people hovering and watching me. I knew it came from a place of caring, but it was not what I needed right now.

I straightened my shoulders, suppressing the urge to wince at the sharp pain lancing through my left side at the movement, and opened the door.

CHAPTER 36

ASTRAEUS

As I entered room number five, my breath stuttered at the sight of her. She lay on her side in the bed, facing me, but she was not awake. A healer sat in a chair at her back, applying some sort of ointment to her skin, and she startled at my entrance.

"Oh," the sweet, innocent-faced healer chirped, "Your Highness. I did not know you would be visiting. I'm almost finished here, and I will be out of your way." Her voice sounded as soft and sweet as she looked. Her light copper gold hair was tied back into a low bun, keeping it out of her face while she worked. Her skin was pale and freckled, but her eyes were the striking green of the Umbra Siderum.

"There we are," she lilted, "all done," pulling her lips back into a soft and kind smile. She began to discard her soiled supplies, humming to herself a gentle tune.

"How is she doing?" I questioned, unable to move from my spot at the door, my eyes glued to Asteria.

At first glance, you wouldn't suspect she was anything but sleeping, but as I studied her face, I saw the tension in her jaw, the

344

slight furrowing of her brow, her eyes fluttering slightly as she moaned quietly. It wasn't the moan of someone who was resting peacefully—it was sharp and laced with fear, with pain. She was exactly as Isa had said: stuck in a nightmare. My heart cracked at the sight of her suffering.

"She's healing," the healer said softly. "The wounds she suffered were quite extreme. They are healing well, and quickly too. It's quite a miracle. I've never seen someone with this extensive of injuries heal like this. Even with our care, though, the marks will remain on her skin, and for that, I apologize. Her mind, though... She should have woken up by now. We have tried everything, but we have not had any success. She seems locked in her own terror. She has fits, thrashing and screaming out. We've had to restrain her a few times to keep her from hurting herself, but even then, she seems to be unconscious."

I tore my gaze from Asteria and looked at the healer, who stood near the foot of the bed. "You've done everything you can, and for that, I am indebted to you..." I paused, realizing I hadn't asked for her name.

She extended her hand. "Calliope."

I reached out, shaking her hand. "Thank you, Calliope, for all that you have done."

She inclined her head, accepting the thanks. Releasing her hand, I turned towards the chair that sat next to the head of the bed. I saw it then, the marred skin of her back. Where there had once been a plain of smooth, silky, pale skin now held the mangled flesh of a sadistic bastard's playground. Her back was a mosaic of pink flesh, scars and cuts in every direction, varying in length and depth. Some of the marks had created trenches, where the flesh had been so badly beaten, it had been ripped from her body. Others were raised, undulating plains of pink tissue where the lashing had not cut as deep. It was... horrific. Not because of the appearance—the scars on her flesh held no weight in my adoration of her—but because I knew what she had suffered to get them. This was not just a flogging to punish someone, to reprimand them for going against your orders or wishes. No, this went beyond that, beyond torture, beyond anything I could have believed a person capable of. This was done out of sheer pleasure in hurting another, in dominating them. It was vile, wicked, abhorrent.

My eyes burned with tears as I forced myself to move to the chair next to her face. I sat down, pulling the chair as close to the bed as possible before I pulled back the covers in search of her hands. I found them, her wrists badly bruised and covered in small marks from manacles that had been used to restrain her. I folded her hands into mine as I bowed my head, resting it on our joined hands.

"I am so sorry," I whispered to her. "I am so very sorry, Little Star. For everything."

The stinging in my eyes gave way as the tears began rolling down my cheeks, landing on her skin like a soft rain. She moved slightly, her head turning so that she would be looking at the ceiling were she to open her eyes. I raised my head to look at her, and I stopped moving. Stopped breathing. I could not process what I saw on her face. I reached up, gently touching her face to see if what I saw was real. There on the right side of her face, three pink lines ran the length of her cheek, beginning above her eye and stopping below her cheekbone. The marks had mostly healed, leaving deep scars she would never be rid of—always there, a constant reminder of what that bastard had done to her.

I doubled over from the shock and heaved; if I'd had anything in my stomach, it would have been on the floor. Everything seemed to close, suffocating, the noises, the feelings, the walls closing in. At the same time, it felt as though everyone was too far away, I was drowning in emotions that warred with one another, battling to make themselves known.

With the help of the healers, I was walked outside, into the fresh air. I sat on the steps that led into the healing wing, elbows on my knees with my head cradled in my hands. I sat there, focusing on my breathing, for a long time. In for four counts. She is alive. Hold for four counts. She is safe. Exhale for four counts. She is here. When the suffocating veil and the tightness in my chest dissipated, I raised my head to find someone I had not expected next to me: my mother. She leaned into me, wrapping one arm around my shoulders, pulling me close and kissing the top of my head.

"You worried us, Astraeus. You were gone far longer than you were meant to be."

I avoided her gaze. "I know, I'm sorry. Things didn't go as planned, and I had to improvise."

"Oh, I can see that." She looked back towards the ward that housed Asteria. "You were supposed to return with information, but instead, you returned with a princess. Care to elaborate?"

I huffed out a laugh, shaking my head as I replayed the many previous weeks in my head. "She ran. I found her. I thought we could use her to bargain with Solaria and Pyrus."

"And then?" she pressed.

"And then things changed. Everything changed. Her *betrothed,*" I spat that title out with pure disgust, "hurt her, Mother. He put his hands upon her. He violated her. I couldn't send her back there, not defenseless. So, we trained." My mother looked at me with a knowing smile as I continued. "I... my feelings changed. Grew. I knew I couldn't let her go back to him. I promised her she would be safe with me, but I failed her. I betrayed her trust, then I let her walk away. I let them take her." Anger began to rear its head, taking charge of my emotions.

"From what your sister said, it didn't seem like you let anything happen. You were found unconscious; it wasn't your fault."

I stopped her, cutting her off as I shot to my feet.

"That's not true!" I yelled, "I didn't fight for her! I should have fought harder, I should have told her the truth sooner."

My mother stood, trying to interject, but I didn't allow it. I didn't want to hear what she had to say, to hear her try and smooth this over, to minimize my actions. It was my fault, and no one could convince me otherwise.

"She was my responsibility!" My anger boiled over, and another emotion began to take hold. "She was my responsibility, and I failed her!" My vision clouded as tears stung my eyes, my face hot with frustration. "I didn't fight hard enough for her. I let her walk away! I let her leave with them! *My* lies, *my* plans, *my* betrayal pushed her back into his hands!" I paced as something gnawed at my stomach. It wasn't anger; no, it was shame, and it tore through my body like a tsunami. The dam broke then—I began sobbing, feeling every ounce of guilt, anger, shame, and hatred, but not towards Stefan.

Towards myself.

"I promised her!" I fell to my knees, slamming my fists in the hard ground as I screamed. "I promised her I would protect her. I promised her she would be safe. I promised her!" My mother knelt before me, pulling me into an embrace, holding me tightly as I continued to break in her arms. "I failed, Mother. I failed her. I failed you. I failed our kingdom."

A deep, concerned voice sounded from behind me. "You failed no one, son." I felt the warmth of my father's hand on my back as he urged me to stand. "Come with me. We have many things to discuss."

CHAPTER 37

ASTRAEUS

It had been two weeks since we had returned to Asphodel. Asteria still had not woken, but the healers said that physically, she had more or less healed, so I had her moved to my chambers. She rested in my bed, and I had been by her side day and night, hoping she would wake for me. I began taking my meals in my chambers, sleeping in a wingback chair I had moved to the side of the bed. It wasn't exactly comfortable, but I wanted to respect Asteria, and I didn't think she would be comfortable with me sleeping in the bed with her. So, the chair it was.

Calliope came by every day to check on Asteria, to make sure her ointments and salves were applied, to see if there had been any change in her status. There hadn't been, aside from the fact that she had stopped having fits. Sometimes, I swore her expression softened, and I could hear my name cross her lips on a whisper, a breath, but she never woke.

The only times I left my chambers was when I met with my father to discuss business. I had relayed all the information I had learned from my time with Asteria. According to our scouts, the Kingdoms seemed to be in a state of chaos. Rumors of the return of the Forgotten Kingdom had set the villagers on edge, and the number of guards patrolling the castles had increased. Pyrus and Solaria were uncomfortably quiet, and we had not heard much from our network of spies. It made me all the more suspicious of their plans.

The biggest piece of information that I had shared, though, was that I was more than sure that Asteria was the one, the key to returning our powers to us, to bringing the Umbra Siderum back to life. Our people would thrive once again, our magic reviving the lands and replenishing our crops. We could once again feel life throughout the kingdom.

"How sure are you of this, Astraeus?" my father asked.

"She bears the mark of Orion. Her eyes are like the brightest moons shining in the darkest night. It's her. I know it is."

"I'm not convinced. You are hanging a lot of hope on a person who may not wake up. It's been two weeks, and she hasn't shown any signs of waking. We cannot hang the fate of our people on the possibility that she is the one. Even if she is, we don't know what will happen. If she wakes, do we know how to trigger the prophecy? If we do, is it something she's willing to do? Would she be willing to help us? These are a lot of unanswered questions, Astraeus." He furrowed his brows as he leaned forward, his palms on his desk supporting his weight. "I know you have a great amount of faith in her, in the possibilities of all this working out, but," he exhaled slowly, "we must plan for more realistic options."

Frustration and anger began to rise from the pit of my stomach. "I understand that, Father, but can't you just trust me? Our people cannot keep going like this. They are dying. The lands aren't producing, and trade with the realms across the sea cannot sustain us."

A fist came down, connecting with the desk, causing the items atop it to jolt. "Dammit, Astraeus! Do you think I don't know this? I am out there working the fields and hunting alongside our people.

I know the state of our kingdom, but I cannot indulge your fantasy! We need to find a real solution, and we need to find it soon."

I stood my ground. "We are out of options! You have heard the intel from our scouts—the people of Leethe fear us. Do you really think they are going to welcome us with open arms after centuries of thinking we didn't even exist? Now Solaria and Pyrus have twisted her escape into a kidnapping by the nightmarish Forgotten Kingdom. They are telling the kingdoms that we have murdered her in retribution for the past. The commoners are terrified of another Great War, terrified that we are going to invade their lands like savages. They would wage war upon us, and that would be the end of the Umbra Siderum. It wouldn't be a war. Fuck, without our magic it wouldn't even be a battle. It would be genocide! So yes, I choose to have faith in her, in the possibility that she could be the answer to our problems."

"Enough!" My father's voice echoed throughout the study as he slammed his fist onto his desk again. "I am done having this discussion about her. Understood?"

I narrowed my gaze at him, his midnight black hair just long enough to be combed back out of his face, peppered with silver and grey. He had grown out his salt and pepper beard, but he kept it trimmed short. His emerald green eyes, a few shades darker than mine, lit with anger as he returned my stare. We shared so many similar features that I wondered if the expression on my face mirrored his.

I flexed my hands at my side, resisting the urge to slam them onto his desk, mimicking his actions. He leaned in further, his arms supporting his weight. Neither one of us was willing to submit to the other, as a light rapping at the door broke our stalemate.

"Your Majesty?" A shy, meek voice floated through the large doors as they slowly creaked open, one of the castle workers peering around the opening.

"I'm sorry to intrude, but there is a matter that requires the King's presence." The younger male's voice was soft, as though he feared whatever confrontation he had just interrupted.

"No need to apologize," my father said in the pleasant tone he used whenever he interacted with the servants. "Lead the way. No need to waste any time." He began walking towards the door, but just as he reached it, he turned back to face me, his tone hard as he spoke. "This discussion is not over."

I stood in his office for a few more minutes after he left, seething. For years, my father had always trusted and respected my instincts. He almost never questioned them or my motivations. So why was he so resistant to them now? The questions rolled around in my head as I stormed off, heading back to my bedchamber. I had not made it more than a few steps out of the study before my sister began following me. She called my name, but I continued to my room, too angry to deal with whatever it was that she felt she needed to be discussed right now.

"Rae!" she called out, frustration evident in her tone. When I continued forward, she kicked out, tripping me and causing me to stumble forward. She used the opportunity to trap my wrist in her hand, twisting and forcing my arm behind my back, forcing me back into the stone wall with more strength than someone of her size should have.

"What the fuck is your problem?" she spat.

Blood boiling at the sudden and unexpected attack, I responded harshly as I tried to push off the wall. "Nothing."

She shoved me back, this time with more force. "That's bullshit, and you know it."

I kept my response short, not wanting to talk. "Nothing. I'm fine." It was a lie, and she knew it.

"Look," she started, leveling her vibrant jade eyes with mine. "Whatever is going on with you, you need to get over it. Walking around snapping at people and lashing out like someone pissed in your wine is unacceptable, and you know it."

I tried to free my wrist from her grasp, but she applied more force, causing me to wince. I did not want to have this conversation.

"There is nothing that you can do to change the past. What you *can* do is fix your piss poor attitude and step up for your kingdom. Whatever anger you are harboring, whatever hatred or guilt you're feeling, you need to drop it." Her face softened slightly as she continued. "You are not responsible for the actions of others. What that bastard did to Asteria was not your fault. Instead of being angry at yourself, why don't you target that anger towards the person who actually deserves it? Stop wasting all this energy blaming yourself. It's not helping you or your people, and it sure as fuck isn't helping Asteria.

"You need to let this go and forgive yourself. You can't go back and keep this from happening, but you can try and help her heal, help your kingdom from wasting away into nothing. When she wakes up, she's going to need you, and the longer you hold on to all that anger, the less help you're going to be. So grow the fuck up, get over it, and stop treating the people who care for you like shit." She released me from her hold and turned to leave, muttering under her breath as she did. "Jackass."

I peeled myself off the wall as I watched her head back down the hall. I started back towards my room, needing the silence and solitude to decompress. I kept my head lowered as I walked, avoiding any interaction with passersby. I was so spent—physically, mentally, and emotionally. The last three weeks had been so tumultuous; I had experienced more life changing events in them than the previous 28 years of my life combined. How everyone expected me to just keep living as if nothing had changed, I didn't understand. I knew my attitude since waking had been different. Gone was the quick-witted, sarcastic man I had once been. Everything felt different, like a heavy shroud of uncertainty had been placed upon my soul. I couldn't seem to shake the anger, the guilt, the frustration. I was hopeful everything was going to smooth over, that things would be fixed, but I had been so weighed down with emotions and stress, I honestly didn't know what I was feeling. I swung between rage and feeling nothing, fearful that if I let any other feeling in, that would be it. I would break. So, I blocked it all out, allowing myself to be fueled by my anger—anything else would be the end of me.

Before I had even realized it, I was at my door. I pushed it open, my eyes drifting straight to my bed—to her. There had still been no change. I made my way to the chair beside the bed and threw myself into it. I closed my eyes momentarily, allowing myself a moment of pure peace. Breathe in for four. Clear your mind. Hold for four. Clear your mind. Exhale for four. Let it go. I leaned in, placing her hand between my own and rested my head on them.

"She's right, you know," I whispered to Asteria. "I do blame myself, for everything. I should have told you the truth that morning. I never should have gone hunting. I tell myself that would have fixed things, but the truth is, I don't think it would have. I still would have betrayed your trust. I still would have done the one thing I never wanted to. I still would have broken your heart." My voice wavered as my emotions fought to be freed.

"I should have never let you leave. I should have protected you. I should have kept my promise and saved you from that monster, but I didn't. I failed, and I hate myself every minute of every day for it. I wish more than anything that I could go back and change things, but I can't." I shut my eyes tightly as tears welled.

"What I can do is promise you a future. Please, let me promise you a future. Don't leave me, Little Star. Give me the chance to show you what it is to love. To be loved. To be free. You're free now —you're safe. Come back to me, Princess. I need you."

I stayed there at her side a few moments longer before the ache in my shoulder had me heading for the bathing chambers. Before walking away, I brushed a shadow of a kiss across her temple. "You will always be my Little Star."

It took time for the sunken tub to fill with water, and I preoccupied myself by reading a book I kept for those nights when sleep evaded me. My mother would often read to me as a child, and it instilled in me a love of literature. It was a nice distraction from the problems and stresses I was currently facing. As the bath finished filling, I placed the book aside and began adding oils and salts to the steaming water.

Stepping into the bath and lowering myself in, I could feel the troubles of the day washing away. I leaned against the side of the tub, submerging my shoulder and allowing the heat to relax and soothe my sore muscles. My mind began to wander to the confrontation with my sister. A small pang of guilt hit me—every word she said was true. I needed to stop blaming myself for what Stefan had done. I knew I needed to clear my head and focus on my duties, find a way to help us prosper, but my heart constantly was pulled towards the woman in my bed, my thoughts consumed by the worry she would never wake up.

I must have dozed off at some point, my dreams replaying that night in the cave when Asteria gave herself to me. I knew that decision was not made easily for her. The memories of worshiping her, exploring the curves of her body, memorizing the feel of her skin, were imprinted on my brain. She had given me something so delicate and treasured, and I wanted nothing more than to spend the rest of my life showing her how much it meant to me and how worthy she is to be worshipped.

The ache in my chest woke me from my memories. The water had cooled, and my skin had pruned. I finished washing up then grabbed the towel that rested on the ledge of the tub before I dried myself off and donned a pair of loose-fitting linen trousers. I walked back to my bedchamber, head down while I dried the mess of curls that fell across my face. I aimed for the fireplace, feeding it logs to keep the room warm throughout the night. I reached for the iron poker that rested on the hearth my body stiffening before I could grasp it. A voice called out from behind me, so soft and weak, that I wondered it it was real. It was the voice I had dreamed of hearing for the past two weeks and had begun to fear I may never hear again.

She gently called out again. "Rae?"

I turned on my heels, whipping my head around and dropping the towel I held in my hand. Her eyes were open, sitting up tall in my bed. Asteria. She was awake. I was stunned, unable to believe my eyes. Unsure if I was hallucinating or not, I uttered the only words that came to mind.

"Little Star?"

CHAPTER 38
ASTERIA

I woke in a dimly lit room I did not recognize. It was lavishly furnished room, with black linen drapes that fluttered in the evening breeze. The large bed I was in was draped with silky sheets in a deep purple, with a black down blanket that kept me warm. Across the room was a stone fireplace adorned with gold accents, the dying fire and fiercely glowing embers the only source of light. I pushed myself up to sit, my arms feeling weak and heavy. I grimaced at the aches that flooded my body with each movement —my joints were stiff, my muscles sore. I tried to make sense of where I was and how I had gotten there.

Panic began to fill my head as the memories of what had happened began to race across my mind. I had left Rae—no, Astraeus—after we had been ambushed by Valdin and his guards. I had gone with them rather than fight. My gut wrenched that the memory of Astraeus laying on the ground, bloodied and still, as we rode away. And then... Stefan.

Everything he had done came rushing back to me. I could remember the feeling of each lash he gave, each hit, each cut. I gingerly ran the pads of my fingers across my right cheek; my

357

breath caught and tears filled my eyes as I felt the remnants of his torture permanently engraved into my skin. Tears streamed down my face, and I thought of how disfigured I must look, how disgusting my appearance would forever be.

I dropped my head into my hands, the movement stretching the skin on my back. Something felt wrong; it was tight, like too little cloth stretched over a too large surface. I shuddered a breath as I lifted my arm, reaching to feel the skin there. The sounds of water sloshing sent my body going rigid, and my pulse began to thrum rapidly in my ears, as my heart tried to beat its way out of my chest and my lungs ceased to function. I sat there paralyzed by fear. I felt so vulnerable—I had no weapon to defend myself, and I didn't know where I was, how to escape, or how many guards there were. There was no chance for me. My blood felt as though it had stilled. I remained glued to the bed, eyes locked on the door as my chest began to rise and fall rapidly.

The door slowly creaked open, and a man emerged with hair so dark, it reminded me of a starless night. He wore only black pants that hung low on his waist. His sculpted chest was dappled with specks of water that dripped from that too-dark hair. His arms were pure muscle as they flexed and relaxed as he dried off. He stopped in front of the fireplace, feeding it more wood—the flames roared to life, the crackling embers burning so brightly, they were almost white. It wasn't until he lowered his towel and reached for the gold poker that I saw his profile. A strange feeling overwhelmed me as I recognized the man who stood across the room from me. The scent of amber and leather filled my senses, causing my heart to skip a beat. Images of him flashed through my mind, of me running and crashing into his arms, of his strong embrace as I faded into the darkness. His was the last face I saw before I was pulled under by the siren song of death.

I tried to call out to him, but my throat was so dry, my vocal cords so raw that his name was barely a whisper as it passed my lips. He stilled in the glow of the flames, and I could see every muscle in his back tense at the sound of his name. I spoke again, this time putting more strength behind the word. "Rae?"

He dropped his towel, whipping around to face me, and his face paled as our eyes met. He blinked at me as if unsure if I were real or a ghost. I stared at him, my skin warming under his gaze.

"Little Star?"

He moved quickly then, darting to the side of the bed. He cupped my face in his hands, gently stroking his thumb over my marred cheek. His eyes glistened as his gaze swept up and down my face, like he was trying to reaffirm that what he saw and felt were reality. His touch was warm against my face, and I leaned into his palm, lifting my hands to cover his. I closed my eyes as I embraced the feel of him, trying to reconcile that he was actually here with me, that this wasn't a dream. I opened my eyes, pulling my face from his hands and lowering his arms, signaling for him to sit. He sat on the edge of the bed, his body angled towards mine. I studied his face; his expression was soft, but his face had hollowed, dark shadows looming under his eyes. He looked exhausted, drained, and I couldn't help but wonder what he had been through to change so much. I reached up, tucking a lock of hair behind his ear.

"You look different," I said as I ran my thumb down his temple. "Tired."

He choked out a rough laugh that sounded more like a sob. "Yeah, well, somebody's been hogging my bed for two weeks." His eyes lit up, and a smile spread across his face. I had forgotten how beautiful that smile was. He moved closer to me, running a hand down my arm. "How are you feeling?" His concern was evident in his voice.

I arched my back, feeling the stiffness in my bones. "Like I've been whipped and tortured and then stuck in a bed for two weeks." His expression changed, his smile dropping as the light in his eyes seemed to dim, his thoughts drifting somewhere else. His entire demeanor had changed, saddened.

"Rae?" I whispered his name, trying to bring him back to the present. He lifted his eyes to me, and a lifetime's worth of guilt and heartache swam in them. He leaned in and wrapped me in his arms, holding on as if he were scared to let go—like if he did, he would lose me forever.

"I am so sorry, Asteria, for everything." His breath caressing my ear as he spoke. Before I got the chance to reply, there was a knock at the door, and the young male didn't wait for a response before barging in.

"Prince Astraeus, there's urgent news regarding the princess!" The man stopped dead in his tracks when he rounded the door and saw us.

"Oh my goddess, she's awake," he said, eyes wide with shock. "I'm sorry, Your Highness, I didn't know... I-I wasn't aware." He stuttered over his words. "The King sent me. He said you were needed in the study immediately." His hands toyed with the hem of his tunic as he shifted his weight from one leg to the other. Rae looked from the man to me and then back to the male.

"Tell him I'll be there momentarily, and then summon Calliope from the healer's wing. Tell no one of her waking. I want her examined by the healers before anything. And by no one, I am including my father." His tone was hard as he relayed his orders.

Astraeus stood, taking my hand and kissing my palm as the man left, looking up at me before he spoke. "I am sorry, but I have to go. I will return as soon as I can. The healer will be here shortly, and I will send for food and drink." He went to the wardrobe and pulled a top over his head. "I know there's so much that needs to be discussed, but I promise, I will answer all your questions when I get back." He shoved his feet into something akin to slippers, readying to leave.

"I want to go." He stopped and turned to me at my statement.

"I want to go. If it concerns me, I want to be there." I began pulling the blankets off my lap, determined to follow him.

"Asteria," he pleaded. "No. You almost died. You've been out for two weeks. There is no way you are getting out of that bed without first being seen by a healer."

"Astraeus," I retorted. "There is no way I am going to sit here while you discuss me with your father. I want to know what is going on. I am going, and you're not going to stop me. If I remember correctly, I was supposed to be your special little bargaining chip. The naive little pawn that you manipulated and used, remember?"

He physically withdrew at my words, as if I had just landed a blow right to his core.

"If it is a discussion about me, I want to be involved, even if it's just to listen." I threw my legs over the side of the bed and looked up at him. "Please. You owe me that much."

He kneeled before me, taking my hands in his and resting his head on my lap. "I will spend the rest of my days trying to reconcile the hurt I have caused you. I know I don't deserve the opportunity, but I will work for it regardless."

"Well then, your first act towards that can be getting me a robe and taking me with you to this meeting. Unless you would prefer me to meet your father in this?" I looked down at the thin black chemise I wore, realizing it was most definitely not the last thing I had been wearing. "How did I get into this? You know what, never mind. That's a discussion for later. Robe, please?"

He let out an exasperated sigh as he got to his feet and retrieved a bathrobe from his bathing chamber. He helped me to slip my arms through, the stretching movements difficult after my prolonged immobility. "It was the healer's, by the way," he spoke as he clasped the front of the robe.

"What?" I asked, confused by his statement.

"The chemise—it was the healer's. They have been coming by

daily to bathe you, tend to your wounds, and keep you in clean clothing. I never saw you unclothed, nor have we shared a bed since you've been here. I didn't feel that was appropriate or respectful."

He fastened the last clasp and helped me to my feet. It took me a moment to get my bearings and steady myself, and he took my arm to ensure I did not stumble as we walked.

"Thank you," I murmured as we headed towards his father's study.

CHAPTER 39
ASTERIA

When we entered his father's study, he was towered over a large desk made of a dark oak, maps and what looked like a stack of letters sitting on it. His father was looking over the maps, pinching the bridge of his nose as his brow furrowed in frustration. He glanced up at the sound of the door, and his eyes widened as he took me in, walking arm in arm with Rae, wearing his son's bathing robe. He was silent as we strode towards him, and despite the large robe covering me, I felt exposed under his scrutinizing stare. When we reached the desk, his father straightened as Rae cleared his throat.

"Father, this is Asteria, Princess of Pyrus." He hesitated a moment before continuing. "Asteria, this is my father, King Elias, ruler of Asphodel and leader of the Umbra Siderum."

I bowed my head. "It is an honor to meet you. I owe you and your people a great debt of gratitude. I will be forever thankful for your kindness, and I hope that someday I am able to repay that debt."

He eyed me incredulously, and the striking resemblance

between him and Astraeus was undeniable. "Pardon my shock, but I did not know you had awakened, much less were up and about. Your face is the last one I expected to see walking through that door, especially since the summons was one of confidential matters." He shot his son a look of frustration and annoyance, and Rae hardened his face in return. Before he could retort, I cut in.

"I insisted on attending. The messenger had not known I was awake. When I heard that the news pertained to myself, I didn't give him much of a choice. He found it simpler to accompany me as opposed to my barging in behind him." I lowered myself onto the arm of a chair. "Considering everything that has happened between the prince and me, and in regard to the other kingdoms, I felt it was only fair that I be informed, particularly on how you planned to move forward and deal with my presence here when Pyrus and Solaria have made such a strenuous effort to retrieve me and return me to Stefan."

I felt Rae wrap his arm around my shoulder, a small gesture that showed he was on my side, sending butterflies swarming through my stomach. The feel of his skin on mine as his thumb gently stroked the side of my neck felt electric. I knew I should be livid with him, but something in my heart warmed at the act.

"If it's not too much to ask, I would like to know why you have kept your kingdom hidden for so long? This land was believed to be barren, that your people did not survive after the Great War. Why not reinstate yourself into politics? Establish trades and develop relationships? Why now? Why develop this elaborate plan to use me as leverage? I don't quite understand."

His father's gaze shifted between the two of us, as if unsure if it would be wise to divulge such sensitive information. He fixed his eyes on Rae, as if silently asking if I could be trusted. Rae gave a curt nod before he took the seat beside mine, resting his hand on my knee.

"What do you know about Leethe's history and the Great War?"

My forehead creased in confusion, not sure what the Great War had anything to do with this. "The shadow wielders used to be a part of the kingdoms, using their magic abilities to aid the people. Higher powered ones would serve in the Royal Guards, protecting the royals and leading their armies during war times. The Prince of Solaria had fallen in love with the Princess of Pyrus, seeking her hand in marriage, forming a united kingdom, but the shadow wielders were worried about the power imbalance if the two kingdoms united, making it the largest court in the realm. One of the royal guard murdered the princess the night before the wedding, the assassination order from the Asphodel King was seen as the ultimate betrayal and an act of war.

When the news of the murder reached the other courts, the people had feared an uprising, scared that the other Royals were next. The Kingdoms banded together and declared war on the Kingdom of Asphodel. The war lasted just more than a month, resulting in the retreat of the shadow wielders behind the Dead Mountains. Their numbers had dwindled down so much, it was believed they died out shortly after the war ended. There's been no contact or activity from here, so we've had no reason to believe otherwise."

Out of the corner of my eye, I could see Rae drop his head, shaking it as he scoffed lightly under his breath. "Of course that would be the version they told."

I eyed him and his father, their faces seeming to harden at the retelling of our history. "What do you mean, 'the version they told'? Is there more than one version?"

"Oh, Little Star." He gave my leg a gentle squeeze. "The version written in your history books differs vastly from the truth."

His father sat, leaning back and relaxing into his chair as he folded his arms over chest. I was so confused as to what they were insinuating. I stood, moving over to fully fit into the chair next to Astraeus.

"I'm sorry, but I don't understand. What other version could you be speaking of? What does it have to do with the present?" My voice faltered slightly on the last word as Astraeus grasped the arm of my chair and pulled it nearer to his.

With our close proximity, I found myself inhaling the familiar scent of him, making my heart jump in my chest. Losing myself in my thoughts momentarily, I startled at the feel of Rae's hand resting on my leg. I turned my attention to his father as he began to tell a different version of the Great War.

"The beginning of your version was correct. The Umbra Siderum worked closely with the kingdoms, aiding them in their healing with the use of our Astra flower, protecting the Royal courts, and guarding the borders of the realm. The Prince of Solaria did indeed fall in love with the Princess of Pyrus. He tried winning the princess' affections by courting her, presenting her with lavish gifts, and throwing elaborate balls in her name, but no matter what he did, he could not seem to get her to return his feelings. He was angered and frustrated, so he recruited one of the human guards to follow her, to see if he could discover why she would not return his love. It was that guard who discovered the princess had fallen in love with another.

The princess had become infatuated with a member of her guard, an Umbra Siderum. They would use his shadow powers, concealing themselves to spend time alone together. The two had fallen madly in love with one another. But, her parents soon promised to the prince of Solaria, and the guard was not of royal blood, so he could not challenge the engagement. Their union, their relationship, was doomed unless they left, and so they forged a plan. During the journey from Pyrus to Solaria, they would stage an ambush. While the guards were distracted, they would shadow stalk to one of the ports and board a boat. What they did not know was that the prince's spy bore witness to their planning. He promptly returned to the prince, feeding him all the information he had learned.

"Overtaken by jealousy, the prince had the guard arrested. When the guard did not appear with the rest of the troop traveling with her to Solaria, the princess began to panic. Heartbroken and terrified of what might have happened, she developed her own plan to run. She decided that the evening before the wedding, she would sneak out of the castle and make for the port to wait for him. Unfortunately for her, she never made it.

"As she readied to flee, the prince caught her. He went mad with anger, and in his fit of rage, he killed her. After the fact, he knew if the murder was traced back to him, it would be the fall of his Kingdom, so he devised a plan. Using the information his spy had gathered, he spun the false story you were fed in your history books. He claimed that shadow wielders planned to force the humans to become their slaves, serving them as the superior race. He had the guard publicly executed, claiming that the murder of his bride had been an official declaration of war, and that the only chance of winning was if the kingdoms banded together to fight the 'shadow demons'.

"The people fell for the ruse, and it became a witch hunt. Women and children were ripped from their homes and murdered in the middle of the night. Soldiers were ambushed and slaughtered. We fought to the best of our abilities, but we hadn't been prepared. Our people were dispersed, our numbers too small compared to combined forces of the other kingdoms.

"Finally, we did the only thing we could think of: we retreated. Anyone with shadow magic fled, returning to Asphodel, but our numbers had been greatly depleted, and as a form of preservation, our magic went to sleep. It has been dormant ever since, asleep within our blood and our souls, waiting to return to our people and become the great kingdom we once were."

My eyes welled with tears as I sat on the edge of the seat, my hand on my chest, grasping at the fabric of the robe. I couldn't believe what I had just heard. It was horrible. Our people had all but wiped out theirs because the Solarian Prince couldn't contain his jealous rage. My stomach turned—I knew exactly what that poor princess had felt, to want one but be hunted by another. I wiped my eyes, clearing the tears from them.

Rae spoke this time. "Our people have been living here. Over time, some made their way into the other kingdoms, starting families, getting jobs. More and more are leaving because we are struggling. The crops and game have depleted. Our kingdom is failing, and I can't allow that to happen. We have scouts and spies throughout the kingdoms who report back to me, but I have been looking for ways to re-integrate our kingdom back into the realm, to establish trade again, to try and save my people. It's all I have wanted since I was old enough to comprehend how critical our situation was."

"So you were going to try and trade me for re-establishment of your kingdom into Leethe, to save your people." It was more of a statement than a question.

His expression changed, and his tone dropped. "Not originally," he admitted. "When I heard about your betrothal, of how massive of a celebration it was going to be, I knew all the courts and their servants would be in attendance. I had planned to masquerade as one of the servants to study the royals, to listen to them gossip, talk about their kingdoms. Plus, the servants are a chatty bunch. Give them a few drinks, and they'll tell you just about anything."

His father cut him off before he could continue. "He came to me with the plan. He thought if we learned enough about the politics of each court and found their weaknesses, we could exploit them, threaten to spill all their secrets to the others."

I laughed. "You mean blackmail them."

He nodded. "In simpler terms, yes. I agreed to Rae's plan under one condition: he was t0 murder your future husband."

I choked from the shock, whipping my head around to look at the man beside me. Guilt was etched deep into his features, and pain swirled in his eyes as he met my stare. "You were going to murder Stefan?"

He lowered his gaze with an ashamed nod.

"So when you told me you are hired to take care of people, and I asked if you were an assassin for hire..." I started to piece together the puzzle that was being laid out before me.

"I had planned to disguise myself as a worker from the kitchen, delivering libations to his room before the wedding. I was going to poison him with mead fermented from mad honey." He began to withdraw his hand from my leg, but I caught it with my own before he could pull away.

"I wouldn't have been forced to marry him?" I asked the question more to myself than to anyone else, trying to decipher my emotions. A strange wave of gratitude washed over me as I laced my fingers with Rae's.

"I ruined your plan by running." The statement caused me a tinge of regret. Had I not run, Stefan would be dead, and none of the horrible things I had endured since I made that choice would have happened. Yet, that choice brought me to Rae. He stroked his thumb across the back of my hand, and for some reason, I felt as though he knew exactly what I was thinking.

"It definitely complicated things." A smirk tugged at the corner of his mouth. "After the wedding had failed, I began my journey back home, with plans to stop in as many towns throughout each kingdom as possible. I would stay a few days, speak with the villagers, try to get an idea of the workings of each court. But before I left, I overheard a conversation, an argument between Stefan, his father, and who I can only assume was your father. Stefan was determined to get you back at all costs, and his father and yours knew the repercussions if you weren't returned to him. When I crossed paths with you at that tavern, after I left you in your room, it dawned on me who you were. It was that night I came up with the plan to help you travel as far away from that sniveling snake of a man as possible. I would bring you back here to Solaria and bargain with Stefan for your return. In the mean time I would train you in self-defense so that bastard couldn't lay another hand on you, all while learning everything I needed to know to be successful in my plan to. So I could, as you so eloquently phrased it, blackmail our way back into trade with the realm."

"I knew that sending you back to Solaria was the wrong thing to do, but I had to do whatever it took to give my people a chance. So, despite my inner turmoil, I had a plan, and I had intended to stick to it."

"Had intended?" I questioned, and his grip on my hand tightened as he inhaled deeply.

"Yes. Had. Everything changed once I got to know you. Slowly but surely, you became a part of me, of my heart. You brought a joy to my life I had never experienced before. I was falling for you, and I knew I couldn't let you go back to him. I would find some other way to help my people, because losing you was not an option."

My breath hitched as he spoke those words. Part of me didn't want to believe that he could feel that way about me. I had convinced myself it was all a game to him, that it had all been a lie. He had shattered my heart into pieces so small, they became dust. I had been so determined to walk away hating him for the rest of my life, but it was him, his voice calling out to me. His voice urged me to fight, to stay. To die at Stefan's hand would have been easy to give up, to allow the darkness to swallow me whole and be free of the pain, but Rae had been my tether to life. The one strand of hope illuminating my path home. To him.

Silence filled the room as I absorbed everything I just heard. I struggled to process the onslaught of emotions that coursed through me, though something the King had said piqued my curiosity. "You said your magic is waiting to return? How is that possible?"

"That is the complicated part that brings us to now, to you," his father continued. "Before our magic slept, oracles throughout the realms received a vision, a prophecy.

"Change comes on two moons bearing the belt of Orion;
When the falling star is enraptured by twilight,
Darkness will fall upon the kingdom.
Out of the dark, a star will rise to remake the realm.
Beneath shadow and light, a new era will emerge, and power once lost
will be returned.
For theirs is a destiny written in twilight and stars."

"I don't understand. What does that have to do with me? With our situation?" As beautifully cryptic as that prophecy was, it didn't answer my question.

"The prophecy has been passed down for years. I passed it to Astraeus just as my father passed it to me, and his to him. Not much has been deciphered from it. There are many different inter-pretations, but my son here—" he pointed to Rae "—seems to think he figured it out."

I cocked an eyebrow at the prince, eager to hear whatever he had gleaned from the utter nonsense I just heard.

"I haven't figured it all out." He turned to face me. "But I do believe the first part is about you."

I almost fell out of my chair. "*What?*" I asked, mouth gaping at the insinuation. "How in the world did you decide that a centuries old prophecy could possibly have anything to do with me?"

He reached up, placing my face in the palm of his hand as he spoke. "The first thing I thought when I saw you was that you had the most enchanting and breathtaking eyes I had ever seen. Even bloodshot and puffy from crying, they looked like full moons cutting through the black of the night sky." He ran his thumb along my cheek. "You were the most stunning person I had ever seen. I didn't want to let you walk out that kitchen door. I wanted to know you, to know why you had been crying, why your face was so bruised. Your lips had been swollen, and every instinct told me to stop you, but you were running from something. I didn't know who you were that night, but had I known then who you were and who had laid their hands on you..." Anger seethed in his eyes. "I would have slit his throat then, consequences be damned."

The world tilted on its axis as the realization dawned on me. He had been the hooded man in the kitchen hall as I fled Solaria. I had been so upset, I hadn't recalled any of his features. All I remembered was the immense fear I felt as I thought I had been caught. When the man allowed me to pass with no attempt to stop me, I had more or less erased the event from my mind.

I couldn't believe it. All this time, I had believed my first inter-action with Astraeus had been in the tavern, when he plunged his dagger into the throat of the merchant who had been harassing me. He had known about the night in the castle all along; he had never needed me to tell him what had happened that night. He didn't need to tell him how I had my virtue ripped from me, how what happened forced me to hate so much of myself. He always knew, but he had let me tell him when I was ready, when I trusted him.

I rose from my chair, looking down at the man who had shown me how to love myself, how to believe in myself, how to respect myself and demand the respect I deserved from others. For the first time, I truly knew how I felt about him. I loved him, with every fiber of my being. With every breath in my lungs, every beat of my heart, every corner of my soul, I was his. I belonged to him, from now until the end of eternity. Before I knew what I was doing, I was kissing him. I kissed him like he was the very reason I walked this realm, because in all reality, he was. He had saved me more times than I could count. I owed him my life.

I broke our kiss when the sound of his father clearing his throat pierced the silence. My cheeks flushed from embarrassment as Rae sat in his chair, spine steeled, in a daze. I clasped his hand in mine, and whispered, "Rae?"

He inhaled deeply, as if he had been drowning and my kiss brought him back to the surface. After a moment longer of silence, his father cut in, "Do you care to continue your explanation, son?"

"There are many things I wish to continue, and my explanation is not at the top of that list right now." My skin flushed, and that familiar heat pooled in my core at his words.

"But, as there are bigger matters at hand, yes, I will continue. I hadn't thought much of it at the time. I never imagined I would live to see the return of power to my people. It wasn't until I saw this." He gently brushed my hair from my shoulder and pulled the neck of the robe slightly down my arm, exposing the constellation of freckles that lived there.

"Freckles?" I asked incredulously. "You think I'm some key because of *freckles*?"

"Orion. Your freckles are the constellation of Orion. You are the only person I have ever encountered with grey eyes, and you are marked with the same constellation the prophecy said you would be." His tone became urgent. "Do you not understand how special you are? How unique? How powerful?" I shook my head; this couldn't be true, none of it. "Have you ever wondered why Stefan was so determined to make you his bride? I would bet my life that he figured it out as well. He wanted to control the key to the prophecy. He wanted to have that power. Why else would your parents agree to such an asinine proposal?"

"No, no." I shook my head repeatedly. "Do you understand how insane this all is? Me, the key to an ancient prophecy? The person to reinstate your powers? There is no way this is true."

Rae stood, and I had forgotten how much he towered over me, almost intimidating as he loomed above me. "Asteria, listen to me. Have you not noticed how similar the events of your life are to what led to this prophecy in the first place? This cannot be by chance."

I sighed. "Even if this were true and I am the magical key to this prophecy, how I am supposed to unlock the door that has kept your magic asleep all these years? How am I supposed to 'remake the realm' when I barely *understand* the realm?" My breathing quickened, and I began to see stars in the periphery of my vision.

"Breathe, Asteria." I was guided back into my chair, a pair of warm hands cupping my face. "Listen to me. Breathe. Focus on my voice. Breathe in for four counts." *One, two, three, four.* "Now hold for four." *One, two, three, four.* I did what he said, trying to slow my breathing. "Good. Exhale slowly." I repeated the exercise until my heart stopped pounding and the tingling in my fingers dissipated.

"You're okay. You're safe."

I was safe, and it was because of him. I hadn't told him how I felt, not in words, but this didn't feel like the time—not with his father standing behind his back, looking down at me with concern.

"Perhaps we should continue this at another time." His father placed his hand on Rae's shoulder. "It will be morning soon, and I feel we could all use some rest. Go take care of her and get some sleep." He gave me a curt nod and Rae's shoulder a squeeze before leaving us.

The intensity of the discussion weighed on me, and I could feel my shoulders begin to sag. I was exhausted. I placed my hand on Rae's shoulder for support as I began to stand. In an instant, my feet were swept out from beneath me as Rae scooped me up into his arms and cradled me to his chest. I giggled slightly at the act, "You know, I can walk."

"Just because you can, doesn't mean you should," he joked, repeating the words I had once said to him. I smiled to myself as I nodded off to sleep, feeling at home in the embrace of his arms.

CHAPTER 40
ASTERIA

I woke in the same large bed to the sloshing of water. I sat up, dangling my legs over the side of the bed, my toes barely grazing the floor. I looked around the room, at the light of dawn filtering through the sheer black curtains, casting soft shadows across the floor. The sound of feet shuffling softly across the tiled floor of the bathing chamber echoed through the room. I pushed myself up to my feet, taking a moment to steady myself before inspecting the noises.

My body felt sluggish, and my head throbbed slightly. I attributed the headache to the stress of the night's events—I wished I had my chest of herbs to make some tea to soothe it. I tread lightly across the stone floor adorned with plush rugs, matching the room's deep purples and blacks accented with gold. It was lavish, but with the deep hues and warm lighting, it was dark and ominous yet warm and comforting.

I reached the bathroom, only to find Rae preparing a hot bath in the most gorgeous sunken tub. It had to be large enough to fit at least four people; my mouth gaped at the sight of it, the steam rising from the hot water beneath the luscious bubbles. I took a deep breath through my nose, the familiar scent of pomegranate and lavender hitting me. My favorite oils. He turned to look at me from where he was perched on the side of the tub, halting his actions. He held a small votive of dried flowers in one hand, salts in the other.

"Good morning, Little Star." He set them down and stood, crossing the floor to close the distance between us. He placed his hands on either side of my neck, caressing my jaw with his thumbs. "I thought you might like a real bath. I was going to finish preparing it and then have food delivered for you. You must be famished."

He inspected my face, his gaze stopping below my right eye before leaning in to place a gentle kiss on the top of my head. "I'll have some brought up for you, as well as a pot of tea. We have a special blend to aid with stress and tension." His expression was so gentle, so caring—I felt my heart stutter at the sight. "I know you've been through a lot, and..." His voice trailed off as he dropped his head. "I know you may need some time and privacy. Your body has suffered a lot, and though you're more or less healed, there was only so much the healers could do."

I cupped his face, lifting his eyes back to mine. "This was not your fault." I rose onto the tips of my toes to place a kiss on his lips. "Thank you for finding me."

He pulled me in, wrapping his arms tightly around me. I could feel him inhale, breathing in the scent of me, committing it to memory, and I hugged him back, relishing in the feel of his embrace. His leather and amber smell overwhelmed my senses, causing my pulse to quicken, my core to heat. He pulled back, releasing me just enough to curl his finger under my chin, tiling my lips to his. His breath warmed my skin as he whispered, his lips brushing against mine.

"I will always find you, Little Star. If I have to plunge myself into the darkness of death to find you, I will. My heart and soul belong to you, from now until the last star in the sky burns out. Even then, in death, I am yours."

My breath was ragged as I closed my eyes, etching his words into the fibers of my heart. He closed the last bit of space between us, his lips crashing into mine. The kiss was deep, long, and tender. He kissed me as though I was his temple, this kiss his confession. I kissed him back, my body begging for more. I gently dragged my tongue across his lips, and he answered me immediately as I pushed myself into him, needing to feel him everywhere. My skin prickled anywhere he connected with me. I wanted more. I *needed* more.

The gentle rapping at his bedchamber door broke our kiss before it could transform into more. His forehead rested against mine as we both stood there, our breath hot on each other's faces as we recovered from the fast escalation. I felt his smile on my mouth before he spoke.

"That would be your meal." His voice was unsteady as he tried to slow his breathing, and the gentle rapping on the door sounded again. "I should go get that," he laughed softly as he pulled away from me, and my skin instantly felt cold at the lack of his touch. "There are fresh towels on the side of the bath, as well as a dressing robe and new chemise on the chaise there." He motioned to the seat near the door before he placed a quick kiss to my lips. "I will be out here if you need me. Take all the time that you need. These here—" He reached for two gold knobs jutting from the wall, connected to pipes that disappeared beneath the floor. "The one on the right is for cold water, and the one on the left is for hot. Just turn them if you need water."

His hand reached for mine, squeezing it gently as he walked past to answer the knocking. I stood there another moment, still feeling cold from his absence, my breathing returning to normal. I reached up, touching my lips—I had forgotten how it felt to kiss him: *intoxicating*.

A gentle voice spoke behind me. "Princess Asteria?" I turned to lock eyes with a beautiful young girl holding a tray of fruits and breads, a pot of tea, and some metal tins. "How are you feeling today?" she questioned as she moved, placing the tray along the ledge of the bath.

"I'm fine, thank you," I answered. She began preparing a cup of tea, humming softly. Once the tea was poured, leaves steeping, she gathered the tins and turned to me.

"I am Calliope." She smiled at me, her eyes creasing. "I'm one of the healers here. When I heard that you had awakened, I wanted to come check on you. I intercepted the worker bringing your tray; I hope you don't mind." She walked over to the large vanity that rested along one of the walls and placed the tins on it.

"I brought you some ointment for your scars. They should help lighten them some. The other one can be used to help relieve any aching muscles or joints." I eyed her from where I stood, watching her work on organizing the things she had brought with her. She had light golden red hair, her skin milky and dotted with freckles that matched her hair, but the feature that stood out most were her eyes. They reminded me of the bright greens of spring, and her smile only brightened them.

"I also brought some herbs for you. Prince Astraeus told me you were a bit of an herbalist yourself. These are some he said you liked." She walked forward, pulling me into an unexpected embrace. "I am so thrilled that you are awake. He was fading without you." She retreated, giving me the most heartwarming and compassionate smile. "If you need anything at all, do not hesitate to call for me. I am at your disposal, Your Highness." She bowed quickly before leaving, the door clicking closed behind her.

I was alone. I looked around, trying to find the courage to confront myself in the mirror. I had felt the scars along my face and back with my hands, but I had yet to see them, and I didn't know if I wanted to. I took a step towards the vanity, and panic began to creep its way into my veins. I could feel my heart pounding, and the air suddenly felt as though it was shredding my lungs. My hand trembled as I clutched the neck of the robe I still wore from earlier. I closed my eyes, taking another step closer, and my skin tingled as the anxiety grew.

Listen to me. Listen to my voice. Rae's voice echoed in my subconscious. *Breathe in for four counts.* I inhaled. *Good. Now, hold it for four counts.* One, two, three, four, I counted to myself. *Now, exhale slowly.* I blew out my breath slowly through pursed lips. *This is ridiculous,* I thought to myself, but it wasn't.

I had been trying to block out the memories of Stefan's pleasure as he cracked the whip across my back, the ache in my ribs a constant reminder of his boots slamming into my sides. Each time I felt the stretch of my skin along my back, or my fingers grazed across the indentions in my face, I was there again. I was chained up in that tent, the smell of the hard earth combined with the iron from my blood and the salt from my tears. I had begged, pleaded with him to stop, but each cry of pain just seemed to urge him on.

I remembered the fear I felt as he held my own dagger to my face, I could feel the remnants of his rage in my skin. It was exactly as he wanted: a physical and permanent reminder of what my actions led him to do. *No,* I thought. *His actions were his and his alone. Your actions were not the reason for his atrocities. His own rage, his malice, his obsession with controlling you—those are what led to his actions. If it were not you, then it would have been another.*

I felt the warmth of my tears as they slowly carved a path down my face. He may have tortured me, scared me, broken me, but he did not own me. He did not control me, and I would not allow him to win by running away and retreating from my scars.

I stepped into the mirror, my head down, willing myself to lift it. Deep down, I knew that this was what he had wanted. He wanted me to feel shame, fear, to feel ruined and unlovable. I knew the only way to win was to embrace the scars, to take the trauma he caused me and twist it into something else. He carved out the hard-won self-love and beauty from my skin, from my face. How would I ever learn to love what I saw now?

I shook, barely holding my sobs back. I let the tears flow freely as I prepared myself. I steeled my nerves, and slowly, I opened my eyes and began to lift my head. My breaths were shallow and rapid as I looked ahead, meeting my own gaze in the mirror as a sob tore itself from my chest.

My face had thinned from the lack of nutrition, shadows settling beneath my eyes and the hollows of my cheeks. I looked like death, but that wasn't the part that had me fighting the urge to turn away. No, it was the three bright pink scars that had dug their way into my flesh, three scars that stretched down the side of my face. They were not jagged or rough; they were smooth, clean marks, evidence that they had been placed intentionally. They began just above my right eyebrow, missing the lid of my eye, ending just below my cheekbones. It was hideous.

I struggled to keep my face forward, to not turn my head and drop it. I cried silently as I dropped the robe I wore and turned my back to the mirror, the straps of my nightgown sliding down my arms and exposing my back. I reached up, touching the scars that spanned over the tops of my shoulders. My stomach churned at the sight of the mess that obscured the flesh of my back. They crossed over each other, an indecipherable map of nightmares etched into my skin forever. Some were raised, while others formed trenches in the skin. My hands covered my face as I slumped to the ground, landing on my knees, hanging my head as I cried. I cried until my eyes felt as though they would bleed if I continued. Only when my self-pity and shame ran dry did I pick myself up from the floor and enter the bath.

The water had gone cold during the time I spent on the stone floor. I turned the knob that Rae had indicated would produce hot water and waited while the water refreshed, replacing the oils and salts that he so thoughtfully added. I lowered myself into the hot water, moaning in pleasure as the heat eased the tension from my body. I fully submerged myself, dipping my head to wet my hair before I rested it on the ledge.

Reaching for a piece of fruit and popping it into my mouth, as the taste of the fresh berry flooded my tongue, it reminded me how famished I was. I struggled to pace myself; I knew I needed to take it slow so that I did not make myself sick. I sipped on the lukewarm tea Calliope had prepared—lavender and chamomile, with what seemed like hints of mint and raspberry. I lavished in the comfort of the bath, momentarily able to forget the stress that had been weighing on me.

As I sat there, thinking over everything that had happened, remembering of all the trauma and hurt, of all the times I had allowed Stefan or my family to degrade me, to belittle me, to hurt me, make me feel small. It was in that moment that I decided no more. I would feel no more shame, hurt, or inadequacy at their hands. I would shed no more tears for my family, no more tears because of the monster who started this all. Stefan would no longer hold any power over me. He was nothing, just a jealous, narcissistic, piss poor excuse for a man, and I was done allowing him into my psyche.

When the water grew tepid, I finished washing my hair and rinsing the soap from my body before I wrapped myself in a plush towel. The chemise that had been given to me was a gorgeous silk trimmed in lace that stopped near the middle of my thighs, the cups cut to fit my breasts perfectly. The color was a beautiful pale lavender, and the dressing robe had been colored to match. I pulled the robe on, the silk cool against my skin, the hem stopping just slightly past the lace of the chemise. I tied the it loosely at my waist and lightly towel dried my hair. The bath had revived me; I felt stronger, my head clearer, and I felt more prepared to deal with what stood before me as I opened the door and stepped into the bedchamber.

Rae sat at a desk in the far corner of the room in front of a large window. Dawn had passed, and the early morning light lit the room more fully. The drapes kept the light from flowing in completely, the room just slightly cloaked in darkness. The air was sweet, the scent of flowers drifting in on the slight breeze. You could feel the winter chill in the air, but the room was kept warm by the fire that had been fed while I was in the bath.

At the sound of my steps, Rae turned his head watching me as I walked towards him from across the room. He sat at the desk, shirtless, wearing those same low hanging, black linen pants that drew my attention to his lower abdomen that disappeared beneath the waistband. He stood, the wooden chair scraping along the stone floor. Goddess he was breathtaking. His body was sculpted, and the way he prowled towards me sent fire sparking through my body. His movements were fluid, like a shadow moving through the early morning light. His hair had grown, his curls dancing across his lashes, nearly obscuring his eyes, though his intense stare cut through his midnight hair like an arrow. The light stubble that had once shaded his lower face was now gone, showing off his impressively sharp jawline.

My arms dropped limply to my sides as he approached, and my breath caught in my chest as he stopped just a hair's breadth away.

"How are you feeling, Little Star?" He gently placed his hands on my shoulders.

"Better," I whispered. "Much better." My voice wavered as adrenaline and desire sparked in my core. I felt my skin flush as he moved his hands down the length of my arms, stopping when he reached my waist.

"Tell me." He lightly tugged at the ends of the sash that tied my robe. "How does the clothing I had made for you fit?"

A cool breeze washed over my skin as he pulled the sash free and the robe fell open. The air sent a chill down my spine, my hair standing on end, as my skin erupted in goosebumps.

"It's perfect." I swallowed the lump of anxiety forming in my throat as one of his hands snaked around my waist, drawing lazy circles just below my breast. The touch heated my flesh, and I felt my face redden. His eyes darkened as he pushed the robe off my shoulders, hooking his index finger under the thin strap of my nightgown.

His voice grew husky and deep when he spoke. "I think I liked them better on the chair in the bathing chamber."

I clenched my thighs together as dampness began to gather between them. He slowly slid the strap down my arm, leaving a trail of sparks following his touch. My breath was uneven and weak as he lowered his head, gently kissing along the path his hand had just traveled. My head dropped to the side, giving him better access to my neck; he brushed his mouth along my shoulder and up the side of my neck as he pulled me tighter to his chest. A small whimper escaped my mouth as he left the faintest of kisses along my jaw, and my eyes closed as I melted into his touch.

"Please," I pleaded quietly.

He stopped his teasing and placed a gentle kiss on my lips. "You never have to beg for me to worship you, Little Star" His hand left my side as he pushed the other strap of gown off my shoulder. "You are my both salvation." He kissed the corner of my mouth. "And my damnation."

He pushed the chemise down my body, the silk sliding to the floor, landing silently, and bearing my body to him. I dropped my head, feeling exposed and insecure at the sudden vulnerability.

"You are my divine goddess, Asteria." Cupping my cheeks, he lifted my eyes to meet his. "And I will die praising you." My heart swelled at his words. "I am your disciple—in heart, in soul, in mind, and body. So please," he pleaded as he kissed me deeply, "let me pray to you."

He kissed me again as he slid his hands down my body. His knuckles gently grazed my breast, the sensitive peaks hardened from his light touch. His hands continued their descent, stopping when he reached the part of me that ached for him, and his breath quickened as he ran a finger through my wet center.

"Let me worship you."

My hands reached up, gripping his arms as I gasped. He brought a hand up, running his fingers through the hair at the nape of my neck as he crashed his lips to mine. I reveled in the feel of him and taste of him, as my mouth opened to him.

He repeated his plea into my mouth as we kissed. "Please, Little Star."

His hold tightened on my hair as he kissed me harder, like he needed this more than anything, more than the night sky needs the stars or the grass needs the sun. He kissed me like he had prayed every day of his life for me, like if he let go, if he stopped, he might lose me. Little did he know, I needed him just as badly as he needed me.

I returned his affection, pressing myself deeper into him, his hand pinned between us as he swirled his fingers through the wetness at my entrance. I could feel the evidence of his need pressed into my hip, and I couldn't deny him any longer—I didn't just want this. No, I needed it. I needed him *now*.

A breathy moan answered his pleas. "*Yes.*"

That was all the consent he needed as he dipped his finger inside me, and my heady moan was immediately answered by a deep rumble of pleasure in his chest. Without breaking our kiss or stopping his sinfully skilled hand, he released my hair and placed his hand beneath my ass. With seemingly no effort, he lifted me, and instinctively, I wrapped my legs around him as my hands gripped his shoulders.

He walked us to the edge of the bed and lightly placed me onto the plush mattress, kissing his way down my body. He continued to curl his finger inside me, hitting that spot that had me arching my back off the bed. He pressed the heel of palm into the sensitive bundle of nerves at my center, expertly working it as his mouth found my breast. He flicked his tongue across the sensitive flesh of my nipple before gently blowing a cool breath over it before he switched to the other breast, repeating the action, sending shivers down my spine. I lifted myself to my elbows as he continued showering my skin with kisses while he moved further down my torso. He placed his free hand on my chest, pushing me back into the mattress.

"No," he grumbled, lifting his heavy-lidded eyes to mine. "Lay back and let me exalt you."

I panted as I followed his command, laying back and pressing my head into the pillows. My hands dug into the covers as the pressure in my core built, and I could feel myself tightening against his fingers as he worked me. He nipped at my hip, and the sting of pleasure from the bite had me arching off the bed as I felt that wave begin to crest. His hand pressed harder into my chest, holding me still as he spoke, hovering over my most sensitive flesh. He halted his movements, the building orgasm plateauing at the sudden loss of his fingers.

"Not yet, Little Star. I'm not ready for you to break yet." He circled his thumb around my center, teasing me as I whimpered, balancing on the edge of pure bliss. In that moment, he had complete control of me.

He smiled as his breathy words flowed over me. "Fuck. Asteria. I could get off on your sounds alone." His eyes darkened, shifting from their usual emerald to a deep forest green. "Make them again for me, louder this time."

He dipped his head, dragging his tongue up my center as he thrusted two fingers inside me, and I came unhinged, every nerve ending in my body sparking to life under every movement of his tongue, every curl of his fingers. I let go, screams of pleasure ripping from my throat as he continued to pledge his fealty to me between my thighs. With each moan, each plea, each scream, he feasted deeper, replacing his fingers with his tongue. My breaths became rapid and shallow as my hands clenched the sheets harder, as if they alone could ground me while I fell over the edge.

My vision darkened as an orgasm tore through me. Stars burst behind my closed eyes, and my muscles tensed as I screamed his name while he continued to drink from me. He slowed his pace as the aftershocks faded, and with one last taste of me, he lifted his head, his lips glistening with my arousal. I tried to catch my breath as I watched him remove the linen pants he wore, freeing his cock. My eyes widened as I took in his appearance: naked, skin flushed, a sprinkling of sweat beaded across his body. His muscles tensed and relaxed, his jaw working as he ran his tongue across his lips, tasting the evidence of my pleasure. He lay beside me in bed, brushing the strands of my hair off my face. He traced a line with his finger down the center of my body, the hairs standing on end in his wake.

He shifted his weight, his body now above mine, pressing into me but not crushing me. "You are so magnificently stunning, Little Star." He traced the curve of my neck and shoulder, his gaze following his fingers. "Just fucking perfect."

The act immediately reignited my arousal, and I felt a rush of warmth between my legs. He ground his length into my hip, and I gasped; I had forgotten his size, and as solid as he was pressed against me, it was a shocking reminder. I began to grind my hips into him as I wrapped my legs behind his back, and I reached between us, seeking to offer him a semblance of the pleasure he had bestowed upon me, but he shook his head instead.

"This is about me worshiping you." He leaned back, untwining my legs and kneeling before me on the bed. His gaze traveled along my bare skin as he bit his lower lip, sending a ripple of butterflies through my core. "Goddess sent." He grabbed my thighs, pulling me close to him. "Did you know that? You are Goddess sent." He dragged the head of his cock through my slick folds, readying himself at my entrance.

I burned with the desire to feel him moving in me, filling me, but I stopped breathing as memories flashed of Stefan forcing himself on top of me, forcing himself inside me. They were gone as quickly as they came, but the feeling of anxiety and shame lingered. I felt a hand push the hair away from my eyes as fingers caressed my face.

"You're here; you're safe." Rae's calming voice reminded me I was free. "I have you; he cannot hurt you anymore."

I opened my eyes to see Rae's face hovering close to mine, his breath on my skin as he continued to return me to the present. I saw his gaze flick to the scars that marred my face, and I instantly felt ashamed. I turned my head, hiding them from his view.

"Don't." He turned my face back to his. "Don't do that. Don't hide from me. These..." He gently ran a finger down the path of each scar. "Your scars do not define or diminish you. They are a testament to your strength, Little Star. Do not try and hide them from me, from anyone." He gently kissed each scar. "A star cannot shine if not for the darkness that surrounds it. You are the brightest, rarest, and most beautiful star, Asteria. You may have fallen, but you are no less powerful. Embrace who you are, scars and all." His forehead rested on mine. "I love you, Asteria, and nothing will ever change that. My heart is yours, Little Star."

A tear rolled down my face at his confession. Love. He loved me —that was the strongest feeling I had ever experienced: to be loved and to love in return. I opened my eyes, bringing my lips to lightly move over his, whispering the words I had felt so strongly but had fought every step of the way, the words I never believed I would say to another. "I love you too, Astraeus."

Suddenly, the earth seemed to shift as a crackling energy hummed and pulsed around us, the heat seeming to rise. I had become so wholly enraptured by the man above me that I failed to notice the room had gone dark—no, not the room: the sky. The entire sky was black, the sun swallowed by the inky black night. The atmosphere felt thick, charged with some strange power that weaved its way into our lungs. I couldn't pull my attention from Rae; his eyes deepened in color, past the forest green, and his pupils seemed to expand, swallowing the whites of his eyes. I couldn't believe what I was seeing: his eyes had gone completely black before they slowly returned to their normal color, hints of black shadows in his irises. It was the most beautiful and intriguing thing I had ever seen.

My skin grew hot, tightening over my muscles and bones. It felt...euphoric, as though a new strength swam through my veins, fueling every muscle and touching every nerve. Suddenly, my vision was obscured by a blinding white light that dissipated as quickly as it came. When I could see again, the night that had blocked the sun had gone, as if it had never been there.

Rae gawked at me, his face a mixture of adoration, surprise, and bewilderment.

"What?" I was confused by not only his statement, but by what had just happened.

"The prophecy... It's been triggered, and you..." A smile of utter disbelief crossed his face. "You are a light wielder. The Queen of Stars, the true ruler of the Umbra Siderum. You..." He pressed his lips to mine, devouring me with passion. A static charge flew between us as he broke the kiss, the tip of his cock pressed at my entrance. "Do you trust me?" he asked.

"With my entire being," I answered, and he pressed into me slowly, making sure I was ready for him.

I exhaled, gripping his shoulders as he thrust into me. I gasped at the sensation of him filling me, stretching me as my body adjusted to him. It was a mixture of pain and pleasure, and I truly knew I would never have enough of this, of him. I lifted my hips, allowing him to sink deeper, the pleasure climbing higher with each thrust. My nails dug into his back as he pressed his chest to mine, needing to feel each other, to touch each other—every movement, every feeling, every sensation. Our bodies moved together in perfect sync, our breathing matched, our heartbeats beating to the same rhythm.

I could feel the undeniable sensation begin to build as my muscles tensed, and he groaned in pleasure as I tightened around him. "Fuck, you feel amazing."

He caught my bottom lip between his teeth, nipping it before he kissed me. "Look at me," he breathed before our eyes met, and our breath mingled as we began to climax together.

"I love you." The words left my mouth just as we jumped off that ledge together, falling into bliss face to face as we clung to each other, moaning as we rode out our intense waves of pleasure.

Around us, small tendrils of shadows and light seemed to emanate from our bodies, wrapping around us, tethering us to one another, binding our hearts and souls. My lights danced with his shadows, as they embraced each other. I gazed into his eyes as we climaxed, the emerald of his eyes surrounded by wisps of black, and I wondered if the light danced in my eyes like the shadows did in his.

Kissing him deeply, I lost myself in the moment. Suddenly, light erupted from body, blinding the room. His shadows answered, bursting forth, cloaking us in darkness before they faded. His movements slowed, and I pulled my focus from the man on top of me to cast a glance around the room. Our powers had become one, entangled with one another, twisted vines of shadow and light, of warmth and cold, of him and me.

It was then I realized together, we could defeat anything. We were now the rulers of Shadow and Light, of Twilight and Stars, and without one, the other could not exist. It was always us, our paths were always meant to collide. We had been made for each other, for ours was a destiny written in twilight and stars.

EPILOGUE

STEFAN

It had been over two weeks since Asteria had escaped. The stupid bitch had caught me off guard when she pulled that dagger from the ground and slammed the hilt into my head. It had knocked me out, lacerating my scalp. I don't know how long it took for those dimwitted soldiers to realize she had run, but it was too long. She had managed to evade them, running straight into the arms of that piece of shit prince from the Forgotten Kingdom. Valdin should have killed him, a mistake that will not be made again.

I had been brought back here to Solaria so I could properly be attended to by our healers, time I could not get back. We had spent the last week looking for a way into that goddess-forsaken 'Kingdom' to no avail. When we had exhausted our efforts looking for a way through the mountains, I had decided on a different plan of attack.

None of the other Kingdoms knew what we had done. They has no idea that for centuries, we had monitored the villages, tracking the influx of Asphodel families as they traveled into our realm.

I had spent years—*years* —organizing the union between

392

Asteria and me. I didn't care that it meant I would eventually be crowned king of both Solaria and Pyrus, making me the most powerful ruler in Leethe. No, none of that mattered. The only thing that mattered, had ever mattered since that day under the willow, was her. My family had been trying to find the key to the prophecy since the Great War, and that day, when I saw her little patch of freckles that made the constellation of Orion, I put it all together. It was Asteria who would be the key to returning power to the realm, something I could not allow. I had always felt a strange attachment to her growing up, but that is when I knew we were meant to be. She was meant to be mine, and from that moment on, she was all I wanted.

I never wasted time truly courting anyone else. I had my fun, but I never committed, knowing the only person who could ever satiate my needs would be her. She was mine and only mine, and that bastard prince touched what belonged to me. He *defiled* what belonged to me. She was not his to have, and I would stop at nothing to get her back. I had hoped that our time at camp would have taught her a lesson, but it seemed I was wrong. She would need to be punished again, and this time, the price of her betrayal would be paid in his blood—his and every last one of those sad excuses for 'humans' who descended from his kingdom.

A knock at my door drew my attention from where I stared out the window, towards the Dead Mountains.

"Your Highness," Valdin, my head guard and most trusted friend, called out.

"Did you find her?" My fingers flexed at my side as my tension and anger rose. Asteria was going to regret her choice to run from her fate. She was going to learn that her place was next to me, and her first lesson was going to begin right now.

"We did." A sinister smile crept up Valdin's face. "She thought she could run, but we made sure that couldn't happen."

My pulse thrummed as my cock hardened, pressing against the seam of my pants. "Bring her in."

Valdin nodded as he stepped out, only to return with her. Dragging her in with the help of other guards, he threw her to her knees, and a short, muffled scream of pain sounded through the cloth satchel they had placed over her head. I stalked towards her, eyeing the distressed state of her bodice and skirt. She had been trying to run and hide in the forests. When I reached her, I noticed the bruises and marks along her ankle—Valdin had broken her foot, and from the looks of it, it was beginning to become infected. I lowered myself down to one knee to face her.

"You never stood a chance," I whispered to her. I could hear her whimpering as I placed a hand on her shoulder and leaned in so my mouth was next to her ear. "The death of the Umbra Siderum has begun. Let this be the first lesson to that disgraceful prince of yours. This is what happens when you try to take what belongs to me."

She tried to scream, but the sound was cut off when the icy steel of my dagger plunged into her stomach. I could feel the warm, wet sensation of her blood as it began to soak her bodice. The scent of iron filled the air as I stood, my hand on her shoulder keeping her upright. I looked at her blood coating my hand, and my cock twitched in excitement. I sheathed my dagger, returning it to its place just inside my boot before I reached down, grasping the satchel that covered her head as I pulled it free. The sounds of her wet coughs as she choked on her own blood grew louder as I fisted her hair and forced her head back, so that I could watch the life drain from her eyes. I inhaled deeply, relishing in the adrenaline that pumped through my veins from the high of the kill. I threw her lifeless body to the ground and returned to the chair behind my desk.

"Dump the body in the foothills of the Dead Mountains. One of their scouts will find it and take it to the prince," I ordered as I pulled a white kerchief from the drawer of my desk and began to clean my hands. Valdin and the guard stepped forward, retrieving the body from the floor. The door snapped close behind them, and I finished cleaning my hands, removing the copper strands of her hair that had wound around my fingers as I held her head, watching the vibrant color of her eyes fade to nothing. I inhaled replaying the scene in my head, my cock hardening at the memory.

My attention shot to the window—the room was cast into darkness as the entire sky went black. My blood began to boil and the realization hit: the prophecy had been set into motion. An enraged scream echoed through the study as I slammed my fists into the desk. My father came running to the office after hearing the crash as I launched the contents of my desk across the study.

"What is the meaning of this?" His voice was raised, full of irritation as he looked around at the destruction I had caused.

I seethed as I planted my fists on the desk in front of me, gritting my teeth as I looked up at my father.

"It's time for war."

ACKNOWLEDGMENTS

There are so many people for me to thank who helped me make this book a reality. Firstly, I want to thank my mother, Lori, and my sister, Sarah. They have always been so incredibly supportive of whatever I have pursued, from nursing school to world travel to writing. Thank you for always encouraging me to never stop reaching for the stars.

Secondly, I would like to thank the group of women I have met on TikTok who were such a huge inspiration for me to start this journey. Faye and Allison, thank you for always being there when I spam you with book development things. If I hadn't met you ladies through our love of books and followed you on your own author journeys, I would never have been inspired to write my own story. Jen, Shana, Mindy, and Rexy, you have been incredible through this whole journey, hyping me up and cheering me on. I am so thankful to have you all in my life.

And, as atypical as this may be, I would like to thank myself. I allowed myself to open up and address trauma I have been shoving down and avoiding since I was a child. So, thank you, self, for confronting your own pain and healing it through this journey.

ABOUT THE AUTHOR

Brieghanna Maye is an author who was born and raised in the state of Texas. Growing up she was known for telling fantastical stories and having a very active imagination. In school she favored her english and writing classes and in middle school was voted most likely to become a famous writer.

As she got older her passions also expanded into medicine and sciences, which led her to obtaining her Bachelors of Science in Nursing from the University of Texas. After completing her degree she rediscovered her love for literature and dove back into reading.

She is a full time travel nurse, exploring the wonders of the United States, but in her spare time she creates cosplays of her favorite characters and makes silly videos for her tiktok. She likes to spend time outdoors hiking and traveling the world when the opportunity arises.

After becoming immersed in her reading and watching her fellow booktok friends write and publish their stories she was inspired to tell her own.

For more books and updates:
Authorbrieghannamaye.com

www.ingramcontent.com/pod-product-compliance
Lightning Source LLC
Chambersburg PA
CBHW021805130726
47987CB00010B/3024